RUNAWAY HEART

Adam tossed several more grapes at Jonquil, until one finally hit its target. She clamped her teeth around the plump, juicy fruit, spewing purple juice across the front of Adam's white shirt. Then she burst into unrestrained giggles.

"So you think it's funny, do you, ruining my good shirt!"

Adam grabbed a bunch of grapes, leaned across, and held them just above Jonquil's mouth. Playfully she nipped at the cluster, but he pulled it out of reach before she could catch it between her teeth.

"Maybe," he said in a whisper, "I should ruin *your* shirt."

Dragging the grapes down her chin, and lower, across the field of white ruffles covering her bosom, Adam pressed himself closer to her. His breath was warm on her neck.

All-consuming fire ignited throughout Jonquil's veins when Adam's palm skimmed her breast. At his deep intake of breath, she felt his arms tighten around her. Then his lips descended upon hers in a deep, searching kiss.

D1601451

TENA CARLYLE

RUNAWAY HEART

ZEBRA BOOKS
KENSINGTON PUBLISHING CORP.

ZEBRA BOOKS are published by

Kensington Publishing Corp.
475 Park Avenue South
New York, NY 10016

First Printing: June, 1993

Printed in the United States of America

In memory of our mothers—
Ruth Lynch Card and Alice Carty Lyle

Special thanks to:

Thelma Taber, Teresa Taber, and Jackie Morris
for their enthusiastic support;
and to Mrs. Gladys Sands of the Eureka Springs
Historical Museum, Eureka Springs, Arkansas

"Here's to the girl dressed in black,
   Who always looks forward and never looks
      back;
   And when she sings, she sings so sweet,
   She leaves things standing that have no feet."
                              —Author Unknown

Prologue

"Old woman, it's time you and that black bastard you live with get off this land."

Jonquil looked up from her sheet music and tried to peek through the lush foliage of the mulberry tree. The shouting came from the other side of the house, a good fifty yards away. Sinister laughter accompanied the threat. The best she could tell, two or three men bent on intimidation threatened her mother. She couldn't see a thing.

Crumpling her paper, Jonquil bit into her fist to keep from yelling out. Dear God, why couldn't she have come when she'd first been called? With her banjo slung over her shoulder, Jonquil wrapped her arms around the tree trunk and scampered down to the ground, pushing her blond hair out of her face.

Booted footsteps moved across the wooden porch and stopped. Jonquil heard a scream. A loud thud sounded on the charged air.

Mother! The wail caught in Jonquil's throat. Intuition warned her not to scream and reveal her whereabouts.

A second voice chimed in. "You got anything left for us white boys? Or has that old nigger poked you

7

so much you're done worn out?" The man's cruel taunt whipped upward from beneath the porch's tin overhang.

"Leave her be, Jack," a third voice intervened. "She's old enough to be your granny. Look at 'er. She can't even speak."

Running across the back yard, Jonquil made for the side of the house, then moved unnoticed along its worn boards. Where in heaven was Gabriel? She eased to the corner of the shack until she could see the porch.

"Jack, she's done passed out," ventured the second man.

The first assailant looked down at Jonquil's mother in disgust. "Shriveled up old buzzard ain't good for nothin'." He aimed his filthy boot at the frail body. "I heard she's crazy in the head anyhow."

"Leave her."

Jonquil's gaze flew to the third man. His face held a menacing expression.

The boot stopped in midair.

"All the boss wants is the deed."

"Shut your trap, Thompson," the man called Jack thundered. "I ain't taking no orders from the likes of you. The boss said me and Leland was in charge. Said we could do as we pleased with these here squatters."

"She's an old woman, Jack. She doesn't have the strength to swat a fly. Let's find the deed and get out of here." Looking over his shoulder, Thompson opened the door and disappeared inside the tiny house.

Her ear pressed to the weathered wood, Jonquil could hear the stranger rummaging through their belongings. At least he wouldn't find what he sought. After the pesky preacher first turned up, asking so many questions about the farm, Jonquil had hidden the deed in the barn.

Her heart caught in her throat when she saw Jack

fumbling with his pants. Dropping to his knees in front of her mother's prone figure, he threw the bottom of her skirt up over her head. Obscene curses spilled from his mouth as he yanked aside layers of petticoats. Jonquil had to do something fast.

She stepped into full view, holding her concealed banjo in the folds of her skirt like a shotgun aimed at the two men on the porch.

"Move another inch and I'll fill you full of buckshot." Jonquil knew that by herself she had little chance against the ruthless characters facing her, but she couldn't allow them to hurt her mother. Any moment now Gabriel would show up with a real shotgun.

"Lookee there, Jack." Leland's voice broke the stunned silence. "Now that's a fine-looking sample of womanhood."

Jack's toothless grin spread across his pocked face. Shifting back on his haunches, he jerked to his feet and left the unconscious woman. Cautiously, he started for the edge of the porch.

Jonquil stared the man down, afraid to call Gabriel's name and thus surrender any advantage she might have. He was in the barn with his friend, Keely. Surely he heard the commotion.

Adjusting her aim, she clenched the covered banjo neck to still her trembling hand. "Make one wrong move and I'll blow your eyeballs out. We don't take kindly to strangers around here. Now get in your wagon and get off our land."

"We ain't going nowhere, girlie. I'd suggest you put that weapon down, or I'll shoot this old woman's head off."

Jerking his pistol from its holster, Jack aimed it at her mother's head. "Hear me, gal? Drop it, or I'll blow her to bits."

The man's venomous words convinced Jonquil he'd kill her mother in the drop of an eyelash. Slowly she slid the concealed instrument from the folds of her skirt.

Where in God's name is Gabriel? she prayed. He should have been here by now.

"Lookee there, Jack, it's a banjo." Leland howled and slapped his thigh. "She done hoodwinked us with a banjo."

Jack dived for Jonquil's feet, coming up short when the instrument crashed against his head. Enraged, he wrestled her to the ground and pinned her beneath his bulk, ripping her bodice from collar to waist.

Jonquil raked the man's neck and face with her fingers, drawing blood. Fighting for all she was worth, she felt her last bit of strength ebb away. Then all motion stopped. The animal astride her froze.

Jonquil shifted her eyes to the gun barrel pressed firmly against Jack's head. The man holding it was not one to reckon with.

"Move it. *Now!*" Thompson's steely voice ordered, and with booted foot, he pushed him off her. "I'll be no party to rape."

Jack stumbled to his feet, holding his ribs, moving cautiously against the gun still fitted against his skull. "You're as good as dead," he stated matter-of-factly. But he made no sudden moves. As the one man led the other out into the yard, locked in verbal combat, Jonquil crawled to where her mother lay and hugged her still form.

The two men began wrestling in the dirt. Jerking into action, Leland aimed his gun at them and pulled the trigger. When his bullet found its mark, Thompson collapsed atop Jack.

With a look of disgust, Jack thrust Thompson's body aside. "Took you long enough, you damn fool. He was going to kill me." He charged past Leland toward Jonquil, who knelt, still sheltering her mother's body.

His gait unsteady, he yanked her up by the hair. "Now I'll finish what I started."

A second shot rent the air, and the man called Jack toppled at Jonquil's feet. Through the haze of hysteria, Jonquil caught a clipped, black image standing at the end of the porch. His shotgun still smoked.

"Lawd, Miss Jonquil, I'm sorry. I was with Keely. Never knew you needed me." Anguish showed in the black man's face.

A motion at her periphery turned Jonquil's head. "Gabriel, look out!"

Leland's gun was now aimed at her caretaker's head. "Say your prayers, nigger, you're about to meet your maker."

A gunshot echoed in the air and Leland fell. The man called Thompson, straining against death, had killed the second accomplice.

Jonquil ran to the stranger's side and eased his head against her lap. Bright, sticky blood covered his shirt. "Sorry, miss, I meant you . . . and your mother no harm." Closely set eyes the deep color of currants looked up into Jonquil's own. Then they stilled.

Her tears fell unchecked against the man's face. "Thank you," Jonquil whispered through salty tears. She drew her fingers across his lids and closed the lifeless eyes, eyes she knew would haunt her throughout her lifetime. Her champion, the stranger Thompson, was dead.

Wrapped in oblivion, she sat staring with unseeing eyes at the deathly quiet scene which only moments before had stormed with conflict.

Absently, she swatted away a green fly. *Bzz-zzz-zzz.* The annoying bug would not leave her alone. Jonquil thrashed again at the pesky insect. *Bzz-zzz-zzz.* Her gaze followed its descent to the heavy wetness in her lap. Then she screamed, feeling herself sink into welcome darkness.

11

Hours later, the old farm wagon pulled out of the front yard. Draped in a worn quilt, Jonquil sat as stiff as a mummy beside Gabriel on the buckboard seat.

Numbed by the afternoon's events, she refused to dwell on her mother's demise. She couldn't afford the luxury of despair, of sinking into that world that had shielded her mother from the pain of reality. She had to be strong for Gabriel.

When he'd presented her with the strangers' belongings, Jonquil knew they'd made the right decision in leaving. Among them was the silver badge of a United States special deputy marshal. It had belonged to the man who had tried so valiantly to help. Intimidating evidence, to say the least. No court in the land would believe how the lawman had died.

The other items were of no real value—an inkwell, a pocket watch, mismatched cuff links, and a silver toothpick, but Jonquil and Gabriel could use them to barter for food if their meager savings ran out before they could find work.

As the wagon rolled beyond the house, Jonquil saw that the old mulberry tree shaded her mother's freshly dug grave. At the head of the mound stood a rough-hewn wooden cross.

Out of sight, in the woods, three other graves lay in a row, indistinguishable but for a small cross at the head of one.

And in the wagon, their sparse belongings tucked behind them, Jonquil and Gabriel headed against the late day into tomorrow. Jonquil clutched her mother's purse beneath her breast, the deed to the farm secure inside.

Why, she lamented, was such an insigificant paper so important that it brought strangers to their door, destroying their lives in the process? What had they done to be the target of hate and to have to flee the only home they'd ever shared?

The townspeople had never befriended them. They'd made it clear enough over the years that they didn't much care for the idea of a white woman, not quite right in the head, living with an ex-slave. There was no reason to think they'd come to their aid now or believe a word they said.

So, with the probability of the law at their back and uncertainty ahead, Jonquil and Gabriel drove into an unknown future.

Chapter One

Pine Bluff, Arkansas, 1882

"I won't do it, Gabriel. I just can't."

Jonquil Rose Trevain paced back and forth in front of the carnival tent, her blond hair whipping against her face. "I will not cheat innocent people out of their money."

Her lifelong friend sat, holding two cups of coffee, before a small cook fire. Against the brightness of the firelight, the whites of his eyes stood out in his ebony-colored face. "This'll be the last time."

Jonquil stopped her pacing and flopped down on the log next to him. "I never knew he was using me."

"Then you're not cheatin' folks, not the way you think."

"But if I run today . . ."

Jonquil reached her hands out to the fire's warmth. It would be hours before the bright sun chased away the late September chill. With a sigh of resignation, she accepted the cup Gabriel thrust into her hands. "You promise?" she asked.

The man nodded. "One last time, then we'll be gone."

*   *   *

Dressed in oversized, stuffed overalls, Jonquil looked like a thickset lad waiting with the other boys for the race to begin.

Orange and peach-colored leaves drifted downward from the canopy of flaming trees. Beneath a wide-billed cap, Jonquil's eyes drank in the distant yellow-gold fields where patches of tasseled corn stood waiting for the harvest. A soft autumn breeze stirred the goldenrod growing beside the road and sent milkweed tufts adrift against the clear blue sky.

The late September sun mellowed the afternoon of a perfect day. Not a day, Jonquil decided, to spend worrying over something beyond her control. The carnival manager's duplicity had been hard for her to accept, but her own gullibility bothered her more. To think she had actually believed Bailey had enjoyed seeing her win the extra money. All along he'd been padding his pockets by soliciting bets for the fastest runner.

After today she could put the whole miserable affair behind her. Gabriel had promised they would leave the carnival. But now she had to concentrate all her efforts on winning this race. If she lost, she couldn't predict what Bailey would do.

For the past year, every race Jonquil had entered had filled her with excitement. She usually won the purse, adding it to their growing cache. A harmless enough ruse, she submitted, unable to understand the discrimination against her the first time she had attempted to purchase an entry ticket. Revenge had been sweet. No one ever suspected that the fat boy who took the prize was a girl. Now she wished they had. Then Bailey could not have profited from her abilities.

The foot race was about to begin.

Adam Coulter stood with the other spectators and

16

watched the racers line up. Behind him the streets of Pine Bluff bustled with people who had come to enjoy the county fair. Booths along the town square were stocked to overflowing with homemade relishes, sweet and hot jellies, pickles and various other culinary delights. Adam had ridden into town early and hungry, had eaten his way through a sack of sweet taffy, a candied apple, lemonade, and an entire cherry pie.

His appetite sated, he now stood with the locals to watch the competitions. In a field about a hundred yards away, a fire blazed in a large open pit. The smells of wood smoke and pungent, roasting pig filled the warm afternoon with the promise of a mouth-watering barbecue supper. Not even the pie could diminish his eagerness to sample the meal planned for later.

According to a billboard, the dance to be held after the day's festivities would last into the early morning hours. Come sunup, tired and happy parents would pack their exhausted families into wagons and head for home. This fall outing was the last big social event before the cold winter months drove every man close to his own hearth until spring planting.

He envied the parents who chased after their children, showing the little ones off to neighbors. They shared a sense of community, of belonging. It was at these times, while returning a smile or the tip of a hat, that Adam tried to forget he was the outsider, just passing through.

Now, standing shoulder to shoulder with the townspeople, he brushed aside the familiar stab of loneliness that always pestered him in a congenial group such as this. Pushing his black felt hat off his brow, he mentally sized up the racers.

As a Pinkerton detective, Adam made it his business to study the habits and mannerisms of people. Anything out of the ordinary captured his

17

attention, and right now he stared at the most curious-looking fellow he'd seen in a long time.

He studied the hefty lad who headed with the other boys to the starting line. No kid with such girth could possibly move with the gracefulness and agility of a cat. Why, with his small hands and feet, his long, thin neck and delicate jaw, the lad was almost dainty. Something about him just didn't add up.

Crouched in a starting position, Jonquil waited for the signal, her usual calm shattered by an immense case of nerves. Today she felt as jumpy as a basketful of bullfrogs, now that she knew Bailey was no more than a fraud, a petty crook.

Taking huge gulps of air to still the pounding of her heart, she scanned the crowd. Expectant faces stared back, and she felt lower than scum on a pond. The prize money no longer mattered. She wanted to get on with the race and be done with it.

Dressed in black, and with a week's worth of trail dirt on his clothes, a tall man stood out among the other spectators. He stared at her with such intensity that Jonquil knew he could see through her disguise. Something in his bearing—she couldn't tell what— made her feel even more uncomfortable, and she shifted restlessly on her feet.

If Bailey hadn't warned her she wouldn't be paid if she lost this race, she'd walk off right now. He had left her no choice but to run and win. She'd do almost anything to protect Gabriel's fragile existence and her own, and hoarding their meager savings was high on her list. There was no telling what a thug like Bailey might do if angered. Taking several more breaths, she tried to calm herself.

A gunshot split the air and Jonquil vaulted into motion. The stranger faded into a blur as she forged forward with renewed determination. Tomorrow she

18

and Gabriel would be gone.

The dry roadbed coughed up dust, enveloping the racers in a powdery cloud. On long, coltish legs, Jonquil outdistanced the others, her rhythm unhampered by the feather pillows secured around her middle.

Growing up on the isolated farm, ostracized by neighboring families, Jonquil had found early release in running free with the wind. Now her running skills worked to her advantage. Disguised as a boy, she won most of the races she entered.

The spectators cheered when she bolted across the finish line. Slowing down and drawing in deep gulps of air, Jonquil accepted the unfeigned congratulations of the onlookers and her prize of twenty dollars. She tucked the money inside her overalls' pocket and moved with the dispersing crowd.

Her guilt at having won grew heavier when she bumped into Bailey. He grinned down at her, winked, then turned and strutted away like a prize rooster. She could see no joy in cheating people. Rebuking herself for her part in his despicable deed, she stalked off toward the creek.

Stripped to her drawers and camisole, Jonquil waded into the narrow inlet that branched off the Arkansas River. Her pillows, shirt, and overalls lay in a heap at the water's edge. Hidden by a camouflage of hickory, ash, and poplars, the cove was a perfect place for her bath.

"Brrrr." A quick plunge was best, but the icy liquid lapping around her thighs delayed her normal zeal. She inched deeper into the water in short, jerky motions.

"Now, ain't ye some funny-looking boy."

No longer concerned with the water's chill, Jonquil dropped chin-deep into the stream. Uncertain if it was the speaker's surprise visit or the bone-chilling water that made her heart hesitate, she tried to regain her composure.

"What do you want?" she demanded, lowering her voice an octave. She turned to face a scruffy man in old work clothes.

"People in this here neck o' the woods don't take kindly to cheats." The man picked the plump pillows from her discarded clothing and shook them.

Clearing her throat, Jonquil assumed an air of control she didn't feel. "You better get on out of here, and leave a lad to his bath."

"Ye take me for a fool, missy?" He dropped the telltale pillows back onto the ground and laughed, rubbing his grizzled chin. "We both know there ain't no lad in them fancy drawers ye be a-wearing."

A violent shudder traveled down her spine as Jonquil remembered other strangers who'd threatened her not so long ago. She glared at the man. "I don't know what you're talking about."

Caught in her vulnerable state, she hoped against hope that this man still carried a shred of doubt that she was a woman. Dirt caked her face and the hat still hid her long hair. But his next words convinced her he was less a fool than she suspected.

"If the good, upstanding citizens in this here town learned ye be a female in men's clothing and in cahoots with yer boss to cheat people out of their money . . ."—he paused to allow his meaning to sink in—". . . they might not take kindly to yer winning that foot race."

"You're mistaken, mister." Jonquil's heart was racing. "My paw, he'll be along any minute now, and I think I should warn you, he's a right ornery fellow."

"Really now, missy, I believe I'll wait right here fer yer daddy." He squatted next to her clothes and draped them over his arms. "Or maybe I should jes' take yer clothes and that twenty-dollar prize I see'd ye stuff in yer pocket."

"Don't you dare." Seized by anger, and with no regard for her state of undress, Jonquil bounded toward the shoreline.

"Oh, I dare, missy," he mocked, "but I might be persuaded to forget what I knowed when I relieve ye of this here prize money." He stood up, a sneer hovering on his slack lips. "I get the money, and ye get yer clothes, and maybe I won't turn ye over to the law for cheatin' decent folks. What ye say, missy?"

"I say take it, and get out of here." Jonquil clenched her fists into tight balls. The law. That was the last thing she and Gabriel needed.

The man's perusal slid down the length of Jonquil's body as he stuffed the twenty into his pocket. "I guess ye ain't no lad." He scratched his head, squinting at the revealing body beneath her wet underthings. "More like a woman."

Jonquil recoiled from his heated perusal and covered herself with her arms.

He chuckled and licked his lips. "Maybe ol' Gig's been a mite hasty." His feverish gaze bore into her. "Maybe I kin think of a better way for ye to earn me silence." He moved closer. "I ain't had me no woman in a powerful long time."

Old, familiar terror exploded into a million fragments. "No," Jonquil ordered, on the verge of panic, "just take the money and leave."

It was the farm, the other men, all over again. If he touched her, she'd be forced to scream, and Gabriel and everyone else would come running to her defense, full of questions and unwanted attention.

Jonquil retreated into the water, but not fast enough to escape the lunging man. Too late, he locked her wrists in his massive fingers.

"I'd suggest, mister, you release the lady while you still can." Several feet away, a tall man stood with a pistol aimed toward her attacker's back.

"Hell, she ain't no lady." The man thrust her aside and turned toward the threatening stranger. "She's an imposter," he added, his tone meant to solicit his foe's help.

Jonquil collapsed to her knees in the shallow water. When her heartbeat slowed, she looked up at her rescuer. It was the same man whose scrutiny had unnerved her before the race. Up close, behind the barrel of his gun, the deadly gleam in his eye made him even more intimidating.

"Imposter or not, she's still a lady. She doesn't deserve to be molested by the likes of you."

"Aw, shucks, I didn't mean her no harm."

"And I guess you didn't mean to steal her money either."

The drifter gave Jonquil a deadly look and swiveled his head back to her rescuer. He reached inside his pocket and tossed the twenty dollars at the meddling stranger. "Here, take her money."

The tall man's expression never wavered, nor did the gun pointed at the other man's chest. Jonquil, still kneeling in the water, began to shake uncontrollably.

"If you're smart," he bargained, "you'll hightail it out of town and not mention this to anyone."

"But, she's a fraud . . ."

"Not only are you stupid, you obviously can't hear either," the guntoter growled.

Jonquil heard the hammer click on the pistol, and the weasel's eyes dropped to the gun barrel.

"I'm a-goin'," he stuttered, "I'm a-goin'," and he clambered away from the stream's edge.

"Remember, nothing about this incident leaves these woods. If I hear anything bad about this lady, I'll hunt you down and blow your head off."

Branches crunched and popped beneath the man's escaping feet. Jonquil watched him disappear, leaving in his tracks a hushed, unsettling calm. She raised her eyes to find the stranger watching her. Overhead, a crow's raucous cry split the strained silence.

For a moment Jonquil forgot she was in sopping wet underwear. The man's dark eyes, the color of chinquapin nuts, stared back at her from beneath straight, bushy brows. They had turned gentle and carried an indefinable wistfulness. For an instant she thought she recognized him, then shrugged off the idea.

"Ma'am," he greeted her, removing his hat and bowing his head ever so slightly.

Jonquil had never seen such a thick crop of hair. Slivers of sunlight highlighted its rich chestnut color. Damp, wispy tendrils hung in half-circles over his forehead. For a man, he had a most satisfying face, with high cheekbones and a well-formed nose. But it was his mouth that made Jonquil feel weak in the knees. It was perfectly chiseled, with a full bottom lip and corners that turned up into a charming smile.

Suddenly she remembered herself and jerked to her feet.

The man moved toward the water's edge, replacing his gun inside its holster. "Are you all right?"

As Jonquil's gaze followed the gun's descent, she wondered what kind of man would carry a pistol strapped to his leg. The thought forced her another step backward, afraid to venture a guess. As an afterthought, she threw her arms across her chest.

Adam caught the sudden response, saw the sway of the full, rounded breasts before they settled into the grip of her wet camisole. Her nipples shimmered like tiny, blush moons beneath the flimsy fabric.

He understood fully the reason for her chubby disguise. To conceal the lush ripeness of her body beneath the guise of a slim, young boy would have been impossible. With a sharp intake of breath he

23

concentrated on the dirt-streaked face partially hidden beneath the flannel cap. He bent and picked up her shirt.

Confusion sucked Jonquil's toes into the mire. Heaven help her, whatever was she to do? This man from nowhere had rescued her from her would-be attacker. Now how should she respond? Caution whispered that he, as the others, was not to be trusted.

The proof of her trickery lay at his booted feet. Incriminating evidence, indeed—clothes made for a lumberjack, the feather pillows, and the twenty-dollar banknote fluttering in the grass. At least her hair and face remained in disguise.

The stranger held her shirt open at the shoulders. Shaking it slightly as though attempting to remove the wrinkles, he gave her a broad grin.

"Come on out before you catch pneumonia." In a deep baritone, he urged her to come toward him and slip into the shirt.

What kind of fool did he take her to be? Jonquil's feet remained frozen to the muddy bottom of the creek bed.

"I won't hurt you. I promise."

He waved the large shirt like a flag, and under different circumstances Jonquil might have thought his movement comical.

Adam stood with his arms extended, waiting for the girl to leave the water. Was she witless? Or afraid? Of him? Confronted by the drifter, she had spoken with determination, but now she hung her head as though she didn't understand simple conversation.

"What's your name?" he coaxed, trying to allay any fear.

Still no reply. She remained rooted in the water and refused to look at him.

"Would you like me to close my eyes until you're dressed?" Hell, he'd had just about enough of this

24

mollycoddling. Couldn't the girl see he meant her no harm?

She cocked her head to one side and stared back at him from beneath the hat's brim.

At last he was making some progress. Pleased with himself, he made a big show of squinching his eyes tightly closed.

"See, just as I promised," he added for assurance, his eyes squeezed shut.

The wind whistled past his ear a split second before the blunt instrument met the side of his head. Adam tried to turn around, but too late. The ground seemed to jump up to meet him. Fighting the dizziness, he felt his legs crumple. Overhead, red and gold leaves faded and blurred together.

"Is he dead?"

Adam could feel the damp heat of the girl as she bent over his prostrate form.

"Naw, but he's gonna have a mighty big headache when he wakes up."

Damnation! He'd been a fool for not watching his back. If he hadn't been so preoccupied with the forest nymph, he wouldn't have let down his guard.

Adam blinked several times, trying to clear the cotton from his brain. Already he felt the powerful headache coming on. Shadows and sunlight merged. A smudged face swam before his eyes.

"You sure he won't die?" the soft feminine voice asked again. Warm breath fanned the air with the fragrance of mint.

Die, he might. He felt as though he'd been hit with a petrified tree stump. Only blurs crossed his face; the blow had probably caused permanent damage to his sight.

The soft voice blended with the deeper voice of a male. Their words muted, unintelligible.

Adam's head hurt like hell. A dizzying wave of nausea washed over his limp body. He drifted on a white fluffy cloud, looking down on the tops of flame-colored trees.

"He'll be fine; I didn't hit him too hard."

Too hard! You nearly broke my damned head. Adam willed the man to listen, but no words came. The more he fought the feathery lightness, the more he felt himself pressed deeper into weightlessness. *I've got to be stone-cold dead.* When the delicate face of an angel hovered only inches from his, he was sure of it.

"Gabriel," she called.

Adam searched for the trumpet-blowing spirit. He must have flown away, he thought through his haze. Again he captured the face of the one whose golden halo glowed like the sun. Spun gold spilled over her shoulder, escaping an oversized crown. And her eyes—he'd never forget those eyes. They were the color of a blue jay's wing.

Adam reached out to touch the vision. "Am I in heaven?" His voice sounded hollow, unfamiliar to his own ears, and the vision slipped silently from sight. He wanted to laugh and protest that he was too young to die, but he could only manage a feeble smile. Then he felt himself drifting, floating away on the blue-jay cloud.

Twilight settled on the small town, bringing with it the cooler temperatures of evening. Chinese lanterns, strung across the interior of the livery stable, added to the ambience of the makeshift theater. Bales of hay, covered with patterned quilts, waited for their audience.

Jonquil wandered through the empty building, familiarizing herself with its layout. The smells of hay, horses, and wood filled the interior. She walked to the platform that had been erected at one end of the large barn. Dried corn stalks, tied together to form stage wings, leaned against the outer wall on both sides of the stand. Hay bales supported overstuffed scarecrows wearing men's overalls and grinning pumpkin faces.

The overalls immediately reminded Jonquil of the seamy vagrant, and with that thought came the image of the man who had come to her rescue. The man Gabriel had slammed upside the head. After assuring themselves he was not badly hurt, only passed out, they had scurried back to their campsite to lie low for the remainder of the afternoon. Why was it that misfortune always found them, two people who never asked for trouble?

Jonquil was plagued by a vague disquiet over this evening's entertainment, but Gabriel had insisted they do the show as usual. Bailey must not suspect that after tonight's performance, they would be parting company with the carnival troupe that had housed them for the last few months.

Gabriel had also assured her the man he'd clobbered probably would have such a walloping headache he'd be holed up in some quiet room tonight, away from loud activity. If worse came to worst and he did show up, he'd never recognize Jonquil as the dirty-faced waif he'd seen today.

Jonquil hoped the last was true. Though she was certain he'd seen neither face nor hair, he'd certainly viewed every other part of her anatomy. At least tonight she'd be fully dressed.

Adam walked on shaky legs down the street toward the livery barn, where music and laughter floated on the crisp night air. How he'd managed to find his way back to his hotel after the blow to his head, he'd never know. Only after a long nap, a hot soak in a tub, a shave, and clean clothes did he feel almost human again. But his brain still banged against his skull.

27

He couldn't understand how he'd allowed himself to be bamboozled by the woman in the stream. Seeing her standing there with all her secrets so lushly revealed had clearly affected his judgment. The wallop to his head had been his punishment for letting down his guard. It wouldn't happen again.

His fingers coiled around the twenty-dollar bill inside his pants pocket. Apparently anxious to escape, the woman and her accomplice had overlooked the prize money.

Well, he hadn't. Adam might not recognize the lady if he saw her again, but if he should, he would enjoy watching her squirm when he returned her money.

Nearing the entrance to the livery, he paused outside the open door. His throbbing head made him as spiteful as a skinned snake. If he had any sense, he would return to his hotel room and forget the lady, but something about the quaint music flowing from the barn expelled any thoughts of leaving.

Faint circles of light from the hanging lanterns warded off complete darkness inside. In their soft haze the darkened silhouettes of the audience were no more than a long chain of paper people, connected at the shoulders as they swayed to the music.

As the tune became more lively, so did the spectators. It was the kind of sound that caused rumps to shake, hands to clap, and feet to tap, and made everyone want to join in with good-time abandon. Mesmerized by the music, distracted from his headache, Adam maneuvered along the side walls, among the standing observers, until he stood at the bottom of the makeshift stage.

Against a backdrop of dried corn stalks, hay, and pumpkin-faced scarecrows, a young woman sat cross-legged on a high stool. Oblivious to the alluring picture she made or the effect of her hiked-up skirt on the men, she plucked away at the banjo snuggled beneath her bosom.

The black bombazine material of her dress embraced every recognizable curve. And there were plenty, Adam thought, envying the banjo's position.

Protruding from a sea of black ruffles on the underside of her petticoat, her silk-stockinged knee and upper calf shimmered in the dusky lantern light. Her foot tapped to the music, her boot tassel swinging back and forth like the pendulum of a clock.

Adam felt the large room close in around him, and his head pounded against the dull, throbbing ache. He kept his eyes riveted on the enchanting entertainer, absorbed in his fantasy of removing that stocking from her long silk-covered leg.

With nimble fingers she plucked the five strings, captivating her audience as she ripped out the tune. Her hair, the color of golden sunshine, hung loose and flowing to her waist. It picked up the brilliance of the large, yellow silk rose pinned to her shoulder.

Faster and faster, her fingers flailed and rapped away at the strings, raising the hairs on the back of Adam's neck with their musical magic. Focused only on the notes she turned loose on the air, she softened her expression as her tempo shifted and she produced a sweeter, more melancholy sound.

And then she opened her mouth to sing. Her haunting, vibrant voice, filled with emotion, stilled the enraptured crowd. Its richness would have put a nightingale to shame.

Adam stood, unable to move, in the semidarkness and listened to the sweet, intense words of her song. When the ballad ended, the woman rose and walked to the edge of the platform to cheers and a standing ovation.

She bowed slowly in Adam's direction. For a brief moment, eyes the color of a blue jay's wing met and held his own.

Adam Coulter had found his blue-eyed angel.

Chapter Two

Horsefeathers.

Jonquil's eyes locked on the man glaring up at her from the foot of the stage, and she wished she could disappear into the hay-infested air.

He knows, she thought.

Gabriel had been wrong about the stranger's not being well enough to attend the festivities. Thinking he looked none the worse from the blow he'd received on his head, she wrested her eyes from his accusing stare.

You fool—the inner voice tried to calm her—*of course he doesn't recognize you. How could he? He saw only your wet underthings, not your face and hair.*

Somewhat bolstered by the reassuring thought, Jonquil turned her attention back to her audience. Bestowing on them her most devastating smile, she took one last bow.

When the crowd began to ready the livery for the dance, Jonquil glanced at the porcelain vessel that always sat at the edge of the stage when she performed. Her mother's heirloom chamber pot, long ago retired from its functional duty, now served as a receptacle for contributions from her appreciative audience.

Her eyes slid over its crackled, glazed surface decorated with vines of trailing yellow roses. Always filled with wildflowers when her mother was alive, it had brought beauty to their home's threadbare interior. Now, spilling over with notes and coins from Jonquil's enraptured fans, it represented security.

Judging from its contents, she'd never miss the twenty dollars she'd purposely left with the stranger at the stream's edge—the man who still hadn't moved from the stage area.

When she stooped to retrieve the pot, she saw him drop the disturbing twenty-dollar note on top of the other money. Tilting his head back, a wry grin on his face, he looked her straight in the eye as though gauging her reaction.

"You left this."

He does know. Unable to control her runaway heart, Jonquil concentrated instead on the soft henna-colored hairs that sprouted from the backs of his fingers and hands. Whatever was she to do?

Again, that calming inner voice rallied to soothe her: Play innocent. He didn't see you.

Jonquil stood and rested the cumbersome pot on the curve of her hip. Forcing a calmness she didn't feel, she managed to reply, "Thank you for your generous gift."

"Gift?" He chuckled, then mumbled, "Not hardly." He rubbed the side of his head and quirked one eyebrow.

"Excuse me?" Jonquil stared back at his face, strong and handsome in the orange, lantern light. His eyes were dark, unreadable. She had the strange sensation that he could see clear through to her soul, and the idea unnerved her. "I really must be going," she said.

His tone coupled with a sudden stormy expression. "I think not." Jonquil saw that escape would not be

31

so easy this time.

She mentally calculated all the charges he could bring against her if he so desired—fraud, assault and, after investigation, finally murder. She felt the noose tightening around her neck.

"Do you dance?"

The question caught her by surprise. "Dance?" she asked. The macabre image of a hanging, jerking corpse flashed before Jonquil's eyes.

"You do know how." He looked at her as though his question had gone unheard.

Regaining her thoughts, Jonquil pulled her focus back to the man's face. "Most certainly. But usually I don't dance with the locals."

She lied. On many occasions such as this, she would grant an enamored admirer or two a waltz around the floor. Single women were always in demand at dances on the carnival circuit. But this man—to allow him a dance, to walk into his arms after what he'd seen of her—this was entirely different.

"I'm not local." He stared at the chamber pot resting on her hip. "Now if you'll put down your thunder mug, I'll allow you to dance with me."

"Thunder mug!"

Jonquil's eyes sought the painted vines on the object in her arms, and she blushed with humiliation. Never had she thought of her precious chamber pot as anything but a vase. The man's haughty attitude angered her. "I think not, sir." She turned away.

"You and your friend damn near knocked my brains out this afternoon. I believe you owe me an explanation."

"Shhhhh!"

Glancing nervously about, Jonquil swung around to face him. No one appeared to have heard his accusation. She was caught. All she could do was apologize.

Sighing, she moved closer to the edge of the stage. "I'm sorry. We meant you no harm." She grabbed the twenty-dollar note and thrust it in his direction. "This should more than make up for your pain. Now, if you'll excuse me."

The stranger gave her an appraising look. "I don't think so." In one effortless stride, he mounted the platform and frowned down at her. Standing on the ground, he hadn't appeared quite so intimidating. Now Jonquil had to tilt her head back to look into his face.

Struggling for control of her emotions, she replied, "I told you I'm sorry, so please take the twenty and—"

But, not to be thwarted, he interrupted. "Look," he said, "I did save your pretty little hide. Don't you think you might repay me with one dance?" He gave her a broad wink. "It's not as though I plan to kidnap you."

Jonquil studied the tall stranger with the teasing eyes. He was nothing like the other men in the barn, spiffed up as he was in his fine, pleated shirt and striped gray-and-black trousers. No, she decided. Dancing was the last thing she wanted to do with this man. His presence was much too disturbing. He knew far too much about her already.

"If you refuse me"—his pause sounded ominous— "I might have to confess to these fine citizens what I know about a certain lad who won the foot race this afternoon."

"You wouldn't!" Jonquil searched his face for confirmation.

"I would, and will. Now, if you please, I fear the music is about to begin." He extended his arm toward the floor on which others had begun to mingle.

"You deserved that blow," Jonquil muttered beneath her breath. Too late she realized he'd caught the murmur. His dark, black stare pierced her.

Her mind reeled. If only she could distance herself from this unsettling man. The heat of temper crept up her neck, and she bit her tongue to keep from telling him exactly what she thought of his attempt at extortion. He was no better than the vile little man he'd saved her from earlier, only cloaked in a prettier wrapping.

"If you insist," she countered, "but first I must dispose of my *thunder mug*." She shot him an angry look, then turned on her heels and marched toward the shadows at the back of the stage.

Never in all of Adam Coulter's thirty years had he been forced to browbeat a lady into dancing with him. He watched the woman sashay across the stage and nearly disappear into the dark shadows. Her hair, glowing like spun gold in the darkness, was his only assurance that she had not kept on walking. It was evident she wasn't pleased with his request, if one could call a threat a request. But the lady intrigued him. He wasn't about to let her escape again.

He couldn't believe his good fortune, if one could include in that a near-fatal blow with a tree stump. How long had it been since he had taken a beautiful woman in his arms just for the sheer pleasure of dancing with her? Clearly, she had resisted with every fiber of her being, but he preferred to think she had been motivated by guilt.

He chuckled under his breath. If he'd truly wanted to make an impression, it would have been so simple to flash his badge in return for the bump on his head. But, from what he could tell, the lady had a protector, someone who was not about to see her come to harm. Adam couldn't blame anyone for that.

Just for a while, however, he wanted to forget that

he wore the cloak of the law, had just left one trail in pursuit of another. Tonight he wanted to be like any other man, to inhale the sweet scent of a woman, this woman, if for only one dance. Then he'd be on his way.

Jonquil hated the helpless position in which she found herself. Fuming, she swept toward Gabriel, standing at the back of the platform. He strummed his instrument in tune with the other musicians. With great effort Jonquil plastered a shallow smile on her lips. No use in causing him worry.

Gabriel's face softened as she approached, his deft black fingers picking away at banjo strings. Depositing the money beneath his chair, Jonquil stood up again and smiled affectionately at her mentor.

She hoped he wouldn't recognize her dancing partner and allow his concern for her to overrule his good judgment. The less attention they received in crowds, the better.

The biggest lesson Jonquil and Gabriel had learned in the last months was that people didn't take kindly to a white woman traveling with a black man. Experience had taught them to keep a low profile for fear of retribution.

Now that she had this stranger to contend with, she would deal with him herself. Or at least try. If she could get past his dark, flashing eyes, the upturned smile whenever he looked at her. He must never suspect Gabriel as her accomplice.

Jonquil walked back to the edge of the stage where the towering stranger waited.

He hopped down from the platform. "Don't look so frightened," he teased, extending his arms.

Jonquil ignored the gesture and moved unassisted down the makeshift stairs onto the dance floor. Sending him a look that clearly stated he was as bothersome as a skunk at a picnic, she stood in silence, waiting for the music to begin.

"You do have a name, don't you?"

With arms folded across her bosom, Jonquil stared defiantly at the buttons on his shirt.

"Shall I call you Godiva?"

A sudden heat rushed through Jonquil at the mention of the medieval, naked noblewoman. In the afternoon this man had seen nearly as much of her. "Call me whatever you wish," she countered with a light shrug. Stealing a second glance at his face, she saw the crinkle lines around his eyes and mouth crease into the beginnings of a smile.

"Well . . ."

The man was trying to be amiable. After all, it was only one dance. If she searched her soul, she did owe him something for saving her from the slimy little despot at the stream.

As hard as she tried, Jonquil had never been able to hold a grudge. She forced a smile as the first strains of "Little Rosewood Casket" floated across the livery. The pleasing notes encouraged even the most unskilled dancers to the floor. Sensing a certain safety in the crowd, Jonquil relaxed. This time, when the stranger offered his hand, she took it.

He felt good against her, solid and strong. He danced as though he were born to music. He was so different from the single men who usually wanted the favor of a dance. After imbibing the local moonshine for most of the afternoon, they could hardly stand by the time the music started.

Where his fingers balanced at the slight indentation of her waist, Jonquil's skin burned beneath the layers of fabric. She was aware of the hot, moist air cupped in the space where her hand rested lightly on his. She felt like a summer moth gliding on a warm breeze as he steered her around the crowded barn.

"A forest nymph without a name."

Jonquil's heart fluttered at his words. She met his teasing brown eyes, not yet prepared to forgive him for coercing her into dancing. "If I don't tell you, will you have me drawn and quartered for withholding information?"

"Now, that might prove interesting."

His playful expression tugged at her heart. "I'm sorry I bullied you." When he apologized, the look on his face was enough to make an unbeliever believe. "I wouldn't have turned you in."

At the statement Jonquil nearly stumbled.

Relax, she scolded herself. He couldn't possibly know anything, so she settled her arm around his neck to savor the man who smelled like cedar and pine needles.

"What about you, sir? Do you have a name?" She held his gaze, waiting for his answer. Certainly, anyone who carried the essence of mother earth on his person couldn't be all bad.

"Adam Coulter," he replied. "I'd be pleased if you called me Adam."

Jonquil thought of all the names she could have called him earlier, but now she only smiled at the sound of his name. It fit. Adam, the man of the red earth. His scent reminded her of the little piece of ground she'd called home all her life. The small farm at Prater, near Murfreesboro, where they could never go back. Ah, well, that was the past. She must not dwell on things she couldn't control.

With practiced effort, she pushed aside her melancholy and studied her partner. Even among the "carnies," Jonquil had never met a man who wore such a fancy shirt—stark white with starched, pressed pleats running in rows, like a newly furrowed field, down its front. So intent was she on his attire, Jonquil almost missed a step.

"Your name?" he asked again.

"Jonquil," she answered, her eyes briefly meeting his.

His tanned, chiseled features stood out in dazzling contrast against the whiteness of his shirt. Soft umber shadows played beneath his deep-set eyes, around his full lips, and in the deep cleft in his chin. His chestnut hair smelled as though it had been freshly washed. Curls hung in wayward strands over his forehead. If somewhere under that thick hair a goose egg still remained, she prayed it no longer hurt.

"Jonquil who?"

"Rose." Her eyes locked with his momentarily, then slipped again to his wide shoulders. He was fine looking, indeed.

"Jonquil Rose." He repeated her name, allowing it to roll off his tongue. "Last name or stage name?"

"What?"

"Rose."

Her chin lifted a fraction of an inch. "You ask too many questions, sir."

Adam looked apologetic. "Sorry." He played with the name again. "Very pretty. It suits you."

"It does?"

He only smiled.

Margaret Trevain's love of flowers had given birth to her daughter's name, not to mention her baby's shock of golden hair. Capturing the memory of the stories her mother would endlessly spin, a sudden sorrow gripped Jonquil now. No longer her mother's fair yellow rose, she was, instead, a woman with no future, always looking back.

The music stopped. The other couples drifted away before Jonquil realized she was still locked in Adam's arms. Jerking from his embrace, she felt her face color and quickly looked toward the stage. Gabriel sat studying her.

Adam's attention followed hers. "Now I understand."

"Understand what?" Surely, he hadn't figured out Gabriel was her accomplice.

"The yellow rose. It fits your name." He nodded his head toward the huge blossom pinned to her shoulder.

With a sigh of relief, Jonquil answered, "Yes, you might say that. Now if you'll excuse me, I really must be going."

"Oh, but you can't." Adam took her arm in his. "I've never met a live rose before, and I feel you need a drink of punch to keep you from wilting." He steered her toward a far corner, to the refreshment table.

Though he did seem pleasant enough, she really shouldn't linger. There was danger in involvement, no matter how brief. However, she told herself, it was only for this one evening.

Throwing caution aside, Jonquil accepted the punch he offered. Together they walked toward the front of the livery to the inviting cooler air. "Oh, Them Golden Slippers" pealed out from the stage, the tune more lively than the others. Several couples joined in a fast spin around the dance floor.

"Who taught you to sing and play the banjo?" Adam asked, stopping at the door. "You're gifted, you know."

She gave a soft laugh, "Hardly. I have a wonderful teacher and friend. He taught me everything I know about music . . . and a lot of other things, as well. He's the truly gifted one."

She looked above the heads of the dancing men and women to Gabriel. Such talent, she thought, as she watched his nimble fingers move up and down the neck of the banjo. But because he's a man of color, he's only allowed to play for white folks in some obscure little place where musicians are in short supply. Bitterness swelled inside her.

"He must have been a fine teacher." Adam's gaze

39

strayed to the musician whose finesse with the banjo was equal to Jonquil's own. The teacher, he decided. What a strange pair.

Adam had been moved by Jonquil's talent. "You should be performing somewhere besides a livery stable."

"And where might that be?"

"The Fourteenth Street Theater in New York, for example."

She shrugged her shoulders as if he were daft. "Really, Mr. Coulter, I have about as much chance of getting to New York as I do of getting to London." Her deep blue eyes twinkled.

Adam caught the formal use of his surname. Nevertheless, he wanted to know everything about this woman. She spoke through a guarded veneer, but her whole being betrayed her, exuding a warmth she obviously tried to keep under wraps. Warmth was a quality he'd found sadly lacking in other females he'd known.

"Where are you headed, Miss Rose?"

"Headed? Why, nowhere."

"By that, I take it to mean you intend to stay with the carnival, running races as a boy and singing your heart out at night. Not much of a life for a lady such as yourself."

"I like my life, Mr. Coulter." She held his eyes with hers. "But let me assure you my racing days are over."

"Why? You're very fast."

Jonquil burst out laughing, remembering all the races that had come before. "You could say that."

When she laughed, her eyes sparkled like sapphires.

"I promise I won't breathe a word of your ruse to anyone," he said, "and if you choose to continue racing, you should have no fears about that little rat who threatened you this afternoon."

Jonquil gave Adam a quizzical look. Why, the man

40

almost sounded as if he approved of her trickery. If it were only that easy, she thought. After tonight she could no longer stay with the carnival, not after finding out about Bailey's scam. Tomorrow she and Gabriel would be on their way, and she'd never see Adam Coulter again. The intrusive thought saddened her.

Jonquil couldn't remember when she'd ever had more than a two- or three-word conversation with any man other than Gabriel. Usually she avoided all contact with outsiders. But tonight was different.

After all, Mr. Coulter had saved her from heaven only knew what kind of fate, and she owed him this small return. In spite of herself, she found his company most congenial. She wanted to know more about him, where he was from, how long he'd be staying. But she didn't dare ask. In truth, it wouldn't matter. Not after tonight.

Adam's next words shattered her fanciful thoughts. "I'm leaving first thing in the morning for Fort Smith. I'm visiting an old friend there."

Jonquil felt the color drain from her face. *Fort Smith. Isaac Parker, the hanging judge.* She had read of the federal court and the judge's dedication to justice. The mere mention of the fated place conjured up all sorts of emotions.

"Miss Rose?"

"Sorry?"

"You seemed to be miles away. Are you all right?"

Jonquil dispelled the disturbing thought and gave him her most appealing smile. "I'm fine. Just contemplating. You were saying?"

"Where does the carnival go from here?"

"Little Rock," she managed to answer, hoping she didn't sound as nervous as she felt. His mention of Fort Smith had shaken Jonquil more than she thought possible. No matter where she went, an innocent word or inquiry would suddenly remind her that she was always on the run. Would it never end?

A new tune started, this time a ballad. Adam smiled down at her, taking the empty glass from her hand. "How about one more turn?"

Jonquil had to keep herself from escaping the livery. "All right, but then I really must leave." Accepting his extended elbow, she allowed him to escort her toward several other couples. Only this dance, then she'd rejoin the performers. She had tarried much too long.

The melody of "Wildwood Flower" floated on the soft air as the two waltzed among the other dancers. The familiar words sounded in Jonquil's mind, playing out their own message as she stared at the plowed pleats on Adam's fancy white shirt.

I'll think of him never, I'll be wildly gay,
I'll charm every heart and the crowd I will sway,
I'll live yet to see him regret the dark hour,
When he won then neglected the frail wildwood
    flower.

A mournful shadow drifted across her heart, and Jonquil tried to focus her thoughts on tomorrow. But the refrain, "I'll live yet to see him regret the dark hour," played over and over in her head. Fighting against her morose thoughts, she stole a glance at her dancing partner. When his gaze locked with her own, her heart nearly stopped its natural beating, and Jonquil was engulfed with yearning for the handsome stranger.

A cream cheese moon hung low in the early morning dawn. Jonquil dozed in half-sleep on the wagon seat next to Gabriel. The air felt brisk and damp against her face. She snuggled deeper into her flannel jacket.

Gabriel turned from staring at the mule's rump to his companion. "You all right?"

Jonquil jerked upright and pulled her wide-billed cap tighter against her head. Tucking under a couple of wayward strands, she stretched her arms high over her shoulders.

"Right as rain," she quipped, sneaking a sideways glance at him.

"Rain ain't always right," he harrumphed, "especially if you're caught in a storm without cover."

"You think it's going to rain?" Jonquil glanced toward the sky, pretending to take his statement literally.

Gabriel's licorice gaze adhered to her like sticky candy. "I ain't speakin' of the weather, miss."

"Then, whatever do you mean?" Jonquil's chin jutted out in determination. Her feelings about the previous evening were too confusing for her to even think about, much less discuss. But Gabriel refused to let the subject drop. He returned his attention to the animal ahead.

"Wha'd your dancin' partner say about his sore head?"

She gave a nervous laugh, but her forced glee sounded hollow to her own ears. "You were right, Gabriel; he didn't recognize us. We're safe from his calling in the law."

Again the driver's stare settled on her. He probably saw right through her lie. Sometimes the man knew her better than she knew herself. After all, he'd nurtured her most of her life, both her and her mother.

But now she saw their roles reversed, and the responsibility fell to her to protect him from the hangman's noose. Therefore, little lies were justified. She'd keep up the pretense that the stranger hadn't recognized them. If Gabriel found out Adam Coulter

43

had coerced her into dancing with him, there was no telling what he might do.

"Girl, I wasn't born yesterday, you know." Distractedly, Gabriel slapped the reins against the mule's rump. "I'm more concerned about the moonstruck look you wore on your face while he skipped you around the floor."

"Oh, Gabriel, you're being ridiculous." Jonquil was thankful that the boy's cap hid her bright red ears.

"It's jest I worry about you, Miss Rose. Without your mama there ain't no one to explain those mixed-up feelin's young ladies have to cope with." Concern was written on his brown face. "You jest ain't experienced enough to deal with such a dapper-looking man."

How true that was. Yet, Gabriel was in a position too vulnerable for her to discuss this with him. "It was nothing but a dance." Jonquil reached over and patted the black man's knee. "Trust me."

Shrugging his shoulders and shaking his head, Gabriel turned his attention back to the driving of the wagon. "*One* dance I wouldn't be worried about, Miss Rose."

Sinking into the tense silence that followed, Jonquil fought her own disquieting thoughts.

Last evening, begging exhaustion, she had left Adam, promising to see him before the carnival pulled out this morning. Then she had tossed and turned most of the night, wrestling with her fib and her emotions.

But Gabriel's life and her own were fated, and by morning they would be long gone. It saddened her to think she'd never see the handsome stranger again, but in the reality of day, their magical encounter seemed more like a dream.

The buckboard wagon that had been their home for the past months carried them westward. As the

44

new sun rose over the horizon, it warmed Jonquil's back and shoulders. A good sign, she thought. Maybe Hot Springs would be a place where she and Gabriel could settle down.

The man in the fancy white shirt floated before her sleepy eyes like a distant mirage, and Jonquil felt a wrenching loss. But he was only an illusion, and like all illusions he, too, would quickly fade away.

Chapter Three

Adam pushed his Stetson off his forehead and eyed the carnival manager, who stood squinting up at him. "You have a Miss Rose in your employ?" Dropping the reins across the saddle horn, he allowed his horse to crop the grass at its hooves.

"Shee-it. That little singer?" The soggy cigar clamped between the man's teeth garbled his speech. "Why, she skedaddled outa here early this morning. She and that man of color she lives with were gone before sunup."

Adam cursed beneath his breath. Damn it to hell. He should have known that wily female would slip away before he had a chance to see her again.

"Are you certain?" He tried to mask his disappointment. "When I left her last night, she informed me she'd be leaving with the carnival this morning."

"Naah . . . good riddance to bad rubbish, I say." The man named Bailey scratched his watermelon-shaped belly, then moved grimy fingers to his armpit.

The image of a baboon came to mind. The man's bloated face and slack lips flaunted his inclination toward the excessive. Excessive in everything but cleanliness. Disgusted, Adam forced his gaze from the carny's discolored armpit. "You have any idea where the lady may have been headed?"

"Lady, ha! Ain't much of a lady that'd travel unchaperoned in the company of a darkie."

This nauseating excuse for mankind wasn't suitable for Jonquil to wipe her tasseled boot upon, Adam decided. But here the man stood, handing out judgments as if he were God Himself. He bit back his anger. He'd learned a long time ago that the best way to obtain information was to remain amiable.

"You know anyone who might know where they went?"

"Naw . . . her kind come and go." Bailey winked at Adam, and shifted the sodden cigar to the opposite corner of his mouth. "Want my advice, sonny? Forget the little singer." He edged closer and spoke in a conspiratorial tone. "She made it real clear she sleeps only with the darkie."

Bailey's sour breath sent Adam up straighter in his saddle, his fist clenching the pommel for patience. *To fend off the likes of you, I would imagine.*

"No, sir, you don't want to be plowing in that black man's field."

Adam fought the urge to scatter Bailey's teeth across the dirt. *Ignorant bastard!* Apparently, Jonquil had scorned his lascivious advances and wounded his warped pride. In return, he'd retaliated the only way he knew—by casting aspersions upon her character.

As a detective, Adam had met plenty of men like the one before him. Lowlives, no-accounts, predators. They were all the same. The only brain they had resided in the crotch. The sooner he distanced himself from this fool, the better.

In one respect, however, the man was right. Adam might as well forget the fascinating woman of last night. Obviously, she'd intended all along to forget him. Right now he had more pressing matters on his mind. Judge Parker was waiting for him.

Anxious to be on his way, Adam focused his attention back on Bailey. "This darkie. Does he

47

have a name?"

"He might," Bailey answered, ogling Adam's finely tooled saddlebag, "but that information will cost you." He folded his arms across his ample belly and waited.

Not bothering to ask how much, Adam tossed a silver coin at his feet.

The man bent over to pick up the piece before he answered.

"Gabriel." He spat on the coin and rubbed it against his rough sleeve. Satisfied he'd been well paid for his information, he continued. "Named after one of God's angels, I s'pose, although there weren't nothing angelic about him."

Adam expelled a deep sigh. By now he'd had his fill of the pugnacious little man. He yanked the reins of his horse, jerking him into motion, volleying rocks and pebbles at a surprised Bailey. The carny stumbled backward and landed on his meaty backside.

"You, mister, ain't no better than those two you're looking for," Bailey shouted to Adam's back. "You just better hope we don't meet again."

"My sentiments exactly," Adam muttered to himself, urging his horse into a gallop. "There's no telling what I might be tempted to do to your stinking hide."

Taking the road out of town, Adam tried to forget his disruptive obsession with the blond-headed woman. Interesting, he thought. Had he not been on his way to Fort Smith, he never would have run across her in the first place. Setting her image aside, he tried instead to focus on the trip ahead.

Nearly a year had passed since Adam's younger brother, Simon, had written to his mother. A United States deputy marshal with Judge Parker's court, Simon could find himself in some remote area of the Oklahoma Territory, where mail would be a problem. But his last letter had placed him in the southern part of Arkansas.

In order to relieve his mother's anxiety, Adam had begun looking for Simon on his own. Now he hoped the judge would fill him in on his younger brother's remiss behavior. Afterward, he would take a well-earned vacation.

Apprehending a slippery bank robber had taken the starch out of Adam. Wanted in four states, Tom Haskins had given him a merry chase from Kentucky to Mississippi. But, in the end, seeing the look in the outlaw's eyes when he had been cornered outside of Greenville had made the effort worth every muscle-aching mile.

Since then, all Adam could think about was having some time to himself in the Ozarks before returning to Chicago. That was before he'd met the elusive little songbird.

Now he toyed with the idea of sporting for bird instead of fish. It had been a long time since any woman had kindled his interest the way Jonquil Rose had. Here one minute, gone the next. A pretty piece of fluff with golden hair and deep blue eyes.

A narrow stream tagged along with the road for some distance. From time to time Adam gave his horse the lead and his mind permission to wander. After a few miles, the horse would head for the bank and both rider and animal would refresh themselves.

At one such spot, Adam rested on his haunches beside the cooling water, wiping his brow. Unwillingly, his thoughts returned to the first time he had seen the real Jonquil Rose.

She had stood in the stream, defying the threat of danger, all her womanly secrets revealed beneath the clinging wet fabric of her chemise and drawers. A woman with those curves had to be experienced with men, especially traveling with a carnival. The thought brought a quickening to his loins.

Imagining the type of woman she could be, however, just didn't quite ring true with what he wanted to think of her. He replayed the carny's words. Bailey's hostility had been obvious, and the more the man said, the more Adam had doubted her lack of respectability. Fighting his imagination, he stood, slapped his hat against his thigh, and forced his mind's eye from her tempting body back to her face, attempting to dwell on her comeliness.

Grabbing the reins, Adam remounted his horse and headed for the road. Where the hell had she gone?

The fact that she wasn't alone eased his mind a little. Now that he had rescued her from the scoundrel at the stream, he was surprised that he felt a certain protectiveness toward her.

Arkansas, bordering on the Indian Territory to the west, invited all sorts of reprobates into the state to prey upon innocents. Before Judge Parker had taken his seat on the federal bench, anarchy had ruled. No law-abiding citizen was safe from one who would claim his life with a gun.

Now that Parker had been around a few years, outlaws thought twice before drawing attention to themselves. But there were still a few who, for a while, could outrun his marshals. The judge had elaborated on this in his last letter.

Worldly or not, Adam felt Jonquil could handle any situation she encountered. He'd witnessed the lady's mettle, had felt the power of her companion's blow, so they probably could take care of themselves. A dull headache served as a painful reminder of just how formidable the two could be.

Adam reined in his horse at the top of a small rise and looked down on the Arkansas River. The loading platforms at the wharf were congested with people and cargo. Packets moved like lumbering snails through the water toward their destination. The Fort Smith steamer waited for its shipment to be loaded.

Guiding his horse toward the wharf, he scanned the crowd of travelers for a blond woman and her black male companion. When no one matching their description materialized, he admonished himself for searching for her. For all he knew, she could be posing as a boy, hiding among the other wide-bills milling around the water's edge. She could also be halfway to Louisiana by now.

Adam realized just how little he knew about Jonquil. She'd been far from accommodating when he'd quizzed her about her background, as well as her reason for impersonating a lad in the foot race. Damn, she'd been fast.

He supposed any female, to profit from such an unexpected talent, would have had no choice but to lie. But, why, after he'd saved her from the weasel back in Pine Bluff, had he been knocked nearly senseless and left for dead?

And why had Jonquil stolen off before dawn? Was he so threatening that he'd frightened her off? He wiped his hand along his jaw. So loathsome that she wanted nothing to do with him?

The possibility sickened him. Well, it wouldn't be the first time. Wasn't that why he stayed away from women in general? Last night, however, he'd really thought it had been different, that she had enjoyed his company as much as he had hers.

Hell, he didn't have time to worry about the lady or her lack of a courteous farewell. He was expected in Fort Smith within the week. Then why did she keep haunting him?

As hard as he tried, Adam couldn't banish Jonquil from his thoughts. Slowly her vision merged with that of another woman, taller, with darker hair. But they both had the same ivory and pink coloring, similar slender build.

Katherine.

An anguished sigh escaped his lips. Thrusting aside emotions he'd long ago buried, Adam swore under his breath. Jonquil Rose spelled trouble, no matter how he perceived her. His lips thinned. And now she'd managed to stir up painful memories he thought he'd conquered.

He had enough troubles without adding new ones to a list of many. Like finding out why his delinquent brother hadn't written his mother in a month of Sundays.

Jonquil, with her baffling contradictions, was too distracting for the life Adam had chosen for himself. He preferred his solitary existence. After his visit with Judge Parker, he'd stick to his original plan—fishing. It was a hell of a lot safer.

"Wha'd I give for hair like yours." Flo stood behind the stool, pulling a brush through Jonquil's hair.

Meeting the girl's reflection in the cloudy mirror that hung above the dressing table, Jonquil reassured her. "Your hair is just as nice as mine, just a different color."

"It's the only thin thing about me," Flo answered good-naturedly, flashing one of her toothy smiles. She dropped down on the seat beside Jonquil and stared at her own reflection in the mirror. "Why God saw fit to make me as big and clumsy as a workhorse, I'll never know."

Jonquil tried to console her new friend. "Don't belittle yourself so. You're just wholesome, that's all."

"Wholesome is right," Flo quipped, meeting Jonquil's gaze. "When those fellows downstairs pay a buck to skip me around the dance floor, they get to hold some . . . and then some." The look on Flo's face sent both girls into riotous laughter.

The two young women slumped against the dressing table covered with jars of face paint and powders in every shade under the rainbow. Their wheezing laughter sent clouds of gossamer powder into the air, coating everything, including their faces, in a fine dust. Jonquil bubbled with uninhibited glee.

It had been three days since she and Gabriel had arrived in Hot Springs. And for the first time in her life Jonquil could say she'd found her first girlfriend. The other two hurdy-gurdy gals who worked in the saloon were pleasant enough, but Flo, with her warm manner and big smile, had soaked up Jonquil's reserve and had seeped into her thirsty heart.

Finding employment had not been as hard as Jonquil and Gabriel had anticipated. They had covered Main Street, learning the town's layout and noting the many saloons that dotted it. As she'd read the signs of The Ohio and The Kentucky, Jonquil had wondered if they catered only to people from those states. One saloon named The Office had really confused her. Who frequented it?

The largest hurdle she'd faced was Gabriel's objection to her performing in a saloon. But Jonquil had insisted it was the only thing she wanted to do, then had gently reminded him it was the only thing she could do well.

Gabriel had reluctantly agreed, but only on the condition that he make the final decision concerning the place they chose. He had wanted to be sure Jonquil's position was for singer only.

Most of the saloons had had permanent entertainment, but at the last place they'd tried, the owner had announced he'd just lost his piano player. He'd agreed to try their act for a week, paying them a salary of three dollars and all the tips they earned. If they were well received by the saloon's patrons, he would hire them full time, he'd said.

Jonquil now shared a room and bed with Flo, over the saloon, and was happier than she had been since she and Gabriel had been forced to leave their farm. Perhaps here, with so many people coming and going, they could make a home for themselves.

Gabriel took a job in the bath house as a day

attendant, and slept in the livery at night in exchange for mucking out the shed once a day. Saving every penny they earned in tips, they stashed these away in case they had to move on.

The girls' costumes were varied. Each had certain frills, but their type and extent depended on how popular she was. French styles were fashionable among the managements of the "thirst parlors," as were silks, ostrich feathers, and fancy hats. The proprietors shortened hems and lowered necklines to expose more leg and bosom.

Although Jonquil was not a "honky-tonk" gal, the owner insisted that she dress as one. So, with Flo's help, she restyled a black dress the two found in an old trunk.

It showed a trifle more bosom than Jonquil felt comfortable revealing, but at least it covered up most of the striped silk stockings she'd agreed to wear. After her first performance, Jonquil waited for the owner to express his objections to her alterations. None were forthcoming.

From the moment Jonquil appeared onstage and uttered her first throaty note, the men in attendance bought more drinks, stayed longer, and tipped bigger to watch the golden-haired, blue-eyed singer. Later that evening, she and Flo lay on their lumpy mattress in the early hours past midnight.

"Honey, you sure brought the menfolks in tonight." Flo's quiet voice carried no hint of envy, only open admiration.

In the darkened room Jonquil fretted, unable to savor her success. "I kept waiting for Mr. Haskell to complain about my gown."

"Haskell?" Flo gave a light chuckle. "Why, that man may not look so smart, but he knows the jingle of coins when he hears it." The bed creaked as Flo settled into her pillow. "Just ignore him. With your talent, you could stand on the street corner dressed in long johns, and Haskell wouldn't have a customer left in the place."

At the image of long underwear flapping against her legs in the late autumn wind, Jonquil smiled. "Thank you, friend," she said in a sleepy voice, "you do know how to ease the mind."

The second night the saloon filled to capacity. From the upstairs landing Jonquil scanned the smoky hall, taking in the crowd awaiting her appearance. To think that these people actually paid to hear her sing. What a heady feeling! Quietly she stole back to her room and defiantly secured her yellow silk rose to the plunging vee of her black gown.

Once downstairs she caught the boss eyeing the blossom with its intent to conceal. Raising her chin a little, she gave him a challenging nod, and he said nothing. But later, when his vulturish stare followed her every movement, fear replaced her earlier victorious mood.

That night as Flo dozed beside her, Jonquil lay alert to every night sound. Crickets chirped in defiance of the approaching dawn, and somewhere in the sleeping town a dog's lonely howl echoed off the surrounding mountains.

Jonquil slipped from the bed and walked to the window, where a soft breeze rippled the faded lace curtain. Pulling a chair over, she propped her arms on the sill and looked down into the narrow alley. The waning moon left an oblique design across its path, velvet shadows sliced by metallic light.

She felt so homesick. She missed the security of her little farm. The more she thought about her former life, the more desolate she felt as she sat staring out into the night. Nearby, an unidentifiable creature scurried across the valley, ruffling discarded rubble in its path.

An errant tear escaped her eye. Suddenly, she thought of Adam Coulter and the dances they'd shared the night of the county fair. She'd hated sneaking away the next morning without a proper goodbye.

The moon peeked back at her through the fading night sky and Jonquil imagined that it also stood guard over him while he slept. Where was he? she wondered. Did he ever think of her?

Judge Parker stood and extended a hand across his cluttered desk. "Son, it's nice to see you again."

"You too, sir."

Adam returned the judge's firm handshake. "How are Mrs. Parker and the boys?" He took the chair the judge indicated.

"Everyone's fine." Parker sat behind his desk. "Mary keeps busy with her volunteer work, and the boys are involved with their studies."

Adam felt the judge's scrutiny.

"Last time I saw you, Adam, you were studying law at Northwestern."

"Yes, sir, ten years ago. Seems like another lifetime now." He laughed, recalling how at the young age of twenty he'd tried to impress his stepfather's important visitor with his own tender grasp of the law.

"How green I was." With a nod, he met the judge's smile. "Humbling, isn't it, when we reach maturity to find we aren't as smart as we thought we were?"

Parker chortled. His eyes twinkled as he leaned back in his chair and locked long, tapered fingers across his flat stomach.

At forty-plus, the judge cut an imposing figure. His arresting face, dignified by a tawny mustache and thick goatee, was enough to make anyone sit up and listen. Adam had heard that Judge Isaac Parker could quiet the most quarrelsome attorney by merely pointing a finger toward him. Seeing Parker now, he believed it.

"Your mother, how is she?" The older man's voice filled with concern as he leaned forward in the chair,

56

propping his elbows on the wooden arms.

"She's fine, just concerned about my rascal brother." Adam's smile felt out of place as he watched Parker's expression turn serious.

The judge stood and moved to a small cabinet. After filling two crystal glasses with port, he turned and crossed to the front of his desk. Stopping before Adam, he thrust one glass into his hand. "You're going to need this."

Adam stilled. Never taking his eyes from the older man's face, he raised the glass to his lips and let the cool liquid quench his suddenly parched mouth. Before the judge spoke again, he knew something had happened to Simon.

"It's your brother." Parker hesitated before continuing. "We've identified his remains here in Arkansas."

Adam's gaze dropped to the contents of his lowered glass. A heaviness lodged in his chest. His eye sockets burned as he fought to conceal the gathering moisture behind his lids. "How?"

"We don't know that, son."

"You're certain it was Simon?"

The judge moved behind his desk and pulled open a drawer. He placed a bundle wrapped in brown paper in the center of his desk. Sitting down again, he leaned forward in his chair and unwrapped the parcel as he spoke.

"Simon was working undercover, posing as a geological surveyor for a railroader named Innes Ball. Ball has a contract with the government, a joint venture for a new spur of track to be laid near Prater, outside of Murfreesboro."

Adam listened, his mind half-tuned to the judge's words as he recalled his half brother Simon's last letter. He'd mentioned grubbing around in rubble and dirt in southwest Arkansas and how much he'd hated the dirty, hot work.

The judge removed a man's striped work shirt

from the brown bundle, but not before Adam noted the garnet-colored stain that discolored its front.

He had witnessed much bloodshed during his stint as a lawman, but nothing had prepared him for what he felt at the sight of his brother's blood, puddled and dried like a large inkblot. Forcing down the bile in his throat, Adam scanned the remaining articles.

The gaudy silver buckle, tarnished over time, caught the window's light, reflecting a rectangular prism on the wall. Adam recognized it immediately. On a trip across the border before his last visit home, Simon had ordered the buckle fashioned by a Mexican silversmith.

"Does this belong to your brother?" A thorny frown creased the judge's brow.

Adam sighed. "It's Simon's." He'd often teased his baby brother about his garish taste. "I'd know that god-awful looking thing anywhere."

Parker's expression mirrored Adam's. Each man knew the buckle's wearer well. Adam suspected his clown of a brother had purposely had his initials monogrammed in the metal to resemble the spelling of the word *shit*. Only Simon Hector Thompson would have enjoyed shocking an observer and then pretending innocence at comprehension of the elaborately scrolled letters. There was no doubt; the buckle confirmed his brother's death.

"I'm sorry." The judge pushed back from the desk, stood, and walked toward the window. "If I'd known it would come to this, I'd never have sent the boy down there."

"It's not your fault, sir." Adam studied the tall, straight-backed man. "I'm sure Simon knew the risks when he pinned on the badge. We all do."

Parker turned from the window, regret in his eyes. "We'll bring his murderer to justice."

Adam watched the man who had sent many outlaws to the gallows. This judge's task was never easy, not today or anytime. Would anyone believe that this alleged sternest of judges was the gentlest men? he wondered.

The judge cleared his throat. "Innes Ball may not have delivered the killing blow to your brother. But, Adam, I have no doubt he had a part in it. The man is a crook. The worst sort, because he's so wealthy. Who knows how many people he's manipulated into his pocket? Washington is investigating his business dealings, and fraud is at the top of their list."

Anchoring his hands on the lapels of his coat, Parker reviewed the facts about the industrialist from New York. "It seems our Mr. Ball has been milking the government out of large sums of money by misrepresenting the price of equipment and land purchased to construct the rail line through southwest Arkansas. Working undercover, Simon had hired on with Ball as a surveyor."

Adam sat up straighter and listened intently.

"Ball owns several acres in the area of Prater, down in the south of the state. Donating his land as a show of good faith to the government, he then agreed to pay half the purchase price on any other land needed to secure the right-of-way for the railroad. Next he hired local contractors to supply wooden ties for the rails. Word has it, he's charging the government their fifty percent plus and adding the plus to his pocket."

Parker returned to his chair and leaned back. "Ball doesn't suspect he is under investigation. But when he couldn't produce the deed to the property he claims he owns, the government became suspicious. That's when they started investigating his business dealings and found him less than upstanding. Now he's claiming the woman who lives on the property is a squatter and stole the deed from him."

The judge ran his palm over his jaw. He seemed so tired. Simon was his loss as well. "We can't check Ball's word against a title because some of the records from around the beginning of the war are missing

59

from the Pike County Courthouse."

"Why not approach the woman? Maybe she has a copy of the deed."

"Simon was to have done that before he disappeared. On the property where we discovered your brother's body, we found three other graves as well. Two of them were in a thicket, along with your brother's, a good distance from the house."

Adam leaned forward.

"My men immediately suspected foul play. It was as if the graves were never meant to be found."

The judge paused as though in deep concentration. "The other two buried there had also been shot."

Silence settled in the room. The only sound was the creak of wood when the judge again settled his large frame into the chair.

"Then, how were they found?"

"That's the interesting part." Parker folded his arms across his chest. "You know as well as I do, when a lawman loses a comrade, he doesn't rest until he's uncovered every stone. When my men located the farm where Simon had worked, they scoured every part of it until they turned up whatever they could find.

"That's when they came upon them. Of the three graves lined up side by side, only your brother's had a makeshift cross at its head." He lowered his voice. "Almost as if the gravediggers knew there was something good about him."

He brought his chair upright. "I swear, if it hadn't been for that cross, those bodies would still be out there."

"You mentioned three other graves." Adam's question was little more than a whisper. "Where was the last one?"

"Not more than twenty feet from the house. We dug it up and it contained the body of a woman." The judge picked up a pencil from his desk and ran it absentmindedly through his fingers.

"It would appear that she died of natural causes. The small cross at the grave's head had crudely carved initials in it. *MMT*. She's probably the old woman Ball claims stole his deed."

"I want to take my brother's place." This time Adam stood and propped his hands on the judge's desk. "I want to find the son of a bitch who killed my brother and see him hanged."

The judge's eyes drilled into his. Adam could have bitten his tongue off because of his poor choice of words. After all, Parker's reputation preceded him far and wide—the "hanging judge" of Fort Smith.

"I'm sorry, sir, I meant no disrespect."

Charged with suppressed emotions, the air in the room could have been sliced with a knife.

A tight sigh escaped the older man's lips. "I never hanged a man, son. It was the law."

"I'm fully aware of that, sir, my comment was not directed at you. I, too, believe in an equal and exact justice." Aam waited for Parker's reply. When none was forthcoming, he ventured, "That's why you've got to allow me to take up where my brother left off. My record with Pinkerton can attest to my abilities."

"Your record is spotless. I'm not concerned about that."

"Sir?" Adam dropped into his chair.

"It's your mother. You're the only one she has left, now that your brother . . ." His last words faded into the air.

"I can handle my mother. She's a strong woman. If I know her, she would want to see my brother's killer brought to justice. My stepfather practiced law right up until his death."

"Your father was a fine lawyer and my friend." Parker gave Adam a direct, honest regard. "All right. I know he would feel the way you do about this."

"Are you saying I'll be working for you for a while?"

Parker beamed. "I'd like that very much. In fact, even with my reservations, I was hoping you'd insist."

"I'd like to accompany my brother's remains home to Chicago, but I can be back here in two weeks."

"Certainly, but you won't need to return to Fort Smith."

Rummaging through a stack of folders, the judge found the one he sought. "After finding the graves, several of my deputies did some snooping on their own. They found the woman Ball spoke of did live on his property. But not alone. Supposedly, the woman had a daughter around the age of eighteen. Townfolks said a Negro man lived with them. He farmed and sold vegetables and looked after the two women. Seems the old woman was simpleminded. She and the girl rarely went to town."

"This girl and the man, did your men question them?"

Parker thumbed through the folder and stopped. "About the time I lost contact with your brother, the two had disappeared."

"Could be they're connected to Ball in some way."

"In my job, son, you suspect everything until evidence is given to change your mind." The judge picked up a letter and handed it to Adam. "We found this in your brother's things. It was addressed to you."

Adam took the letter. "Thank you, sir. If you don't mind, I'd prefer to read it later."

"Certainly, son, I understand." The judge rose and handed Adam the folder. "All the information on the investigation is in here. After your personal business in Chicago is finished, let me know where you'll be. Then we'll talk again."

"About those missing folks . . . does anyone know where they may have gone?"

"Sources from town said a carnival passed through around the time we believe the murders were committed."

At the news a chill rushed up Adam's spine.

"Find them," Parker added. "They may hold the key to this whole sordid affair."

The judge paused, then added as an afterthought. "I heard both the girl and the black man played the banjo. My guess is they may have joined up with a vaudeville troupe traveling with one of these carnivals."

For the second time in one day, Adam felt as though he'd been slugged in the chest. First the news of his brother's death and now this.

He refused to believe that Jonquil Rose might be the missing lady in the judge's scenario. With more composure than he felt, Adam bid the judge farewell.

Alone with his thoughts, Adam stood at the rail of the packet headed north. Could it possibly be he'd already encountered his brother's murderer? A beautiful songbird who had warbled her way into his heart?

He let his head drop into his hands and watched the muddy current flow past. The image of Jonquil Rose, his beautiful blue-eyed angel materialized. There had to be an explanation.

Chapter Four

Light diminished behind the lace curtain as day gave way to darkness outside Jonquil and Flo's window. Downstairs in the saloon a crowd of boisterous males had gathered early to be assured of ringside seats for the forthcoming entertainment.

Preoccupied with tying on her last petticoat, Jonquil stood in stocking feet, only half-listening to Flo's chatter. Like the universal deluge recorded in the Old Testament, an outpouring of conversation flowed abundantly from her roommate's mouth.

"And then I told him," Flo rattled on, "if he expected me to go downstairs and dance with those men, he'd have to find me a costume that covered up my assets better than this one." Flo pulled and pushed at her fleshy pink bosom that threatened to spill over the top of her neckline.

"And you know what that old goat said?" Flo paused at Jonquil's sideways glance. "He said, 'You better be glad you got udders big enough to draw their attention away from your ugly face. Now get upstairs and get dressed.'"

"Oh, Flo, he didn't!"

Jonquil crossed the room and flung her arms around her friend's shoulders. "You don't have to put up with his nasty remarks. He's a mean and heartless man."

"And the boss, remember. Besides"—Flo's face gushed with mischief—"I told him he should be so endowed where it mattered most. I swear his ding ain't as big as a peanut."

"You didn't!"

An immediate heat sizzled up Jonquil's neck. In the week and a half she'd known Flo, the girl's coarse remarks still managed to throw her off balance. But, in spite of Flo's gutter jargon, Jonquil loved every strapping inch of her new friend. She especially envied her roommate's ability to meet adversity with a smile and a good laugh. This girl was a survivor.

Someone's fist boxed the door. "Heist your carcasses to their majestic heights. The boss wants you beauties downstairs, *now*."

"I'm coming, sugar," Flo shouted as the caller moved on down the hall, pounding on the other doors. She crossed the room and rested her hand on the doorknob, looking every ounce the hurdy-gurdy girl in her tight-fitting costume. Then she turned to wink at Jonquil. "Now there's a man I could snuggle up with."

"The bouncer?" Jonquil's brows shot up in surprise.

"Beneath that gruffness and brawn lies a heart bigger than my aa—uh . . . behind."

"Flo!"

"And we both know how big that is." Flo winked, turned, and opened the door. On a rush of cold air the noise from downstairs lambasted the room. "Good luck with your performance. I'll be cheering as loud as the next fellow." With that, she slipped through the door and was gone.

Instant quiet settled in the small room. Jonquil walked to the bed, picked up her black dress, and slipped it down over her head. Silk rustled and squeaked as it settled snugly around her curves.

Using the looking glass above the dressing table, she worked to secure the tiny onyx buttons. Then, turning from side to side, she eyed the plunging neckline. What had the lecherous saloon owner thought about her own set of udders? From the looks he'd been giving her the last few days, and the way he always managed to brush up against her with his "little peanut," she imagined he thought of her too much.

Jonquil shivered with revulsion and wished she could brush off his lewd advances as easily as Flo did. But she couldn't. He frightened her too much. All men frightened her. All but Gabriel. She ran a finger along her bottom lip, in thought. And possibly the stranger, Adam Coulter.

When their act had proven so successful the first week, the owner had hired her and Gabriel permanently. The man's idea of permanent probably meant as long as they continued to bring in more patrons. Jonquil delighted in the steady income and the tips the customers thrust into her chamber pot every evening, but she didn't like the saloon owner, not one whit.

Gabriel clucked over her like a mother hen, voicing clear protestations to her performing in a saloon before dozens of men. Each night brought on renewed disapproval, and each night she found it harder to pull him out of his brooding objections.

But they desperately needed the money. Their small savings wouldn't last long in Hot Springs. Everything was so expensive. So, for the moment at least, Jonquil held Gabriel at bay, convincing him it would be only until they found a more respectable position, perhaps in a music hall.

Besides, Jonquil reflected, Gabriel had found work as an attendant in a public bath house. He was so excited about his success, she didn't have the heart to tell him her misgivings about their employer.

The smell of melted tallow floated upward from the open jars of face makeup, tickling Jonquil's nose. She reached across the untidy rows of paint and grabbed the large yellow rose she always wore on her shoulder whenever she performed, pinned it to her plunging neckline. Fluffing its silk petals to camouflage her cleavage, she felt a little twinge of victory.

She took one last look in the mirror. *That'll show the old goat!* She turned and strolled smugly from the room.

When Adam stopped at the livery in Hot Springs, he felt as if he'd washed in a mud puddle and combed his hair with a towel. The liveryman eyed him as though he'd crawled out of a prairie-dog hole and candidly suggested the Arlington Hotel, boasting it had its own bath house.

Some thirty minutes later, he sat immersed in steaming hot water. Inhaling a long, audible breath, he slid deeper into the overly large wooden tub and sank beneath the water's surface. Only when he thought his lungs might burst did he jerk upward, spewing air like a spouting whale. Lord, it felt good.

Temporarily blinded by the water dripping from his hair and eye lashes, Adam squinted at a shelf at the foot of the tub, over which bold lettering read Bottled Remedies for the Hair. He perused the labels, Dr. Cook's Bandoline; Borax Dandruff Cure, Cure for Baldness—with ingredients Adam knew for sure would have the opposite effect—and lastly, A Hair Restorative. Adam reached for the last.

He dumped the contents over his head and gasped at the distinct odor of carbolic acid. Diving below the water's surface, he scrubbed his head with a vengeance. The stench alone would have killed any unsuspecting lice within a mile. With only a trace of the foul odor remaining, he slumped back against the tub's rim.

"The fellow who made this ought to be shot." Adam rose and tossed the empty bottle to the black attendant who had entered the room.

The man laughed and held up a Turkish towel for his client. "Yes, sir, it shore do stink." He proceeded to empty the soapy water from the tub, then turned on a spigot to refill it.

Adam eyed the assistant's crisp white coat and graying hair. For an instant he thought he recognized him, then as quickly dispelled the notion. This town was pretty remote from any place he'd ever been. He looked again at the faucet. "Pretty fancy operation."

"Yes, sir, fanciest thing I ever seen. Much better than the shanties that used to sit over the springs." The man went on to explain how the water now flowed into open troughs down the mountain to the bathhouses.

"You must have seen a lot of changes over the years."

"Let's just say I saw how it used to be, and how it is now." The aide shook his head in obvious admiration. "Yessirree, shore beats the old days." He let it go at that.

When water again filled the tub, Adam stepped back into the hot steam bath and sat down.

"I'll be leavin' you now, sir." Replacing Adam's used towel with a fresh, dry one, the attendant prepared to go. "My shift is over, but Samuel will be checkin' on you."

"Fine, fine." Adam closed his eyes and savored the water's warmth. "Oh, wait a minute." He motioned over to where his pants hung on a peg. "There are some coins in my right pocket." Adam pointed with his wet hand.

"Just reach in there and take a couple for your

trouble. I appreciate your help. This bath is making a new man of me."

Without hesitation, the attendant eyeballed him in return. "No, sir. I couldn't do that." He waved off any insistence. "It's been my pleasure. Good day, sir."

Adam watched the man move toward the entry, surprised by his response. He was a rare one, indeed. Rusty hinges creaked as the door swung open, then closed, with a soft thud, against the warped frame.

Alone in the wooden stall, Adam felt almost weightless in the hot water. A welcome respite for one who'd oscillated in a whirlpool of motion for the past two weeks.

He hated leaving his mother so soon after Simon's funeral. But, for all she'd lived through, she was remarkably strong, and had long since made up her mind to handle what life sent her way.

Maybe, Adam rationalized, when this assignment for Parker was finished and his brother's killer brought to justice, maybe he'd return to Chicago and settle down. He owed his mother that.

Not one to dwell on his problems, he focused his thoughts on the future and the job he had to do.

Little Rock had seemed the logical place to begin looking for Miss Jonquil Rose. The nearest town to Pine Bluff, from which she had so mysteriously disappeared, it had failed to lead him any closer to the banjo-toting singer and her partner.

He'd canvassed every Little Rock saloon and place of entertainment, and turned up nothing to indicate the two had ever set foot in the town. But everyone he'd questioned had talked about Hot Springs and how fast it was becoming a popular resort.

It was entirely possible he'd find them here. In a town that sported so many thirst parlors, a good entertainer would have no trouble finding work.

Steam swirled upward, unclogging his nostrils,

and formed tiny beads of perspiration on his upper lip. A mental picture of himself in a cannibal's black cooking pot rippled through his mind before he dismissed it and sank earlobe deep in the heated water.

From the hallway outside his stall came two voices. Adam half-listened to their conversation.

"Sammy, thanks for takin' the late shift."

Adam recognized the attendant who had waited on him earlier.

"No bother, Gabe. I need all the extra money I can get my hands on. My missus, she's expectin' our fifth this month."

"Must be real nice to have a family and be settled in."

Adam pushed up, resting his head at an angle on the edge of the tub. He understood the wistfulness in the man's voice when speaking of family. On those rare occasions when he let down his guard, he had felt the same yearnings.

"Ain't we funny niggers." The man called Sammy laughed. "Here you is, wishin' you was in my position, and I'm standin' here wishin' I was in yours."

"Mine? Oh, no, brother. You shore don't wanna be in my shoes."

"Why, man, you is talented, both you and that lady banjo player. I heard you both from out back of that saloon. You is good." He stressed the last word.

Adam jerked up so fast he sent water sloshing over the rim of the tub like a waterfall. He strained to hear their next words, but the two men proceeded down the hall and out of hearing distance.

"Gabriel." Adam mouthed the word. He *knew* that man looked familiar.

Adam jumped out of the tub and grabbed the clean towel, so excited he nearly slipped on the wet floor. He attacked his damp scalp, trying to rub out the remaining stench of the hair restorative.

The door to his bath stall opened, and the man named Samuel entered.

"You need some help?"

"No, I'm just about finished. Thank you."

Adam slipped his arms into his newly pressed shirt. Another appreciated service offered at the Arlington Hotel, he thought.

"What does this town offer in the way of night life?" He stepped into his striped black-and-gray trousers and buttoned up the front.

Samuel handed Adam his newly polished boots and waited until he had them on his feet before he handed him his dusted and brushed hat.

"If you want to enjoy a real treat, go to the Traveler Saloon."

"What's so special about that place?" Adam asked, certain he already knew the answer.

"A little blond songbird there is meltin' the wax in all the gentlemen's mustaches." Samuel laughed at his own statement and slapped his thigh.

"If that's the case, I'm glad I don't sport a mustache." Adam winked at the attendant and dropped a silver dollar into his palm. Settling his Stetson upon his head, he exited the bathhouse, a clean and satisfied man.

> "I'm discarded, disregarded, and as distant
> as the hills of Tennessee;
> No one wants me, no one needs me,
> I'm as lonely as a girl can be."

Jonquil's deep throaty voice floated across the room, weaving a spell over her male audience. Some men sat and others stood transfixed, while all eyes focused on the blonde standing atop the piano. A heavenly apparition on her pedestal of wood. On the

71

stool in front of the keys a black musician plucked the strings of his banjo in accompaniment.

Adam shoved open the swinging door to the saloon and scanned the clientele. At the far end of the room a woman stood head and shoulders above the crowd, her sultry voice stopping every glass and bottle in midair.

Her long hair gleamed in the low light of the smoke-hazed hall, and her black gown accentuated her ivory skin. Again Adam stared at the woman who'd played havoc with his emotions since he'd found her, alluring and defenseless, at the water's edge. He felt his breath catch in his throat as he watched Jonquil move to the music.

The familiar yellow rose shielded the revealing neckline of her costume. Like the last dress he'd seen her in, this one, too, left little to the viewer's imagination. The scantily cut black satin clung to her curves like skin on a ripe tomato, with room for nothing in between. Her rounded breasts strained against the plunging neckline. It seemed only the restraining rose prevented them from spilling over.

Adam reluctantly pulled his gaze from the flower and trailed it downward to the center knee-high slit in the skirt. Jonquil's calves, covered in zebra-striped stockings, shimmered as she toe-tapped to the rhythm with her booted feet.

Since the day he had pulled himself out of the bottle, years ago, Adam Coulter had considered himself a man in control. With his senses reeling at the sight of the little songbird, he now felt anything but.

Irritated with the explosive current surging through him, he ran a finger beneath his collar and tried to bring a breath of cooler air to his clammy flesh. Instead of worrying about mustache wax melting, he was more concerned about a certain part of his anatomy solidifying instead.

"As lonely as the river that flows to the sea,
Alone, I question, how it might be,
If someone, somewhere . . .
Could only love a girl like me."

The last heart-rending words whispered on the charged air and stabbed deep into Adam's heart. As if she didn't know that every male in the saloon would gladly volunteer to be that someone. He felt as foolish as every half-soused, lovesick swain in the room appeared for allowing the little singer to get under his skin.

Jonquil bowed her head and the last strains of the music melted into nothingness. She straightened and smiled. Her audience applauded and hooted and this time she bowed deeper. Her long hair rained down over her shoulders like a golden sun shower.

Gabriel stood and bowed. Again a roar of applause filled the room. He extended his hand to assist Jonquil down from her pedestal. Adam lost sight of the princess as her subjects swarmed around her.

Disgusted with himself and the whole scene, Adam strode over to the bar. Over the din of the hoots and hollers of ogling, bleary, pie-eyed males, he ordered a beer. He propped an elbow on the varnished surface and stared at the painting of a rotund half-nude woman sprawled in a bed of pansies.

"Mister, how 'bout a dance?"

Adam turned and appraised the girl who had sidled up to him, swishing her ample feminine wares in his face. She would have been a handful for sure, but tonight he was in no mood for dancing.

"Sorry, but I think I'll just drink."

"Suit yourself, honey, but if you change your mind, just holler for Flo." The girl had an infectious grin, and Adam was forced to return her smile.

She leaned forward and whispered in his ear, "I won't even charge you." And then she disappeared into the crowd.

Searching the room again for Jonquil and not finding her, Adam turned back to study the nude. He needed a plan. He needed to get close to Jonquil and her male companion without their knowing his purpose.

This afternoon the man named Gabriel had waited on him in the bath long enough to have remembered him. The attendant had said little, but he hadn't run out. When Adam hadn't quizzed him, it must have been a relief to realize that the man he had knocked on the head and abandoned couldn't place him.

Adam hoped now that if Gabriel spotted him, he'd merely see him as another customer, come to drink the liquor, gape at the half-clad women, and hear the new singer perform.

He'd have to work undercover until he could learn where the two stood in relationship to Innes Ball— and if they knew anything about his brother's death.

He took a big swig of the beer and plopped the mug back down on the bar for a refill.

Conversation buzzed around him. He listened, then turned again to search the crowd for Jonquil. Leaning back against the bar, Adam caught sight of the black-gowned singer, headed up the stairs.

Minutes later a bloated, balding man followed in her footsteps. Adam's interest was piqued. He glanced around the room, looking for her black guardian. Gabriel was nowhere to be seen.

The man who'd followed Jonquil paused on the landing and glanced down over the crowd as though he, too, searched for someone. With a satisfied look, he turned and slipped down the same hall Jonquil had taken only moments earlier.

Adam refused to dwell on what might be going on in the room upstairs. Despite his own weaknesses, he considered himself a good judge of character. Jonquil Rose might have secrets to hide, but it

74

pained him to think this could be one of them. He just couldn't bring himself to believe that his own blue-eyed angel might earn her keep on her back like the other "fallen" angels that usually worked the saloons.

Again he scanned the room for Gabriel, but the man was nowhere in sight. He looked back to the landing and waited. Jonquil's customer hadn't been up there more than a few minutes, but to Adam it seemed an eternity.

He turned back to the bar and took another swig of beer. Maybe it was for the best, thinking she was not the young innocent he'd envisioned her to be. After all, hadn't she lived among the carnies long enough to learn what life was really about? And wouldn't the thought help harden him to the job that lay ahead?

It wasn't as if he'd intended to become involved with the mystery woman anyway. His days for such entanglements were long over.

Nevertheless, Jonquil didn't need to entertain men in private, not with a voice like hers. Whatever else she might try to hide, she couldn't hide that talent. All she needed were the right breaks, and help from someone who knew the business. The woman could become another Lillian Russell.

Then Adam hit upon an idea. He would pose as a promoter. He'd convince Jonquil that he could make her a star. Hadn't he hinted at the possibility of her performing on stage in New York when they'd first met?

If she agreed, he could dog her every footstep while he continued his investigation of Ball. Damn, it was a perfect idea. Adam chastised himself for not thinking of it sooner.

The fat, balding man appeared again on the landing. He dabbed at his shiny pate with a handkerchief, nervously scanned the room, then hastily tramped down the stairs and disappeared.

75

Adam waited, expecting Jonquil to appear at any moment. If she was a prostitute and the man had been visiting her room, he must have changed his mind before the deed was done. He hadn't been up there five minutes.

Ten minutes later, Adam checked his watch again. Convinced she wasn't coming back downstairs, he approached the staircase. No one seemed to notice. Most of the men were cheering on the dancers and anxiously waiting for their dollar turn around the crowded floor.

He reached the landing and stopped, craning his neck. Then he started down the dim hallway.

Pausing outside each closed door, Adam listened before moving on to the next. At the end of the passageway one door stood partially open. He eased toward it and came up short when he heard a woman weeping. Dread squeezed his heart. Could it be Jonquil?

Adam moved closer and concealed himself in the shadows. From his vantage point he could see her at the dressing table, wracked with sobs, clutching the remnant of her gown's bodice to her. The yellow rose lay smashed at her feet.

Gabriel stood with his back to the door, trying to console her.

"I'll kill that bastard—"

"No!" Jonquil protested. "He did nothing but ruin his own gown."

"You sure, Rosie? He didn't hurt you or force you?" Anguish bubbled up from the man's throat.

Jonquil swallowed back a sob and shook her head. "When I threatened to leave and demanded the money he owed us, he only laughed at me. He said if we left before he could replace our act, we'd never see a penny of that money."

"Damnation," Gabriel grumbled. "I knew the man couldn't be trusted. When he refused to pay us

76

the first week, we shoulda turned our backs on this place."

"But I thought he would pay us. He seemed so pleased with the crowds we were drawing."

"We're leavin'," Gabriel mumbled. "Tonight. You pack your things and I'll be back for you in less than an hour."

Jonquil picked up the crushed rose and cupped it to her face. "I'll miss Flo, but I know we have no choice." Her eyes fastened on Gabriel. "Thank goodness we have our tips and the money you earned at the bathhouse."

"We'll have more'n that." Turning on his heel, Gabriel tramped toward the door.

"What do you mean?"

Adam backed farther into the shadows.

"Don' worry your head none. We'll be fine. You just get ready . . . and lock this door."

Adam ducked into a window alcove when Gabriel pulled the door to Jonquil's room shut and hurried down the hall. Reaching another door, the man looked around, then opened it and disappeared inside.

For several seconds more, Adam stood in the shadows. Then he tiptoed to Jonquil's door. Soft footfalls. Back and forth in her room. Drawers scraped open. Thudded shut. Several loud sniffles grated on his ears before he turned away.

With silent steps he moved toward the exit Gabriel had taken moments earlier. He paused, then very quietly cracked the door so he could see what lay beyond it.

The door opened onto another set of stairs. Adam moved down them. Hearing a creak or two, he tried to proceed silently. At the bottom the stairs gave way to a small storage room. A lantern glowed amber in the otherwise darkened interior.

Slowly his eyes adjusted to the dim light. He could

make out crates of whiskey piled ceiling high in disorderly stacks. Across the floor a door stood partially open. Past it, a cluttered desk in front of a bare window showed this to be the saloon owner's office.

His nerve endings suddenly aware of the touch of the fabric of his clothing, Adam moved to the door and listened. Soft scraping sounds came from beyond the entry, out of sight. Sounds of someone busy at his task.

Slipping his hat off his head, he tried to peer around the door, then opened it farther and slipped through. Black smoke from a lantern's wick flickered and streaked upward on the sudden draft. Cast in shadow on the opposite wall was the silhouette of a man—so intent on searching through a file cabinet, he didn't detect another's presence in the room.

Gabriel lifted a small strongbox from the cabinet and walked to the desk, where he placed it on top of strewn papers. Picking up a letter opener, he pried the lid and studied the box's contents.

He lifted out a stack of notes, counted several off and pocketed them, then returned the rest to the box. Shutting the lid, he turned back toward the cabinet. In that precise moment his eyes locked with Adam's and he stopped dead in his tracks.

Indecision masked his ebony face. Across the supercharged air each man waited, assessing the other. After an indeterminable period of hesitation, Gabriel backed toward the cabinet, his coal eyes never straying from those of the intruder.

Adam's intuition held him immobile. Rosie, the black man had called the woman upstairs, in a tone near that of a father's. If he wanted to win Jonquil's trust, Adam knew he had to first earn Gabriel's confidence. Without a word, he backed quietly out of the room and closed the door.

Chapter Five

Adam left the building and hid in the shadows of the dry-goods store to watch the back entrance of the saloon.

He didn't have to wait long before the door opened and Gabriel and Jonquil peered out. Then Gabriel stepped into the night, leading the way to the end of the alley. A street light caught Jonquil's boyish disguise when she slipped into step behind him. The two hurried toward the livery.

Keeping to the shadows, Adam hightailed it to the stable, shielded behind the row of structures that fronted Main Street. He waited outside until the pair led a mule and wagon from the barn. Catlike, they skulked down the street until they were well away from the main part of town. Then they boarded the wagon and stole away into the dark.

When Adam passed the saloons some ten minutes later, the sounds of laughter and music spilled out through swinging doors, then faded as he reached the outskirts.

Up ahead, the two runaways were making good their escape. He reined his horse to a slower pace so as not to overtake them.

*　　　*　　　*

"Wha'd you tell Miss Flo?" Gabriel asked, his voice muffled by the clopping of the mule's hooves on the hard, packed road.

A wagon wheel dipped into a large washout. Jonquil clutched the wooden seat to steady herself. "I didn't see her. But I did leave her a note. I said only that the old goat was trying to graze in private pastures."

"Goat? Pastures? What kinda note is that?"

"One Flo will understand."

Jonquil didn't elaborate, and Gabriel didn't press.

She felt terrible about leaving her new friend. She'd wanted to say goodbye in person, to give Flo one last hug. But when she'd learned from Gabriel that he'd taken their wages from the manager's office, there had been no time.

Even now the sheriff could be in hot pursuit, although the money Gabriel had taken was rightfully theirs. Again, who would believe the word of drifters, a pair of wanderers, over that of the saloon owner?

Enfolded in the darkness of the lonely road, Jonquil succumbed to the matching gloom that shrouded her heart. What had happened to the moon that only last week had been so bright?

She stared straight ahead, trying to make out the distant trail against the inky shadows of the woods. With the bad luck that constantly dogged their trail, like a hound nipping at their heels, they'd probably both be killed in a wagon accident before this night was over.

Her thoughts kept returning to her roommate. Every night after work, Flo had returned to their room tired but full of stories about her dancing partners. They had laughed and giggled until they'd fallen into exhausted sleep.

Tonight she'd expect Jonquil to be there, waiting for her as usual. *Damn and double damn!*

80

"He saw me." Gabriel's voice prodded her from her thoughts.

"What?" Jonquil whipped her head around to face him. "Who saw you?"

A crack of the whip above the mule's head urged the creature to a faster pace. Leaving the woods behind, the wagon rumbled on through a wide clearing. The road ahead looked like a charcoal ribbon in the shadowy darkness.

"Giddy-up, Cantank."

Again the whip cracked, and for a split second the "family steed" stepped up his pace. He soon dropped back to his arthritic gait, however. "Stubborn ol' mule," Gabriel mumbled under his breath.

Fear gripped Jonquil. "Gabriel, who saw you?"

Dear Lord, she despaired, if Gabriel had been seen taking the money, the law would be right behind them.

"The man we walloped on the head."

Totally taken aback by Gabriel's words, Jonquil froze. Suddenly, her palms felt wet. Her heart dived to her stomach, where it tumbled around like popcorn about to explode.

She fought to control her rapid breathing. "You mean Mr. Coulter? That man at the stream?"

"If Coulter was his name."

"Of course that's his name!" Jonquil tried to control the panic bolting up her spine. "In Haskell's office?" She trembled, imagining the saloon owner's reaction when he found them and his money gone.

Gabriel only nodded.

"I see."

She bit back any scolding words, knowing they wouldn't solve anything now. Gabriel couldn't be blamed for being discovered in that man's office. He'd only been trying to help.

Instead, she chided herself for divulging the stranger's name. Up to now, her friend hadn't known that Adam Coulter had been more than a casual dance partner at a county fair. Now he had to realize that the tall, handsome man had affected her in ways she couldn't explain.

What had taken hold of her, she wondered, to cause the mere mention of the stranger to put her on the offensive, to set her heart to whirring at such a feverish pitch?

Taking a calming gulp of air, she let the dregs of disappointment wash over her. Adam Coulter had been in the saloon and hadn't bothered to approach her.

With deceptive calm, she asked, "What did he say?"

"That's the funny part," Gabriel droned. "He didn' say nothin', just stood there. And then he closed the door and disappeared."

"Disappeared?" Jonquil paused, then demanded, "Where?"

"I don' know, missy." Gabriel's tone bordered on petulance. "Would you have me chase him down and ask him?"

"No, of course not." Although Jonquil couldn't see Gabriel's face, she sensed his rebuke.

She found herself again questioning Adam Coulter's behavior. Since their first encounter, he'd witnessed nothing less than disreputable conduct on her part and on Gabriel's. Now this last act—seeing Gabriel help himself to money from the saloon owner's strongbox—what did he think of them now?

"Do you think he's going to turn you in?" Jonquil twisted in her seat. In the darkness her friend was but a shadow.

"I don' know, Rosie, but we shore ain't gonna hang around to find out." Giving the mule its head, they plodded on toward their unknown destination.

*   *   *

In the blunted night Adam heard, more than saw, the wagon he followed as it plodded through the darkness. After a while, the rising trail swerved, and in the clouded light of a waning moon he had a view of the now-distant valley. The lights of Hot Springs twinkled like cookfires in an encampment.

"Dark as pitch," he grumbled. He followed along, through the dense woods, worrying over the safety of the wagon and its occupants. Soon the trail left the cover of trees and stretched out flat across a clearing.

It had been a motley pair he'd watched flee the livery earlier, their cases and meager belongings piled into the back of an old farm wagon. Their mule moved with a heavy clumsiness. The wheels and fittings of their wagon creaked like an old man's joints. If he could rely on his intuition, the ragtag lot of them couldn't continue much longer without a rest.

A few hours before dawn, his hunch paid off. The spent, weary team had pulled off the trail into the cover of bushes.

Adam stole quietly to the perimeter of a small clearing. The wagon stood partially hidden, in a thicket. The mule's wheezing snore blended with the chirping of crickets and tree frogs. An owl hooted from a nearby tree.

The two hadn't chanced building a fire, but in the predawn light, Adam could see two misshapen lumps of humanity on the ground. Covered in blankets, Gabriel lay beside the camouflaged wagon. A short distance away was Jonquil's smaller form.

Adam hobbled his horse and decided to snatch a few winks himself before sunrise. It was obvious the runaways wouldn't be going anywhere for the next few hours.

Facing the sleeping bodies, he slid to the ground and settled his back against the tree's curved trunk. He lowered his hat over his face, snuggling deeper into his canvas duster. Before long, his exhausted body gave in to sleep.

Only seconds later, it seemed, his eyes jerked open to take in cold metal jabbed into his chest. Through the first blush of light a shotgun barrel pinpointed his heart.

He didn't move, but he knew he'd have to do some fast talking if he didn't wish to be sprouting grass come next spring.

Before he could speak, his hat spun off his head like a child's cone-shaped top, then stilled on the flat ground. A looming silhouette looked down on him. A smaller figure stepped backward and gasped.

"What you want, mister?" Gabriel's menacing voice cut like a razor through the quiet.

Adam caught the ebony glare of the man he'd been following. He felt the shotgun muzzle dig deeper into his chest. Instinctively, he settled his hand on the icy metal.

"I wish to talk," he said.

He hoped his flat tone screened the volatile throb of his heart. Given the reputation that preceded this pair, he, too, could end up in a crudely marked grave like his brother's.

"Talk's cheap."

The shotgun thumped against Adam's chest. Not to be thwarted, he rushed on. "I overheard the conversation between the two of you in your dressing room."

"And?"

"And you know I saw you take the money from the strongbox."

Gabriel glanced nervously around the thicket. "You alone? Or are you ridin' with the law?"

"Do you see anybody else? Would I have been caught completely off-guard if the law was around?"

The two seemed to weigh his answer.

"Sneakin' around in places you ain't supposed to," Gabriel replied, "can get you into lots of trouble."

"Believe me, I don't need trouble. That's not why I followed you."

"Then what do you want?"

"I wanted to see the young woman again." For the first time, Adam allowed his gaze to settle on Jonquil.

In scuffed, worn boots, her feet braced for combat, Jonquil stood beside her comrade. Her masculine trousers hung on her legs like stovepipes, and her oversized shirt tried to—but couldn't quite—conceal the rounded fullness of her breasts. Even dressed as a boy she was a beauty.

"How come?" Gabriel again prodded the gun against Adam's chest.

"How come what?"

Adam tried to ignore the rush of blood searing his skin. It had been forever since a woman had affected him as this half-pint female did. Then, remembering the point he was attempting to make, he put his best foot forward. "I have a proposition." Noting Gabriel's scowl, he continued, "For you both."

"Proposition? Hah! You ain't in no position to proposition anybody, mister."

Jonquil laid a hand on Gabriel's shoulder. The black man hesitated, then relaxed the gun's pressure.

"We are grateful you didn't turn Gabriel in," she said. "You may state your case."

"Thank you, but can he take that gun out of my chest?"

Adam watched the black man swing his head in Jonquil's direction. An understanding look passed between them, then Gabriel conceded and stepped backward.

In rapidfire speech, he tried to put the pair at ease.

He turned his attention full on the towering man and gave a chuckle.

"You two sure don't make it easy to negotiate a deal. Why, I've been trying to catch up with you since Pine Bluff." He caught the quizzical expressions on the pair.

"Yes, sir, ever since I took a listen to what you two could do with a banjo"—he gave Jonquil a sideways glance—"and the notes that came floating out of your mouth. I've heard you twice now, the two of you, with your banjo picking, drawing crowds even Stephen Douglass couldn't command for his most eloquent speeches." He shook his head solemnly for effect.

"Lord, everybody loves a good banjo. Why, when this young lady wasn't singing, people couldn't keep still, as if they had a giant case of the twitches. Their clapping was so loud it nearly caved the roof in."

Jonquil and Gabriel said nothing, just stared.

Adam prattled on like a peddler setting up his customers before he made his sales pitch. "Look," he said, appealing to Jonquil, "when I walked into the barn at that county crossroads, I fully expected to hear good old foot-stomping, forget-your-troubles music. The last thing I expected to hear in that wayside was a voice that stopped 'em so cold you could hear a pin drop between your words."

For emphasis he added, "You're both very talented."

"What you say is very flattering, Mr. Coulter, but—"

He cut off her next words. "I believe with my connections, we could make your talents work for you."

Jonquil stepped closer. "And what's in it for you?"

He wanted to say "the pleasure of your company," but instead answered, "I'd get three percent of every penny you earn."

86

Adam tried to catch a reaction. Through the early morning light he could see her glare pinned on him. "Mr. Coulter, why should we trust you? You may be no different from the saloon owner. He promised to pay us but never did."

"The difference is, if you don't succeed, neither do I."

He allowed the words to dangle in the air between them, weighing their effect. Again, Jonquil and Gabriel exchanged looks but said nothing.

"Of late," Adam pressed on, "I've suffered some heavy losses with my investments. I'm so convinced of your abilities to be successful, I'm sure our joint venture will help me to recoup my funds."

"You lost money at the gaming tables?" Jonquil sounded appalled.

"Certainly not!" Adam's response held censure. "I assure you, I'm not the predatory card shark and confidence man who exploits human weakness." But he knew plenty who were, from the riverboats on the Delta to Jonquil's sleazy carnival manager.

Jonquil appeared satisfied with his answer. "Let him up," she said to Gabriel. "We'll talk about this over breakfast."

Adam stood and brushed off the seat of his pants. He bent over, picked up his hat and dusted off the debris, then placed it back upon his head.

The threesome walked beyond the wagon toward the clearing, Gabriel following behind. Adam checked over his shoulder and noted with relief that he no longer appeared to be the man's target.

"I invest large sums of money in stocks, people, and companies." Adam continued his pitch. "I'm very well connected, and I assure you, you would be at no risk if you allowed me to manage your career."

Jonquil studied Adam Coulter. He'd ridden as far as they had and had slept propped up against a tree half the night. Yet, in the early morning he looked as fine as he had the first night she'd met him.

When she'd awakened to see a man braced against the tree, her first thought was that she and Gabriel were about to be arrested. But he'd made no move to challenge them and appeared to be sound asleep. So she had relaxed somewhat, deciding that he must be a weary saddle bum who'd wandered into their presence during the night.

When she'd whirled the Stetson from the man's head, Jonquil's breathing had nearly stopped. The blood that pumped through her veins had felt like heated syrup, and her heart had settled to the bottom of her stomach like too many flapjacks.

Never in her wildest dreams had she thought she'd ever see Adam Coulter again, especially after he'd witnessed Gabriel stealing money from the saloon and they'd made their getaway. But here he was, bigger than life, flashing his pearly white teeth and inviting them to allow him to be their promoter. Whatever that meant.

Gabriel motioned him to a tree stump and sat down, resting the shotgun across his lap.

Adam settled himself, resting his elbows on his knees. He looked over at Jonquil. "Do you recall when we first met?" he asked. "I mentioned that you should be performing in New York."

Jonquil nodded her head. She did remember his absurd statement.

"I meant it. You have so much talent that New York remains a possibility. But for starters, what I have in mind for you is not on such a grand scale."

Jonquil, wavering between suspicion and vulnerability to flattery, weighed his words against his direct gaze, the sincere look an honest person laid upon another. Finally forcing herself to turn from his compelling eyes, she moved to the back of the wagon and brought out an enamel coffeepot.

Adam watched her build a small fire, then measure

out a portion of ground coffee. Adding water from a canteen, she set the pot over the fire to brew. While she worked, her hair, braided in one thick plait, fell forward over her narrow shoulders and trapped itself in the wide valley between her breasts. Adam's eyes riveted on the silken strand, envying its place in her private vale.

Before long, the rich aroma saturated the small clearing.

"We don't have many staples, Mr. Coulter, since we had to leave in such a hurry. But you're welcome to share what we do have."

She reached inside a sack and brought out three apples. She gave one to each of them. Then she unwrapped a checkered towel and withdrew a crusty loaf of bread. Tearing the loaf into big hunks, she passed it among them.

Adam downed a swallow of coffee from the cup Jonquil pressed into his hands. "So what do you say? Are you willing to take a chance with me?"

"Why should we trust you, Mr. Coulter?" Gabriel's deep voice cut across the small clearing. "We don't know nothin' about you."

Adam met his question straightforwardly. "You do know I've caught you both in several shady situations, but I never brought you trouble." He added for emphasis, "Or had you thrown in jail."

His insinuation withered the air. Jonquil and Gabriel looked at each other, then back at Adam.

"Why is that?" Gabriel's fingers clenched his tin cup.

Adam felt Jonquil's eyes on him. He understood full well the importance of helping Parker expose Innes Ball. To do that, he needed to get close to these two. His act had to be convincing.

He laughed nervously. "As I told you earlier, I'm interested in promoting your career and making money for us all."

89

After a long silence Jonquil spoke. "What would that entail, exactly?"

"Have you ever heard of Eureka Springs?"

Adam hoped they had heard of the boomtown in northwest Arkansas. If they had, it would make his hoax a little easier.

"It's a health resort," he said. "People are coming from all over the country to bathe in the medicinal waters . . . people with money. They demand superb accommodations and eating establishments. And they love to be entertained. Some come because they can afford it, others because it takes their mind off their illnesses."

"Of course we've heard of the place. The newspaper in Hot Springs reports thousands of people swelling the town to overflowing." Turning toward Gabriel, Jonquil added, "Haskell even called it a watery gold rush. When he hired us he talked about bringing in good entertainment so his customers wouldn't be tempted to head north." Her voice sounded hopeful.

Adam's face took on an expression of supreme confidence. "I know some of the town fathers there. They'd be mighty interested in your act." He nodded at the twosome.

Turning to Gabriel, he pressed on. "They have bath houses there also. With your experience, you probably could find work." For the first time he acknowledged that he had recognized the attendant for his own afternoon bath. "I'd be your reference, if you're worried about that."

Adam had talked so much and so fast his jaws ached. But he saw his plan spread out before him, like a tablecloth stacked with food just waiting to be tasted.

In Eureka Springs Adam knew a man who could wield more power with words than Paul Bunyan with an ax. One word from him and Jonquil would have a promising career.

At the same time this respected friend of Isaac Parker's would prove invaluable as Adam's contact with the judge while he investigated Ball. He was thrilled by the prospect.

"So?" He took another swallow of coffee. "Shall we join up and attempt to make us all richer?"

"But we still don't know any more about you than we did ten minutes ago." Gabriel swished his own coffee around before taking a long swallow. "Maybe you're as shady as we are."

Gabriel was testing him and Adam knew it. These two were prime suspects in the murder of his brother and more than likely in cahoots with Ball. His cover depended on winning their approval. He hoped his answer was the right one. "And maybe I'm not," he shot back. "But unless you give me a chance, you'll never know."

Again the pair eyed each other, and Adam read indecision behind their staunch veneers.

Gabriel's answer was smug. "We've come this far without help," he said.

"But how much farther will you go? You can't continue to help yourself to the bossman's till. You need a manager."

"We don't need nothin' from a fancy man like you," Gabriel countered. "That money belonged to us. We earned it."

"I figured that out before I ever followed you," Adam consoled. "You're not naive, my good man. You know it's an unfair world. Whites—Southern ones in particular—don't cotton to a white girl traveling unchaperoned with a black man. You'll be confronted everywhere you go."

Gabriel's shoulders slumped forward in defeat. He knew Adam spoke the truth. Though the war was over and blacks were free, they were still in bondage. It was a white man's world, where a black man's word meant nothing. Wasn't that the real reason he and Jonquil had run from the law instead of facing it?

A battle waged behind Gabriel's dark eyes. Adam knew he had touched a sensitive nerve, and as much as he hated playing on a man's vulnerability, he intended to use this to his advantage.

"If nothing else, think of Jonquil's safety. She's a beautiful young woman and because she's traveling with you, she is easy prey for every man she meets."

"Wait a minute!" Jonquil jumped to Gabriel's defense.

"He's right, Rosie; we know he's right. . . ." His words trailed off into silence as they shared a look of silent understanding.

"We'll travel as brother and sister. I assure you, no one will question a man journeying with his sister and his manservant."

"All the way to Eureka Springs?" Jonquil asked, assuming the role of mediator.

"Before I followed you, I took the liberty of telegraphing an old friend of mine there. He promised me, if you two were as good as I said, he'd put you both to work immediately."

"Doing what? Working in another saloon?"

"No more saloons for you, darlin'." You'd be working for the founding fathers of Eureka Springs, the Eureka Springs Improvement Company. The little town is becoming very social, and the community demands entertainment. My friend tells me they feature programs of literary readings and drama—and musical concerts."

"And they'd hire us?"

"All you have to do is agree to give it a try. I promise you, when they hear you sing and play that banjo, they'll hire you so fast your pretty little head will spin."

Jonquil raised her brows.

"I . . . I don't know."

"What do you have to lose?" Adam asked, using his most persuasive voice. "If you go and hate it, you can always leave."

"I don't think . . ." Jonquil turned to her mentor. "Gabriel and I have to discuss this alone. Will you excuse us?" The two stood and walked to the edge of the clearing, out of hearing distance.

Taking a large bite from the shiny red apple, Adam felt very satisfied with himself. He'd baited the hook, and it looked as though the two were going to nibble.

The tree branches overhead trembled with nesting birds that trilled their early morning songs. Adam strained to hear Jonquil and Gabriel's conversation through the cacophony created by mockingbirds and yellow-billed cuckoos.

Jonquil stepped once more into the clearing. "Mr. Coulter," she announced with a most businesslike air, "Gabriel and I have decided to accompany you, but we insist on paying our own way."

"I assure you, that's not necessary. When I made this offer, I intended to take care of the expenses."

"No, sir," she insisted. "We have some money, and that way if we get there and don't like it, we won't be beholden to you."

"Would that be so bad?" Adam's eyes locked with Jonquil's. "I mean we will be working together."

"No." She stood tall, portraying complete composure. "We'll do just fine."

They watched Gabriel douse the campfire with water, making sure the coals were thoroughly covered with dirt, before he turned to the old mule and the wagon.

"I figure that team of yours will bring a respectable sum. We'll sell them in the next town."

"I beg your pardon?"

"What'd you say?"

Jonquil and Gabriel had exclaimed in unison.

"We'll sell the mule and the wagon to buy your stagecoach fare to Eureka Springs."

The air crackled. Even the roosted birds seemed to sense the tension as they fluttered their wings.

"We won't sell them."

"Won't sell them? Why not?"

"If they don't go, neither do we." Gabriel and Jonquil nodded in agreement.

Adam couldn't believe what he was hearing. "Have you looked at those two lately?" The one thing he didn't need was to escort a broken-down mule and wagon through the Ozarks.

"We won't sell." Jonquil reinforced his worst fears.

"It won't be an easy trek through these mountains."

"If you prefer, you take the stage, and we'll meet you there."

The last thing Adam could afford was to have them disappear on him now that he had tracked them down. "Have you forgotten why we decided to travel together? It was for your protection."

"I don't need protection."

"Little sister," Adam taunted, "everything I've seen up to this point contradicts that statement."

Bejeesus! With the turn of events, Adam saw his role of avenging angel take on a new dimension— that of guardian angel as well. And it did not go down easy.

This assignment is going to be anything but dull, Adam thought as he watched Jonquil and Gabriel board the rickety wagon. If we're lucky, he mused, we might make it to Eureka Springs before the first snow flies.

Chapter Six

Dawn was hours away, but Jonquil lay wide-awake and shivering beneath the parked wagon. *Some protection!* she thought, as she curled into a fetal position to avoid the rain that drooled insistently through the floorboard cracks. She cursed the day the three trespassers had stormed into her life and uprooted her from the little farm in southwest Arkansas.

The downpour had started soon after they had crossed the Arkansas River the evening before and had continued its punishment throughout the night. Coaxing a flame from the few soggy pieces of wood for a campfire had proven impossible. With only a shared can of cold beans to stave off hunger, they had bedded down early for want of anything better to do.

Chilled to the bone, Jonquil now listened to the rain drum down around her. She strained to see Gabriel and Adam's sleeping forms, but in the all-consuming blackness couldn't find them. Would this night never end?

Turning over, she stared into the surrounding gloom, seeing nothing but mud and bone-chilling rain. An icy drop of water splattered on her forehead and she tunneled deeper beneath the musty wool blanket.

Her damp clothes clung heavily. She wiggled her toes against the inner soles of her boots, to make certain she could still feel circulation. When morning came, she'd be either frozen to death or covered with mildew. Jonquil groped for a diversion to take her mind off her discomfort.

Like a beam of warm sunshine, Adam Coulter appeared in her mind. During the two days he'd been traveling with them, he'd proven himself to be an excellent guide and traveling companion. He was a man, Jonquil decided, who was very comfortable with himself and the environment.

Occasionally, he complained about their "beast of burden," but did so in a teasing way that always managed to solicit a chuckle from Gabriel. The men had arrived at a camaraderie, and Jonquil was glad that, at long last, her companion had another male for company.

Adam's periods of silence, when he seemed preoccupied with his own thoughts, suited Jonquil's quiet nature. She was not one given to idle chitchat and he, too, seemed disinterested in empty twaddle.

He had to be the most handsome man she'd ever known, and the only one besides Gabriel she'd ever liked. Just thinking about him evoked a rush of sudden warmth.

But Adam Coulter confused her and left her vaguely disturbed. Sometimes, when she stared into his deep brown eyes, she felt as though they'd met somewhere before. But then she'd dismiss the feeling as absurd, knowing that was an impossibility.

"Horse feathers!" Jonquil raised her head when a sheet of cold rain gusted beneath the wagon. She tried to settle the damp blanket around her. "I'll freeze for sure."

"Now what's wrong?" Adam whispered to her across the span of darkness.

"Nothing," she lied. Flopping back down on the cold ground, Jonquil clamped her teeth together to still their chattering.

In the velvet darkness where seeing was impossible, she felt movement next to her. Across the abyss, a hand fumbled and groped, until it came in contact with Jonquil's waist.

"Damn it, you're freezing to death." His voice sounded as cold as the rain. "Why didn't you say something?"

Meekly, she reached out and touched his arm. "I'm not the only one."

His hand blotted the soggy curve of her hip. "I'm a helluva lot drier than you are." With one swift movement, he settled himself beside her and dragged her against his body.

Jonquil found herself within the folds of his waterproof duster. Suddenly frightened by his nearness, she stiffened and tried to pull away.

"Do you want to catch pneumonia?"

Chills wracked her and she couldn't stop shaking. She tried to sit up, but he clamped an arm around her waist and hauled her close against his front. "Where's Gabriel?"

"The last time I checked on him, he was snoring away in the hollow of a downed tree. He's probably a heck of a lot drier than you are."

"But I can't stay here," she argued.

"You can, and you will."

One last attempt to free herself from Adam's embrace met with uncompromising restraint. What he said was true. She was going nowhere.

His body felt as warm as a baked potato, and in spite of her resistance, her tremors slowly began to subside, her muscles to relax.

Buried in the cocoon of Adam's embrace, with his warm breath swirling the hairs at her nape, she thought of hot summer days, of running barefoot on

97

sun-toasted ground.

The rain continued to pummel the forest around them. But it no longer existed for Jonquil. For the time being, her little sphere was centered beneath the cover of Adam's duster.

Enveloped in his warmth, she snuggled her curves against his until they fit together like pieces of a puzzle. Soon the earlier agonizing hours faded into oblivion, and Jonquil fell into a restful, relaxed sleep.

Relaxed was not what Adam was when Jonquil finally settled her rounded bottom against his lap. Involuntary spasms had tormented her body until his arms had encircled her, warming her. With her feminine parts pressed so intimately against his manly ones, he found himself craving her softness.

Yearnings he'd channeled to his mind's secret place surfaced and gushed through him. The slip of a woman who lay soft and yielding in his arms was, without knowing it, the fountainhead for his long-buried desires. Against all judgment he wanted her.

In the two days they'd traveled together, Adam had carefully held their relationship to neutral ground. Knowing what he did about his new companions, he was determined to keep it that way.

But at times during their journey, he'd pondered the strange relationship his two companions shared. Gabriel exercised his position as "guardian" of his young charge with the devotion of a loving parent. Jonquil, in return, treated the black man with the honored respect of a trusting child. They simply didn't fit the profile of cold-blooded killers.

Jonquil sighed, then nuzzled closer. Smelling like rainwater and crushed grass, her warm body saturated his senses. How long had it been since he'd held a woman? Far too long, he thought, as her hair tickled his nose and upper lip, reminding him of the pleasure of connecting with another human.

Her fresh, sweet scent became an aphrodisiac, drugging him with its seductive powers. With every breath he took he knew he slipped into a more dangerous situation. Calling on supreme determination, he stilled his growing passion.

Tomorrow they would be near the town of Russellville. From there he could telegraph Powell Clayton that they were on their way to Eureka Springs. And while they were there, they'd outfit themselves for the trip north.

He'd purchase enough canvas to keep them all dry, separately, in any future rainstorm. If his partners insisted on camping all the way to Eureka Springs, then he'd be damned sure he didn't find himself in this uncomfortable position again.

The sleeping woman he cradled rolled toward him, then buried her face in the sensitive flesh of his neck. Her warm breath seared his throat, and again he fought his rising desire. Adam groaned and prayed for daybreak.

"Now missy, no need in actin' like a puffed-up toadfrog."

Gabriel gave Jonquil a disapproving scowl as he brought the wagon to a standstill on the edge of a small rise. Below them sat the town of Russellville.

Jonquil glared straight ahead and offered no defense for her silence.

The rain had stopped around daybreak, and cotton-batting clouds now stretched across the horizon, blotting out the sun. A chill wind whipped up the hillside, rippling the mule's cropped mane like shorn wheat and pushing the two deeper into their coats.

"You're not experienced in the ways of the

99

world"—Gabriel's voice wavered—"or in the ways of men."

At daybreak when he'd found Adam and her entwined like the tendrils of a trumpet vine, Jonquil couldn't blame him for believing the worst. She remembered waking to find her limbs coiled around Adam's solid mass and her nose and lips planted in the hollow of his warm neck. She blushed now, thinking of the intimacy of their embrace. Anyone would have believed the worst.

"Nothing happened," she finally said, "and if Mr. Coulter were here right now, he'd tell you so himself."

"I don't need Mr. Fast-talkin' Dandy to explain nothin' to me about my girl. It's your words I care about. Ever since I delivered you, I've felt as liable for you as your mama did, rest her poor soul. And so far, best I can tell, you ain't ever lied to me yet."

Jonquil knew Gabriel had only her best interest at heart. "I know," she said, suddenly feeling as defensive as a six-year-old, "and that's the truth."

As if she hadn't been mortified enough by her own actions, Adam's reaction had complicated the circumstance. He'd jumped up with a half-moon smile plastered on his face and mumbled incoherently before excusing himself from the tense situation. His quick departure to town, barely stopping to saddle his horse, had left Jonquil speechless.

Further determined to clear up the matter, she attempted to justify her behavior. "He only offered me refuge from the cold." As an afterthought, she added, "I promise you, he was a perfect gentleman."

"Rosie, gal, I know that. I just worry about you, that's all."

When she didn't respond, Gabriel concentrated on the reins, sharing the renewed silence. Too clearly he remembered the day of her birth, and long before.

After that no-account river dandy, Innes Ball, had

abandoned Jonquil's mother without benefit of a marriage certificate before Jonquil's birth, Gabriel saw his role of hired hand suddenly shift to that of provider and defender of the small, destitute family. And he had stepped into it lovingly. Margaret Mary Trevain came to rely on him for all the family's needs, from the very food they ate to protection from an ostracizing community.

But like any righteous father figure, Gabriel Sims had no intention of seeing his young charge fall into the same love trap that had caught her mother so long ago. Not as long as he had breath in his body.

"You've been my responsibility since the day you laid eyes on this world," he muttered.

Jonquil felt that, too, as surely as she felt his burden, and she regretted adding to his worries. How many other men in this cold, unforgiving world would have packed up, leaving a woman friend behind? Without one word of complaint, without knowing when he might ever see her again. Jonquil affectionately butted her shoulder against Gabriel.

"We're responsible for each other," she reassured her companion. "Don't worry. I can handle Mr. Coulter."

"I hope so. We don't know him that well and he might turn out to be a handful. You just be careful."

Gabriel gave the mule its lead, and slowly they started down the rise that sloped toward the flat valley and the small town.

Jonquil contemplated her words with every bump and dip along the pockmarked trail. Having spent most of the night in the shelter of Adam Coulter's arms, she questioned whether she really could handle herself.

While the wagon jounced along, Jonquil sat anchored in her private thoughts. Recalling Adam's tender concern sent her heart soaring, even now in the reality of day. His sole purpose had been to ward

101

off her chills, to keep her from becoming ill—nothing more.

But the moment he had settled his weight beside her, she had been struck by a skittish alarm, like a rabbit, suddenly stunned by a strange noise and not knowing which way to run. Even while her mind told her he meant her no harm, her heart panicked at his closeness. When finally her trembling had ceased and she'd settled more comfortably against him, his nearness had unleashed a pensive longing deep within her.

Now, in the cold light of day, confusion and guilt mingled with irritation. Had he truly only been embarrassed at having been discovered in an untenable position?

Adam's quick glance at Gabriel and then at her, the sleep-tousled woman beside him, followed by his speedy departure from camp—in search of canvas and provisions, he'd said—presented a much clearer picture. The man obviously wanted nothing to do with warming her bed a second night.

Jonquil set aside her unsettling thoughts and concentrated instead on the town that sprouted from the grass roots of the prairie land. The rain-soaked structures that comprised the business district of Russellville looked dismal and uninviting in the shrouded gray light. Down the wet street their wagon plodded, mud squishing beneath its wheels. Gabriel pulled the vehicle to a stop in front of the general store.

"Mr. Coulter said he was going to purchase camping supplies," Jonquil remarked. She dragged herself from the wagon. "I'll see if he's inside."

"You all right, Rosie?" Gabriel asked, concern stamped on his face. "You sure nothin' happened you ain't telling me about?"

"Nothing happened." She faced him with less conviction than she felt. "It's this gloomy weather."

She smiled tentatively. "I'll be fine after we eat."

Her friend's black eyes narrowed suspiciously before he jangled the reins. "Cantankerous needs some new shoes. I'll leave him at the livery and join you later."

"You need any money out of the trunk?"

"Naw, I've got enough."

"We'll eat when you finish, then . . . whether we find our traveling companion or not."

Stepping onto the stoop in front of the store, Jonquil waved Gabriel off before she pushed open the door and entered.

A small bell on the door jangled. Pausing just inside the entrance, Jonquil took a deep whiff of the scented air. The aromas of soaps, spices, leather, and molasses hovered pleasantly throughout, and Jonquil wondered how a combination of such diverse elements could smell so inviting.

"Hello," she called, gravitating toward the Franklin stove in the back of the room. "Anyone here?" When no one answered, she backed up to the stove and massaged her cold bottom with her palms.

The heat slowly penetrated her clothes. "Ahh," she sighed. She felt better already.

Jonquil removed her boy's cap, and her long braid tumbled down her back like an uncoiling rope. The warmth of the stove seemed to steam the dampness from her bones, the invisible vapors lifting her spirit at the same time.

She scanned the hodgepodge interior. Shelves were packed with everything from foodstuffs to dry goods. Hardware, leather riggings, and barrels of flour, sugar, and molasses filled every inch of floor space. Axes, log chains, kettles, and pots hung from the rafters on cords and crowded the corners atop kegs of nails. Counters on either side of the room were stacked with coffee, cheese, tobacco, and piles of shirting, Russian sheeting, bed ticking, and cassimeres. Jonquil didn't envy the storekeeper's task of housekeeping.

Warm enough at last to browse, she moved away from the stove and rummaged through a large "shoe box" in which loose, unmated shoes were piled among saddles and harnesses.

A door slammed at the back of the building, and a stringbean of a woman juggled an armload of wood through a curtained doorway behind the counter where the cash register sat. She dumped the logs into a wood box, straightened, whipped long fingers down her flatcake hips, then brought her beaky stare to rest on Jonquil.

"Sister!" she hollered, glancing over her shoulder at the curtained wall. "Where is that woman?" She looked back to Jonquil as if in apology, then sized her up carefully.

"Oh my poor, poor dear. I'm glad you're finally here. Your brother said you'd be in."

The woman's voice dripped sugar as she appraised Jonquil's attire through hook-bow spectacles perched on the end of her nose. "You certainly can use a nice dress."

Before Jonquil could utter a word, the shopkeeper ushered her to a back corner of the room, where an assortment of ready-made dresses hung on a rack.

"You're such a mite, I don't believe we have anything that will fit you." Then she spied Jonquil's ample bosom, and her lips drew up like a puckered prune. "Except for that chest of yours . . . unless Sister can alter it." Again she glanced toward the curtained wall and bellowed across the yards of paraphernalia. "Sister, our customer is here!"

At that exact moment the curtain whipped open and the woman named Sister appeared. As she scurried forward, Jonquil noted she was the mirror image of the lady standing beside her. Having never encountered twins before, Jonquil stood mesmerized

104

while the two women eyed her critically.

"This young woman needs a dress," the first sister contended.

They've confused me with someone else, Jonquil thought. "I'm sorry, but I'm not—"

"My, my, such a little thing," the second sister interrupted. "I'll have to alter." She thumbed through the ready-mades, decided on a navy blue homespun check, and pulled it from its hanger. "Yes, indeed," she murmured, looking it over, "definitely have to alter."

Both sisters turned to Jonquil. "Those filthy clothes must go!" they chimed simultaneously, then broke into high-pitched giggles.

Sister One grabbed the bottom of Jonquil's full, loose shirt and, before Jonquil had a chance to protest, lifted the garment over her head.

"Now wait just a moment," Jonquil demanded, grabbing for her shirt. But the second sister caught it on the fly and stood eyeing the dirty camisole beneath. "Tut-tut. A young woman should never allow her undergarments to become so dingy."

"Dingy?" Jonquil's temper flared. *The nerve of these two strangers.* She'd had about enough of being poked and prodded like a pig on a spit. "I don't want your dress, or underwear, or anything else you're selling." She snatched her shirt from the woman's hand and hid behind a dress form.

"But surely, dear, those lice-infested garments must go."

"Lice-infested!"

Jonquil knew the night spent on the rain-soaked ground probably had left her looking worse than skunk cabbage, but that did not give these women the right to accuse her of being beset by parasites.

Before she could offer a defense, the two women converged on her. With the agility of a racer, she thrust the dressmaker form at the twosome and tried

105

to make her way around the back counter toward the front of the store. Looking from one end of it to the other, she found both means of escape effectively blocked by the shopkeepers.

Undeterred, she jumped onto the counter top, sending bolts of yard goods flying and uncoiling like colored banners before they hit the floor. But before she could make good her escape, the stringy women were right beside her. One sister grabbed one leg and the second sister grabbed the other. Jonquil danced and kicked, trying to release herself from their iron grasp, but to no avail.

The tinkling of the door's bell announced the arrival of another. Please, she hoped, let it be Gabriel. He would rescue her from these grappling women.

Straining to peer through the haze of cords and equipment suspended from the ceiling, she saw the long, lean form of her new manager enter the store. Adam had come for her.

One more time—out of the blue—he was there when she needed him.

"My, my, Sis," he greeted her. "I can't leave you alone for a minute without you getting into trouble."

Adam Coulter stood just inside the entrance, eyeing the bolts of material strewn across the wooden floor. He then stared up at her with an amused grin on his face.

Feeling the women's hold on her legs relax, Jonquil was about to vault to the floor when she remembered the impropriety of her dress. Instead, trying to hide herself behind a huge woven basket hanging from the ceiling, she sidestepped.

Her boot connected with a gum ball jar. Her near nakedness forgotten, Jonquil grabbed for the jar, but was too late. It tumbled forward and gum balls ricocheted off the floor like ice in a hailstorm.

Never in all her life could she recall being so embarrassed. If only she could evaporate into thin air. She turned back to the two sisters. They looked as though they might suffer twin apoplexy attacks. Before her, the incredulous look on Adam's face turned to amusement as he doubled over with laughter.

"I warned you ladies that my little sister would put up a fight about buying a new dress. But I didn't expect an all-out rebellion." Again his full-bodied laughter rumbled throughout the store.

Jonquil glared at him from her high perch. "You . . . you knew about this?"

Anger boiled inside her and all she could think of was wiping the silly grin from the man's face. Reaching for the nearest item she could hurl, she curled her fingers around a palm-leaf fan hanging nearby and sailed it toward Adam's grinning face. "I've never in my whole life been so humiliated." With a frustrated growl, she searched frantically for something else to throw.

Adam ducked with lightning speed, then charged the counter where Jonquil stood. Slinging her over his shoulder as though she weighed no more than a feather, he swirled around to face the gaping women.

"I told these ladies you loved a captive audience; but really, little one, must you upstage everything in the store?"

"I'll get you for this," Jonquil ground out so low only he could hear. She tried to free herself, kicking at his forearm locked securely behind her knees and beating her fists against his back. The harder she hit him, the harder he laughed. In her embarrassing position, her bottom exposed to strangers, she felt blood rush to her head.

While her frustration mounted, the fight in her drained until she slumped like a sack of potatoes in Adam's arms. He relaxed his grip and allowed her feet to slide to the floor, but continued to hold her to his side.

"Sis"—he emphasized the word—"if only you'd given these nice ladies the chance to explain. These are the Shelton sisters, the owners of this fine emporium, and they have graciously offered to allow you to freshen up in their back room before we lunch at the hotel." He gave her his broadest smile.

Jonquil couldn't believe her ears. What in tarnation was he talking about? And where was Gabriel? She glowered at him.

"I explained to them earlier about our unfortunate accident, how we lost our bags in the terrible downpour last night—and how you'd become so soaked we had to borrow a young boy's clothing until we could purchase new garments."

For the first time since Adam had entered the store, Jonquil noticed his dress. No traces of fatigue showed on his recently shaved face, nor was there any evidence of the wet and muddy night they'd shared. With his clean, pressed clothes he looked as though he'd just stepped out of a bandbox. Immaculate. And an enigma as always.

"What do you say, Sis?" Jonquil tried to pull away, but Adam reinforced his grip. "You ready to allow these ladies to outfit you in a nice, *dry* dress?"

So he had set this whole disaster in motion. The ladies in the store were only carrying out his directives—albeit with the most assertive mercantile persuasion. He may have had the best intentions in mind, but Jonquil looked around at the unexpected results. Lord, what he had caused in the process.

She seethed at the humiliation he had brought on her. Her—a grown woman who prided herself on the decorum and gentle ways her mother had taught her in better times. Why, because of him, she had acted like a ten-year-old farm boy chasing his pet pig through his mother's house. And, she thought morosely, she had incurred about the same amount of damage as such a chase would have made.

But, if the truth be known, a nice sponge bath with warm water did sound like heaven. To be rid of the dirty clothes and once again feel clean . . .

Deciding to take advantage of the situation, she spoke directly to Adam. "Only if these nice ladies will allow you to clean up this horrible mess I've made in their store." She looked at the gum balls scattered across the floor and the bolts of unwound material.

"Me?"

"Who else, dear brother?" For the first time Jonquil turned on her most guileless charm. Spotting a broom at the end of the counter, she stepped out of Adam's arms and retrieved it. "Had it not been for you and your meddlesome ways, this would never have happened." She held it in front of him. "You *do* know how to use one, don't you? Think of it as a pitchfork; just don't be quite so aggressive. Gum balls are much lighter than hay."

Before her, Adam looked too startled to offer any objection, while from behind her Jonquil heard a gasp. She turned to the women. "My *brother*, ladies, has a tendency to spring surprises. If I'd been forewarned of this arrangement, I assure you I wouldn't have acted like a hoyden."

"Never you mind, dear," the first sister offered. She rushed over and took the broom from Adam's outstretched hand. "Sometimes men can be so inconsiderate."

The twins exchanged knowing glances until Jonquil's state of undress dawned on them both at the same time. They immediately jumped in front of her and formed a wall to shield her from the tall man's eyes, their loyalties evident by their stance. Brother or not, it wasn't proper for a young man to be aware of his sister's womanly attributes.

"If you'll excuse us, sir, we'll take care of your

sister and return her to you dressed as a proper young woman."

Adam strained to peer over the barrier that blocked Jonquil from his sight. "I thought you wanted me to stay around and help clean up."

One of the sisters shooed him away. "Tut-tut. You be off now. We'll have this cleared away in a matter of minutes."

Adam tried to meet Jonquil's eyes through the maze of the two women's arms. "Don't worry about Gabriel. I've arranged for his needs to be taken care of."

"Fine," she answered, her voice set with defiance. "And where shall we meet?" She peeked over one twin's shoulder.

"I'll pick you up here in two hours."

Gum balls rolled like marbles from Adam's path as he moved toward the door. He paused, stooped, and picked up a handful. Turning again to face the threesome, he said, "Add this to my bill," indicating the damages with his hand. "I'll settle with you later. Until then, ladies."

He popped several gum balls into his mouth, pinged the swinging bell with his finger and disappeared through the door.

Chapter Seven

Adam trailed behind the old wagon, trying to ignore the feminine apparition in navy homespun check poised on the seat up ahead next to her driver. With her banjo on her lap, Jonquil Rose began to sing in her clear, inviting voice.

Her notes wafted on the air, soothing and sensual, and set Adam's mind on a path he didn't care to follow. The more he tried to ignore the magnetic force of her voice, the more his soul became absorbed in its sweetness.

He turned his mind from the captivating tune and the woman who sang it to concentrate, instead, on the wide span of azure sky that paralleled the lush, fertile prairie to east and west. From time to time he had to remind himself of why he'd attached himself to her in the first place—this could be the woman responsible for his brother's death.

The sun, now a large fiery orb overhead, had appeared before noon, burning away the low-lying clouds and with them the cold, damp chill from the air. Hundreds of liquid droplets clung to the swaying grasses and sparkled like diamonds in the bright sunlight, the only visible reminders of the previous night's rain.

And the woman who'd slept in his arms appeared

unmindful to how fetching she looked in her made-over dress.

Adam's eyes roamed over Jonquil's womanly figure. The point at the waist at the back of her dress drew his attention to the curve of hips concealed beneath the skirt's side panniers. The memory of his sleepless night, with that camouflaged roundness planted firmly against his lap, made his body harden.

Until he'd entered the Russell Hotel with Jonquil on his arm, Adam had tried to forget what lay beneath her rough and tumble disguise. But it was far from a boy's body that turned every man's head in the dining room. All her feminine attributes had been rubbed, scrubbed, and shoved into the latest fashion, and the result had been breathtaking.

She'd even smelled different. All traces of the previous rain-soaked night had disappeared. Instead, the delicate scent of lavender soap, talc, and woman's honey had touched his nostrils in a most pleasant way, and he'd indulged himself in her fragrance throughout their meal.

The wind flirted with the blue ribbon that now secured Jonquil's golden mane. Her narrow shoulders moved slightly as her fingers plucked notes from the banjo's heart. Needing to distance himself from her, Adam spurred his horse forward to escape the inexorable pull of Jonquil's voice. With a grumbled excuse about searching for a place to camp, he bolted forward, aiming for the distant mountains.

"Crotchety, ain't he?" Gabriel declared.

"Maybe his lunch didn't sit right."

Jonquil watched the path of trampled grass snaking behind Adam's mount. When horse and rider appeared no larger than a black speck against the distant peaks, she turned her attention back to her banjo.

"Somethin' shore didn' sit right, but I ain't convinced it was the food." Gabriel regarded her and

112

waited for a reply.

Acting indifferent to her companion's prodding, Jonquil drop-thumbed a familiar tune on her banjo. She was in no mood to talk about Adam Coulter.

She thought she'd behaved admirably during lunch—her mother would have been proud. But inwardly, with every bite she'd taken, she'd seethed over the audacity of the man. The nerve of him, acting as though he'd done nothing wrong—that he'd had nothing to do with causing her to conduct herself like a mindless country bumpkin.

Well, she decided, the town and the meal were part of the past. Right now the sky was blue, the grass green and gold, and the distant mountains were purple. With a view like this, she refused to think of the man who twisted her insides and made her feel things she'd never felt before. She'd concentrate instead on the beautiful dry afternoon.

Her sullen veil lifted with the words to "Cluck, Old Hen." Gabriel's deep bass voice joined in, and for the moment Jonquil's troubles lay in the dust.

"Make your banjo talk, girl!" Gabriel shouted above Jonquil's vigorous plucking. Soon the mocking sound of barnyard chickens echoed across the empty, rolling grassland.

A good distance ahead of the wagon, Adam swung around in the saddle, half-expecting to be set upon by a flock of squawking prairie grouse. Above the brittle sound, Jonquil's tinkling laughter joined with Gabriel's own, and their uninhibited joy rang out across the vast expanse.

Through the haze of long-ago childhood, Adam groped for the song's forgotten lyrics. Tunelessly, he croaked out the notes:

"'My old hen's a good old hen . . .'"

Chuckling at the foolishness of his efforts, he found himself grinning like Alice's Cheshire cat, and his earlier black mood lifted considerably. He could well imagine his own flat notes carrying back to his two traveling companions, and their ears being assailed by his caterwauling. Why, they'd laugh themselves right off their seat. He'd stick to things he knew best.

His horse suddenly neighed.

"What in thunder?" Adam cursed. A dozen or more cottontails, their tails snow-white against the lush grass, scampered away from Ranger's prancing hooves.

Too late, Adam realized he'd strayed upon a rabbit burrow. His mount stumbled, and Adam struggled to hold on. The flurry of activity sent the frightened horse rearing up on its hind legs, shaking its rider, as if it were an unbroken colt. Caught unaware, Adam found himself hurled from the saddle. He hit the hard ground shoulder first, then skidded for several feet before he stopped.

Moaning, he rolled onto his back. He tried to sit up but streaks of lightning ripped through his shoulder. Giving in to the throbbing pain, he flopped back down, his left hand hugging his right arm against his side. The earth vibrated with the thundering hoof-beats of his fleeing stallion.

The light, pristine sky overhead belied the black pain in his shoulder. A low moan escaped as Adam tried to steady his breathing, but the pulsating torture would not subside. He lay there, nailed to the earth while sickening waves rolled through his gullet, the carefree voices still floating across the prairie. Not for the first time, he questioned his sanity for becoming involved with these two less-than-respectable characters.

From his first encounter with Jonquil Rose and her companion, Adam's stable world had been on a volatile downward spin. In only a couple of weeks, he'd witnessed a fraudulent act against innocent country folks, been knocked senseless and left for dead, and been party to a cover-up of what the law would certainly term a robbery. Now, because he'd been concentrating on the little singer's voice instead of on the trail, he found himself in the middle of God's green acres, minus his horse, with what felt like a dislocated shoulder.

Pushing up with his good arm, he searched the horizon for his horse. Where the hell was that confounded animal? In utter frustration, he collapsed back down on the hard, unyielding ground and shielded his eyes from the bright sun. Sooner or later, Ranger would come meandering back, after he'd run off his fear and realized his master was no longer with him. The horse was the one friend Adam could count on.

Never in all his years as a detective had he encountered such a hell of an assignment. For christ's sake, he thought to himself, if he had any sense he'd just throw the two of them in the nearest jail and let the courts decide who was who and what was what.

He squinted up into the wide expanse of sky. "Simon," he growled toward the heavens, "you never did listen to me as a kid. So listen well now, you hear?" He held fast to his arm. "I wouldn't be putting myself through this hell for anybody else. If I come through this thing in one piece, I'm gonna expect some sign of real gratitude. You got that clear?"

Damn, if he weren't so bent on bringing his brother's killer to justice, he'd walk away from this case and never look back.

Oh, Lord, his shoulder hurt. He dropped his good arm across his brow and closed his eyes. Any minute now he expected to pass out.

The jingle of a harness and the squeak of wheels

brought Adam out of his haze. Flinging his arm from his face, he tried to sit up. But the half-ton mule poised above him effectively blocked his attempt.

Soulful brown eyes returned his exasperated gaze. With teeth that resembled petrified wood, the animal dropped its large head and shredded a clump of grass only inches from Adam's face.

Besieged by the rank breath of the stubborn, drooling creature, Adam shouted, "Get this beast off me."

Gabriel pulled hard on Cantankerous' bit, but the mule wouldn't budge. With its hooves firmly planted and its head lowered, it continued to crop the grass around the fallen man as if alone in a barren land.

Certain he was about to be trampled—or eaten—by the obnoxious brute, Adam tried to scoot backward. A sharp pain shot through his shoulder, sending more black waves through his gut. This time, when the ground met the back of his head, it felt like a hammer blow.

Blue checks swished across his line of vision. Turning onto his uninjured side, Adam squinted up the length of checked fabric.

"Are you all right, Mr. Coulter?" Jonquil asked, leaning slightly toward him.

"I'm swell, *Miss* Rose." Adam forced a smile and saw on her face a look of surprise at his use of her purported surname. "But I'd appreciate it if you'd move this hunk of meat before I become his next meal . . . or drown in his spittle." He cringed when a large drop of green drivel splattered close to his head.

"Not such a bad idea . . . considering," Jonquil responded.

"Considering?" Adam lifted his chin so he could better see Jonquil's face. The quick movement made him flinch.

"Considering, *dear brother,* how you placed me in a most embarrassing situation at the general store.

116

You left me defenseless and without the slightest warning that I was to be set upon by those groping women."

"Maybe I should have warned you," he retorted, "but I knew you'd protest."

Cantankerous' head hung suspended within inches of Adam's own. Nostril holes as big as silver dollars blew hot air against Adam's neck.

"Please," he pleaded, "would someone move this ornery beast?"

"Only after you apologize." Jonquil met his accusing eyes without faltering.

"Look, I'm in no mood—" Damn, but the woman was stubborn. She and that old rickety animal of hers deserved each other. "All right." He almost choked in exasperation. "I'm sorry."

Gabriel's shadow lengthened across the grass. He stopped inches away from where Adam lay sprawled and took one look at the expression on their downed companion's face. "Rosie," he said, "the man is hurtin'."

"Well, he ought to be." Jonquil propped her hands on her hips. Addressing her words to Gabriel, she glared down at the man at her feet. "You weren't in that store this afternoon, and you didn't see the fool I made of myself."

"Rosie," Gabriel protested, "this ain't the time or place for this discussion."

Intervening, he pulled an old bandana out of his pocket, blindfolded the mule, grabbed its harness, and carefully manipulated the animal away from the injured man.

With his adversary a good distance away, Adam eased himself into a sitting position. Holding his arm immobile against his chest, he stumbled to his feet. Red-hot pain shot through his shoulder and he reeled unsteadily. Only steely determination kept him from buckling. That and the support of the soft

117

woman in blue checks whose arms suddenly wrapped around his waist.

Adam sat propped against the wagon wheel, small beads of sweat dotting his forehead and upper lip. Jonquil sat beside him to keep him from falling over, her hands free to help with the difficult task ahead.

"Here," she said, guiding the whiskey bottle to his lips. She turned away from the foul alcoholic odor. "Drink up."

With deft fingers, Gabriel unbuttoned Adam's soiled shirt and slipped it down over his shoulders.

"Appears to me you dislocated that bone when you fell." The older man eyed the alteration in shape of the injured shoulder. The rounded upper end of Adam's arm bone protruded forward from its socket. Gabriel probed the deformed area around the injury. "Only thing to do is put it back where it belongs."

Adam's gaze, glassy with pain, centered on the man before him. "Then what?" he asked.

"Then, if you're lucky—and there's no other damage—you'll be right as rain in a couple of weeks."

"A couple weeks!" Adam stared at the whiskey bottle, his words slurred. "I got things to do. Got no time to be laid up." He looked up suddenly and focused on the black man. "How many humans you treated for this ailment, anyway?" His voice was skeptical. The tautness of stomach muscles, bunched in hard knots beneath his bared skin, confirmed his distrust.

Shielding her eyes from both men, Jonquil helped lower Adam's shirt past his elbow and covertly studied his back. Several strange-looking scars marred the otherwise satin smoothness of his skin. They looked red and puckered—like old burns. She felt an unexplainable sorrow at the thought that this

118

present pain could not possibly be worse than whatever tragedy had left these vengeful marks.

Gabriel's honest response interrupted her perusal, and Jonquil dragged her gaze from Adam's back.

"Not many," he was saying, "but I'm real good with animals."

"He really is good with animals," Jonquil blurted out, trying to forget what she had just seen. She caught Gabriel's watchful expression and flushed at her boldness.

Adam nodded his head toward the family mule, now tethered some ten feet away and oblivious to the charged currents traveling between his companions. "So I noticed," he said. "But how many of their shoulders look like mine?"

Gabriel seemed to ignore the caustic comment, attributing it to the effects of the liquor. "There ain't much swelling," he said. "But I'd advise we get that bone set back in place soon."

"Well, let's get on with it," Adam barked.

"It's gonna hurt like hell."

"It already hurts like hell." Adam grimaced, favoring the injured shoulder. "Since you're the only doctor I've got, I don't have much choice. What next, Doc?"

Gabriel looked at Jonquil. "I'll need your help, Rosie. But I must warn you, it ain't gonna be pleasant."

The words resounded through Jonquil's mind. They needed her help, both of them. After the countless times when she'd been on the receiving end of rescues, it was now her turn.

She shifted uneasily. A nervous fluttering filled her stomach as if she'd swallowed too much ginger beer—her mother's fizzing home remedy for whatever ailed any of them.

"I can handle it," she said stoically. "Just tell me what to do." One deep breath later her voice rang

119

with confidence. "I'm ready when you are."

"That's my girl." Gabriel beamed widely, confirming his confidence in her. He turned to Adam. "Think you've had enough painkiller?"

Adam held up the half-empty bottle. "We'll soon know, won't we?" He took one last swallow. "At least I'm warm." He looked up at Jonquil. "As warm as you finally got last night, darlin'."

The loose-lipped reference to the night before provoked another show of color. Jonquil glared at Adam, but he merely stared back, sporting a silly schoolboy grin across his flushed face.

Hopefully, she thought, when he finally regains a clear head, he'll never remember that scandalous remark. She listened intently to Gabriel's instructions.

"You're gonna help brace him, Rosie," the man said.

"Braishe?" Adam protested through his stupor. "Why, a good shtrong wind could roll her across the prairie." He laughed at his own joke. "Jus' like a tumblin' tumbleweed."

Jonquil and Gabriel exchanged glances. The whiskey was working. Adam might be hurting, but he was happy.

"Never you mind," Gabriel said. "She may be little, but she's strong."

Adam harrumphed. "Let's get on with it," he mumbled.

"I think the easiest way to do this," Gabriel was saying, "is to lay him down on his back. We'll cushion his head and his hurt shoulder."

Jonquil pried the whiskey bottle from Adam's good hand, placed a rolled blanket under his shoulder and head, then looked to her friend.

"Okay," he said, seemingly satisfied with her work. "Now here's what we're gonna have to do: I gotta pull that arm, as slow and gentle as I can. And

120

when I do, you're gonna have to see if you can help set that bone back in its socket." His coal black eyes looked to Jonquil for reassurance. "Think you can do that for me?"

Jonquil knew, out here in the middle of nowhere, on a godforsaken trail she'd insisted upon, that she had no choice. "Of course I can."

"Good girl." Gabriel's approving voice gave her the confidence she needed. "Now I want you to sit on top of him so you can put pressure on that shoulder and help hold him down."

"What!" Jonquil's face grew crimson. "Sit on him? Why, when you start pulling on that arm, he'll buck me off faster than his own horse did him."

"Don' worry," Adam assured her. "I promish to behave. Jus' gimme somethin' to hold on to." He reached out and grabbed her ankle.

"I've got a better idea," Jonquil snapped, dreading his strength, but fearing the intimacy of his touch more. She helped Gabriel rearrange their patient so he could curl the fingers of his good hand around the spokes of the wagon wheel.

Then reluctantly, she saddled herself across the hard planes of his bare stomach and, trying to avoid contact with his skin, braced her knees on either side of his body. She knew her expression was strained to say the least, but the nature of the injury had left her no alternative.

Amusement crossed Adam's face when he looked up at her. "Ever see a grown man cry?"

"Only when I sing," she countered, a reassuring smile plastered on her face.

"Well, my angel, I suggest you sing now!"

His endearment brought an odd tingling to Jonquil's depths.

Gabriel took off his own boots and, positioning one foot beneath Adam's right armpit and the other against his neck, braced himself with Adam's arm

121

between his legs. "Here," he said, handing Jonquil a rag-wrapped stick. "Put this in his mouth. Biting on it should help take his mind off his shoulder."

With shaky fingers, Jonquil placed the stick between Adam's teeth. She gently traced her hand down the side of his face—an automatic gesture of comfort against what was to come. The pulse in his neck throbbed beneath her fingertips.

Gabriel anchored his massive black hands around Adam's elbow and began to pull.

"Shing," Adam ordered, through clenched teeth.

Jonquil groped for an appropriate song. The haunting words from "Beautiful Dreamer" filled the tense air.

"There ain't no easy way to do this," Gabriel apologized, as he pulled on the injured arm. Adam uttered not a sound, but Jonquil could feel the trembling of his body beneath her own.

She watched his eyes, now tightly shut, wishing she knew some magical potion that might reduce the agony she felt certain he was trying to conceal. His face remained set, his jaw clamped around the stick. The pulse in his neck pounded in cadence with Jonquil's own.

In the still of the late afternoon, the only sounds on the prairie were Gabriel's hard breathing and Adam's muffled grunts as the painful treatment continued.

Beads of moisture popped out in the space above his upper lip. The muscles in his jaw hardened like stone. Her song became a mere whisper, then stopped.

Adam's eyes opened and centered on her. Moisture filled the corners of them. Again the resonant voice rasped out the command: "Shing."

And Jonquil did, realizing how heavily focused he was on her words. "'Beautiful Dreamer" surrounded them, as with a shaky voice Jonquil issued forth the

122

lyrical words she hoped would be the balm for this man's pain.

The gentle pulling increased and Jonquil watched Adam's tears slip down to his hairline. "Now, Rosie," Gabriel pronounced. "Try pushin' the bone back in place."

"But . . ." Jonquil thought her heart would burst from her own sympathy. She wanted so badly to absorb Adam's suffering—all of it—so he could finally rest. Pass out, she prayed. Please—just pass out.

"No buts, girl." Gabriel's tense words hit her like iron on an anvil. "The sooner we fix this thing, the sooner it'll be over. Now push!"

And without further thought, she did.

Amazingly, the rounded tip of the humerus gave under her prodding and slipped obediently back into its socket.

"It worked." Jonquil stared at the shoulder, her words coming in a rush. "Oh, my God, Gabriel. It worked!"

"Awww right!"

The black man eased his hold on Adam's arm and placed it gently on the ground. "Now keep him still," he instructed. "I'll be right back." He stood up and in his stockinged feet walked to the back of the wagon to retrieve Jonquil's petticoat for bandages and a sling. The sound of ripping linen accompanied his satisfied whistling.

Jonquil continued to stare at her handiwork, trembling in the aftermath. The shoulder now looked intact. As long as she lived, she knew she'd never forget the sound of Adam's arm bone slipping back into place. It was a hollow grating thud, that rumbled through layers of muscle and flesh, finally fixing itself securely in place.

Against her legs was Adam's sweat-slickened torso. His bulk felt clammy against her inner thighs. His eyes were closed, his breathing deep and hoarse. He no longer flinched, and for a moment Jonquil silently thanked her Maker for easing him into an anesthetic sleep.

She gently removed the wrapped stick from his mouth and started to lift herself off his waist. But in that same moment Adam again caught her right ankle in an iron grip and she stilled. His eyes flew opened, their depths struggling for lucidity. Then, as quickly, they softened and his lips quirked upward into a halfhearted smile.

Jonquil held her breath and looked at him, at the glassy eyes that mirrored the excruciating pain he had just endured, and wondered that he could absorb so much with so little complaint.

When she didn't pull away, Adam reached up with his good hand and held it against her cheek, brushing away an errant tear with his thumb. Unable to move, Jonquil sat, frozen, on his stomach, mesmerized by the deep, searching voyage of his eyes into her own. His touch felt warm, soothing, and if at that very moment the earth had chosen to rumble with a life of its own, she knew she could never have moved against it.

"Thanks," he whispered, wiping her tears with his fingers. "That helped."

At his touch Jonquil's world stopped, and she knew with certainty what he had meant. Not that she had held him down, or fixed the stick in his mouth, or even manipulated his shoulder. But because she had sung for him.

In an involuntary gesture, she cupped his hand in hers and held it tight against her face, relishing the rough texture of his fingers on her skin. The unexpected lump in her throat choked off any inane remark she might have made in her embarrassment. Instead, she merely nodded and returned a broad, genuine smile.

Tomorrow, she knew, when he'd completely sobered from the medicinal emptying of the whiskey bottle, he'd never remember any of this. Not his words or his actions. But she reveled in the sweet exchange between them before he again closed his eyes and his hand slipped out of her grasp.

Jonquil leaned down and rested her head against his neck, unmindful of the intimacy of her impulsive action. Suddenly it was her turn to give him the comfort of human touch, to send him her strength; and she made no move to sit up.

Adam's bounding heartbeat slowed to a steady rhythm. The smells of horse, sweat, starch, and salt besieged her. And beneath them all, she took in the slight lingering scent of bay rum and remembered the previous night she'd spent secure in his embrace.

His own strength, she thought, had been more than that of any man she'd ever encountered, except perhaps Gabriel. Guilt washed over her when she recalled how she'd stood over him, badgering him about the episode in the store. How childish she now felt.

Adam's arm rose to settle across her back, and when she looked up, she saw a weak smile turn up the corners of his mouth. His warm breath caressed her earlobe with his whisper.

"Aren't angels supposed to sing?" he teased her.

"Only in heaven," she replied, smiling back at him.

"My loss. My soul's too black."

His head lolled sideways and he collapsed into exhausted sleep.

Night fell upon the camp set up in a grove of shortleaf pine. The tangy fragrance of burning pinecones, bark, and needles scented the air around the small campfire. Jonquil and Gabriel sat just within hearing distance of where Adam lay, their voices joined in a whispered exchange.

Disjointed bits of their conversation floated to Adam above the wind that rustled through the trees. A charred branch shifted position in the glowing coals, shooting rubious sparks heavenward and causing the pine's resin to pop and sizzle like hot grease.

"We'll be fine," Jonquil's voice insisted. "You have to ride back to Russellville for the medical supplies we need."

"But I hate leavin' you alone with him."

"I assure you, I can handle Mr. Coulter. He'll be no problem in his weakened condition."

"You know it'll be two good days."

"The two days will fly by. Really. And I'll be fine. Now, please don't worry. Go on to sleep. You need to get an early start in the morning."

From his position within the sleeping bag Adam watched Gabriel rise from a tree stump and stretch his arms overhead.

The man looked tired. The way his fingers massaged the small of his back as he walked away revealed just how much of a load he'd carried today. Adam guessed him to be about forty, though he possessed the solid muscles of a much younger man. His black curly hair was touched with gray at the temples, and Adam wondered ruefully how much of that gray had developed since knowing the woman who traveled with him.

Since Adam's fall, Gabriel's burden had doubled. Now he not only had to perform the work of two men, he had a patient to contend with as well—one he was not at all happy to leave alone with his charge.

The big man moved away to his bedroll and lay down on the cushioning pine needles he had pushed into a heap earlier. He drew up his blanket, rolled so his back was toward Jonquil and the fire, then stilled.

Once more Adam searched out the young woman.

She rose from her cross-legged position, bent to add more branches to the fire, then sank down upon her own blankets. Unmoving, she sat mesmerized by the flames.

He thought about what she'd said to Gabriel—that she could handle him. Adam smiled to himself. After what she'd accomplished this afternoon, there was no doubt in his mind that she could do exactly that. Right now he felt as weak as a newborn babe, and with the whiskey wearing off, his shoulder ached like hell. He'd dozed in fits and starts most of the evening, thanks to the headache that threatened to burst his brain. But because of these two, the bone was back in place. For that he was immensely grateful.

He moved his arm slightly and squeezed his eyes tight against the excruciating pain in his shoulder. Exhaling a low groan, he hoped the damage wasn't permanent. What the hell good was a lawman with a dead gun arm?

As an afterthought, he flexed his fingers and felt a slight tingling in the digits of his right hand.

The reflected light flickered against the surrounding trees and encroaching mountains. Glistening shadows settled over the parked wagon and the two animals tethered several feet away.

Jonquil stared at the fire as though hypnotized by its leaping flames. Her face—tomato red from the heat—looked young and vulnerable in the soft light. He'd never asked her age, but the way she looked in the fire's dancing shadows, she could have passed for fifteen.

She'd braided her hair in one long golden plait, and her blue check dress had been replaced with boyish clothing. Unaware that she was being observed, she removed her boots and stretched her legs out in front of her, lifting her bare feet to catch the heat of the flames. After a moment she lowered her feet and glanced over in Adam's direction.

127

With his lids half-closed, Adam remained immobile. He had no wish to intrude upon her privacy or to engage himself in conversation that could only send his head spinning in torment. He wished that he hadn't drained the bottle in the hours after his shoulder had been wrapped, but the dulling effects of the whiskey had helped somewhat.

If only the damned stuff didn't have to demand retribution. A good ten years had probably passed since he'd downed more than a social glassful at his mother's holiday gatherings, and hard liquor no longer held much appeal. But in this case, a one-time-only shot, he would have considered trading his horse for another bottle.

Apparently satisfied that he was asleep, Jonquil pulled out a canteen, poured water onto a rag, and pulled the oversized pantlegs up past her thighs. The simple act seemed logical enough. The prairie this day had been a grueling mixture of whipping wind and sweeping dust, and by now Jonquil's skin surely tingled like needles from the punishing dryness it had endured.

A woman's skin should be soft and supple, Adam thought, reliving the times he had experienced the satin smooth touch of a female in his arms. But that had seemed a lifetime ago.

Until he'd met Jonquil Rose, he'd long ago given up the fantasy of holding another woman, her smooth, pliant skin meshed with his own. But he would never forget how a woman felt. And, like a drunk taking the cure, he knew he would never stop craving it.

He dismissed the morbid thoughts he usually kept at a safe distance and allowed his mind to wander, back to how this young woman before him had looked when he had first seen her in the stream. He remembered how she'd looked when he had held her in his arms and, still later, in her low-cut gown with

128

the camouflaging yellow rose. The memory sent a smile to his lips and a quiver through his veins.

Damn. His eyes snapped shut and he cursed himself for being so lustful. He fought his body's urgings and tried to steady his breathing. Determined not to open his eyes again, he found instead, like his namesake, that he could no more resist the forbidden fruit than he could stop his next breath.

His eyes flew open.

Jonquil wiped the wet rag over her legs, then opened a bottle of oil. Pouring a small amount into the palm of one hand, she recapped the container and started to massage the tops of her thighs. With slow, deliberate strokes, she rubbed the oil down, around, and over the tops of her legs.

The fragrance of lily of the valley wafted across on the night air, drawing Adam toward its intoxicating scent. He could well understand how the plant had earned the reputation of being able to lure the nightingale from its nest to seek a mate.

Her legs still parted, Jonquil lifted one, worked the emollient over her knee and proceeded down her calf to her toes. Picking up the other leg, she ministered to it in the same attentive way.

The scene, Adam knew, was never meant to be erotic, but wildfire raged through him nevertheless. He felt scorched to the core, as though he might melt beneath his heavy covering. Desperate to throw off his covers, he lay perfectly still, cursing his invalid state.

He knew he should close his eyes, but he was helpless to do so. From his hiding place beneath the blanket, he continued to observe her cleansing ritual.

Jonquil worked on her arms, first wiping the rag over them, then massaging and kneading the scented liquid onto her pale flesh, upward to the rolled-back sleeves of her shirt. Her damp skin took on a golden sheen in the firelight. Then, she rewet the rag and released the top buttons of her shirt. First wiping the grime away from her neck and shoulders, she polished her skin with more oil.

Her fingers slipped the last button through its hole, and the shirt opened to reveal perfectly formed breasts—to the birds, stars, night critters, and the one lone man who dared to watch. Adam was consumed with renewed heat, and deafening hammer blows struck him within his chest.

Jonquil lightly cleansed the ravages of the prairie dust from around, over, and under the fullness of her breasts—first with water, then with the liquid balm. Firelight again burnished her oil-dewed skin, and Adam found himself struggling for breath, unable to close his eyes or to keep from imagining the touch of his own hand on her nipples.

Powerless to control his growing arousal, he forced a strangled groan from his lips and turned over as far as his injured shoulder would allow. The searing pain would surely be lighter than that to which he had just subjected himself, lighter than the aching desire for something he couldn't have.

Chapter Eight

Jonquil saw Gabriel off the next morning at dawn, after an early breakfast. She was now wide awake. Rather than try to go back to sleep, she walked about the encampment, thinking how she could fill the two days until his return.

Once during the night she had heard Adam fitfully moaning, but before she could rouse herself, Gabriel had already reached his side. Tonight she'd have to remain more alert. No one would be there to help.

She looked over at Adam's unmoving figure, nestled in his bedding, and saw a second whiskey bottle sitting upright in the dirt within easy reach. Gabriel had produced it. Jonquil remembered the false bottom in their trunk and the compartment underneath, where they hid their earnings. Leave it to a man, she thought, to always be prepared.

But Jonquil was quite sure there were no more concealed bottles for pain. Otherwise, Gabriel would never have considered leaving her at the mercy of a stranger he didn't begin to trust. Assuming Adam would sleep well into the morning, she set about exploring the area beyond their camp.

Several hundred yards away, she followed a narrow stream to its headwaters deep in the earth. There, to her delight, she discovered that hot water gushed from a crevice in the mountainside. Centuries of rushing water striking the sandstone had formed a near-perfect bowl, more than a foot deep. Large enough for Jonquil to sit in with her legs outstretched, this would be the perfect bathing hole.

Exploring further, she found a hollow "bee tree" where wild honey was stored. Abandoned in the golden brown sweetness were great squares of honeycomb, rough and uneven, just waiting to be gathered. These would provide a perfect accompaniment to a big batch of biscuits for supper. Perhaps the sweet surprise would ease the pain lines etched into Adam's face.

Jonquil returned to camp and checked on her patient. Other than the even rise and fall of his chest, he lay as still as death beneath his blanket. Keeping her distance, she stalked about the camp with catlike stealth, determined not to wake him.

Adam's body needed to repair itself from the shock of his injury, and while she did not approve of whiskey in general, she blessed the bottle beside him for its dulling powers and the healing sleep it brought.

She'd seen the effects of alcohol on many men during the past year. As the spirits took over, their behavior turned unpredictable.

Strangely enough, looking at Adam, tucked into his covers in blessed oblivion, she harbored no such fear. Since the previous afternoon he'd garnered a steely control over his own body to prevent lashing out at her, had instead harnessed the raw pain and carried it within. No, she decided. This man, whatever else he was, was no threat to her.

She retrieved her soap and towel and, gathering clean underthings, headed back to the spring for a much-needed bath.

A few minutes later she sat submerged in the hot basin. The water fizzed and frothed around her before spilling over into the shallow stream she'd followed earlier. Leaning her head back against the smooth surface of the rocks, Jonquil stared at the powder-blue sky overhead. The sun would reach its zenith in a few hours. In her soothed, relaxed state, she lathered her hair with soap and tried not to think of the mountain of laundry that awaited her back at camp.

She sighed and dropped deeper into the tepid water. Bubbly warmth surrounded her limbs. Her chemise and drawers inflated around her like a life preserver, making her feel weightless in the liquid buoyancy of the pool.

Considering the heavy dousing of whiskey Gabriel had given Adam before leaving camp, she doubted the man would be able to rise from his pallet for several hours. But if he did, the most he'd see was what he'd already seen twice before. Catching her in her underwear was fast becoming a habit.

Jonquil glanced through the trees toward their small camp. Sunshine streaked golden light across the heavy layer of pine needles on the forest floor. A bushy-tailed squirrel flounced among the white oak trees, gathering acorns for the coming winter. Blue jays fussed, hidden from view beneath the painted leaves. Enjoying the tangy touch of fall, Jonquil breathed in the aroma of wood smoke and coffee from their cooking fire.

Gabriel would be gone for two days. Never in her twenty-two years had Jonquil been more than a stone's throw away from her black guardian for longer than it would take him to haul eggs, vegetables, and her mother's tatted lace into town to sell to the locals. At times he would stay and visit with his woman friend, Keely. But he was always home by nightfall, sometimes bringing Keely with him.

He'd been the father she'd never known, the rock in

her crumbling world.

She gulped hard, feeling her confidence waver. Within hours the gentle chatter of morning creatures would give way to the menacing sounds of night prowlers. What if Adam worsened or something threatened them? Even with a shotgun and a pistol between them, he was certainly in no shape to use either; and she would have a dickens of a time trying to protect the two of them.

How would she ever make it through the night?

Jonquil forced away her pensive reflections and concentrated instead on Gabriel's return. With him, he'd bring more whiskey, more horse liniment, and whatever the doctor in Russellville offered to keep down the swelling of Adam's shoulder.

For now, after she finished her bath, she'd do their laundry, and possibly coax her patient into the warm pool. The heated water would soothe his muscles and wash away the soggy bread-and-milk poultice she'd applied the night before.

Dipping her head beneath the water's frothy surface, Jonquil rinsed away the remaining soap. Reluctantly, she gave up the warmth of the enveloping pool and perched on the edge of its natural bowl to twist the water from her hair.

"Well, I b'lieve I've dishcovered a mermaid."

Whipping her head around toward the slurred voice, Jonquil focused on the bloodshot eyes of Adam Coulter. A silly, lopsided grin shaped his mouth. Ungainly as a newborn colt, he stood across from her on long wobbly legs, his arm in the sling Gabriel had made from her dingy gray petticoat.

"Mr. Coulter, get back to bed," she scolded, dropping the long hank of hair.

Adam only stared at her and made no effort to move. His red gaze raked down the front of her wet chemise. Jonquil blushed under his perusal, but, not to be bested, tossed her head and settled her long

134

mane across her bust like a golden curtain. Then she glared back at the unsteady man.

Disappointment creased his face. Under different circumstances, Jonquil thought, his expression would have been almost comical. At the moment, however, she didn't feel like laughing. She was too concerned with watching the way he swayed unsteadily on his feet. If he fell and aggravated his injury, she would never be able to get him back to bed.

"You shouldn't be up," she chided him again, coming to her feet in the pool when he looked as though he might topple over.

Adam's gaze dipped down her front and rested on the shadowed triangle at the apex of her thighs. He licked his parched lips and stepped into the warm water, shoes and all.

"Mr. Coulter, get out of here!"

Realizing she sounded like a harpy, Jonquil watched the water gurgle over the tops of Adam's boots.

"Cain't," he mumbled. He looked down. "M'boots are full."

Water rings circled Adam's calves and crept upward like the incoming tide on a beach. Soon his trousers were wet from the tops of his fancy brown boots to his knees.

"M'legs won't work." He looked at her again, the silly grin lighting his face. "M'pants are in the way." He stumbled to keep his balance. "I know," he said, "I'll take 'em off." His mobile hand fumbled with the top button of his fly.

"No!" she screamed. "You can't!"

Suddenly Adam's legs buckled. Jonquil lunged to steady him, her arms surrounding his waist for support.

"Now tha's better." He sank to his knees, dragging her down with him.

"But your shoulder—"

She tried to avoid contact with the sling that held Adam's arm close to his chest. His free arm circled her back. Panic sliced through her. If the man fell over, in his besotted and injured condition, she'd never be able to lift him.

In her concern, she tightened her arms around his waist and rested her forehead on his chest. One burgundy nipple peeked at her from a patch of russet hair.

Lord have mercy! Jonquil thought. Blushing, she snapped her eyes shut. *Whatever am I to do?*

Adam held her in a viselike grip. They knelt, knees touching, thighs touching, and with her stomach resting intimately against his crotch.

Hot water swirled around them, its gentle pressure forcing them closer. At the feel of Adam's erratic heartbeat against her temple, Jonquil's blood rushed like a dangerous current through her veins, threatening to sweep her away from all reality.

In spite of herself, she made no move to break their intimate contact. In the midst of attempting to save him from himself, she suddenly had no wish to save herself from him. Instead, caught in his eager embrace, her face only inches from his, she thought she might finally be kissed by a man. And she found herself wanting to know how that first kiss would feel.

Her skin burned clammy hot. Her heart thumped wildly against her ribs. Across the stream's pebbly bank she heard a bullfrog croak, then *kerplunk* into the water. Reason screamed that she should flee while she still could.

But she couldn't.

Instead, she kept her arms locked firmly around Adam's waist and hid her face against his half-bare chest. The contact sent tingling sensations exploding through her. His heated skin smelled of salt, musk, and the poultice she'd applied to his shoulder.

Keeping his good arm around her waist, Adam sank back upon his haunches, pulling Jonquil with him. Her legs floundered out behind her, her upper body bowed against Adam's torso.

"Let me go," she pleaded.

Jonquil was sure her back would break from the contortionist's pose Adam held her in. Torn between fear of drowning and concern for his injury, she dropped her legs over his thighs and struggled to regain her balance.

"Tha's nice," he commented, his eyes smiling devilishly into hers. He shifted closer, settling her against his lap, and she couldn't escape the steely hardness of the muscles against her own. Or the bulge that pressed firmly against her wet drawers.

"Nice," she croaked. "Release me this minute."

Playfully, he teased, "First you haf' to pay the piper."

"Pay the piper? Whatever for?" Jonquil's earlier fascination with the man completely disappeared. "You, Mr. Coulter, should be paying *me* for not allowing you to fall and break your fool neck."

"If you insist."

Air exploded from Jonquil's lungs when she was suddenly hauled against his chest. His long, hot fingers hooked behind her head and steered her mouth to within inches of his own. His warm breath, mixed with the spray of the bath, misted her face and sent scorching sensations to her toes.

And then he kissed her.

Opening his mouth, he probed her lips with his tongue, silently inviting her to follow his lead. Innocently, reverently, she closed her eyes and explored the smooth hollow of Adam's mouth, savoring its warmth and texture.

His kiss became more urgent, more demanding, his breathing more labored. His hand swept down and cupped her bottom.

Adam's heated fingers kneaded and pressed her in a way she'd never been touched before. It felt wonderful. Breathlessly, she squirmed against his lap, trying to release the unexplained pressure that tightened her lower regions.

With the expertise of a practiced lover and the agility of a sober man, Adam lifted Jonquil slightly, settling her firmly against his aroused flesh.

"You're driving me mad," he whispered. His lips dropped to her throat, to the center of her pulse. Jonquil's insides felt as liquid and warm as the water that percolated around them.

"I've wanted to kiss you this way since the day we met." His low voice drifted and he began again to nuzzle her skin.

Jonquil's eyes widened at his words. Her delicious stirrings screeched to a halt with the lucidity of his tongue. With a will she didn't realize she possessed, she bolted upright and tottered backward.

Shock doused the passion on Adam's face. He lunged at her, but missed as she leapt, dripping, from the pool of water. For a man who only moments before appeared to be a staggering drunk, he had the reflexes of someone clear-headed and stone-cold sober.

She watched him steady himself against the slippery rocks, with a grimace that bespoke raw, primitive pain. "Hellfire and damnation!" he growled, grabbing for his wounded shoulder.

Gone were his slurred speech and blank gaze. Other than the fact that he favored his injury, Adam Coulter was very much in control of his faculties. And Jonquil knew she'd been played for a fool. Having been twice duped made her temper hotter than the water that perked around Adam's crouched form.

"Not worth a bucket of warm spit," Jonquil

138

mumbled, grabbing her clothes and darting behind the nearest rock. Ignoring her wet undergarments, she tugged on her dry clothes.

Color gushed to Jonquil's skin as she recalled her unladylike behavior of a few moments earlier. Dropping to the ground behind the rock, trying to conceal herself from further scrutiny by Adam, she struggled to stuff her wet feet into the rough cowhide boots.

". . . allowing me to believe you're woozy and not fully alert." The boot folded itself around Jonquil's toes and refused her foot entrance.

"What's that you say?"

Jonquil swung her head around only to find Adam slumped over the rock, his eyes almost even with her own.

"I say, *Mr. Fancyman*, you're not the gentleman I mistook you for." Jonquil jumped to her feet, her body rigid, her hands clenched on her hips.

Adam vaulted to his own feet, his tensed expression betraying the pain from his recent injury. "Why? Because I kissed you?"

Seeing him wince nearly made Jonquil forget her anger. "No, not because of the kiss," she answered truthfully. "But because you pretended to be something you weren't. Now I'm not certain I can trust you." Jonquil turned and tromped back to camp.

God, deliver us from the fury of the Northmen. Adam's subconscious called up the ancient prayer of the churches of Europe. He could still see Jonquil standing before him, her feet braced, her hands on her hips, and determination stamped upon her face.

If it weren't for her slight build, he thought, she could have passed for a Viking raider. Her mane of golden hair had settled around her shoulders like a thick pelt, and her wet underthings had wept against

139

the front of her khaki-colored shirt, forming a perfect circle over each breast. To complete the picture of his Viking warrior, Adam mentally conjured up a horned helmet atop her flowing blond hair.

The swiftness with which she had delivered her accusing words had cut him as deeply as a Norseman's lance.

If his brain hadn't been overruled by his crotch, the episode in the pool would never have occurred. Too much of Gabriel's liquor and too much of Jonquil's flesh—she'd unknowingly paraded it in front of him the night before—had caused his lapse in judgment. Disgusted, he kicked a rock, skipping it across the water's surface, before he turned and headed away from camp.

Following the path bordering the stream, his feet made a squishing sound as he walked. Not only had he diminished himself in Jonquil's eyes, he'd probably ruined a good pair of boots as well.

"Boots be damned," he grumbled. Boots could be replaced, but getting Jonquil to trust him again was another story. The success of his undercover assignment depended upon her belief in him.

He was wet from the waist down. His trousers clung to his legs, the air chilling him through. After yesterday's fall, his muscles were as taut as a bowstring. His head ached like the devil, his shoulder throbbed, and he felt meaner than a cornered razorback hog.

But could he really blame his bad mood on his physical condition? Or on the breaking up of their little tryst? Adam had had enough experience with women to know that this yellow rose was ripe for the picking—if he hadn't been such a damned fool and revealed he wasn't as drunk as she thought. Now he wondered if he'd ever be able to mend the rift between them.

He wandered for a while, attuned to the waiting

stillness filling the woods. The only sounds came from the animals that pawed beneath pine needles and leaves when Adam passed. Stopping beside the stream, he hunkered down and dipped his finger into the cool water, sending outbound ripples along the surface until it again stilled. A smallmouth bass appeared and hovered over a hole in the stream bed.

"Now you'd be a good peace offering for the lady," Adam said aloud, thinking he wouldn't mind supping on the fat fellow himself. The fish, seeming to understand Adam's suggestion, quickly darted beneath an overhanging rock.

"Don't trust me either. Can't say I blame you."

Adam stood again. Snapping a twig from a bush, he stuck it in his mouth and found a nearby tree stump. He sat, crossing his ankles out in front of him, and scanned his surroundings.

Sunlight reflected off the crystal surface of the water, its sparkles winking at the sky overhead. His pants no longer felt cold and damp, but had begun to dry against his skin.

For a while he lingered, inhaling the crisp autumn air as the sun rose higher overhead. This had always been his favorite time of year, when nature was covered in a rainbow-colored blanket. As the sun beamed down on him and his clothes dried out, his muscles no longer felt stiff, and he found the pain in his head and shoulder had lightened, along with his mood.

It had been well over an hour since Jonquil had turned on her heels. Adam couldn't put off the inevitable any longer. The time had come to return to camp and apologize for his earlier unseemly behavior.

She'd been as mad as a hornet when she'd stomped away from him, and rightly so. To begin with, he'd had no business taking advantage of her. But she'd been so beautiful, sitting on the side of the pool, and so challenging when she hadn't backed away from him.

When he'd reached out for her, he couldn't be sure of her reaction, but his body had rejoiced when she'd returned his kiss with uninhibited passion. They had both relished the encounter until his lust had weakened his bogus inebriation.

The sooner he returned to camp and apologized, the better. Otherwise, when Gabriel returned they'd probably send him packing. His only hope was to convince Jonquil he wasn't the scoundrel she believed him to be.

He'd be honest. He'd tell her he had no regrets about the kiss, only about his trickery. Searching the landscape for a token of his sincerity, he sighed. No flowers this late into the season.

And then he saw it! The perfect peace offering for Jonquil Rose.

The smell of lye soap filled the warm early afternoon as Jonquil wrung out the last piece of laundry and stretched it across a nearby bush. Her hands and knuckles burned from the intense scrubbing she'd dealt the wash, but the exercise had provided her with plenty of time to think.

After mulling and stewing over Adam's deception for a good half-hour, the scene in the pool struck her as being more comical than serious. She needed only to close her eyes to call up the picture of Adam stepping into the water with his boots on.

Watching those shiny brown boots fill up with water, Adam acting no more concerned about them than a fisherman over waders, was something she'd not likely forget for a long time. His expression had been priceless.

True, he'd led her to believe he was drunk, but she'd been as deceitful in her own thinking as he'd been with his actions. He'd used his guise to kiss her, and she'd used his guise to allow it. So the way Jonquil had it figured, they were both guilty of deceit. The realization sapped her anger.

As one hour turned into two, she began to worry. She peered through the trees in the direction she'd last seen him head. With his bound shoulder and no weapon she envisioned all kinds of terrible things happening to him. Maybe he'd fallen again or been attacked by some forest animal. Or maybe he'd strayed too far from camp and was lost.

Lost, she thought. Heaven forbid! Jonquil had grown up on a farm, but in this strange environment, if Adam were indeed lost, she'd never be able to find him. And how long would a fancy man like Adam Coulter survive in the wilderness? Hadn't his accident yesterday proven his bad judgment? Really, she reflected, guiding your horse across a rabbit burrow.

Jonquil looked again toward the trees and the small pool beyond. It would be dark in a few hours. If Adam were not back by nightfall, she might never find him.

Even now, he could be lying somewhere, unable to move, his body twisted and broken. She had to find him. She was responsible for Adam's well-being until Gabriel returned.

One more quick glance around the camp convinced Jonquil that Adam had not returned. His horse stood tethered to the same tree Gabriel had tied him to yesterday, the feed and water buckets within reach. The only thing to do now was return to the pool and track him from there.

Jonquil hastened toward the trees, her eyes searching the landscape. When she'd spied him leaving, he'd taken the path beside the stream.

Turning in that direction, she started down the same trail and came to an abrupt halt. A glint of

143

mischief on his face, Adam approached her from the trees. He cradled a large piece of bark in his one good arm.

Bowing before her, he held out his gift. "I bring you a peace offering," he said, giving her a magnanimous wink.

Jonquil scrutinized this maddening, resourceful man, whose sudden appearance made her heart flip-flop in her chest. From the tips of his tanned fingers up to his shoulder, across his chest where one rosy nipple peeked from behind a thin veil of russet hair, and across the sling of his anchored arm, Adam Coulter was covered in a thick golden ooze. A fly buzzed around his syrupy form, but he seemed indifferent to its pesky drone. His eyes never leaving hers, he thrust the slab of bark toward her. He'd found her honey tree.

Jonquil's gaze slid over the honey-coated man as she accepted his offering. "Why, Mr. Coulter, I'm speechless."

Adam raked sticky fingers through his hair, spiking his deep brown curls like a porcupine's quills. Color came to his cheeks. He tilted his head and looked at her from beneath his raised left eyebrow. A smile played at the corners of his mouth.

Jonquil's heart softened, and a warm glow suffused her. Adam looked like a small child who'd been caught with his fingers in the honey pot—and he had!

Her own lips fluttered into a smile as she stared at him in astonishment. No longer able to contain her emotions, she burst into laughter.

"You're not angry?" he asked, returning her smile with a devastatingly beautiful grin.

"Noooo, I'm not angry," Jonquil teased. Their eyes met and held across the distance of sun-dappled shade.

"But I do believe, sir, you could use *another* bath!"

144

"Bath?" Adam's brows lifted in surprised solicitation, then he tried to apologize. "About this morning—"

Jonquil silenced him with a movement of her hand. "But this time, I suggest you take your boots off."

"Anything . . . everything . . ." Adam replied, before the innuendo of his words penetrated.

"That won't be necessary," Jonquil countered, enjoying the deepening color on the man's face. "All I'm interested in removing is the honey coating. We can't have the ants sniffing you out, now can we?"

Setting aside the bark tray that contained the honeycomb, Jonquil linked her arm in his and steered him toward the small pool.

Gabriel entered the Russellville General Store to the welcoming tinkle of a tiny brass bell. At four o'clock, he was grateful to find the place still open for business. The afternoon had grown chilly, and a shopkeeper couldn't be blamed for closing up and heading home to a warm kitchen fire.

A tall, thin-framed woman appeared from a back room and stepped up to the counter. "May I help you?"

"Yes'm."

Gabriel unbuttoned his heavy coat and pulled out a paper. "My—uh—boss, he fell about a day's ride from here and hurt his shoulder. We were through here yesterday on our way north, and we figured it would be too hard on him to bring him all the way back."

"You were here?" the woman asked.

"Yes'm. He came in to buy supplies. Said you was real helpful, that maybe you might have some things to ease his pain."

"You wouldn't by chance be with that nice farmer

145

who came in with his sister, would you?"

"Yes'm, that's the one." He thrust the list into her hand.

The woman studied the paper as if it were a personal letter from her customer of yesterday. After a moment she looked up. "We should have what you need." She started along the wall. "You do have money . . . ?"

"Oh, yes'm," Gabriel replied, trying to blend into the woodwork. "He gave me plenty."

Better not to draw any unnecessary attention to himself, he thought. Better to let the town think they were a farmer, his sister, and a hired hand heading north to buy stock.

"You really ought to stop by and see Dr. Mosby before you leave. Let him know how your boss is injured. It could be serious."

"Yes'm, I'll do that."

The shopkeeper began wrapping the assortment of items from the list.

Gabriel studied a stationery box on the counter and suddenly thought of his female companion back home. Maybe tonight, while he had some quiet time alone, he would write her a note, just to let her know he was all right. Lord, he missed his woman. He wondered if fate would ever bring them back together.

"And, ma'am? Could you add some paper and a writing pen?" He pointed to the box. "And some ink?"

The woman gave him a studied glance.

"For my boss. He forgot to put that on his list."

"Certainly," she said. "Did he say whether he needs an inkwell or just a small bottle?"

Gabriel thought of the two carpetbags strapped across his mule's back. Packed into the depths of one were the crystal inkwell and the silver badge they had taken from one of the intruders at the farm. He might

146

have had to leave Rosie in the hands of a stranger, but he would never leave incriminating evidence with her for the man to find.

"Just a small bottle should be enough, ma'am."

The shopkeeper added the items to her price list.

When he had paid, Gabriel headed for the door and put on his hat. "Ma'am, could you direct me to the doctor's office?" he asked.

The woman seemed smugly pleased that he would take her sage advice and see the doctor before leaving. "Certainly." She held the door open and pointed up the street. "But you won't find him in town tonight. He's out at the Livsey farm, preparing to deliver a baby. Knowing him, though, if everything goes well, he'll be back after sunup and sitting in church before ten."

She turned back to Gabriel. "You can stay in town tonight, can't you? Surely you weren't going to try to ride all night in the dark?"

"Oh no'm, I'll stay." He nodded, agreeing with her wisdom.

"Good." She pointed in the opposite direction. "Go on down and see the blacksmith. Tell him I sent you. He's got a room in the back of his place. Should be nice and warm after he's been working all day."

She watched Gabriel stuff the package into one of the bags on Cantankerous' back. "Hurry on over, now," she warned, her arms fluttering in the breeze. "He closes up early on Saturdays."

Gabriel untied the mule from the hitching post. "I'll do that, ma'am. And thank you." He touched his finger to the brim of his hat. "Bless you, ma'am."

Later that evening, from a warm room in the back of the smithy shop, Gabriel listened to the Saturday night revelers who rode, whistled, sang, and brawled their way up and down the main street of Russellville.

147

By the light of a tabletop lantern, he finished a hot meal of ham, potatoes, turnip greens, and canned peaches packed for him by the hotel cook. Then, untying the mercantile package, he withdrew the paper, pen, and bottle of ink.

He considered setting the bottle contents into the inkwell itself, but he couldn't shrug off his fear of repercussions at flaunting a dead man's belongings.

If Rosie wanted to use the inkwell, it would be her decision. Unless he was forced to sell it, pawn it, or use it for a bribe, he wanted nothing to do with it. So he left the inkwell where it lay hidden in the carpetbag.

With his new pen he made a list of his purchases, including the two bottles of whiskey he'd picked up at the saloon before dark. If the liniment, poultice, and pain powders from the mercantile didn't help Mr. Coulter's shoulder, the liquor would at least get them as far as they had to go. Perhaps in the morning this Doc Mosby would have advice of his own.

He took out a fresh piece of paper and moved the lantern closer. For a moment he sat studying the pen, remembering the freedoms he had gained since his fifteenth birthday. That was the year Rosie's mother, Margaret, ran away with that rapscallion, Ball, that no-good card shark and slave-ship captain. Miz Elizabeth had granted Gabriel his freedom if he would leave the security of the Natchez plantation and spend one year looking out for her daughter Margaret's welfare. It was a bargain he couldn't afford to turn down.

But if it hadn't been for Miz Elizabeth and her threats to Ball as her trusting daughter left with him for an insecure future, the man would have stolen Gabriel's papers and had him sold by the end of the first day. Gabe was sure of it. Too bad the missus was gone now, he thought. She'd really have taken to her granddaughter.

Gabriel grinned as memories churned in his mind. He was recalling when Ball had taken one look at the wretched, abandoned Arkansas farm he had won in a card game, had given his pregnant bride-to-be the deed as a farewell gift, and had skedaddled out of the picture.

The agreed year of indenture came and went, but Gabriel stayed. Stayed and helped raise his Rosie, keeping his promise to her mother that he'd never reveal the circumstances of her birth. The little girl would have a hard enough life as it was without adding a shame that she hadn't earned. To this day he'd kept that promise, backing up Miz Margaret's tales of how the child's father had died in the war.

In spite of their poverty, Gabriel had been a happy man. He couldn't imagine life without the two women he so loved. And while he might have inherited a greater burden than he'd expected, he was in fact free. Free to move, free to learn to read and write, free to earn a living for his tiny makeshift family.

And over the years he shared his idea of freedom with the few black friends he made. He was most proud of teaching his special woman, Keely, to read and write.

He put his pen to the paper. "Dear Keely . . ."

Chapter Nine

Dr. Josiah Mosby stood in his upstairs office over the furniture store, dressed in trousers and undershirt, drying his hands on a fresh towel. His black bag sat open on the table before him. Mosby's eyes were bloodshot, his facial lines were deep. He looked like a man who had been up all night.

"You say Mr. Coulter dislocated his shoulder? How do you know?"

Gabriel explained the malformation of the arm and the subsequent action he had taken. He added that Adam could move his fingers, that they were warm to the touch, and that so far he appeared to have no fever.

Dr. Mosby stilled the towel and shook his head. "That's some story. Ordinarily," he said, "I'd say rig up a pallet Indian-style behind his horse and bring him in here anyway, but at this point I suppose there's no need. It would appear you accomplished what I would have done anyway."

The physician pulled a jar of salve from a shelf and took a small envelope of powder from his black bag. "Here," he said, scratching instructions onto a piece of paper. "Use this"—he handed Gabriel the jar— "on the shoulder three times a day, then keep it covered with a dressing for warmth." He held out the envelope. "Use this when he bellyaches about your manhandling his arm. Little by little he'll have to move it to keep the shoulder from freezing up on him."

"How long, Doc, till he's feelin' better?"

"What Mr. Coulter had, my friend, was a dislocation. Sometimes they take as long to heal as a break. My guess is, if he takes care of himself, he should be up to snuff in about four weeks. While you're traveling, he'd do best to keep his arm tight to his body. He'd do even better if he'd remember to stop to rest and use this stuff I've given you."

Gabriel was taken aback by the physician's words. Not only had the man complimented him on his work, he had addressed Gabriel as he might have any man, as though taking no notice of his dark color.

Throughout his life, Gabriel had become a master at paying respect, his seemingly passive resignation convincing all that he not only knew but accepted his "place." This time, however, he actually did feel respect for this man of science who, more than most, could so easily have reminded Gabriel of who and what he was—black, uneducated, even uppity. Instead, the doctor had even called him "friend."

Gabriel paid Mosby for the medications and pocketed the written intructions. "Thank you, sir. I'll be on my way." He retrieved an envelope from his pocket. "By the way, sir," he said, "bein' this is Sunday and there's no place to take this, could I trouble you to post this letter for me tomorrow?"

"Be glad to." Dr. Mosby reached behind him and took a clean shirt from a peg. "Just leave it right there. I'll see it gets mailed."

Gabriel laid the letter on the table next to the bag. On top he placed some coins he hoped would cover postage. "Thank you, sir." He opened the door and started out into the bright Sunday morning.

151

The church bells were ringing as Gabriel walked down the main street of Russellville, leading Cantankerous by the reins. He'd ridden for hours yesterday, he'd ride for that many more today. But for now it felt good to walk and move his joints.

The street appeared empty except for the few people climbing into buggies in front of the hotel. They would be heading for the church, no doubt. There, he thought to himself, they'd join other townspeople and farm families and sing their praises to the same God Who'd put up with all the ruckus of the night before.

On the outskirts of town he adjusted the mule's blinders, then mounted, securing his knees behind the two full carpetbags. Without the flaps attached to his bridle, Cantankerous would become so distracted by passing objects that Gabriel would never be back to camp by nightfall.

Slipping his feet through the improvised rope stirrups, he jiggled the reins. "Giddup, boy." The mule started forward.

The river they followed gushed and tumbled, splashing its objections against boulders stuck in its path. Gabriel settled back and listened to the soothing music of nature. He closed his eyes for a moment, only to hear new sounds mingling with those of the stream. From somewhere along the bank, voices raised in song drifted his way. Up ahead, people were gathered.

As he approached a grove, he came upon parked wagons and horses. The voices were much clearer now, and he recognized the words to the hymn that rose from the water's edge. Through the trees he could see a dozen or so people, prayer books in hand, facing the water, while four men, white garments draped over their clothes, snaked hand in hand out into the river toward a man who stood waist-deep, waiting for them.

His interest piqued, Gabriel pulled the mule to a stop and watched the ritual. For all the solemnity of the scene, the thought of how cold that river must be about now kept occurring to him.

His eyes rested on the preacher in the water, whose speaking voice grew thunderous as he addressed the now hushed gathering. "Do ye," he roared, his arms lifted skyward, commanding the attention of the group, "renounce Satan?"

The crowd answered in unison.

The preacher continued, waving his arms about as if calling upon all within miles to listen to his words. Gabriel studied him, caught by the boisterous commands the man issued in the name of religion. The voice sounded strangely familiar. He tried to get a closer look without drawing undue attention to himself. Digging his heels into the mule's flanks, he urged the animal forward until he had an unobstructed view of the preacher.

Hatless, the man looked to be about his own age. With a bony face, he sported a straggly beard and stringy, pale yellow hair that blew about in the sharp breeze. From a distance, Gabriel couldn't make out the color of the preacher's eyes, but he recognized instantly their narrow beadiness. So the Reverend Cates, circuit preacher, was covering the Russellville area this time of year.

Perhaps out here the preacher promoted himself as the messenger of God, but Gabriel couldn't help wondering how many of his followers he had garnered by intimidation. That same intimidation he had used on Miz Margaret whenever he had called at the farm those few times before she had died.

If those souls who trusted him with their shivering bodies out in that river could've heard his pounding on the spirit of a frail woman like Miz Margaret, they'd run in the opposite direction. Cates might persuade everyone else he met that he was a true man of the cloth, a spiritual leader, but Gabriel would never be convinced. Not in a lifetime. This man had other fish to fry.

After the first preacher-come-to-call visit, supposed to be so reassuring to a poor soul, which instead left his mistress weepy and withdrawn for days, Gabriel vowed to stick close by whenever the man came again.

After that Cates had shown up twice more, each time ranting and raving about how a sick woman who really loved the Lord would turn over the farm to him out of charity and move into town where she could receive "good care."

The man was nothing more than a crook.

Cantankerous began nodding his head, seeking direction from his rider. "Come on, boy," Gabriel urged, giving him his lead. "You're probably as tired of listenin' to him as I am. Anyway, he's got nothin' to do with us now."

Jonquil and Adam had nearly finished their supper when Gabriel rode into camp. While Jonquil greeted his return with relief, she was surprised to find her happiness mixed with a sense of regret, for since Adam had presented her with the store of honey, they had fallen into an easy companionship that would now regress into more formality.

Only when she had touched Adam—to remove his shirt to rewrap the bandages, to dry his back after the healing soaks in the warm pool—had the memory of their one fiery kiss assailed her and left her shaken. But Adam had done his best to keep the rest of their time alone light-spirited.

Still, when it had come time to bed down for the night and Jonquil had dragged her pallet closer to

154

Adam's bedding, the odd stirrings crept up again and her senses became heightened. Lying near him, she had listened for his every breath, had almost felt his energy pulling her nearer to his body. In spite of herself, she thought again how secure she had felt nestled against him in the rainstorm. As she lay with her back to him, hugging the barrel of her rifle against any threatening night creatures, a feeling of emptiness engulfed her.

Now Gabriel was back, dismounting and looking from one to the other as if searching for any changes in their relationship since he had been away. And Jonquil, hearing nothing but praise from her patient, nonetheless felt exposed, transparent, as though her raw emotions were stamped across her forehead.

When he'd unwrapped his supplies, Gabriel repeated the physician's orders to a studious Jonquil and a grimacing Adam. After doling out some pain-relief powder and waiting for it to take effect, Gabriel removed Adam's confining sling and proceeded to move his upper arm in small circles as wide as Adam could tolerate. He then left Jonquil to redress the shoulder and sat down to a hot meal topped with half a dozen honeyed biscuits.

When she turned in for the night, Jonquil climbed under her covers, a proper ten feet from where Adam lay, and felt an acute loss of warmth and familiarity with the man she had cared for so diligently since yesterday. Now that Gabriel was back, she would have no excuse for physical contact—for bathing his shoulders and back, drying his skin, and helping him dress.

Even as she strained against sleep to count the ways she would miss the small intimacies she had enjoyed with Adam Coulter, Jonquil felt her lids drop from exhaustion.

*   *   *

"Eureka!"

Adam's zealous inflection made the word sound more like an invocation of divine blessing than the name of a town.

As though sensing Jonquil's confusion, he smiled and clarified his declaration. "Archimedes was said to utter this very exclamation on discovering a method for finding the purity of gold. Simply stated, Eureka means 'I have found it!'".

"Found what?" Jonquil asked from the wagon seat. "Surely not gold."

"Everyone felt this wonderful place of healing waters was going to flourish as a town, so they named it Eureka Springs."

Gabriel pulled the wagon to a stop, and from the mountaintop on which they sat, Jonquil stared across sloping hills to the rough plank buildings crowded together to form a town. Excitement tingled in her veins.

Maybe, she thought as she listened to the sounds of industry echoing from the treed hillsides, this indeed was a place for healing the body and spirit as Adam had suggested, maybe she and Gabriel would have a chance. Perhaps at last they would be able to put the past to rest and be welcomed into this new community.

Jonquil turned to Adam, his leg pressed companionably against her own. Remembering too well how her family had been ostracized by the town of Prater, she didn't put much faith in these people being any different. But when she looked into Adam's eyes, something about his expression made her think this time just might be different.

Since the episode at the spring, their relationship had changed. While they had become fast friends, Jonquil wondered at her compelling attraction to this man.

Adam's reassuring smile reached his eyes, and they

156

sparkled like golden topaz in the morning sun. Jonquil's heart swelled beneath her ribs until she thought it might explode. With growing anticipation she looked from one man to the other. "Well, what are we waiting for?"

"Waiting for this ornery beast to descend on the valley . . . God help them all," Adam groaned.

Gabriel chuckled and snapped the reins against the mule's rump. "Giddy up!" he shouted.

Braying from the slap, Cantankerous swung his large head around and rolled back his upper lip to expose yellowed teeth and waxy gums.

His harsh snort evoked ripples of laughter from the threesome as the mule grudgingly moved forward with the rickety wagon in tow. Headed for the center of town, they joggled down the washboard road, falling in line with many other pilgrims making their way to the "city that water built."

Jonquil stood on the second-story balcony of the Perry House, looking down on the constant stream of traffic that rattled along Spring Street. With Adam searching for lodging for Gabriel and the mule, she was on her own until supper. Free to explore the town and check out the many shops that lined the business district of Eureka Springs. The prospect both thrilled and terrified her. Again she and Gabriel would be separated, not by choice, but by circumstances and the order of society.

The severing of this deep-rooted tie tugged at her heartstrings, but Jonquil knew she and Gabriel had to look to the future. Only after much soul-searching had they come to grips with the fact that they had no choice but to close the door on their former lives.

The death of their rescuer at the farm, a man whose name they would never know, weighed heavily on their hearts, and they both felt sure that somewhere

157

someone grieved for him. But there had been no one to trust with their report of the incident, no one to come to their defense when they would have been charged with murder.

For Jonquil and Gabriel, today marked a new beginning. For them the past no longer existed.

So she stood dressed in her newly pressed, blue checkered dress, a crisp breeze furling the blue ribbons of her straw poke bonnet. She was sure she looked as much a real lady as the women who passed on the street below.

Leaning over the railing, she stared at the strange flatiron building at the top of Spring Street. With Bank of Eureka Springs printed in large letters across its facade, it looked as though it had been erected directly in the middle of Spring Street. The roadbed swerved sharply to the left and another street branched off to its right. Strange, she thought, this city built on the up-and-down swells of the Ozarks.

She decided she'd dillydallied long enough. The sooner she descended the stairs, the sooner she could feel a real part of the town. Her first stop would be to visit Basin Springs and partake of the "magical waters."

Following the balcony that led around the corner of the hotel, Jonquil ambled toward the wide stairs that zigzagged down to the street below. Several fashionably attired ladies and gentlemen nodded in her direction as she descended toward the ground. At the bottom, she moved with the throngs of visitors who had come to receive the curative waters.

People were everywhere, milling about the planked boardwalks and reclining on the many benches scattered around the parklike area. Some even perched upon limestone rocks that jutted out from the high natural wall behind the springs.

Jonquil paused on the boardwalk and read the large

arched sign that marked the entrance to the site—Balm of Life, Eureka Water Condensing Company.

She studied the crowds standing in line, waiting to drink the water. They were a varied group from all walks of life and in all conditions of health. In their hands they carried buckets or cups. It was then that Jonquil realized she'd not brought a container for herself. Suddenly embarrassed by her careless planning, she turned to leave.

"Miss!"

Jonquil turned to the woman who addressed her; a very well-placed lady, she thought, several years her senior. Dark eyes twinkled from an arresting face. But it was the woman's smile that captured Jonquil's attention. It was like a dose of sunshine, and Jonquil was immediately drawn to its warmth.

The woman extended a hand in a welcoming gesture. "You're new to our city?" she asked in a culturally refined voice.

Hesitantly, Jonquil offered her own hand in greeting. "Yes, I've only just arrived."

"Well then, you must sample our water." Smiling, the woman thrust her own cup into Jonquil's hand and ushered her toward the basin, hovering over her like a mother hen.

Like an obedient child, Jonquil filled the metal container with the clear, cold liquid and raised it to her lips. Her eyes met the other woman's over the cup's brim while she drank. The water tasted deliciously pure and sweet.

"Everyone's taking the cure," the woman explained as Jonquil finished swallowing the cup's contents. "They're drinking, and bathing in, the magical waters of our sixty-three healthful springs."

"That many?" Jonquil asked, as she relinquished her place in front of the basin.

"Oh, yes, my dear. And if you'd care to hear of their successes—"

159

A child of four or five skipped over to the woman and grabbed her hand, urging her to follow. "Sam's arrived, Mama. Come on. It's time to go!"

The woman prodded the child into silence. "Kathleen, where are your manners?" The little girl darted behind her mother's skirt and peeked at Jonquil from behind a black serge ruffle.

"This little minx is my youngest daughter, Kathleen." The woman's hand lovingly patted the child's head while encouraging her to abandon her hiding place. At her mother's affectionate insistence, the little girl relinquished her position and curtsied in Jonquil's direction.

"Pleased to meet you, ma'am."

"Pleased to meet you, too, Kathleen." Jonquil smiled down on the adorable child. "My name is Jonquil Rose."

"Your name sounds like my mama's garden."

Both women laughed at the child's response. The little girl blushed a bright pink, and Jonquil tried to smooth over the awkward moment.

"That's why my mother named me so. She loved flowers as much as your own mother must, since you seem to be so familiar with their names." Jonquil's gaze returned to the child's mother, and again she was warmed by a friendly smile.

"Just look at me." The woman scolded herself. "I reprimand Kathleen because of her absence of manners when I myself am remiss." Thrusting a hand forward, she announced, "I'm Adaline Clayton, and I hope you'll enjoy your stay in our city."

"It's a lovely place," Jonquil returned, "and I like it already."

"Good, dear. Will you be staying long?"

The little girl again nudged her mother. "Mama, the buggy's waiting, and I mustn't miss my nap."

"From the mouths of babes," Adaline replied. "If you'll excuse us, we really must be going." She then

160

allowed the little girl to pull her toward the waiting carriage.

"Wait!" Jonquil hurried after the twosome. "Your cup."

"I insist you return it to me in person." Adaline thrust the cup aside and pressed a small calling card into Jonquil's hand. "Come for tea tomorrow at two. There will be other ladies present as well, and I'd so like you to meet them."

"But . . ." Jonquil tried to delay Mrs. Clayton, but the woman climbed into her carriage behind her daughter, and her driver maneuvered the vehicle into the busy street.

"Please come," she called back. "We must become friends."

"I'd like that, too! Until tomorrow!"

Jonquil crossed Spring Street and perused the calling card in her hand: Clayton House, A Fine Hotel, Mill and Main, Eureka Springs, Arkansas. Imagine that, she thought, not in town a day and already I've been invited to tea.

Suddenly, she felt the decison she and Gabriel had made to accompany Adam Coulter to Eureka Springs had been a wise one. The promise of a new beginning bubbled up from somewhere deep inside her and poured forth like the water gurgling up from Basin Springs.

Adam sat across from Powell Clayton in his private study at the Clayton House Hotel, which also served as the family's private residence. Their chairs faced the marble fireplace, where a small fire burned away the room's chill. Adam puffed on a cheroot, sated and relaxed after a light lunch of duck breast and Arkansas pears.

"Your cook is wonderful," he complimented.

"Thanks to my lovely wife," the former governor

161

agreed. "Addie oversees the planning of all the meals served to our guests and our family."

"Pass on my regards, if you will."

Clayton nodded and smiled at the praise.

Adam blew a nearly perfect halo of smoke and watched it rise. A log shifted on the grate, shooting sparks up the chimney.

Clayton stood and moved across the highly polished hard pine floor, grabbed a brass poker, and resettled the errant log before turning again to face his guest. Although the general was missing the lower part of one arm, his dexterous movement was to be commended. That along with everything else Adam had learned about the man.

After extensive study of Clayton's biographical profile, included in the papers Judge Parker had given him, Adam felt he knew the man almost as well as he knew himself.

Clayton had served with the United States Army during the Civil War, much of his duty having been here in Arkansas. A brigadier general when the war ended, he'd married Adaline McGraw, the daughter of a Confederate officer from Helena. Their first child, Lucy, had been born in 1868. By now, he thought, she must be about fourteen.

After serving as the state's first Republican governor, Clayton completed a term with the United States Senate, then moved his family to Eureka Springs. Here again, according to Judge Parker, Clayton used his leadership skills, this time to build his dream town, boasting the newest advances in urban planning and engineering.

And of all the titles Powell Clayton had earned over the years—General, Governor, Senator—he still preferred to be called General.

"So, my friend," the older man asked, "how are our fugitives?"

Adam shifted in his chair, pulled from his reverie

by his host's question. After all that had occurred since he had met Jonquil Rose and her partner, it had been a while since he had thought of his traveling companions as fugitives.

Now the question forced Adam to focus on his true purpose for being in Eureka Springs. Striving for objectivity, he replied, "Truthfully, sir, they don't fit the profile."

From beneath raised, bushy brows Clayton's eyes drilled into his own, though he said nothing.

"I spent a good month trailing those two, and the last week or so traveling in close quarters with them. I'm certain they're hiding something, but what it is I can't put my finger on."

"Murder, most likely." Clayton's remark was to the point, no beating around the bush.

"No, sir. I don't believe they're capable of taking a life."

Adam went on to relate Jonquil's impersonation of a lad at the race, the knock he received on the head, and his watching Gabriel remove the money from the saloon owner's office in Hot Springs; all suspicious acts but, on their own merits, justifiable.

He told Clayton about his accident and of how Gabriel, with Jonquil's help, had reset his dislocated shoulder. But the one thing Adam failed to mention was his growing affection for those two, one of them in particular.

"These might be desperate people," Adam admitted, "compulsive and misdirected, but basically they're kind and caring . . . and much too trusting for their own good." He lifted his right arm, still in its sling. "If they were the type they're made out to be, they could easily have ridden off and left me to the wolves. But they didn't."

"They also didn't know you were on their trail," came the gentle reminder. Clayton sounded not at all convinced. He left his spot in front of the fire and returned to his chair. "You said they're hiding something. I can't help thinking they've somehow joined ranks with Innes Ball."

He recounted the facts as they both knew them. "We know they lived on land that Ball claims to own. Suddenly they take off for parts unknown without telling anyone, leaving behind fresh graves. I tell you, Adam, those two either crossed Ball in some way and got caught at it"—Clayton was silent for a moment—"or they saw something they weren't supposed to see." Fingering the goatee that sprouted from his chin, he drew his own conclusion. "Until I learn differently, I tend to believe the former."

"Why do you say that, General?" Adam remained poised in his chair, interested in the second speculation.

"Because an innocent bystander would have gone straight to the law and received its protection. And because innocent people don't lie, and cheat, and *steal*."

The words made sense, but the circumstances surrounding Jonquil's actions hadn't seemed to impress the man a bit. So, until Adam learned more about his "fugitives," any argument to the contrary would serve no purpose.

Clayton leaned closer. "Ball's our enemy, son. He's the one to flush out. His fall will bring down his scavenger battalion, and we'll know soon enough how these two fit in."

Adam couldn't help but smile at the general's military jargon. It was hard to imagine a black man like Gabriel and an angel like Jonquil being referred to as a battalion.

The general's next words interrupted Adam's thoughts. "I met Innes Ball in the seventies . . . after I left the Senate. It was in Little Rock." A smile pushed up his large shaggy mustache and twitched his goatee. "Our youngest child, Kathleen, was born there. What a little heartbreaker, that one."

Adam returned the general's smile, enjoying a glimpse of the indulgent side of what he knew to be a stern personality.

Clayton continued, the tender moment forgotten. "Fancied myself as a promoter of railroads and hotel projects." He winked. "Still do," he said. "Hope to have our own railroad here in Eureka Springs in the next year." He digressed for a moment onto his latest project before remembering the point he was trying to make. "Well, anyway, it was when I was president of the Little Rock, Mississippi, and Texas Railroad, that Ball and I crossed paths for the first time."

Flicking a large gray ash into a satin chase dish, Adam returned the Havana to his mouth to savor one last draw before snuffing it out.

The older man stood, and from a crystal decanter on the table between them poured two glasses of port. Handing one to Adam, he replaced the stopper. He again took his seat.

"It was in Little Rock in eighteen seventy-eight. He visited the capitol, lobbying for the right-of-way for the railroad from the town of Malverne to the southwest. In seventy-five, the Hot Springs Line had started operation and Ball wanted to connect the two."

Adam listened, then nodded. "Judge Parker mentioned this to me when we met in Fort Smith."

"I pride myself on being an astute person, normally a good judge of character." Clayton's bushy brows knit together and wrinkles ebbed upward into his receding hairline. "And from the moment I met him, something about Innes Ball sat wrong with me. He tried to appear to be a man's man. But the first time I shook his hand, I knew the man was a weasel, not to be trusted. But clever and a user."

Adam almost choked on his port. The general didn't mince words. Adam decided he liked him.

165

"It doesn't matter what I think of Ball," Clayton was saying. "That's not the issue. Just threw that in for your information."

Adam returned the general's smile with one of genuine approval.

"The future of this country lies in its railroads." Clayton leaned forward to make his point. "And don't get me wrong. I'm for making a dollar just like the next fellow. But I believe in honesty and integrity, and I'm convinced Ball doesn't even know the meaning of those words. I'd wager everything he owns he came by dishonestly."

Clayton turned up his glass, drained its contents, and set it back on the table. On a more personal note he added, "I'm sorry about your brother."

"Thank you, sir," Adam answered. Bitterness clawed at his insides. "You can understand, then, why it's so important for me to bring the people responsible for his death to justice."

"Certainly, certainly. Innes Ball is a fraud of the worst kind. I'll enjoy bringing him and his followers to their knees."

The man's face turned serious. "Tell me about your singer. Jonquil Rose, I believe, was her name."

Adam was about to respond when the door opened and a little girl bounced into the study.

"Papa, are you here?" she called out.

Both men rose at the same time. The child, spying her father, ran across the room toward them. Skidding to an abrupt stop, she bobbed a quick curtsy before she spoke. "I didn't know you had a guest, Papa."

"That's quite all right, dear. Come, I'll introduce you." Clayton motioned his daughter over with his hand.

The child, no longer a whirlwind of energy, moved toward them with the practiced grace of a young lady. Stopping beside her father, she hugged

166

his chair arm while he bestowed an affectionate pat on her head.

"Adam, this is my youngest daughter, Kathleen."

Adam stooped to take the small hand she extended and bowed his head in her direction. "I'm pleased to meet you, Kathleen."

"Pleased to meet you too, sir." She looked toward her father for approval.

He beamed down at her. "Is your mother with you?"

"I'm behind her, as usual." The rather winded woman paused at the doorway long enough to remove her cloak and hat before she walked toward the threesome who waited in front of the fireplace.

"This is my lovely wife, Adaline."

Again the affection the man held for his family did not go unnoticed by Adam.

"Addie, this is Adam Coulter. He has only just arrived in town."

Adam bowed his head. "Mrs. Clayton."

The woman extended her hand and smiled. "Addie, please. It's so nice to meet you at last. I've told all our friends about your endeavors to bring us entertainment during the off-season. We are so looking forward to our first recital."

"I'm sure my talented companions will afford you and yours a most memorable entertainment." Adam returned the woman's smile and released her hand.

"We met a lady at the spring who'd only just arrived in town, too."

All eyes turned to the small child standing next to her father, her shyness and manners forgotten as she proceeded to tell her father about her experience.

The child giggled and wriggled with delight. "She had the funniest name."

"Now, Kath, don't be fresh," her mother reminded her.

"I mean, she had the . . ." The child groped for the

appropriate words. "It was just like Mama's flowers."

"It was a lovely name, Kathleen, just like its owner." The woman looked to her husband. "Jonquil Rose. And I've invited her to meet with the other ladies for tea tomorrow."

"Jonquil Rose," Adam repeated the name. Clayton just stared at his wife.

"Yes. Unusual, isn't it?" Mrs. Clayton replied. "But lovely."

Adam could hardly believe his ears. Of all the newcomers entering the town hour by hour, the governor's wife had apparently met his very own Jonquil Rose. His "fugitive," as Clayton had so aptly pointed out earlier.

His gaze locked with the general's. This was a turn of events neither of them had expected.

Addie Clayton may have been informed of Adam's ostensible purpose for being in Eureka Springs—to supply entertainment during the off-season and to promote a young singer and banjo player of great promise. But she had no idea of the real nature of his sojourn in the town. Only he and Clayton knew that, and until Adam's mission was complete, they would have to keep it that way.

In the meantime, how was Clayton going to take to having his wife hobnob with a murder suspect?

"If you'll excuse us, Mr. Coulter," Addie said, "it's time for Kathleen's nap, before the children return from school."

"Adam, please," he returned. "It would be my honor."

"Then Adam it is." Her eyes smiled at her husband. "General." With that, Adaline Clayton turned and ushered her daughter from the room.

Adam watched the two females disappear through the doorway. A moment later a door slammed at the back of the house and their muffled words and footsteps faded into silence.

He assessed his host for a reaction. When none was forthcoming, Adam attempted to apologize for the complication. "Sir, I don't know what to say. I will tell Jonquil that she needs to spend tomorrow rehearsing and looking for a permanent place to live. She'll send her regrets to Mrs. Clayton."

Clayton waved Adam to silence.

"My Addie would play hostess to everyone who sets foot in this town if given the opportunity. Tomorrow afternoon the Invalid's Association will hold its regular meeting here. She obviously sensed the young woman was in need of friendship and that's why she invited her to attend."

Still, Adam knew the general, with his convictions, had reservations. "For what it's worth, sir, I don't believe Jonquil is guilty of murder. I hope that will ease your mind somewhat."

Clayton's expression was deliberate. "That, young man, is for the evidence and the law to determine, when and if charges are brought against the twosome." Then, on a gentler note, he added, "Is there something you're not telling me?"

The unexpected question clanged like a warning bell in Adam's head. Did the man suspect he harbored feelings for Jonquil? With a candid stare he met the general's eyes. "Excuse me, sir?"

Clayton whacked him on the back and draped an arm over Adam's shoulder. "Don't mind me. I'm a suspicious son of a gun."

Adam forced a laugh, knowing full well that Clayton's misgivings were close to being right. He did, indeed, have trouble focusing on Jonquil Rose as a killer. Especially when he considered her gentleness, her refinement of speech and manner, and an innocence he couldn't explain to himself, much less prove.

"After all," the general was saying, "our job is to keep the little fishes swimming until we can reel in the big one. That means you and I will have to work doubly hard watching out for my Addie."

Adam left the Clayton House and started back up the street toward the hotel. Although the general's suspicions had no credence, he wondered if his jumbled feelings were really so transparent.

Tomorrow evening Jonquil and Gabriel would audition before the founders of the Eureka Springs Improvement Company. He knew the associates would recognize and appreciate the lady for the gifted artist she was—a talented banjo player who sang like an angel. Only he and Clayton would know the truth . . . that Jonquil Rose was an angel in disguise.

Chapter Ten

"Surely you're not wearing that!"

Adam's expression bordered on the incredulous when Jonquil approached him from across the hotel lobby.

Her ears burned as she looked down at her now clean, blue check dress, painstakingly pressed in preparation for Mrs. Clayton's tea. With one caustic statement Adam had reduced her morning's worth of nervous anticipation to acute embarrassment.

Jonquil held her chin high, searing him with a fiery look. "And what, sir, would you suggest I wear?" Her neck scorched with combined anger and humiliation. "My pants and shirt have been freshly laundered. Will they do?"

Adam's thoughtless remark had cut to the core. Jonquil inspected her hands. After the arduous journey, she had managed to scrub away the last of the imbedded grime and had smoothed her nails with the emery board her mother had always insisted she keep handy.

Her hair had been brushed until it gleamed, then plaited and pinned at her neck, leaving softening wisps about her face. And now, because of Adam she felt as unattractive as a wilted flower, her plans for attending the tea shattered. Feeling tears well in her eyes, Jonquil turned, eager to escape before she made more of a fool of herself.

Adam grabbed her arm, stopping her retreat. "I'm sorry," he apologized. "I didn't mean that the way it sounded. You look beautiful as usual, but surely you must have another dress. That one has been through more than I'd care to remember."

Jonquil pried his fingers from around her arm and brushed away his effort to console. "Please give my regrets to Mrs. Clayton. Tell her I'm too ill to attend her tea."

"Too ill mannered, I'd say," Adam retaliated when she again tried to leave. "Didn't you hear my apology?" His deep voice resounded throughout the lobby, and Jonquil was suddenly aware that all eyes in the room were on the two of them.

"Must you shout?" she whispered, anger making her words grate across the silent room.

"I won't give your regrets, Jonquil. You will go to that tea." Adam's dark brown eyes challenged her. "It's a matter of courtesy—and the least you can do for the wife of the man who is hiring you. Cultivating the Claytons' friendship and that of their circle of friends means money in your pocket as well as mine."

Stunned by Adam's condescending attitude, Jonquil took further offense. She met his stalwart gaze without flinching. "I didn't know I should be trying to impress Mrs. Clayton."

She paused, gulping a great draft of air. "My making friends has nothing to do with padding either of our pockets. And you have no say whatsoever as to the clothes I choose to wear. Maybe I'll wear my black saloon dress. Would that please Mr. Clayton's close circle of friends . . . and my employers?"

Adam remembered all too well the dress she'd worn the night he'd found her in Hot Springs. Her

172

sultry image would be engraved in his mind forever—the way the black fabric molded itself around her curves, the way the yellow silk rose nestled against her creamy flesh. And the way his body had responded to such a vision.

Recalling that night, he knew she'd look beautiful in anything . . . or nothing at all. But he wasn't willing to risk another word that might send her scurrying to her room.

Adam's fingers fumbled with the neckline of his shirt as though his collar had become unbearably tight. "All right, you win," he croaked. "Of course, that dress will never do.

"Besides," he said, "you look most presentable as you are." He caught Jonquil's suspicious glare. "Honest."

He turned to the more serious issue. "And another thing," he warned, "don't tell Mrs. Clayton's friends about your background. They think very highly of their entertainment in this town, and wouldn't understand or approve of your having worked in a saloon or traveled with a carnival."

"Then what should I tell them, Mr. Coulter?" Jonquil faced him without wavering. "That I was raised in a convent and taught to sing by the nuns?"

Jonquil's chest felt clogged, an emotional reaction. But she was determined, even if she had to bite her tongue off, that Adam Coulter would never know how much his words had injured her. In her family, manners and etiquette were as important as reading and numbers. Her home may have been shabby, but her education was anything but.

Adam continued, engrossed in his concern for appearances. "Just tell them I discovered you singing in one of the hotels in Hot Springs. That should satisfy them."

The careless words continued, effectively beating Jonquil's spirit into the ground. This new manager

173

of hers, she supposed, had every right to push her career, but what gave him the right to make her feel ashamed when she had in fact done what she could to keep herself and Gabriel from starving?

She almost wanted to laugh at the man's attempt to hide her past from the fine, upstanding ladies of this new community. If he knew her true extraction, then what would he think? An accomplice to a murder and on the run from the law.

Finally Adam looked at her, brought up short by her lack of response, and Jonquil could no longer hide the distress now mirrored in his eyes.

"Look," he said, "I'm sorry about the dress, it was rude and thoughtless of—"

Jonquil interrupted the apology she couldn't bear to hear. "I'll tell them nothing . . . unless they ask."

Silently she questioned why she had thought this town, with its magic waters, would be different from the countless other towns she and Gabriel had encountered in their travels. With crippling awareness, Jonquil knew she would always be on the outside looking in. Suddenly the irony of her situation hit her full force, and she burst into uncontrollable laughter.

Adam quirked an eyebrow, confusion stamped across his forehead at her unexpected humor. "I'm glad you're no longer angry with me." He offered her his elbow.

Jonquil gave in to her laughter, drawing curious looks from strangers, unable to rein in her emotions. Little did Adam Coulter know she feared at any moment her hysterics might switch to tears.

Dabbing at her eyes, she took his arm and proceeded outside to the carriage he'd hired for the day. Bolstered by her sudden mood swing, Adam seemed to have recovered his own good nature.

"Tomorrow, my dear, we'll go shopping," he announced over the clopping of the horse's hooves as

174

they rode toward the Clayton residence. "We'll buy you all the dresses you could want." He looked over at her with a wry grin. "If I don't have to tie you down to try them on."

The memory of the calamitous scene in the Russellville General Store brought fresh giggles from Jonquil.

"When we're finished," he continued, "you'll be the best dressed lady in Eureka Springs."

"And you'll be the poorest man in town."

Jonquil teased Adam, trying to appear enthusiastic about the tea and the shopping spree he'd planned for tomorrow. It was clear he thought everything between them had returned to normal.

But deep inside, in the smallest corner of her soul, she harbored the bitter disappointment that she'd never be anything more to Adam than just a saloon girl. And a way to increase the contents of his pocketbook.

Well, it wasn't enough for her. Tomorrow, unknown to him, she planned to seek employment to fill her daytime hours. In this bustling town, with so many new businesses springing up, surely she could find a position befitting a "pretend" lady. Besides, all those gowns and dresses Adam wanted to buy would require a lot of money. Money she didn't have and wasn't about to accept from him.

"I heard of a small cabin for rent on the edge of town." Adam guided the carriage around a parked wagon. "When I leave you at the Claytons', I'll ride out and take a look at it. Since we'll be here through the winter months, I'd prefer to have my own place."

He pulled the carriage to a stop in front of a large three-story building. Wide, terraced steps led up to the entrance. "This is it," he announced, turning toward Jonquil. "While you're visiting this afternoon, perhaps you can inquire about a respectable boarding house where you can take a room."

He jumped down from the driver's seat and offered Jonquil his hand so she might exit the rig. Together they moved toward the stairs.

Jonquil, full of unbridled laughter only moments ago, stilled the moment Adam pulled to a stop in front of the imposing structure. Now, as she ascended the stairs on his arm, she wanted to turn tail and run.

How could she ever have imagined that the women inside would accept her as an equal? Fear of rejection, coupled with Adam's insinuations about her past, made her feel as volatile as grease on a hot griddle.

Still wounded by Adam's low opinion of her, Jonquil couldn't resist one last gibe before he departed. "Why, Mr. Coulter, if it's a respectable boarding house, they won't allow the likes of me to stay on the premises."

Adam's hold on her arm tightened, and for a brief moment they exchanged smoldering glances. He was opening his mouth to speak when the front door flew open and Addie Clayton rushed out.

The woman threw her arms around Jonquil, giving her a welcoming hug. "My dear, we've been waiting for you." Greeting Adam, Mrs. Clayton dismissed him and ushered Jonquil into the wide entrance hall.

Stung by Jonquil's last remark, Adam stood on the porch and watched the two women disappear inside. Obviously he had hurt her more than he'd thought when all he'd meant to do was caution her about her past and the ways of the world. The whole argument had started with a simple observation on his part. For that he could have bitten his tongue.

When he had suggested the day before that she browse through the shops while he attended to business, he was sure she would have purchased at least one new frock. What woman in captivity could have resisted the fashionable garments in the windows along Main or Spring Street?

He then thought just how harshly life had treated Jonquil and Gabriel this past year, and realized she would hold onto every coin she made as if it were the last she'd ever earn. Though a frugal woman, she had spruced herself up for this tea as proudly as a banker's wife.

When she'd walked into the hotel lobby, she had looked breathtaking. After all the worn dress had been through, she'd tended to it until neither stain nor wrinkle remained.

Her hair had glistened and, pulled back to her nape, had exposed a very kissable neck. Her complexion had been smooth and silky, her lips inviting with a light touch of color, as though she had kissed rose petals.

At the sight of her Adam had felt slightly off balance, and what had he done? Ignored his natural male response to make disparaging remarks. What the hell was the matter with him?

Though he'd have to temper his statements in the future, Adam knew that while he still had to consider Jonquil a criminal, there remained an innocence about her that would require protecting. One wrong utterance from her and she could very well experience rejection by the community.

And the one thing Adam wanted to insure was that Jonquil felt right at home here while he gained her confidence. Until he was ready to bring her in.

After the general had approved of a friendship between his wife and Jonquil, Adam could see the advantages such a relationship would allow. The woman's approval would guarantee Jonquil's acceptance by the genteel ladies of the town. And once they heard her sing and recognized her talent, her reputation would be established.

177

Jonquil's acceptance into the mainstream would make his job easier. His relationship with Clayton could be more open, allowing him to converse with the man at will. It was an ideal situation for a man forced to wait—to study his subjects—before drawing a conclusion on their guilt or innocence.

His brother's killer had to be brought to justice, and ruthless men like Innes Ball and his followers had to be stopped. Then why, Adam questioned, did he feel as though he'd just delivered a lamb to the sacrificial altar?

Could Jonquil, his delicate rose, be the thorn that had pricked the life's blood from his brother?

Lord, he hoped not.

Adam turned and walked down the stairs to the waiting carriage.

Hustled into the parlor, Jonquil nearly forgot she wore the same dress she'd had on yesterday. Left standing just inside the doorway while her hostess excused herself to wipe up a spilled cup of tea, Jonquil held her breath. Instinctively, she reached out to touch a nearby chair.

Never had she seen such a beautifully appointed room. The parlor alone was three times larger than the farmhouse where she'd been born. Twelve-foot walls supported flocked red and gold paper and held paintings of pastoral scenes, along with several kinds of fancy work and decorative trifles.

In the middle of the room, a lavish Oriental rug anchored a large seating group that could easily accommodate fifteen to twenty people at once. Around the room's perimeter, highly polished dark floors reflected other ornate furniture arranged for smaller, more intimate seatings.

Suddenly Jonquil remembered her mother's descriptions of the ancestral home she had left to marry the man she loved.

She ran her hand along the carved back of the chair, feeling the richness of the wood. So this was the beauty that had surrounded her mother on the plantation. How sad that she'd spent her last days in such humble circumstances, when she'd had, and still deserved, so much more.

Gold velvet fabric crowned tall windows from which gathered panels of lace fell to the floor. A stark contrast to the lace tatting that her mother had lovingly made and hung in the windows of the little farmhouse—to bring their home a touch of "opulence," she remembered her mother saying.

Diverse scents drifted across the room; lemon wax, pine, cedar, and the many different fragrances the women had sprinkled on themselves before leaving their homes.

A large marble fireplace stood majestically in the middle of a long wall. Poised upon chairs and stools in front of a glowing fire were a dozen or so ladies engrossed in quiet conversation.

"There you are, my dear," Addie declared, returning to her side. "Allow me to introduce you to some of the others." She ushered her into the middle of the group. "Ladies, I'd like you to meet my new friend, Jonquil Rose."

All chatter ceased, all eyes focused on the newcomer. Names Jonquil knew she'd never remember were rattled off as she was introduced to each lady in turn. Jonquil said a silent prayer of thanks to her deceased mother for being able to draw upon the manners she'd been taught.

She recalled the many "play" tea parties she and her mother had shared when she was but a small child, and the later ones, when she had grown into a young woman. At least once a week they would both dress in their Sunday best and go through the ritual of high tea. Today, because of her mother's persistence, Jonquil knew how to conduct herself like a proper lady.

"Jonquil is the gifted artist I told you about."

Addie's effervescence over her talents was surprising as Jonquil knew full well her hostess had never heard her sing one note. As though the older woman read Jonquil's thoughts at that precise moment, she smiled encouragingly over the head of a stump-shaped woman.

Strangely enough, Jonquil felt very comfortable with these ladies. She listened to them talk of the latest fashions, their children and husbands, and the many newly formed civic organizations. Everyone present seemed concerned with presenting the town positively and, with an open-door policy, welcoming all visitors to their fair city.

Eventually the ladies were directed to the tea table where bone china and accountrements were artistically laid out. The silver tea service glistened in the glow of the candles placed around the table.

China and crystal dishes were filled to overflowing with scones, cucumber sandwiches, cheese biscuits, date-nut bread, fig preserves, and orange marmalade. Jonquil had never seen such an array of food served.

With their plates filled, the ladies moved to the center seating area. Here the conversation turned to intellectual topics, spiritual advancements, and social reform. Jonquil wondered why these women, who'd apparently never worked a day in their lives, would be interested in social reform. Her friend, Flo, would probably have some choice words on this subject.

She learned about the Invalid's Association, the reason for the meeting. Though only women were present today, membership was open to both men and women who were interested in hearing of or sharing the good news of healing from the waters.

The speaker, a middle-aged woman, declared that

for years she had thought she was going blind. Her eyes itched and burned, and she suffered daily with blurred vision. She proclaimed that after having bathed her eyes repeatedly in the spring water—every day for a month—she no longer suffered with this malady. Jonquil listened with rapt attention, wishing there had existed some wondrous cure for her mother's depression and constant fatigue.

The clock on the mantel ticked away the hours until Jonquil realized Adam would soon return to pick her up. So engrossed had she been in the conversation, she'd completely forgotten about inquiring about a suitable boarding house. If she didn't do it soon, everyone would be gone and she'd never find a place to live.

Summoning up her courage, she asked, "Can anyone recommend a boarding house where I might rent a room?"

A gray-haired, motherly looking woman turned her way. "My dear child, you've asked the right question. I'm Mrs. Stanford, and my husband and I own a boarding house on Owen Street, across from the Daveys'." She acknowledged the woman beside her. Jonquil supposed the two were friendly competitors.

"We have some lovely rooms," she continued. "We run a very respectable house and"—she blushed right up to her gray hairline—"we don't allow any shenanigans." Mrs. Stanford suddenly stopped, apparently aware that she sounded like an advertisement board. Instead, she extended a hand toward Jonquil. "You'd be most welcome. I feel we suit each other fine."

Addie Clayton interrupted. "Weren't you telling me just the other day that you needed help in your dining room?"

"Why, yes, I certainly do." Mrs. Stanford looked to her hostess, then back to Jonquil. "I can't seem to keep good help with all the new places opening up. We can't afford to pay much, so consequently our people come and go."

Again the governor's wife spoke, her eyes resting on Jonquil. "I don't suppose you'd be willing to exchange one of those fine rooms for the chance to allow a real lady to help you out in the dining room."

"Lawsy, yes, but who would that be, Addie?"

"Well, I don't know right offhand, but I believe I have someone in mind."

Once more Jonquil found Mrs. Clayton's benevolent gaze on her. Again it was as though the woman had read her mind.

When everyone had left except Jonquil and the prospective landlady, the issue of the boarding house again came up.

"I believe, Elizabeth, I've found you the perfect lady."

"Why, Addie Clayton," Mrs. Stanford responded, "I believe that tea you've been drinking was laced with something more than sugar cubes. Who in this crowd would want to help me in my boarding house?"

"I would," Jonquil replied, returning her hostess's smile across the table on which they stacked empty tea cups.

"You, child?" The woman looked Jonquil up and down, not certain she'd heard right. "I thought you were a singer, dear."

"I am, but I also need a place to live. I'm a hard worker, and I learn quickly." Jonquil turned on her most enthusiastic smile. "And I'd only be singing maybe one or two evenings a week."

Or maybe not at all, she thought, if the Eureka Springs Improvement Company doesn't approve of me after they hear me sing.

The two older women exchanged conspiratorial looks. "I believe you've found your helper," Addie encouraged Mrs. Stanford.

Her friend winked back. "I believe you're right."

Turning toward Jonquil, she stopped her busy work. "Room and board in exchange for your help in the dining room at breakfast and the noonday meal. Any tips you earn will be yours and Sundays off. We close the dining room on the Lord's day."

"Thank you, Mrs. Stanford." Jonquil gave the older woman a grateful hug. "I'll do you proud."

The doorbell rang and Adaline moved toward the hallway. "It's Mr. Coulter," she called over her shoulder.

Left alone, Mrs. Stanford turned back to Jonquil. "You may move in tomorrow and take the next day to get settled before you begin your duties in the dining room." She reached over and patted Jonquil's hand. "We'll get along fine, dear. I'm so glad I've found you."

In a spontaneous gesture Jonquil gave the woman an affectionate squeeze. "No, Mrs. Stanford, I'm so glad I found you." With a light heart she then excused herself and hurried to where Adam waited, just inside the parlor entry.

Everything had fallen into place. Truly, she thought, it must be the magical water.

Chapter Eleven

"You sure you're all right?"

"Right as rain."

"Are you eating well and taking care of yourself?" Jonquil fixed her eyes on Gabriel and absent-mindedly rubbed the long neck of her banjo with her hand.

His voice empty of all emotion, Gabriel answered, "Yes'm, good food. I get it up from the Perry House kitchen after I finish work. The cook there, he looks after me."

Instead of me, Jonquil thought. She and Gabriel had looked after each other for so long, it stung that she'd already been replaced by a stranger.

She fidgeted on a stool beside her friend on the Opera House stage. The men who'd hired them, the founders of the Eureka Springs Improvement Company, had walked outside with Adam, leaving Jonquil and Gabriel alone in the empty building.

"Real private, too," Gabriel continued, avoiding her gaze and concentrating instead on the frayed cuff of his shirt. His nut brown fingers with manicured nails picked at the fabric.

"Private, huh? You like having your privacy?" Jonquil dreaded his answer.

"Oh, don't mind too much." A momentary silence

veiled their position in the center of the stage. "Rent's right." He laughed. "Free for muckin' out the horse stalls once a day. I'm close to old Cantank, too," he added as an afterthought.

"Cantankerous." Jonquil's voice quivered. It had been two days since Gabriel and the mule had trotted off with Adam, leaving her behind at the hotel. But to Jonquil it now seemed a lifetime ago. "How's he faring?"

"Ornery as ever, but he's fine, too."

Jonquil noted how he'd emphasized the word "too." *If everyone's as fine as Gabriel claims, then why am I feeling so dreadful?* She gave him a forced smile.

"Your job, do you like it? Adam told me you're working at the Basin Street Bath House."

"Like it a lot." Gabriel's eyes lit up. "My boss, Mr. Jackson, he's a fine fellow . . . easy to work for."

"You're an attendant?"

"Same as in Hot Springs. I help the patrons."

"Gabriel . . ."

Jonquil heard the tremor in her voice. Gabriel must have noticed, too, because he rushed on with his next words.

"Yes'm," he ended, "everythin' is right as rain." He shook his head and quickly looked away. But not before Jonquil noticed the rheumy glaze in his eyes.

It was that woeful look that was Jonquil's undoing. She loved this man, who was the father she'd never had. He'd been a part of her life for as long as she could remember—too long for her to have to pretend indifference over their separation.

Tears flowed warm and unchecked down her cheeks. "I miss you." Her misery resonated throughout the empty house.

"Now, Rosie, stop that snivelin'," Gabriel scolded, again exercising his parental authority. He glanced toward the door through which Adam and the others had disappeared only moments before. Then on a softer note, he said, "You hear me?"

"I can't," Jonquil wailed. Seized by a bout of homesickness like none she'd experienced since she and Gabriel had left their farm, Jonquil blurted out, "I hate it here. I want to leave."

Once she started to cry, it was as though someone had opened the floodgates. All her pent-up emotions rushed forth like a current out of control.

Gabriel spoke with desperate firmness. "Rosie, that's enough! Mr. Coulter was right. It ain't proper for a young lady such as yourself to be a-travelin' the countryside with an old colored man like me."

"I don't care what Adam Coulter said. We did just fine until he came along."

"Rosie, we'll still be fine."

Reaching inside his shirt pocket, Gabriel pulled out a clean white handkerchief and thrust it into Jonquil's hands.

Jonquil buried her face in the snowy folds, inhaling the smell of hay and musk. Then she blew her nose.

"Those gentlemen, Mr. Coulter's friends, they liked our act." Gabriel reached across and patted Jonquil on the shoulder. "I've got good feelin's about this place, Rosie. Here you'll be treated with respect, not like some saloon entertainer."

Jonquil inhaled noisily and lowered the handkerchief. "And how will you be treated? Receiving your meals from the back doors of hotels, sleeping in a room behind the livery, and kowtowing to white folks during the day." She squared her shoulders and leaned toward him. "Doesn't sound like a change for the better to me. At least before, we had each other."

"We'll still have each other," Gabriel insisted, "we just won't be sharin' the same campfire. And you remember, missy, there ain't nothin' wrong with doing an honest day's work."

Even though Jonquil hated to admit it, what Gabriel said was true. From what she had seen of Eureka Springs, she felt comfortable among its inhabitants. They could make a life here, separate but equal, in their own little niches. It was the "separate" that hurt so badly.

"Look," he countered in a soothing voice, "earlier you were babblin' away about your tea party, the nice ladies you'd met, and your new boardin'-house job. Who'da thought two weeks ago, you'd be attendin' a tea party at the ex-governor's house? Now you tell me, child, how you can be faultin' such good luck."

"But I'll never see you, or Cantankerous."

Gabriel tugged at the hanky. "Now, gal, you know better'n that. We is family, and family don' go about forgettin' each other." He forced Jonquil to look at him. "Look," he reminded her, "we both agreed to accompany Mr. Coulter here in hopes of maybe startin' over." There was a gentle assurance in his voice. "This Eureka town, it shows a lot of promise for us both."

"Promise. You mean *surrender*." Jonquil couldn't keep the inflection from her voice. "Surrender to a way of life that neither of us wants." Again she buried her face in Gabriel's handkerchief. "You'll be busy, I'll be busy. . . ."

"Sure, we'll both be busy, but not so's we can't visit at least once a week."

Jonquil straightened on her stool. "Once a week?" She sat quietly, contemplating Gabriel's words, then added, "Every Sunday?"

"Fine with me. I don't have to work at the bath house on that day." A large smile lit up his black face. "And I guess you've gotten to be such a good singer and banjo plucker, you don't need to practice no more."

Once more Jonquil was the student and Gabriel the teacher.

"But of course," she trilled with enthusiasm. "We'd need to rehearse at least once a week." Already she felt better.

"I'll always be here for you, Rosie. You should know that by now."

"And, I'll always be here for you," she confirmed, sealing her promise with a smile. Just talking with Gabriel had made her feel better.

Unable to control her happiness a moment longer, Jonquil jumped down from her stool and threw herself into Gabriel's arms. "This is not the *death* of our relationship, but only the *beginning*." They both smiled in agreement.

Surrender . . . death . . . only the beginning. Jonquil's words stabbed at Adam's heart like an ice pick.

Having stepped back in from the sidewalk, he remained in the back of the theater, picking up only bits and pieces of the conversation between his two "clients." But there'd been no mistaking some of the words, spoken as clearly as an actor's practiced lines.

So as not to intrude on his partners' privacy, Adam had politely waited in the shadows before interrupting the scene being played out on the Opera House stage. But as the full implication of Jonquil's words penetrated his brain, what had first appeared to be no more than a parental hug—a display of affection—now looked and sounded like a conspiracy.

Whose death were they speaking of? His brother's?

Adam's blood ran cold. It took all his self-control not to rush down the aisle and demand the truth.

Only yesterday Clayton had indicated their records showed them to be less than law-abiding citizens. And he had argued in their defense. Were these two such masters of deception that he, too, had been duped by their performance? Well, he had news for them. He was nobody's patsy.

He continued to mull over the incriminating words. Surrender to whom? he questioned. Whose death? And the beginning of what? The words replayed themselves in his mind. More than casual conversation, they had been spoken with a heightened sense of urgency.

Lately, Adam had fallen into a sense of complacency, needing to believe in the innocence of the beautiful woman before him. Both her compassion and her feisty temperament had, against his better judgment, found their way into a corner of his heart. Now, with a sinking feeling he watched her, imagining her dressed in the bewitching, black gown, capturing the admiration of all who saw her. Like a black widow spider, Jonquil Rose had woven her web, thick and sticky. And up to now Adam had allowed himself to become securely trapped in its hold.

Well, not anymore.

Checking his rising bitterness, Adam turned his focus toward his mission. With renewed determination he felt driven to obtain the truth about what really happened on the little farm in Prater. And to do so he'd use every trick he'd learned as a detective for the Pinkerton Agency.

He'd start by playing on their growing friendship. Then, when he learned all he needed to know about the mysterious twosome, he'd go for the throat. He'd do whatever it took to crack this case, even if it meant seducing Jonquil Rose Whatever-her-last-name-was. He wasn't beyond that either.

Retracing his steps, Adam slammed the outer door to announce his presence. Then, bursting from the shadows like a happy man, he rushed down the aisle toward the two entertainers.

"Just like I said." He rubbed his hands together for effect. "They loved you. You're both going to be stars."

Reaching the stage, he took the steps two at a time until he joined Jonquil and Gabriel in the small ring of light.

"Really?" Jonquil looked from one man to the other, trying to absorb the news, then clasped her hands together. "They loved us!" she exclaimed, and danced around in excitement, first hugging Gabriel and then Adam.

In response, Adam picked her up in his arms and swung her around in a circle. When he finally stopped and allowed her to slide down his length, Jonquil flushed, feeling small, hot, and lightheaded from the unexpected intimacy. For a moment, as their eyes met and held, it was as if they were alone in the large auditorium.

Gabriel cleared his throat and Adam met his disapproving gaze over the top of Jonquil's head. Surprised at his own exuberance, Adam released Jonquil and stepped backward. Now that he'd taken control of the situation, he felt anything but in control of his emotions. Regardless of what he thought of this little vixen, he couldn't seem to keep his hands off her. What kind of magic did she weave?

Gabriel's black eyes drilled into him, leaving him feeling as transparent as rain. Adam forced a nervous laugh. "Tomorrow it's new clothes for you both."

"We'll pay you back," Jonquil insisted, "as soon as we get our first paychecks." Her face glowed with happiness.

"Don't worry about the money, honey," Adam answered. "Just consider it a worthwhile investment for us all. Now I think we'd better vacate the premises before they lock us in here overnight."

Jonquil grabbed Gabriel's arm and chattered like a magpie as they preceded Adam down the aisle toward the entrance. As Adam followed close behind, he watched the erotic swing of her hips beneath the blue check material.

190

If it takes the ultimate sacrifice to gain the information I need to bring Ball to trial, he thought, I'll have that delightful little body in my bed before the month is over. The action itself would be no sacrifice at all, but he couldn't say the same about the consequences to his sanity.

As the door to the Opera House slammed shut behind them and the threesome walked shoulder to shoulder toward the hotel, Adam was suddenly overcome with regrets. One glance at the blond beauty walking beside him made him feel he might rue the day when he learned the identity of his brother's killer.

Wind bells of delicate etched glass announced Jonquil and Adam's arrival at the dressmaker's shop. Pausing just inside the door, she blinked, allowing her eyes to adjust to the room's natural light. Behind her, Adam removed his hat and hung it on a wicker rack beside the door.

Slowly, Jonquil scanned the room. Behind the lace-draped windows and door, against the palest of ivory walls, the room glowed with diffused sun from an overhead skylight. Blue sky filtered through hazy panes, glazing potted ferns on wicker stands and creating a garden of subtle hues out of the fabric-filled shelves.

Scents of lavender, orange, and lemon teased her nose, carrying her back to another time when, as a small child, she and her mother had played dress-up with the discarded flimsy materials stored inside one of her mother's old trunks. The same fragrance had clung to the old dresses packed away with sachets, to scented pillows and the few keepsakes from her mother's other life.

Not wishing to dwell on her past, Jonquil moved toward a large glass case in the middle of the room.

Displayed inside, on a field of snow white velvet, were all manner of female fripperies—pearl and crystal necklaces, brooches, cameos, and rings with filigree as fine as lace.

Hairpieces in every shade were curled, poufed, and frizzed into the latest designs and adorned with a rainbow of ribbons. Jonquil couldn't imagine so many fine things being displayed together in one place. Purses, fans, and an array of other items which Jonquil didn't recognize completed the collection.

"What do you suppose that is?" Jonquil pondered, pointing to a carved wooden bear the size of her hand, seated next to a writing pen.

"Probably an inkwell," Adam explained. "I've seen a few like him. The head flips backward on a hinge to allow access to the ink bottle. Cute, isn't he?" He nodded toward the item. "Allow me to buy—"

"No!"

Cut off in midsentence, Adam snapped his head toward Jonquil with a look of surprise.

Suddenly reminded of the ill-gotten inkwell she carried to this day, Jonquil felt her throat go dry. "I mean, thank you, but I really don't need it." She tried to still her racing pulse, but was sure Adam could see the beads of sweat forming on her upper lip.

"Got one already, huh?"

"Yes." With a weak smile, she added, "Besides, we've got enough to spend our money on as it is." She moved to the other end of the case and tried to focus on other items. Still, she could feel her hands trembling beneath the folds of her skirt.

Small, tasseled booklets with numbered lines caught her eye. "Dance cards," Adam informed her when she raised her eyes in question.

Dance cards. Now there was something Flo and the other hurdy-gurdy girls could have used in the saloon in Hot Springs. Since Jonquil had arrived in her new home, her mind often turned to the friend she'd left behind so suddenly. I'll write her soon, she thought. Maybe I'll buy those dance cards and send them to her as a surprise.

"Why, Adam, I see you've arrived. Right on time, too."

Tugged from her reverie, Jonquil focused on the voice and then on the woman who stepped out from behind a partition at the back of the store, noting the familiarity with which she greeted Adam. Obviously they'd met earlier.

As the woman moved with fluid grace toward them, Jonquil thought that never in all her life had she seen anyone more beautiful. A sudden, unexplained wave of jealousy swept over her.

"Elise, this is Eureka Springs's newest talent, Jonquil Rose."

Elise. Disconcerted by Adam's informality with the dressmaker, Jonquil shot him a curious, surprised look.

"Elise Dupree is the proprietor of this fine shop and comes very highly recommended for our task."

Task indeed, Jonquil thought, meeting the large onyx eyes of the dressmaker. To change a weed into a rose.

The woman stood so that both Jonquil's reflection and her own were mirrored in a large pier glass that hung on the opposite wall. Oblivious to the mirror's existence until that moment, Jonquil spied her own bedraggled blue check beside the other woman's buttercup silk.

Suddenly seized by shyness and an urge to run, she instead forced herself to stand her ground and assumed her best stage pose. She placed her gloved hand in the woman's extended one. "Pleased to meet you, Miss Dupree."

Elise Dupree had skin that looked like fine porcelain with touches of light vermillion coloring its pale ivory glow. Blue-black hair hung in thick tendrils around her delicately boned face, and several curls had escaped their confining combs to hang in long ringlets about her neck.

Her hair seemed so thick and heavy Jonquil expected her delicate neck to break beneath its weight. Surely this one would need none of the fake hairpieces displayed in the glass case.

Jonquil thought of her own tresses hanging straight as a poker down her back. This morning before leaving the hotel, she'd hastily tied it at her nape with her only blue ribbon. A ribbon frayed and worn from repeated use on the trail and the constant pulling of the wind.

Elise Dupree smiled at Adam before stepping back and studying Jonquil like a painter about to make the first stroke on an empty canvas. "I'm sure we can fix this little lady up in no time." Jonquil felt as flat as the endless white background, and just as insignificant.

She'd never before been jealous of another female. But then, she'd never before traveled in the company of such a handsome male as Adam Coulter. Again he was the meticulously dressed man she'd first met. Funny, she thought, she'd become so accustomed to looking at him during their weeks on the trail, she'd forgotten how dashing he was.

And from the way the dressmaker cooed and fluttered around him, it was apparent that the porcelain beauty standing beside her confirmed Jonquil's opinion.

Adam no longer wore his shoulder sling. Out of pure stubbornness, Jonquil imagined. She'd certainly reminded him enough about the doctor's instructions. But she also knew the support would mar his polished appearance, and she suspected Adam Coulter was vain.

Today, instead of his usual white ruffled shirt,

Adam wore a plain one beneath his short gray frock coat. The ruffles had been replaced by a gold silk vest. At his neck was a black cravat. His black trousers had been cleaned and pressed, and the crease that ran the length of each leg appeared to be sharp enough to cut any finger run down its knife edge.

"Where do you want us, Elise?" Adam asked the brunette, holding her captive with his outrageous smile.

In her bed, most likely, Jonquil surmised.

She watched the woman turn provocatively in front of Adam, allowing him a better look at her silk-encased assets, before motioning for the two of them to follow her beyond the partitioned wall.

Elise, indeed. When did they become so chummy?

The dressmaker ushered Adam to a couch at the rear of the room. It was a beautiful setting, appropriate for its owner. A combination of delicate colors woven into a masterpiece of perfection.

A shiny flowered fabric trimmed in beige-colored braid covered the wide-armed, button-tufted sofa. Floral and needlepoint pillows, all framed in gold braid, were scattered about the settee.

Sitting, Adam leaned his long frame back naturally against the soft pillows. From across the room Jonquil saw him wink encouragingly at her, and her heart expanded till it was near exploding.

She studied the man who seemed so comfortable with himself in such a richly appointed place. With his flawless dress and perfect manners, he looked like a well-placed ornament added to enhance the room's beauty.

The dressmaker handed Adam a delicate china cup filled with steaming black coffee, then turned her attention back to Jonquil. Jonquil dragged her eyes away from Adam and forced herself to concentrate on the woman who would transform her into a lady. But the look on Elise Dupree's face, stinging as a sharp slap, was intended for Jonquil alone to see.

Why, she considers me a threat.

Jonquil nearly laughed at the irony of the situation. *The woman is everything I could hope to be, and she considers me a threat.*

Out of the corner of her eye Jonquil watched Adam sip coffee with his little finger extended, then replace his cup on its saucer, the way her mother often did. "So, Elise," he asked matter-of-factly, "what do you suggest we do for my client?"

The silken butterfly turned again toward her guest, then announced in her most businesslike voice, "I think we should get to work. We have a lot to do to make this young woman presentable."

Jonquil wanted to tell Elise Dupree what she could do with her fine manners and superior airs, but one look at Adam's scowl told her he'd read her thoughts and dared her to make a scene.

His lecture about her background was still fresh in her mind, as was his warning: if she wished to be accepted as a lady in this community, then she must present herself as one on all occasions. Success depended on their being accepted by those prominent in the town.

Jonquil bit her tongue and allowed Elise to usher her behind a rosewood screen across the room from Adam.

Here she was stripped and fitted with corsets, silk stockings, drawers, camisoles, and petticoats. Her already small waist was tightened even more until Jonquil feared she might pass out from the binding stays that held her in and pushed her out in what the dressmaker considered to be the right places.

Jonquil stood like a statue while the dressmaker displayed swatches of the finest fabrics, obviously trying to impress Adam with their names. Tulles, batiste and sheer lawns, satins and velvets, finely crinkled piqués, surahs, moire taffetas, alpacas, and chenilles were one after another draped around her weary form until Jonquil thought she would drop.

She felt like a pincushion where the Dupree woman had stuck her—too many times for it to be accidental. But she stood quietly and endured the dressmaker's abuse, watching with fascination her metamorphosis in the large cheval mirror.

Three hours later, spent from being pulled and tugged beyond her endurance, Jonquil was allowed to escape the pawing hands of the dressmaker.

She'd been measured and fitted for several day dresses, three skirts with interchangeable bodices, and two evening gowns, while Adam had issued orders like a general as to the colors that complemented her blond coloring.

Only when he'd suggested a color other than black for the evening gowns had Jonquil put her foot down. This was the one link she still had to her mother.

Unwilling to explain her passion for the black costume with the yellow rose, Jonquil stood firm in her conviction until Adam finally agreed.

Allowed at last to slip into her checkered dress, Jonquil listened behind the privacy screen to Miss Dupree's soft laughter. She peeked over the divider to the couch on which Adam still lounged in princely splendor.

The silken butterfly had landed beside him, as close as propriety would allow in the presence of another, her arms outstretched and thrown back above her head. A more provocative position Jonquil had never observed.

And Adam, with a broad smile plastered across his face, seemed to be observing and enjoying the full display of Miss Dupree's rounded breasts as she flapped and stretched her arms in animated conversation. Jonquil's skin prickled.

For heaven's sake, did the woman have no scruples?

Unable to stand another moment of the sensual display, and not understanding her own aversion to it, Jonquil stomped from behind the screen, past Adam and his brazen hostess, and toward the front of the store.

"Rose." Adam's deep voice demanded that she stop.

The hairs on her neck tingled at the use of her second name. That name was much too personal—used by her family for affection, and by her mother when she demanded Jonquil's attention. Spoken, it had always stopped her.

It didn't stop her now, however.

In hot pursuit, Adam and the dressmaker followed her to the front of the shop where Jonquil had her hand on the door, ready to open it and escape.

For the first time she noticed the flowery, scripted sign above and read out loud the penned words of John Donne, a seventeenth-century poet.

"Come glad from thence, go gladder than you
    came,
  Today put on perfection, and a woman's
    name."

"Haa!" she screeched. Then she turned and glared at Elise Dupree. Overcome with jealousy, Jonquil released the pent-up green-eyed monster for which she had no name. "In your case," she announced, her nose in the air, "I believe the last word should be *shame*."

On that note, Jonquil yanked open the door, stalked outside, then slammed it, leaving a bewildered Adam and the dressmaker behind.

Chapter Twelve

Adam stood in the doorway behind his stage-side box, listening to the buzz of conversation in the Opera House that was filled to capacity. Glancing over the prosperous men and women in the box, he wished instead he were standing in the wings so he could watch the entertainers from his own private spot. Reluctantly he moved forward and took his seat.

Elise Dupree looked up to acknowledge him, touching his sleeve before turning back to the matronly woman on her left. She sat regally straight, as though holding court in her garnet satin dress. Bobbing her head in an ardent display of zeal, she called attention to her thick, black curls anchored with violet-red feathers. Despite his overriding distress, Adam had to admit the dressmaker was beautiful.

She was also quite cunning.

Adam smiled ruefully as her eyes sought his. With Elise Dupree, the sister-in-law of one of the town's leaders, on his arm, a man's success in the community would be confirmed.

Adam cringed at the thought, knowing full well he had swallowed that bait. But for Jonquil's sake he had been given no choice.

More than two weeks had passed since he'd seen the dressmaker. Totally engrossed in Jonquil, he had escorted her all over town, keeping her company, urging her to talk. All for business, he'd argued. But whatever his excuse, he knew he'd simply wanted to be with Jonquil.

Knowing, however, how she felt about the dressmaker, he had not insisted she accompany him the day before when he'd stopped in to settle Jonquil's account.

In retrospect, he wished he had. For by the time he'd left the shop, Adam had agreed not only to escort the seamstress to the recital but to the reception for Jonquil that would follow.

Within a matter of minutes Elise had lured him onto her line as a fisherman would an unsuspecting fish. Pleading chagrin over the last-minute absence of an escort, she had woven a tale about how her position as one of Eureka Springs most sought-after modistes could be at risk.

Explaining that she had disappointed numerous customers of her brother-in-law's acquaintance, she had whined that her seamstresses—under her own expert direction—had worked long hours for the last two weeks just so they could finish the superb gown Jonquil would wear for tonight's performance. The least Adam could do in return, she suggested, was to escort her to the recital.

Suddenly the picture had become very clear. The fact that Adam had spent great sums in her shop meant nothing. His position had changed—from client to ornamental object to be dangled before other women. And remembering Jonquil's parting shot in Elise's salon, Adam knew she had one particular woman in mind.

With refusal on his lips, he caught Elise's warning gaze upon him. Sputtering on about the influence her sister enjoyed among the local society maidens, she'd implied that her sister could make Jonquil's stay in Eureka Springs most unpleasant.

Adam had nearly laughed. He considered bringing the Claytons to his defense, but decided against it. The governor's wife had already made known her approval of Jonquil and had accepted her for what she seemed.

But danger lay in stirring up trouble in any corner. Both Jonquil's happiness and his cover depended on the friendship of the powerful locals. For that reason alone he had decided to tolerate Elise Dupree for one evening. The image of holding Jonquil in his arms as she walked off the stage vanished.

But he now had another problem. Jonquil's blatant dislike for the brassy shop owner. If his luck held, Jonquil wouldn't notice the brunette during her performance. At the reception following, however, there would be no denying the woman's presence on his arm. That would surely hinder his progress of the last few days.

After her uncharacteristic behavior at the salon, Jonquil had apologized to Adam, declaring her profound distaste for the brazen, shallow minx. At his own admission that he shared her opinion, Jonquil's eyes had sparkled with relief—exhilaration even—and their relationship had once again reached an even keel.

As Jonquil adjusted to her new position of helping out in the boarding house, she'd become decidedly happier. Her relationship with Adam had taken a turn for the better. Often he would find her looking at him with those soulful blue eyes, hungry for his comments regarding the most trivial of matters. Daily he gained more and more influence over Jonquil's opinion. His plan was proceeding nicely.

So how was he to explain the presence of Elise Dupree on his arm when he knew Jonquil harbored such distaste for the woman?

As the house lights dimmed, a qualm born of nervousness stabbed Adam. It would be so easy, he thought, to blame it on sympathetic stage jitters rather than a pang of conscience.

But, in fact, he knew he was no better than the scheming woman beside him.

Deafening applause accompanied Jonquil's pacing in the small dressing room backstage, where she and Gabriel waited to be called. As was customary with such billed acts, theirs would follow the performances of several gifted townspeople and visitors.

"Jitters?" Gabriel asked, his chair propped against the wall.

Jonquil's eyes lighted on her friend, admiring him in his dressed-up finery. "A little," she replied.

"Appears to be a lot, the way you been wearin' a path in that rug."

Jonquil halted her pacing and dropped her worried gaze toward the floor. Then, feeling the fool, she met Gabriel's gaze and burst out laughing.

"Laughter always chases the flutters away," he replied.

"I've done this many times, but tonight I have a case of stage fright like none I've had before."

"Ain't no different than before. You'll see. Jest take a few deep breaths and you'll feel better in no time."

Jonquil took several large gulps of air, and some of the tension left her body. Shooting an appreciative glance toward Gabriel, she teased, "You're so spiffy-looking in your funeral finery, I thought you might know something I don't. Are you expecting me to die of stage fright?"

"Funeral finery!"

Gabriel harrumphed, his hands brushing with

reverence the fabric of his new black suit and white shirt. He cocked his graying head to one side and stared back at her.

"Or are you to be the corpse?" Jonquil persisted in her playful sparring.

A pumpkin grin spread across Gabriel's face as he accepted her teasing with a shake of his head.

"Corpse or not," she parried, "you do look marvelously handsome."

Gabriel fingered his daffodil-colored silk vest and bowknot as though he weren't quite sure they were real. "I guess I do at that. Mr. Coulter, he sure do have a knowledge about fashion."

Jonquil's eyes roamed over the new Gabriel. He seemed so proud and confident. From his accounts she knew he loved his work in the baths. Many people she'd met in the dining room of the boarding house had reported on what a fine job he'd been doing there.

At last, both their lives seemed to be filled with purpose. The person most responsible was Adam Coulter. And to think, Jonquil had nearly refused to allow him into their lives.

No longer troubled by the resentment she had experienced in the Dupree woman's shop, and her awareness of Adam heightened, Jonquil realized the stabs of jealousy over the brazen dressmaker had all but disappeared.

For reasons she couldn't explain, her heart sang every time she saw Adam. Tonight, she thought, I'll sing for him.

A hand pounded on the closed door. "Miss Rose, we're ready for you."

Jonquil's heart dropped to her stomach.

"Now, gal, you go out there and sing like you was back in your favorite tree on the farm. You pretend all them folks out there ain't nothin' but birds. Old Gabe, he knows you'll knock their feathers off."

With the picture of featherless birds in her mind, Jonquil walked out the door smiling.

A hush fell throughout the theater when Jonquil and Gabriel took their positions on stage. Adam sat up straighter in his chair, and for the first time that evening felt better for having agreed to escort Elise Dupree to the opening. They occupied some of the best seats in the house—thanks to her brother-in-law's connections.

The four boxes, two on each side of the Opera House and level with the stage, provided their lucky occupants with ringside seats. Glancing across, Adam noted the Claytons were seated in the opposite box. Addie Clayton waved a gloved hand in acknowledgment, then turned her attention back to Jonquil and Gabriel. Adam's gaze followed hers.

Gabriel, looking as proud as a peacock in his new clothes, sat about a foot away from Jonquil. He and Jonquil whispered softly between themselves while they tuned their banjos.

Jonquil had never looked more beautiful. In the soft glow of a hundred lanterns, and against the painted backdrop, an Ozark landscape, Jonquil's loveliness blossomed like the first gardenia of the season. Like a bee drawn to nectar, Adam felt powerless against her allure.

Her bared shoulders and arms appeared as pale as moonlight against the midnight black of her velvet and lace dress. A yellow silk cabbage rose adorned one of her shoulders, while clusters of smaller roses trailed down a panel of black lace on her skirt front. Her golden hair, swirled up and secured on top of her head with a spray of yellow roses, gleamed in subdued radiance in the hazy lantern light.

"You outdid yourself, Elise," Adam heard the

woman beside his companion exclaim as she stared at Jonquil.

"I did at that," Elise confirmed haughtily, leaning toward Adam as though awaiting his confirmation. When none was forthcoming, she complained, "'Twas not an easy task considering what I had to work with."

Adam shot her a glaring look, but bit back his retort when Jonquil began to sing. Even the woman he was escorting became speechless when Jonquil's husky voice suffused the house.

The music soon had toes tapping, hands clapping, and mouths flapping with approval. The audience loved her, just as Adam knew they would.

Jonquil was a born entertainer. She carried her listeners to such feverish heights that their exuberance almost seemed combustible. When she switched to a sleeker, twangier pace, she brought her listeners down to a sensual low and they smoldered in their chairs.

As Adam was doing. Almost to the point of embarrassment. Listening and watching, he ached to have Jonquil's sultry voice crooning her runaway desires in his ear, to have her curvaceous body with its uninhibited movements awaken willingly beneath his own. Lost in his imaginings, he became aware that the evidence of his lust was on the rise.

Adam squirmed uncomfortably in his chair, trying to forestall his arousal. Elise, her hands clasped together in a choke hold, sent him a scathing look. He fought to slow his racing pulse and refused to meet her eye.

When he looked up again, Jonquil had left her chair beside Gabriel and was walking around the stage. Lost in the strains of a slow, mournful ballad, she wandered toward Adam's box, strumming her banjo. Stopping directly in front of Adam, Jonquil fingered the last chord. With lowered lids, she let her voice trail off, the trebly note lingering across the room's silence.

Jonquil opened her eyes to a round of applause and looked directly into Adam's face. When she recognized him, her luminous blue eyes crinkled into a smile. Then, as though remembering where she was, she quickly looked to the others seated around him. She came up short when she saw Elise's gloved fingers curl possessively around Adam's arm.

Surprised by the discovery, Jonquil seemed to freeze. Adam watched emotions play across her face before she chilled him with a look that could have created snow. Then she turned and stormed back to center stage.

Adam disengaged Elise's fingers from his arm and leaned forward against the spindle rail of the box, his eyes never leaving Jonquil. He felt like a traitor.

Only fragmented pieces of Jonquil's speech reached his ears before she again began to pick at her banjo strings. This song, she announced, would be her last.

Adam had seen hurt, then blue anger blaze in Jonquil's eyes when she'd discovered Elise at his side. That his vexing companion had decided at that moment to cling to him like moss irritated him more than he realized. But right now he had bigger concerns.

Jonquil's exit from Elise's shop raced through his mind, and he almost trembled. Could he expect another childish outburst, this time in front of an auditorium filled with people? Surely not. Then he heard the tune Jonquil strummed on her banjo and his concern tripled.

Everyone familiar with the song sat up straighter, no doubt remembering the sensation *The Black Crook* had caused when this extravaganza had first opened in New York. The words of its hit song, "You

Naughty, Naughty Men," flowed emotionally from Jonquil's mouth:

"When you want a kiss or favor,
 You put on your best behavior,
 And your looks of kindness savor,
 Oh, you naughty, naughty men."

As Adam watched, his worst fears materialized.

Jonquil lifted the skirt of her elegantly designed gown and placed one booted foot on her empty chair. Resting her banjo across her raised thigh, she plucked away at the tune while she revealed her black silk calf to anyone interested in looking. And they all were, especially the men.

Jonquil's unorthodox behavior brought the crowd to their feet. Those not too shocked to move joined in, clapping their hands in time with the music. Adam watched, frozen in place, not believing what he saw as she continued the teasing song:

"Of love you get us dreaming,
 And when with hope we're teeming,
 We find you are but scheming,
 Oh, you naughty, naughty men."

Lord have mercy, Adam thought, they'll run her out of town on a rail.

"We've no wish to distress you,
 We would sooner far caress you,
 And when kind we'll say 'Oh, bless you,'
 Oh! you naughty, dear, delightful men."

Bedlam broke out in the auditorium when the last notes of the chorus died. The boxes and chairs began to empty as the crowd surged toward the stage on which Jonquil and Gabriel were taking their bows.

By damn, she pulled it off, Adam thought as he watched the cheering throngs push forward. His chest filled with immense pride and relief, and he started to leave the box, disregarding Elise and the others behind him.

"Nothing more than a saloon tart, I'd wager," one dowager whispered from behind her fan for Elise's approval. At Adam's condemning look, the dressmaker merely pressed her bosom closer to his back.

Adam cursed silently. With this crowd he'd never get to Jonquil, and at the moment all he wanted was to sweep her into his arms and tell her how wonderful she was. And that— What? That he hadn't meant to hurt her? That she was the one he wanted?

Good Lord, he thought as Jonquil's pained expression floated before his mind's eye, he'd violated the most fundamental rule of his profession —no emotional ties.

Then he remembered the prearranged plan—that Jonquil and Gabriel would ride back to the boarding house with Mrs. Stanford. He'd have to wait until the reception to explain to Jonquil why he was escorting Elise. By then, perhaps, he'd be able to think more rationally.

Men and women moved toward the back exit, chatting amiably among themselves. Adam sent Elise and her family ahead, watching them exchange comments, wondering what the stylish people of Eureka Springs had thought of Jonquil's ribald display of leg.

Most, he decided, would consider it a memorable experience and chat about it over dinner for weeks to come. But a few old busybodies would condemn Jonquil for unseemly behavior. These were the ones he worried about. Gossip. He deplored it.

Unable to reach Jonquil, Adam stepped back into his box and stood at the railing, watching her greet her admirers with the grace of a high-bred lady. She accepted one compliment after another, never looking his way, unaware of his feeling of isolation.

At that moment Elise returned, giving Adam no more time to contemplate the stranger Jonquil had become.

"Darling, they're waiting," she announced, her voice clearly audible above the conversations buzzing around Jonquil and Gabriel.

"I'm not your darling," he managed to mumble out of the corner of his mouth, before his eyes finally locked with Jonquil's above the others' heads.

Elise completely ignored his remark while she fluttered around the box, collecting her program and fan. Thrusting her wrap into his hands, she positioned herself between him and the stage to allow him to drape her velvet cloak around her shoulders.

Adam fairly dropped the mantle around her, wishing as he did so that he could strangle her. Instead, however, he forced himself to act the gentleman when all he wished to do was distance himself from her suffocating presence. "Miss Dupree," he mumbled, "shall we?"

Damn, he'd be glad when this night ended.

Elise raised a gloved hand and waved to the remaining assembly onstage. "Liz, we'll see you at your house."

Standing beside Jonquil, Elizabeth Stanford waved back. All members of the group turned in their direction, but Adam noticed only the two pairs of eyes stabbing him across the space—deep blue ones and coal black ones. If looks could kill, he knew he'd be laid out dead on the floor. He turned and followed Elise out the door.

So, Jonquil thought, Adam Coulter lied about his opinion of the Dupree woman. Shallow indeed.

Jonquil seethed, lodged between Liz Stanford and another woman as the Stanford carriage clopped along the street toward the boarding house. She should be basking in the good wishes of the townspeople. Instead, like a lifeless marionette she felt drained. Her success this evening had paled the moment she'd spied the beautiful brunette on Adam's arm.

"The town loved you, dear," Liz Stanford declared, patting Jonquil's velvet-covered knee. "Why, I can't remember when I've enjoyed myself more." The woman on Jonquil's left nodded her head in agreement.

"When you sang 'You Naughty, Naughty Men,' so help me, I thought the house might tumble down with the applause."

Thankful for the dim light within the carriage, Jonquil felt herself color. "About that song, I hope I didn't offend you."

"Don't be silly, child. It would take more than a risqué number to offend me." Again she patted Jonquil's knee. "Why, Mr. Stanford and I saw *The Black Crook* in New York years ago."

"But, perhaps I shouldn't have revealed my leg." Jonquil pondered the reason she'd done it. She had her friend Flo to thank for the tune and the lyrics, but the devil himself had made her slap her foot upon that chair. The devil in a red dress, if the truth be known.

"You know, a minister in New York claimed the show was responsible for the male members' slackening interest in the affairs of his church's congregation." Liz chuckled at the memory.

"You see," she said, "the corps de ballet were buxom girls, dressed in low-cut, tight-waisted bodices, abbreviated skirts, and pink tights." She paused as though trying to remember. "The minister claimed, instead of listening to the 'pealing of the bells,' the men had their eyes fixed on the 'peeling of the belles.'"

This brought unsolicited laughter from all three ladies.

"I do declare," Liz continued, "people can be so stodgy."

She gave Jonquil a beaming smile. "My dear, don't you let anyone accuse you of acting dishonorably." Their carriage pulled to a stop in front of the boarding-house walkway. "If someone does, child, you tell me and I'll put that person in his place." With that remark, Liz exited the carriage and the others followed.

Jonquil lingered at the end of the pathway that led to the wide front porch of the Stanford home. From behind the lace-curtained windows, yellow light beamed a warm welcome. She could see a myriad of silhouettes behind the sheer panels and knew Adam Coulter and Elise Dupree would be among them.

How would she be able to walk into that room and face the man she had come to trust? Her disdain for the dressmaker aside, she'd never be able to look Adam in the eye and hide the jealousy that threatened to suffocate her.

If she had a choice, she'd sneak right up to her room and never make an appearance. But she knew she couldn't disappoint Elizabeth. In the two weeks she'd been at the boarding house, Jonquil had grown very fond of the elderly Stanfords, and they had chosen to honor her.

Jonquil moved slowly up the path behind the other two women. Soft conversation, laughter, and Gabriel's banjo music greeted her ears as she neared the porch.

Her conscience cheered her on when she mounted the last step and started across the wide porch. *Courage, Jonquil, you must have courage,* the voice reasoned. After all, you are a master of deceit.

The thought sobered her. Since her arrival in Eureka Springs, Jonquil had nearly forgotten that she and Gabriel were fugitives from the law. Her acceptance by the honest, hardworking townsfolk had at times made her question her own identity. And Adam Coulter, more than anyone, had made her feel like the lady she impersonated.

"Child, do come in." Liz beckoned from the doorway. "We're waiting for you."

Taking a deep gulp of air, Jonquil moved toward the group waiting just inside. Fine, she thought with determination. She'd walk into that room and act as though Elise and Adam were not even present. What was one more deceit in a list of many?

The leaded-glass door closed behind her, and she was ushered through the arched opening into the parlor.

"She's here, everyone," Henry Stanford announced.

Conversation ceased, and a round of applause thundered throughout the drawing room.

Gabriel, who'd been asked to furnish music for the event, sat in the window alcove and greeted her with a big smile. They both knew this reception was held in his honor as well, but because Gabriel was a man of color, he'd never be accepted as a guest by the whites of the community. This was the Stanfords' way of including him, and Jonquil appreciated their ingenuity. She quickly moved to his side.

Again the room hushed. Jonquil stared at the group of people gathered in their honor and her heart went out to them. Some faces she recognized, others she did not.

The Claytons were present, as were several ladies she'd met at the tea. All the Stanford boarders had come, along with several regulars from the Stanfords' dining room. But nowhere in the room could she find Adam Coulter and Elise Dupree.

"Speech!" someone shouted from the back of the room.

Jonquil smiled in that direction and cleared her throat.

"I'm not very good at speeches," she began, trying to collect her thoughts. Then she found words.

"Since first coming to Eureka Springs, I've heard this town called many things—The City That Water Built, City of Magic and Healing Waters, Emerald City of the Ozarks." Jonquil's voice broke. She swallowed and then proceeded.

"But there are two names that are very close to my heart. They express my deepest feelings on what Eureka Springs means to me. First, God's Gift to Humanity, and second, Land of a Million Smiles." The glowing faces of the people around her warmed her.

"I'm not sure the first name refers to the water or the people, but I do know I've never been anywhere where I've been treated with such kindness and compassion. You, the people of Eureka Springs, have greeted me and countless others with open arms and smiling faces. This is a town beaming with love and acceptance. So, to you all I say thank you."

Tears flowed in earnest down her face as everyone cheered and applauded.

Liz Stanford quickly moved to Jonquil's side and put an arm around her shoulders. She thrust a lace handkerchief into Jonquil's hand and turned to the group. "This *is* a city of water." Laughter broke the emotion-filled room. "Now," she said, "I suggest we all enjoy the refreshments and mingle with our good friends."

She squeezed Jonquil one last time. "Dear, you stop those tears and get you and your friend here something to eat." Reaching for Gabriel's hand, she shook it, then moved to talk with her many guests.

Eat. The very thought of food made Jonquil's

stomach tighten. The tears had only enlarged the huge lump lodged in her chest, and she knew not one ounce of food could bypass it. What with her emotional acceptance by the townspeople and her bitter disappointment in Adam, it took every bit of self-control she could exert to speak normally to those who stopped to shake her hand and Gabriel's.

Then from the corner of her eye she saw them. With Elise clinging possessively to his arm, Adam entered the room. They were surrounded by the same people Jonquil had seen in the theater box. She watched the beautiful couple with something almost akin to envy, until Adam's eyes locked with hers. Then she quickly looked away.

Damn my Judas heart, Jonquil silently cursed. Here she'd sworn to act as though the man didn't exist. But the moment he appeared, her heart pounded as though she'd just finished a foot race. It defied good sense, but once again she found herself watching Adam.

He maneuvered through the gathering shaking hands, exchanging pleasantries, while Elise continued to clutch his arm like a drowning female.

For the first time that evening, Jonquil noticed Adam wore a red silk vest and tie with his black jacket and trousers. As usual, he looked devastatingly handsome. Like a figurine atop a wedding cake. The thought pierced her like a knife's stab. As the twosome advanced closer to where she and Gabriel stood, all she wished to do was run.

Disregarding her shaking limbs, Jonquil moved closer to Gabriel. He peeked around her, spotted Adam, and understanding dawned on his face.

"Rosie, you all right?" he whispered.

"Right as rain," she answered, then to herself mumbled, "in a flood."

"What's that you say?" Gabriel prodded.

"I said, I wonder if they planned their outfits."

Jonquil's temper bristled, and Gabriel shifted uneasily in his chair.

"Now, gal," he warned, "don't you go and do somethin' you might regret later."

"Why, Gabriel, I was only admiring the near-matching colors of their clothes." She turned toward him. "Why, if one didn't know better, one might think they were the performers instead of us."

Gabriel passed a warning look to Jonquil. "Gal, your claws are out."

They were . . . and Jonquil felt ashamed. She stared at her shoes, trying to regain her composure. But at this moment she could think of nothing she'd enjoy more than raking those claws across Elise Dupree's lily white skin.

Gabriel's dark eyes never left Jonquil's face. "I believe, missy, we both could use some fresh air." He started to rise from his seat.

"Not now, Gabe . . ." Jonquil's voice trailed off. Her breath rushed from her lungs when her eyes alighted on the red velvet skirt and black trousered legs of her tormentors.

"Evening, Gabriel."

Adam's voice cut through Jonquil's consciousness like a steel blade. Gabriel stood and nodded. Adam then bent forward and whispered for Jonquil's ears alone, "You look lovely this evening."

His warm breath caressed her neck, causing goose bumps to prickle her arms and shoulders. Damnation. Adam Coulter could drive her to distraction by the mere touch of his words.

"You, too," she managed to mumble before stepping backward against the window seat.

Elise's greeting broke the spell. "I must admit, dear, you certainly surprised me with your talent."

"Really?" Jonquil asked, her eyes never leaving Adam's face.

"I mean, Adam told me you were gifted, but I

215

wasn't certain until this evening in what capacity he meant."

"Oh?" Jonquil turned to Elise, her interest piqued.

Adam's head snapped in Elise's direction with a warning look. Unconcerned, Elise leaned provocatively close, her fingers delving into the space between his upper arm and ribs.

"I think we should mosey on, Elise."

But it was clear to Jonquil that Elise wasn't ready to do that.

The woman ignored Adam's attempt to steer her away. "After your last number I was convinced," the dressmaker persisted, her voice as deadly as venom.

"Convinced? Of what? That I could actually sing?" Jonquil bristled at the woman's audacity.

"And that you are probably as talented horizontally as vertically."

Jonquil nearly choked on the implication in the woman's words. She saw Gabriel's big hands tighten into fists at his sides before he stepped closer to her.

"There is no need for such talk," Adam insisted, his face a mask of fury. "Let's go."

Elise refused to move, drawing herself to her full height, a victorious expression on her face.

Jonquil glanced nervously around the room. Elizabeth Stanford stood close to the foursome, engaged in conversation with another woman. Jonquil prayed she hadn't heard Elise's underhanded remark.

"Why," Jonquil asked, feeling her face grow crimson, "would you assume such a terrible thing?"

"Elise, let's go," Adam insisted again. "This is not the time or place."

Elise released his arm and leaned closer to Jonquil. "Because, my dear girl, I saw the way his eyes watched your every movement that day in my shop. He claims to be your manager. But I'm sure he lusts

216

for your favors as well. Has he already sampled them?" Her dark brows went up in question.

Jonquil now understood the woman's malicious look two weeks before. But, certainly not even she could be so spiteful as to suggest such a thing, even if she thought it.

"Miz Dupree, I—" Gabriel started to protest, but Adam cautioned him to silence and tried once again to steer the dressmaker away from the alcove.

"Elise, we'll talk about this somewhere else."

"Why? Because your little tart's upset?"

Stunned by this last jab, Jonquil gaped at Elise, then glanced uncertainly around the room. She had spent most of her life being ridiculed by cruel and hateful people, and she had learned how to handle them. If the dressmaker wouldn't leave, then she would.

Leaning close to Elise's face, she tapped a finger on the smooth velvet of the woman's dress. "You, my dear, are a witch."

Turning back to Gabriel, Jonquil held her head high. "I believe I could use that fresh air you mentioned earlier." When her friend moved to accompany her, she gave him a brilliant smile. "No," she said. "These good people came to hear you play. I'll be fine."

With that she turned and, with as much aplomb as she could muster, headed toward the back of the house. Several well-wishers slowed her progress, but Jonquil politely averted their advances. Concentrating instead on the rhythm of her footsteps, she counted each one, fearful that at any moment she would break down.

After what seemed an eternity, she reached the back entrance, thankfully turned the icy knob, and was greeted by a rush of cool air. Stepping out onto the landing, she closed the door behind her and welcomed the black embrace of the night.

217

*   *   *

Left in the room amid happy conversation, Adam, overwhelmed by regret, regarded the rigid set of Gabriel's jaw. At feeling a feminine hand on his sleeve he stepped away from its touch and turned to face his companion.

Up to now Adam had behaved as a gentleman, but the diabolic barbs thrown at Jonquil and the pain he had seen in her eyes had been his undoing. Jumbled curses threatened to spill from his tongue while his mind reeled in disgust.

In that instant there was a light touch on his shoulder, and he turned toward it. Elizabeth Stanford stood behind him. He barely heard her whispered command.

"Go to her, Adam. I'll take care of this little she-devil." She gently nudged him with her hand.

Adam looked the landlady full in the face and caught her acknowledgment of the fiasco. His hostess had heard everything. He wanted to hug her. Instead, he gave Elizabeth Stanford a grateful smile and then his gaze went to the opposite side of the room. Without glancing back, he practically ran toward the door and the woman who had disappeared beyond it.

If only he wasn't too late . . .

Chapter Thirteen

Leaning against the clapboard siding of the house, Jonquil stopped to catch her breath and rein in her galloping emotions. For someone accustomed to accusations and ostracism, she had been staggered by the Dupree woman's vehement attack.

Worse than that, after declaring his own objections to the dressmaker, Adam had dared to accompany her to Jonquil's opening. The stinging humiliation of seeing him with her hurt more than Elise Dupree's cruel insinuations.

Taking a deep, ragged breath, Jonquil held back her tears. I won't cry, she charged herself. Adam Coulter and his serpent-tongued friend aren't worth it.

Then why, she silently questioned, did her heart weigh so heavily in her chest?

Suddenly conscious of the bite in the air, she rubbed her arms and fretted. She could not possibly go back inside and act as though nothing had happened. For her the reception was ruined. She only hoped Liz Stanford would forgive her absence of manners. Stepping away from the wall, Jonquil hurried toward the corner of the porch and the darkness beyond.

A brisk wind set the wicker swing into motion and

nipped at her bare skin when she passed it. Hugging herself against the cold assault, she raced down the porch steps into the side yard and headed toward the covered arbor.

Henry Stanford's grape vines had turned brown and lost most of their leaves. But they still provided a refuge of sorts from the evening air and a place for Jonquil to hide. Entering the vine-covered tunnel, she spied a garden bench. In misery she flopped down upon the seat and buried her face in her palms.

"What now, Jonquil Rose Trevain?" she whispered to the breeze that whistled softly through the latticed stems. Seized by anger she demanded, "What now?"

"You could go back inside and face the witch."

Jonquil jerked upright on the bench just as Adam's shadowed figure appeared before her.

"I'll leave that to you, since you're so enamored of her." Jumping up from her seat, Jonquil tried to dart around him, but Adam's fingers clamped around her arm, forbidding her escape.

"Let me go," she insisted, trying to shake his grip.

Adam stood towering over her, his expression clouded with anger. "Not until you listen."

"I'm tired of listening to you. Everything you say is a lie." Jonquil fought his hold, but Adam held her firm. "You know that woman insulted me, yet you condoned it."

"Condoned it? How, Jonquil? How did I condone it?"

"By allowing her to say such hateful things, and by escorting her to my opening." It was to have been a special time, she thought morosely.

Only one other time in Jonquil's life had she wanted to release her wrath upon another person—when the strange men had come to their farm and hurt her mother. She recalled the small rush of pleasure as her banjo had made contact with that horrible man's skull.

Now she wanted to lash out at Adam for inflicting pain upon her by flaunting Elise Dupree in her face. With all her strength, she slammed her free hand against his injured shoulder.

"Yee-oow!" Adam yelped. He slumped forward into a half-crouch and cradled his injured shoulder with his good arm.

As soon as she had delivered the blow, Jonquil was filled with regret. Bending to him, she moaned, "I'm sorry. . . . Oh, Adam, I'm so sorry."

"Gotcha."

His voice was low, husky, and full of easy wit. Jonquil watched him straighten to his full height, his eyes never leaving hers. A new tension intruded upon her anger, prickling her skin, as though with the one word he had gently goaded her nerve endings to tormenting, pleasurable sensations. She found the unfamiliar feeling discomfiting.

Reaching out, Adam surrounded her with his arms and pulled her snug against his length. "See," Jonquil snapped, her breath coming in short, anxious bursts, "you even lie about your injury." She kicked out at Adam's shins, but layers of petticoats and velvet blunted her blows. "Let me go," she ordered, struggling to get away.

But Adam held her fast in the circle of his arms. "Will you listen to me?" he demanded. Against her face, his breath smelled of cinnamon sticks and apple cider. Liz's cider. The same beverage Jonquil had helped to ready for serving that afternoon.

"Why should I listen when I can't believe a word you say?"

"I'm sorry—"

"You certainly are. The sorriest excuse for a human that I've met yet."

At the heavy reprisal Jonquil saw Adam still and his expression change. In the muted light a touch of sadness crossed his face. But as quickly as it came it disappeared, and Jonquil questioned whether she'd

221

only imagined it.

Adam started in again. "I'm sorry that I allowed Elise to dupe me into bringing her tonight."

"I find that hard to believe—a big, strong man like yourself being at the mercy of a woman, even one like *Miss* Dupree." Her emphasis on "miss" implied the woman was anything but a lady.

At her retort Adam brought her up hard against his chest. The action nearly slammed the breath from Jonquil's lungs. He leaned within inches of her face, and in a low, ragged voice added, "You, my delicate Rose, are the most stubborn female." His arms tightened around her.

"Don't call me Rose," she ordered, "and release me this minute."

He didn't.

Instead, Jonquil felt the hard contours of Adam's body pressing against her. His hot nearness and the way he'd said her name released strange ripples in the depths of her stomach and made her feel lightheaded.

I should flee, she thought. But the simple truth was that she no more wished to relinquish her place in this man's arms than, to her mind, the surrounding grapevines would wish to give up the fertile soil that nourished them.

So Jonquil stood rooted, consumed by Adam's closeness until the growing, aching emptiness in the pit of her stomach longed to be filled with something that had no name.

Leaves rustled in the night wind, crickets chirped, and Jonquil's heart thumped so loudly she fancied Adam could hear it.

He pulled her nearer and bent his head forward. With his forehead resting against hers, their noses touched. His lips, poised so close to her own, invited her to sample the cinnamon and cider taste of his mouth.

Please, Jonquil silently pleaded, let me go. *No, kiss me.* But Adam did neither. He held back, tempting her with his nearness, his dark eyes reflecting the moonlight.

Riveted against Jonquil, he drank in the softness of breasts melded against the hard planes of his chest. God, how he wanted to devour the beautiful mouth only inches from his own. To probe the hot depths beyond Jonquil's sensuous lips and have his own tongue mate with hers.

But instead of doing as his body willed, he remained firm in his resolve. As much as he wanted her, he wanted even more for her to willingly return his embrace, to press her length into his, their clothes the only barrier keeping them both from paradise. He would wait for Jonquil to make the first move toward accepting him as her lover.

From the depths of his mind Adam's scheme once again surfaced—to learn Jonquil's secrets, any way he could. Again he reminded himself that this seduction was to learn who killed his brother, nothing more.

Jonquil's breasts strained against her chemise. They budded, sending offshoots of longing for something more than the feel of the soft fabric pressing against their sensitive peaks.

Lord have mercy, she silently admonished, I'm no better than Elise. But the sobering thought failed to chase away the hunger that Adam's presence induced. It worsened it instead.

Summoning the memory of Adam's face that day in the dressmaker's shop when the owner had so wantonly displayed herself for his admiration, Jonquil now wished to enchant him with her own womanly mystique.

What's the matter with me? she worried. I should be fleeing this man of so many fabrications. But when his red satin vest brushed against her bare arms, sending a warming shiver throughout her, Jonquil knew she was incapable of escape. She wanted him to kiss her, just as she had the day in the warm, bubbly

223

pool deep in the woods. Again she made the first move. Standing on tiptoe, she tilted her face up to his.

Adam allowed his lips to brush hers ever so lightly before settling them against her mouth. Lips to lips, they lingered until his warm breath fired Jonquil's blood.

His girp loosened, and she was no longer imprisoned in his arms. Slowly Jonquil slid her hands upward, encircling his neck. Pressing her fingers to the back of his head, she drew his mouth closer to hers. Her parted lips welcomed his tongue's feverish invasion and the hunger that came with it.

With the first plunge of his tongue, Adam burned with nearly uncontrollable desire. His whole being was filled with a craving he hadn't realized he still possessed. It seemed a lifetime since he'd been with a woman.

He took her mouth savagely, his tongue curling and swirling with hers, then lifted her roughly against his frame before allowing her to slip slowly down his length.

His hands caressed the smoothness of her bare arms before slipping to her narrow waist. With a growing fever he pressed kisses down the length of her neck, then back up again before grazing the tip of her ear with his tongue. Jonquil shivered, sighed, and clung to him, pressing her softness so close that Adam felt he might explode with the need to become one with her.

Sinking to the garden bench, he settled Jonquil upon his lap. Feathering kisses over her shoulders and down the swell of her breasts, his lips at last touched the shadowed valley that disappeared into the deep plunge of her gown.

Heaven help him but he wanted her. When he'd made the pact with himself to seduce her for information, he hadn't bargained on his own body's response to their lovemaking. The moment Jonquil stepped so willingly into his arms, his unholy plan was incinerated.

He wanted Jonquil Rose in his bed, naked beneath him. Curse the investigation. For the moment it seemed insignificant.

"Rosie, gal, you out there?"

Gabriel's voice came from the porch, silencing the chirping crickets and making Adam's labored breathing seem twice as loud. He felt Jonquil stiffen in his arms.

"Damnation," he muttered beneath his breath, pulling her close with one arm and pressing his fingers to her lips. "Shhh . . . be still. He'll think you went to your room."

They could hear Gabriel's footsteps as he walked the length of the side porch, stopped, waited, then turned and headed back in the direction he'd come. The door slammed, and again the night was given over to the sounds of night creatures.

"Come here," Adam murmured, trying to recapture the moment before Gabriel had interrupted them.

But for Jonquil the spell was broken. She jumped up from his lap and stepped out of his hold.

Adam vaulted to his feet and swept her into his arms. He wanted her soft and yielding, not rigid and balking at his attempts to regain their earlier closeness. "Please," he insisted, "we need to talk."

"You can't call what we were doing conversation." Holding his gaze, Jonquil backed away. "I must go. I've stayed too long already."

"Give me a moment," Adam insisted again, closing the distance she'd placed between them. He clasped her hands, massaging her fingers as he spoke. "You're freezing to death." His hands slid up and down her bare arms to warm her.

No longer able to deny his touch, Jonquil threw herself into his arms. Adam received her, holding her in the warmth of his embrace. He whispered

225

hoarsely, his breath hot against her hair.

"I want you to know that Elise goaded me into taking her tonight by threatening to make your stay in this town miserable." Jonquil tried to pull away, but he clasped her tightly against him. "Hear me, Rose, when I say I can't abide the woman."

Jonquil looked up at him, wanting to believe his evening's companion meant nothing to him, but a skeptical inner voice cautioned her to be careful.

"What about the next time? If the woman is so intent on having your affections, she'll have everyone in this town believing I am your tart." Jonquil pushed against Adam's chest and leaned away from him. "Maybe she's right. Look at my behavior before Gabriel interrupted."

"I found nothing wrong with your behavior. In fact, I enjoyed it very much." Adam smiled, placing a light kiss on her forehead.

"I'm sure you did, but what man wouldn't?" The memory of her response to Adam's kiss swept through her as though it were happening all over again, and she was unable to hide her embarrassment. She shifted nervously in his arms.

Over the past months she'd encountered many men who'd made presumptuous advances, and her response had always been evasion, polite but slick. As an entertainer she might be easy prey but she most certainly wasn't easy company. She questioned now how this man differed so from the others.

Never had she wanted a man as she did Adam Coulter. After their first meeting he'd been a constant companion in her innermost thoughts. His nearness always made her senses reel. Perhaps she was a tart after all. Why else would she respond so?

Adam placed his finger beneath her chin, lifted her face, and stared deep into her eyes. "Believe me, my dear, you're anything but a tart."

The assessment brought her up short. Were her

thoughts so transparent that this man could actually read her mind? At the same time his assurance did nothing to convince her. "I'm so confused," she answered, "and what must the Stanfords think?"

"Why, Liz is the one who sent me after you. She assured me she could handle Elise."

"But how . . . ?" Jonquil's voice trailed off, her bewilderment evident.

"Liz Stanford apparently has her own friends in this town."

Jonquil stared past him, hoping what he said was true. She was happier in Eureka Springs than she'd been since they'd left the farm. She loved working alongside Liz in the boarding house. Their friendship had grown over the last two weeks. Not since Flo had she met a more endearing person.

After a strained silence, Adam continued on a playful note. "She also has one very pleased new friend. Remind me to thank her for providing me an escape to pursue you." He tweaked her chin. "I don't believe the serpent-tongued woman will bother either of us again."

At Adam's words a shudder flashed along Jonquil's spine. Again he'd repeated the very words that she had conjured up in her mind. Were they so connected by some invisible thread that he could read her very thoughts? Even when he wasn't with her?

She considered the woman who had sent her fleeing into the night. To think she'd actually envied Elise Dupree. She pondered now how someone with the dressmaker's advantages could have such a hateful heart. The beguiling creature could have had any man she wanted, but her plan to snare Adam had backfired. At his reassurance Jonquil felt like dancing.

"Are you certain?" she asked hesitantly.

"I am. I'm also sure if I don't get you back inside, you're going to catch pneumonia and I'll catch holy hell from your guardian angel."

"Gabriel?" Jonquil laughed, unable to hide her amusement.

"He's the only angel I know."

Gently she reached up and placed a light kiss on his cheek. "Thank you, Adam Coulter, for everything."

"You're welcome." Adam's eyes became dark and turbulent. "And in return, I'd like the same from you."

With those words, Adam pulled her into his arms and kissed her with such force that Jonquil forgot to breathe.

No doubt remained as to the meaning of Adam's words. His "everything" meant more than just the physical gift of herself. It included her openness, her confidence, her vulnerability. But did she trust him enough to surrender all her secrets into his keeping?

Everything, she silently pondered, might be more than she had to give. After all, she and Gabriel were running for their lives. And like a lizard, someday soon she might need to hide behind another disguise in order to protect herself.

Adam stuck his head around the wide arched door and peered into the dining room of the Stanford House. Since Jonquil's debut two weeks before, he had made a habit of taking most of his meals at the boarding house.

By eight-thirty each day the huge dining room would be empty except for Jonquil and her landlady, whom he would find at a table sipping coffee, enjoying the lull between breakfast and preparation for the noonday meal. Subsequently, these encounters had turned into a cozy threesome, with Adam looking forward to a comfortable chat.

Bits and pieces of Jonquil's past surfaced during these early morning conversations, and Adam had learned a bit about the lonely, isolated life she had led growing up.

She hinted of her mother's depression, its cause, and how it had worsened through the years. Because the townspeople considered her mother demented, the small family had been shunned and ignored. The town's name was never mentioned, but Adam knew it to be Prater.

According to Jonquil, after her mother had died of a heart attack in the past year, she and Gabriel had chosen to leave their poor farm in the hope of establishing a better life for themselves as entertainers.

During these conversations Jonquil remembered not to mention the carnival or the saloon, only that they had been working in Hot Springs when Adam had discovered them. Adam found it interesting, too, that Liz never opened up avenues of questioning Jonquil didn't herself volunteer, among these her last name.

Not even the *Echo* had seemed inquisitive when it reviewed Jonquil's debut, referring only to "singer Jonquil Rose and her accompanist, Gabriel Sims."

Except for a handful of troublemakers, these mountainfolk seemed to share a penchant for hard work and good manners and an aversion to idle gossip.

On some subjects Jonquil was quite open, claiming her mother had taught her to read, write, and do numbers. Having been raised the daughter of a wealthy planter before the war, her mother had also instructed Jonquil in proper manners and conduct for a young lady.

But it was Gabriel who'd taught her to sing and play the banjo. And it was Gabriel who'd helped her and her frail mother through the difficult times. He'd been the rock of their shaky existence, the guardian angel Adam had teased her about.

For the first time Adam heard Jonquil's story of the

loss of her father, that he had been killed fighting for the South. With no family left who were willing to take in a widow and her baby daughter, Jonquil and her mother had remained in Arkansas.

The more Jonquil revealed about herself, the more convinced Adam became that she was more victim than hardened criminal. But there were still so many unanswered questions, one being how Jonquil's mother had come to be on the small piece of worthless land in southwest Arkansas in the first place.

Could Innes Ball's claim be true? Had Jonquil's mother stolen the deed to that land from his suitcase? And if the deed had been stolen, could the Jonquil Adam knew be capable of the murder of his brother?

She might be protecting someone. Her mother perhaps? The people of Prater had claimed the woman was crazy and dangerous. The facts he'd gleaned so far swirled around him, like autumn leaves on a wind current. Try as he might he could not grab at enough of them to put together a logical explanation. If Jonquil was in cahoots with Innes Ball, the man's name was never mentioned. And the more Adam learned of this mysterious lady, the more he believed no connection existed between these two.

Though the brunt of the investigation lay with him, Adam knew Parker's deputies would dog whatever trail they could uncover. One of their own had died in the line of duty.

He only hoped they uncovered something soon, something that would free Jonquil from suspicion and free him from the overpowering attraction he felt for her . . . before it turned to something deeper.

Since the accident he'd vowed to march through this life alone. That was why he'd left his law practice for such a transient career. Constantly on the move, he had a ready excuse for not settling down.

Now he needed answers so he could close the door on this investigation. He would not risk inflicting on

Jonquil this thing called love. In the end it brought nothing but pain. The sooner he could distance himself from her, the better it would be for both of them. Or so he told himself.

Following Jonquil, being with her, at every moment wanting to reach out and protect her, aroused feelings he tried desperately to deny. And yet he couldn't.

He liked the way she laughed, the way her temper flared and cooled in the same moment, and the way she looked after him when he came in to eat at the boarding house. It had been a long time since anyone had made him feel special. Or since he'd allowed anyone to. Maybe the damned water did contain some magical power.

The kitchen door swung open, bringing Adam back to the present. He hung back and watched Jonquil hustle through, swinging a large tray. Stopping at the sideboard, she began to shuffle empty dishes onto the tray, humming a tune while she worked. She was completely oblivious to his presence.

Adam studied her. She looked as inviting as a lush meadow on a hot summer day. Her green bodice and skirt were protected by a fresh apron, and a large bow covered the small of her back, its tips fluttering with her energetic movements.

The drapes had been drawn back, and early morning sunlight cast a checkerboard pattern across the highly polished floor. An errant beam catching Jonquil's blond hair reminded Adam of their first meeting, when he'd mistaken her for an angel.

"Morning, sunshine," he called from the doorway.

Startled, Jonquil turned, nearly dropping the dish-laden tray. "You . . . you scared me half silly," she scolded.

"I'm sorry, but I thought you were expecting me." Feigning disappointment, Adam walked to the sideboard and reached out to steady the tray.

"Since you hadn't shown up, I thought you weren't coming." Jonquil continued to remove dishes from the marble top. "Besides, I've been much too busy to worry over your whereabouts. Liz had to leave early this morning for an appointment."

"Too late for breakfast then?" Adam glanced at the dirty dishes.

Jonquil smiled up at him. "Oh, I might be able to rustle up something in the kitchen to tide you over until noon."

Grasping the tray, she sidled up to the kitchen door. Adam held it open and followed her through.

From a bowl on the cupboard he retrieved an apple and took a large bite. "Liz gone, huh?" Chewing, he looked around the sunny room. Yeast dough sat rising in bowls on the work bench.

Jonquil carried the tray to the dry sink. Carefully she manipulated the dishes into an enameled pan filled with hot, steamy water. "Leftovers suit you?" she asked. He nodded.

"We were busier than usual this morning so there's not much left."

Jonquil wiped her wet hands across the front of her apron and ordered Adam to sit on a high stool beside the work center. She poured a cup of coffee and set it before him, then took a clean plate from a shelf and filled it with grits and ham.

Taking several biscuits from the warming oven in the fireplace, she placed them on a second plate for him. She opened a jar of honey and daubed a large spoonful on his plate. A mischievous grin lit up her face when she pushed the dish toward him. "You do like honey, don't you?"

"Only when you help me wash it off," Adam countered, cocking one brow.

Jonquil colored. "I asked for that, didn't I?"

Trying to check her embarrassment, she turned her attention back to the honey container and removed the spoon. Honey dribbled down the handle and over her fingers. Absentmindedly she drew her fingers to her lips to remove the sticky substance. But Adam intervened.

"My turn," he said, his voice low and raspy.

Taking her hand, he placed one finger at a time into his mouth and sucked the sweetness from its tip. His eyes never left her face.

Suspended in the moment, Jonquil watched Adam's chiseled lips mold around each finger, drawing it deep into his private moist space before he released it and moved on to the next one, repeating the gesture. It had the effect of being tickled with a feather, lightly raising goose bumps on Jonquil's skin.

After all four fingers had been thoroughly cleansed, Adam placed his lips to the center of her palm and grazed it with his tongue. The touch caused such a jolt of desire that Jonquil jerked back as though she'd been burned. She rubbed her hand across her apron front, unable to look him in the eye.

"So," Adam prompted, turning to his breakfast, "tell me about your morning." He picked at his grits, as though nothing out of the ordinary had happened.

For a moment Jonquil watched him eat, unable to speak. Trying to interpret her response to his caress of her hand, she turned her attention to the bread dough on the table, sprinkled more flour over its surface, and began to knead the mass. She stared at her hand, surprised she could control its movement.

Two weeks had passed since their heated embrace in the arbor, neither of them referring to what had transpired between them. They had both acted as though it had never happened, and in small ways Jonquil had been thankful.

She'd tried to be rational since then, examining her feelings extensively. In her precarious position she couldn't afford an attachment with anyone. But that didn't keep her from recalling the passion Adam had aroused in her and how much she'd cherished his embrace.

Sometimes when she thought about their encounter, she felt as though she'd imagined the current that had swirled between them. But if Adam's licking honey from her fingertips could start her blood humming out of control as it just had, Jonquil knew that for her the lightning charge still existed. It had not been her imagination.

Clouds of flour rose around her face, settling in white dust over her dress. Lost in thought, she worked the bread with such a vengeance that she was completely oblivious to the man who shared her kitchen.

Suddenly she caught the unmistakable scent of bay rum. Adam stood behind her, his warm breath on her face, his hands reached around her to cover her own.

"My mother always said if you knead the dough too much, it gets tough."

His words carried a teasing ring but that deep, intoxicating voice sent quivers up Jonquil's spine. He stood so close that if she turned her head to answer, she would undoubtedly brush his lips with her own. Without turning, she nodded. "And your mother is right."

When he'd moved away, Jonquil stopped her pounding and squeezing, wishing she could as easily stop the racing of her pulse. Wordlessly she shaped the dough one last time and dropped it into the loaf pans. All the while she could feel Adam's eyes on her.

"I'm sorry about the honey," he apologized. "I didn't mean to embarrass you. It's just that your fingers were so tempting I couldn't help myself." He shrugged his shoulders in mock sincerity. "Forgive me?"

The little-boy look of innocence stamped across Adam's face made Jonquil's heart beat frantically. His behavior had been spontaneous, nothing more. She couldn't fault him for her reaction.

"Only if you dry the dishes," she bargained. Hoping to again establish an even footing between them, she turned toward the dry sink and tossed a dish towel in his direction.

"Tell me," Adam asked, rolling up his shirt sleeves, "how was yesterday's meeting of the Invalid's Association?"

"It was wonderful," Jonquil answered, glad for the diversion. She concentrated on removing caked egg remnants from an especially dirty plate. "I'm always amazed at the stories people have to tell, and how supportive they are of others with ailments. I wish my mother had been able to talk with people like that. Maybe they could have lifted her spirits."

Jonquil handed the dish to Adam for drying, then continued to wash and rinse the remaining ones.

"By the way, did you know that this town has only one undertaker? It seems so many people are cured by the spring water, there isn't enough business to warrant more than one."

"Don't tell me you're feeling sympathy for the undertaker," Adam teased, drying the last pot Jonquil handed him.

"Heavens no! I mean, yes, I'm sorry he's not earning more money, but I'm certainly glad folks aren't requiring his services." They both laughed at the undertaker's plight.

After the last dish was washed, dried, and added to the stack atop the dry sink, Adam lifted the panful of dirty water and carried it outside to the back porch. When he'd tossed the contents over the rail, he hung the pan on a nail by the door and started back inside.

"It's like Indian summer outside," he announced. Tugging at his shirt sleeves, he gave Jonquil a dickering raise of one brow. "A great day for a picnic."

"Who has time for a picnic? Most of us have to work for a living."

Jonquil walked back to the stove, lifted the lid off a

235

large soup caldron, stuck in a spoon, and stirred the contents.

Ignoring her insinuation, Adam followed her to the stove. "Hmmm, my favorite. Beef stew." Adam wrested the spoon from Jonquil, lowered it into the bubbling pot, and lifted out a spoonful of vegetables.

"Every kind of food is your favorite," Jonquil reprimanded. "Didn't you just finish breakfast?"

"I did, but I'm already thinking about dinner. A picnic dinner." Adam continued with a poetic note. "You and me, a jug of wine, a loaf of bread."

"And tomrrow morning one colossal headache." Jonquil's own bit of foolery prompted an appreciative laugh.

But a picnic did sound like fun. This time of year the weather could change drastically, especially in the hills. Perhaps they should take advantage of the warmth before colder temperatures forced everyone to stay huddled around hearths.

"I know a perfect spot," Adam prodded. "I pass it every day on the way back to my cabin. Can I tempt you into joining me?"

Jonquil hesitated. Other than a few buggy rides with Adam to learn something about her surroundings, she hadn't enjoyed a real outing since she'd arrived in town. She'd been far too busy helping Liz in the boarding house and rehearsing with Gabriel.

Her noonday meal chores would be completed by two, and no rehearsal was scheduled for this evening. So what was stopping her? The idea that they would be alone for a couple of hours? That in casual conversation she might let slip some incriminating part of her past? Worse, that the feelings this man stirred in her would suddenly turn her shy, that she'd become tongue-tied?

Still debating whether to accept his invitation, she fussed with her apron sash. Seeing her dilemma, Adam turned her back to him and pulled the ends of the troublesome bow until they unfurled over her bustled hips.

"Why do you women wear such contraptions?" he asked.

Assuming he referred to her apron, Jonquil answered, "To keep our dresses from becoming soiled, of course."

"It's such a pity. . . ."

Adam's voice trailed off, and Jonquil wondered if he'd been complaining about her bustle. It was intended to enhance the figure, but in fact it hid a woman's natural feminine curves. With a slight blush she pretended not to understand.

"Pity? Now why would you think wearing an apron is a pity?" Turning to face him, she pulled the apron off, folded it, and draped it over her arm.

"I mean it's a pity if you won't accept my invitation." Adam boldly met her gaze, and Jonquil knew exactly what he'd meant.

Nevertheless, his was a tempting offer and she found herself out of excuses. As long as she got back before the sun set, before the evening mountain chill descended, what harm could possibly come from sharing a picnic supper with a friend?

"All right," she said. "You've talked me into it. I'd love to go on a picnic with you. We'll call it an early supper."

Adam's instant response was a devastatingly beautiful smile, and Jonquil was glad she'd accepted his invitation.

Chapter Fourteen

Gold and copper leaves floated across the terraced path as Adam strolled back toward the center of town with Powell Clayton. The autumn sun felt warm against their shoulders and soon both men removed their jackets to walk in their shirt sleeves.

"You have information for me?" Adam asked, enjoying the feel of a warm breeze against his face and the sound of acorns crunching beneath his feet.

He tried to concentrate on the general and his purpose in meeting him, but the beauty of the day and the promise of his later engagement made his thoughts wander to less pressing problems.

"I received a letter from Parker in this morning's post," Clayton said, fumbling with the inside pocket of his jacket. He pulled out an envelope and thrust it into Adam's hand.

"Our suspicions of Ball were well founded. The property he claims was stolen never belonged to him in the first place."

His interest piqued, Adam focused on the general's words before unfolding the letter and hastily scanning its contents.

Clayton stopped and motioned toward a bench beneath a nearby tree. "Shall we sit awhile?"

Following the older man through the fallen

leaves, Adam waited for him to settle himself, then did the same.

"It appears your little singer owns the property Ball claims as his," Clayton stated. With the deftness of a man with two arms, he folded his jacket and draped it across the back of the bench.

"If you hadn't given me her last name, we'd still be looking for a needle in a haystack. Parker's deputies have been all over the county asking questions. But folks just wouldn't talk. Claimed they didn't know a thing." The man shook his head. "I just don't understand people like that. It's as if that family never existed."

Adam crossed his ankles and slouched against his seat, remembering when he'd found Jonquil in the grape arbor, alone and desolate. Her misery had pierced him so, he'd nearly forgotten later that she'd mentioned her name. "So my giving you the name helped."

"Helped?" Clayton quipped. "I'd say it did. With that piece of information Parker's men found the record of ownership of the land. Look." He pointed to the paper. "It's all there in the judge's letter. The farm's title was recorded in 1861 in the name of one Margaret Trevain."

"But didn't Ball claim there were no records? Something about pages missing from the deed book?"

"He did and his claim was legitimate. But that was in Pike County, where most of the property is located." The general sat back saying no more, allowing his news to sink in.

Adam's brows rose in appreciative speculation. "Wait a minute. You're saying the property lies in two counties?"

"Exactly. It seems part of the farm lies in Hempstead County, which would have required a separate recording for tax purposes. My guess is Ball wasn't aware of this fact. If he had been, you can bet those papers would also be missing."

"So apparently Margaret Trevain knew Ball well enough to realize she needed to protect her interest in the land." Although Adam would never meet the lady, he appreciated her foresightedness. "Well, I'll be hornswoggled." Adam gave a light chuckle. "Innes Ball isn't as smart as he believes himself to be."

Clayton nodded. "My guess is he underestimated Mistress Trevain."

Adam propped both arms on the back of the bench. "How's that?" he asked.

"In the Record of Births and Deaths, Parker's men found a birth recorded later that same year. The birth of a daughter, Jonquil Rose Trevain. Mother, Margaret Mary Trevain. Father, deceased."

Adam sat up straighter and shifted toward Clayton. "You don't say. So my Jonquil Rose is Margaret Trevain's daughter." He leaned back in thought. The carved initials on the grave at the farm—*MMT*. "Finally, it begins to make sense." He looked over at the general. "You don't suppose . . ."

Clayton met Adam's questioning eyes. "That Jonquil's father didn't die in the war?"

"Right."

"It's certainly a possibility." The older man scanned the scenery before him. "Think about it. One piece of property owned by your little singer, born the year it was deeded to her mother. One angry man hunting her with a claim of ownership he doesn't know we've disproved, a man who says his deed was stolen in that very year. A man who hides behind his big name in New York City. Does it strike you as peculiar that he won't even set foot in our fair state to defend his claim?"

Powell looked over at Adam. "You don't suppose he might find himself accused of something if he came on down, do you?" He gave a light snicker. "Yes, sir, it all seems a little too suspicious, if you ask me."

Adam recalled the stories Jonquil had told Liz about her past, about her mother's grief and depression. This last was the reason Jonquil had been so interested in the Invalid's Association. Indeed, she had expressed fears that later in life such a morbid state could befall her.

"Do you believe," Clayton wondered aloud, "she'd admit she was illegitimate, or that she'd even know it if she was?" When Adam only shook his head in conjecture, the older man added, "I don't believe this is something a mother would tell a child, no matter what the circumstances."

Especially a lady of good breeding. Adam turned thoughtful, recalling again what Jonquil had told them of her mother's past. To fill the silent void, he answered, "We're grabbing at straws."

"True, son, we are. But isn't that what detectives do?"

Their eyes locked in acknowledgment as Adam tried to sort out the connection between Innes Ball and Margaret Trevain's daughter.

"Have you questioned the black man? What's-his-name—Gabriel Sims?"

"No, I haven't, but I'll get no answers from that quarter. He won't tell me anything without Jonquil's approval."

"So I gathered from what Addie has told me about them. There's a story there, son, that neither you nor I know about."

"You're not suggesting . . . ?" Adam's jaw tightened at the general's words.

"That he could be her father?" Clayton laughed. "No, but he certainly does look after her something fierce. He's more than just a devoted servant, I'd say from mere observation. And sooner or later he's going to have to talk—either to us or to the court—if he really wants to protect his mistress."

Both men stood, and Clayton patted Adam on the back. "Now if you'll excuse me, I'm expected back at the house for supper. Addie has some out-of-town friends coming in this afternoon."

"Thank you, sir." Adam shook the older man's hand. "I'll be in touch with you later this week."

Clayton picked up his jacket from the bench and, before turning to leave, added, "By the way, you were right about Miss Trevain's talent. That lady can sing. God willing, she'll have a long and successful career."

The general bid Adam good day, then started back up the sidewalk. Adam watched Clayton, contemplating the truth of his statement as he disappeared from sight.

God willing, Jonquil would be successful, if singing was the only thing she had to worry about. Much as Adam wanted to avoid the inevitable, he realized it was time to confront her with some direct questions about her past.

As he headed toward a nearby hotel to pick up the picnic supper for their outing, some of the warmth had fled the Indian summer day, along with his enthusiasm for the outing ahead.

It is a beautiful afternoon, Jonquil thought, seated in the wicker porch swing. It rocked creakily to the motion of her feet as she waited for Adam to arrive.

The dinner hour had seemed endless as boarders lingered over their noonday meal. The last dishes finally cleared, Jonquil had helped Liz tidy the dining room and kitchen, then had excused herself to freshen up for her afternoon outing.

Promptly at three-thirty, Adam pulled up in his rented buggy. The mere sight of him as he hopped down from the driver's seat and looped the reins around the hitching post prompted an unnatural quiver in Jonquil's lower regions. Striding toward her, he showered her with his heart-melting smile.

"My lady," he announced, "your carriage has arrived." Removing his familiar brown Stetson, Adam held it over his heart and bowed.

Jonquil stood up from the swing and, with a gesture of reverence, dipped into a deep curtsy. "Your lady is ready," she answered, trying not to laugh.

At that moment Liz Stanford bustled out the front door, interrupting the playful display of formality. "Whatever are you two up to?" she asked.

"I've come for my lady," Adam quipped, winking at Liz.

"Well, you'd better hurry up and take her," she answered. "My bones are telling me there's rain in the air." Liz walked to the edge of the porch and peered upward into the cloudless sky.

"Well, your bones are wrong," Adam declared, following in her footsteps. "Not a cloud to be seen."

Jonquil stood back from the two, watching their easy banter.

"Adam Coulter, my rheumatism is never wrong. Child," Liz ordered, turning to Jonquil, "you take this shawl. I feel sure you'll need it before the day is over. Now hurry along and enjoy yourselves while you can."

"The woman's a loon," Adam replied, rolling his eyes heavenward. His action earned him a playful swat from the older woman. Darting to Jonquil's side, he held out his arm to her, and together they headed down the stairs.

After helping Jonquil into the open carriage, Adam unhitched the horse and leapt in beside her. With a jingle of the reins, the rig moved forward.

"We'll be home before dark," Jonquil called to Liz.

"Probably won't see you," Liz called back. "Mr.

243

Stanford and I will be out most of the evening."

Jonquil waved, then settled herself comfortably beside Adam. Her bones told her it was going to be a wonderful afternoon.

Adam cut his gaze from the road ahead and gave her an approving smile. "You look lovely this fine afternoon."

"Get on with you," she replied, shrugging off his compliment. Her heart swelled with pleasure, and Jonquil was glad she'd taken extra care with her appearance.

She wore her green skirt, but had exchanged the flour-dusted green bodice for a white lawn blouse perfectly suited to the mild weather. A bow at the neck and a lace-frilled jabot at the bosom made her feel surprisingly feminine.

Because of the warm, summerlike day, the walkways were filled with people. In spite of the crowds, Adam easily maneuvered the carriage through the streets.

With the warm breeze on her face, Jonquil listened to the rhythmic clopping of the horse, thinking how wonderful it was to be young, carefree, and in love.

Love?

Lord have mercy, she admonished herself, feeling a sudden heat rise up her neck, whatever made that thought crop into her mind?

She stole a guilty look in Adam's direction. Convinced he'd been able to read her deepest thoughts before, she prayed he hadn't done so now. But he stared ahead, the breeze tickling his hair, and seemed oblivious to her ruminations. Dismissing her fear as absurd, Jonquil exhaled with relief and concentrated instead on the passing scenery.

Leaving the town, they headed down a wooded, country road. Adam's voice interrupted her musing, breaking the deepening silence. "You should have brought your banjo."

His long legs were spread, his knees bent, his shiny boots propped upon the dash. He resembled a handsome country gentleman out for a ride. Once more, Jonquil considered the vast differences in their pasts.

Putting aside the disturbing thought, she replied, "No, thank you. Remember? This is my afternoon off."

Adam glanced toward her. "You'll never convince me that you consider banjo-playing work. You love it."

"You're right," Jonquil agreed. "I do. When I play, I forget all my problems."

Adam concentrated on the road, successfully guiding the horse around a large washout. Safely past it, he looked over at her. "How did you learn to read music?"

Jonquil laughed. "I didn't. I can't read a note."

A look of surprised admiration crossed his face. "But I've seen your sheet music. You play by ear?"

Nodding her head, Jonquil studied the multi-colored leaf that fell into her lap. "I only use the sheets to memorize the words."

"I've heard of people with your ability. That's a gift."

Both flattered and uncomfortable under Adam's praise, Jonquil twirled the leaf between her fingers. "I don't know about that, but when Gabriel discovered my 'ear,' he started teaching me to pick out songs on his banjo. Soon I could play all the ones he'd taught me, then I started creating my own. With no friends to distract me, I had plenty of time to practice."

Realizing how her statement of having had no friends might sound to Adam, she quickly steered the conversation away from herself. The last thing Jonquil wanted was Adam's sympathy.

"And you?" she asked. "Do you like to sing?"

Awkwardly, Adam cleared his throat. "Oh, I love music, but I'm not much for singing." The line of his mouth tightened.

Her interest piqued by his reaction, Jonquil pressed for an answer. "Why not?"

"Never wanted to."

"But you said you loved music. Usually anyone who loves music can sound out a few passable notes."

"Not me," Adam insisted, keeping his eyes glued to the road.

Jonquil knew she was bullying him, but that didn't stop her. "Come on," she said, "let's try something simple."

"Told you, I don't sing."

Still she didn't give up. "We'll sing together."

She started humming "Shall We Gather at the River." Between notes, she gestured to Adam to join in, but he sat beside her, as mute as a mummy.

"Please," she entreated, showering him with a coy smile.

With an exasperated frown he blurted out, "When I sing, I sound like a damned bellyaching hog."

"A what?" She couldn't believe she'd heard him right. "Who told you such a thing?"

"The choir director of our church in Chicago, where I grew up." Appearing somewhat relieved by his admission, Adam continued. "I was seven then. Haven't sung a note since." He corrected himself. "At least not where anyone could hear me."

"What kind of person would say such a thing to a child?" Jonquil demanded, her feathers clearly ruffled. "And in a church of all places. Where everyone is supposed to sing praises to God."

Pondering Adam's admission, and her own unhappy experience with the minister who had visited their farm, Jonquil questioned the charity of the Church.

"But you know what?" Adam interrupted her woolgathering, his face aglow with mischief. "He was right."

"Right?" She stared at him. "He still had no business hurting a little boy." With a snap of her head she confirmed her disdain of the choirmaster's lack of charity.

In a small clearing in the midst of the colorful forest, made more brilliant by the sun, Adam pulled their conveyance to a standstill. Jonquil could hear the gurgle and tumble of water rushing over nearby rocks.

"My spot." Adam motioned to the great outdoors.

Jonquil looked around the clearing. "Why, it's breathtaking. However did you find it?"

Mile-high hardwoods formed a thick barrier on three sides of the outdoor room. On the fourth, she spied the water she'd heard. It sparkled like a million diamonds in the afternoon sun before disappearing into the deep shadows of the woods.

"My cabin's not far." Adam pointed south beyond the trees. "This stream has provided me with some pleasurable hours, as well as several sizable trout for my dinner table." As an afterthought, he added, "I love to fish."

Somehow this meticulously dressed, dandified-looking man didn't fit the picture of a fisherman. Where she'd come from, people didn't fish for enjoyment or sport. They fished to put food on their tables. Many times she and Gabriel had fished for dinner, their only meal of the day.

Adam jumped to the ground, tethered the horse to a nearby tree, and returned to help Jonquil down. Then reaching behind the wagon seat, he pulled out a large basket and took Jonquil's hand. A carpet of fallen leaves covered the forest floor, crackling like paper when Adam pulled her toward the stream's edge.

An attempt to help him spread the large red-checkered tablecloth upon the ground brought a sharp scolding. "Didn't you remind me earlier it's your afternoon off?" Yanking the cloth from her hands, Adam snapped out the folds. They both watched it settle upon the ground like a windless kite.

"My lady," he announced with a bow, "your dinner is served."

A few minutes later, seated across from Adam on the makeshift table, Jonquil worried about whether she should sample the wine Adam was uncorking. Having no experience with alcohol other than for medicinal purposes, but well aware of its evils, she fought her conscience. Did she dare?

Adam produced two stemmed wine glasses from the picnic basket and set them out with a flourish. With a final twist the cork exploded from the bottle, expelling frothy suds all over his hands.

"Champagne?" he offered. He poured the fizzing liquid into one of the glasses and handed it to her. She watched him pour himself a glass.

"I've never had it before," Jonquil admitted, holding the glass toward the sky and studying the star-filled liquid.

"You'll like it," he promised. He corked the bottle and placed it at the water's edge to cool. "And now a toast . . ."

She noted his thoughtful expression as he paused to recall the words.

Acting the gentleman, he cleared his throat and raised his glass into the air.

"Here's to the girl dressed in black,
    Who always looks forward and never looks
        back.
    And when she sings, she sings so sweet . . ."

He halted in midsentence as though he had forgotten the rest.

". . . Her talent brings Eureka to its feet."

Seeming pleased with his own creativity, he winked at Jonquil. "They love you, you know."

A blush of pleasure colored her cheeks. "You, sir, should write verse."

He touched his glass to hers before lowering it to his lips and swallowing a sizable amount. Copying his actions, Jonquil brought her own glass to her mouth. When she tipped it upward to taste the wine, fizzing bubbles tickled the underside of her nose.

Her first reaction to the champagne was surprise. How anything so wet could taste so dry was beyond her comprehension. She swished the liquid around in her mouth and swallowed. A stinging sensation scorched a path all the way to her stomach.

She grimaced. "You like this stuff?"

Adam hooted. "I like watching you drink it more." He lifted his glass to his mouth and downed the remaining liquid.

"I'll stick to grapes," Jonquil replied, though good manners prompted her to finish her drink. Thankful the god-awful stuff was gone, she set the glass aside and looked up to find Adam smiling at her.

"Then grapes it will be."

Rummaging through his basket, he pulled out a large cluster of purple grapes. Invitingly, he dangled them in front of her nose before placing them beside a wedge of golden cheese. With his knife he carefully sliced the cheese into smaller pieces. Then reaching back into the basket, Adam brought out a long loaf of French bread for her admiration.

Jonquil laughed. "You weren't kidding when you said, 'a jug of wine, a loaf of bread.'"

249

Her busy morning had allowed her time to grab only a few quick bites. Now, at the sight of food, not only was she starving, but she'd never felt so carefree, so relaxed, and so devilishly playful. And the slightest bit lightheaded.

Crawling across the tablecloth, she peeked inside Adam's basket. "What else is in your bag of tricks?" she quizzed him, then stretched like a curious cat still intent on a better look.

Raw desire ignited Adam's blood as he watched her innocent but provocative display. He wanted to answer "An apple," but kept the wicked thought to himself. Instead, he studied Jonquil's curves while she studied the contents of his basket.

Stretched out on his side with but a few feet separating them, Adam fixed his gaze on Jonquil's rounded breasts, emphasized by the ruffled jabot. All the more alluring, he thought, packaged in such filmy wrapping.

Her rib cage appeared small, her waist smaller still. He cursed the volumes of material in the green skirt that camouflaged her hips and thighs.

Oblivious to his perusal, Jonquil lingered over the basket's contents. She pulled out the few remaining objects for inspection—a tin of nuts, two slices of pound cake, and a fancy box of foil-wrapped chocolates.

"Mmmmm." Her eyes grew wide with pleasure. "I love chocolates." She turned and showered Adam with an appreciative smile.

Finished with her exploration, Jonquil stretched out on the opposite side of the tablecloth, mimicking Adam's relaxed pose. All that separated them was the width of the red-checkered cloth holding their picnic supper. Their eyes locked and held over the mountain of grapes. Jonquil snapped one from its stem and popped it into her mouth.

With abandon, she chewed the grape, turned her

head to spit out the seeds, and plucked another. Every time she licked juice from her bottom lip, Adam's stomach lurched into a tight knot of need.

Only the sound of creaking timber, the gurgling stream, and an occasional bird call broke the tense silence. Every time Jonquil's blue eyes met Adam's, she smiled appreciatively before returning her attention to the food spread before them.

Adam hungered not for food but for the woman across from him. She teased his senses. Her nearness fed the fire that burned in his blood. He wanted her; it was as simple as that.

Jonquil's innocence charmed him as he watched her. No longer the proper young woman she'd worked so hard to be for the last few weeks, she had left the lady she'd become back in town at the boarding house.

This was the Jonquil who dressed as a boy and won foot races, who bathed in her drawers in forest streams, who slept beneath a rain-soaked wagon, and who considered these things her lot in life. Before him, this same Jonquil had become a tempest, stirring his blood with desire. She made him feel like a lovesick schoolboy.

The thought caught him off-guard. Damnation. Lovesick? Was this what he called his present condition? Not likely, he rationalized. Not when he'd forfeited the right to love a long time ago. This was pure lust, mad and untamed.

He watched Jonquil grab a slice of cheese, then a small hunk of bread, and stuff both into her mouth at the same time. She chewed with relish. No longer able to contain himself, Adam burst out laughing. "You look like a chipmunk," he teased, "your cheeks puffed and full."

His remark earned him a grape hurled in his direction. It hit his shoulder and bounced off, landing on the tablecloth. Adam picked it up, plopped it into his mouth, and chewed.

Jonquil giggled and fired another one.

"Watch it, lady," he warned good-naturedly.

"That'll teach you to ply me with star-speckled spirits."

Jonquil sailed another grape at him. This one ricocheted off his forehead and landed in his empty wine glass. She broke into unrestrained laughter.

I'm tipsy, she thought. And on one glass of wine. For the first time in all her twenty-two years, the restraints that had governed Jonquil's behavior were lifted. She was thoroughly enjoying herself, laughing and shooting grapes at the handsome man across from her. She launched another one and smiled wickedly when it bounced off the end of Adam's nose.

"Two, my love, can play at this game."

Adam fired a grape at Jonquil. Feeling young and silly, she opened her mouth and tried to catch it.

"You look like a wide-mouthed bass."

"You did say you were a fisherman," she teased.

Adam tossed several more grapes until one finally hit its target. Jonquil clamped her teeth around the plump fruit, spewing purple juice across the front of Adam's white shirt. Her response was more unsolicited laughter.

"So you think it's funny, do you, ruining my good shirt?"

Adam grabbed a bunch of grapes, leaned across, and held them just above her mouth. Playfully she nipped at the cluster, but he pulled it out of reach before she could catch it between her teeth.

"Maybe I should ruin your shirt," he bluffed.

Dragging the grapes down her chin and lower, across the field of white ruffles covering her bosom, Adam hoped he'd soon be seizing his own fruit.

Fire ignited in Jonquil's veins when his palm accidentally skimmed her breast. At his deep intake of breath she suspected he'd had a like reaction. Just as suddenly, the space between them closed.

Adam had shoved the foodstuffs aside and now lay beside her, pulling her into his embrace. Their lips were only a grape's breadth apart, and Jonquil felt as though she might die of the sweet ecstasy of his nearness.

She was aware that she'd thrown caution to the winds, teasing this man unmercifully as she had. She could blame the champagne all she liked, but she knew full well it had been Adam's easy manner and gentle company that had sent her barriers crumbling. Her woman's intuition had warned her she was playing with fire. Nonetheless, at this moment Jonquil was as anxious as an arsonist to ignite the blaze.

When Adam pulled her close, she clung to him. Soon his hand left her waist and his warm fingers slid upward to caress the side of her breast. Gently he kneaded the soft mound, his eyes never leaving hers. When his fingers brushed the tip, Jonquil felt her nipple bud against his intrusion.

"Rose," Adam groaned. "Oh, my sweet, sweet Rose." He rolled her onto her back and pinned her beneath his length. "Let me make love to you." He looked into her eyes with such longing that his request touched a place deep within Jonquil's heart.

There, he'd said it again. Rose. Her personal name. Only those close to her could use it. Her mother, Gabriel. And now this man. Finally, it seemed so right.

His long legs were planted between hers, and through the material of her skirt Jonquil could feel Adam's maleness pressed hard against her pelvic bone. His arms supporting his upper body, Adam searched her face, awaiting her consent. Again, did she dare?

As little experience as she'd had with alcohol, she'd had even less with men. But in the short time she'd

253

known him, Adam had shown his gentleness in so many ways. From the moment he'd rescued her after the footrace she'd known he was different. Whatever passed between them now, Jonquil was certain Adam Coulter wouldn't hurt her.

The sensations he aroused were new and different, and she wanted him in ways she didn't begin to understand. If allowing him to make love to her would compound all these wonderful feelings, then what could she possibly gain by refusing?

His lips sank to her earlobe, which he nibbled before dipping his tongue into the opening. After laving it with his tongue, Adam dried it with his warm breath. Jonquil's toes curled.

Dizzy with the sensations the intimate act provoked, she delighted in his trailing kisses back to her mouth. Poised and ready to accept his tongue, she parted her mouth slightly.

And then she burped.

Not a quiet, ladylike burp, but such a loud eructation that they both looked toward the stream in feigned search of a bullfrog.

Under normal circumstances Jonquil would have died of embarrassment at such a spontaneous outburst. But the effects of one glass of champagne combined with the heat of the moment instead produced a look of incredulity followed by a bout of hand-clapping, and tension-relieving giggles.

And so, rather than dying, she laughed. Adam's own infectious laughter joined with hers, and their passion turned to glee. Flopping back upon their backs, their fingers tangled, they chortled like carefree children until they were both spent and giddy.

Comfortably entwined, Jonquil's legs woven with Adam's, her head resting upon his arm, they studied the kaleidoscope of colors overhead. The branches were no longer still, but swayed as a breeze sifted through their lofty heights.

An invisible barrier had been hurdled in their romp and the brief passion that followed. They were no longer children playing at games. Adam was man and Jonquil woman, and they had reached an irrefutable turning point in their relationship.

"When?" Adam asked, his hand absently running up and down Jonquil's arm.

She picked a grape from the cluster that now rested in the center of his chest. He was serious about making love to her. "How about right now?" she answered, playfully stuffing the fruit into his mouth.

Adam grabbed her hand and kissed the tips of her fingers, then stilled. A gust of wind stirred the treetops, sailing leaves across the clearing. Barely visible beyond the canopy of swinging branches, the tiny scrap of blue sky had turned violently black.

Adam jumped to his feet and pulled Jonquil up after him. "Liz's bones were right," he said. "We're in for some rain."

The forest became shadowed with murky light as several heavy raindrops pelted the ground around them. Jonquil hurried to pack the picnic basket, while Adam fought the wind to keep it from whipping the tablecloth from his fingers.

A streak of lightning flashed beyond the stream. Exchanging uneasy glances, they both started counting, waiting for the first clap of thunder.

"One, two, three . . ." They didn't have long to wait before a peal sounded.

"Too close for comfort!" Adam shouted above the din.

A second bolt exploded. The echo of falling timber shook the ground.

Adam sprinted to Jonquil's side. "We've got to get to shelter!" He grabbed her arm and started for the buggy. In that instant the clouds opened, and the accumulation of drops turned to a dense sheet of rain.

They broke into a run, huddled under the tablecloth.

"Get in!" Adam ordered. He darted to the tree where the horse was tied, cursing himself for having rented an open carriage. Overhead, thunder rumbled. The clearing had turned dark as the rain cascaded down upon them.

"Thataboy," Adam consoled the nervous animal as he worked his way back to the side of the buggy. All he needed to compound his problem was a runaway horse. With the reins tightly wound around his fingers, he jumped into the carriage.

Wind howled through the trees, slapping great sheets of rain against the conveyance. Adam urged the horse forward at a slow pace. His limited vision made it almost impossible to see the trail that led into the main road.

"Where shall we go?" Jonquil asked, barely making herself heard above the wind and thunder. Her hair had escaped the chignon and hung wet and straight over her shoulders. She mopped rain from her face with Liz's shawl.

"My cabin!" Adam answered, his voice raised against the heavy downpour. He turned the buggy onto the road and headed south. "We'll have to wait there until the storm blows over!"

Jonquil steadied herself on the seat. "How far?" Her skirts, the shawl, the tablecloth—all were soaked.

"Less than a mile!"

For one suspended moment, their eyes locked in silent communication. Then Adam gave the anxious horse his lead.

"Hang on!" he yelled. "You're about to have the ride of your life."

And Jonquil knew he wasn't referring to this one.

Chapter Fifteen

As soon as Adam pulled up to the cabin, Jonquil jumped down and ran for the porch. Safe under the protective overhang, she stood trembling in the aftermath of the bone-chilling wind and rain.

"Wait inside," Adam ordered from the driver's seat. "I'll put this horse in the lean-to around back." He flicked the reins, urging the frightened animal forward.

When the buggy had disappeared around the side of the house, Jonquil turned and walked to the front door. She pushed and it opened with a grunt. Still clutching Liz's sodden shawl, she stopped just inside the doorway to adjust her eyes to the dim interior. Water dripped from her clothing and puddled around her feet.

For a moment the tiny cabin took her back to her own humble home. Trailing water across the pine flooring, she moved toward the back wall. Across it was a huge fireplace. Firewood stood stacked on the grate, ready for lighting. More logs waited on the hearth. Reaching for a matchstick, Jonquil slashed it across a rough stone, then placed its tip to the small pile of kindling. Within moments flame gobbled up the twigs, then licked higher to feast on the remaining logs.

Finding a lamp on a table in the center of the room, she lifted the glass chimney and touched another match to the wick. A string of black smoke snaked its way toward the ceiling. Soon the yellow-blue flame sent soft light throughout the room.

Several loud thuds came from the back side of the house. Jonquil jumped at the unexpected noises, then realized Adam must be settling the horse. A loud clap of thunder rattled the glass windows while overhead rain drummed on the tin roof. That brought back memories of other rainy nights when as a child she'd been lulled to sleep by the same soothing sound.

Moving to the fireplace, Jonquil studied the room. She found it well kept but primitive, containing none of the luxuries she'd expected a man like Adam to surround himself with. In her memory, he would always belong in the richly appointed salon of the dressmaker, sipping tea from a bone-china cup, his little finger crooked. She'd been surprised that he hadn't sought lodging in one of the hotels in town. A man with his background would be accustomed to a certain amount of pampering.

But, she thought, just what did she know of his background, other than that he was a successful business manager? Perhaps there was a simpler side to him, one about which she knew nothing.

Here, stripped of his fancy clothes, Jonquil could imagine Adam a different kind of man—quiet, rugged, purposeful—answering to no one but himself. He certainly was as adaptable to sleeping under a wagon in a downpour as to sitting in a fancy theater box. He could charm the skirts off every woman in town, then concern himself with finding a black man a decent job. And he mastered a spirited horse as well as he handled the reins of a carriage. Somehow this place seemed to fit the Adam Coulter she wished she knew better.

One side of the room served as the kitchen, the other as the bedroom. Beneath the kitchen-side window, a table functioned not only for eating but also as a desk, if the papers stacked upon its top were any indication. On that same wall stood a dry sink, a small mirror hung above it. This also, she decided, served two purposes—dishwashing and shaving. Just as she'd remembered from her own home—all things practical, functional, and compact.

What had once been a beautifully colored Turkish rug covered most of the heart-pine flooring in the middle of the room. Though its blue and red design had faded to threadbare insignificance, it still added a touch of warmth to the setting. Adorning the rug, was an overstuffed chair, with footstool. It sat facing the fireplace.

As if she couldn't deny her eyes any longer, she finally allowed her gaze to settle on the bed at the opposite side of the room. Nothing more than a daybed, it was covered with a woven blue jacquard coverlet, a feather-ticked pillow at its head. With its simple wooden frame, the bed looked hardly long enough to fit Adam's length . . . and much too narrow for two people. At the realization, a sudden blush crept up Jonquil's neck.

A massive two-door wardrobe stood against the same wall, nearly touching the ceiling. How such a large piece of furniture had ever been carried through the door of the wee cabin she couldn't imagine. One of its doors held a mirror the height of a man. Anyone who peered into its silvered depths could see a complete image of himself.

Lost in thought, Jonquil jumped when the cabin door banged open to reveal a dripping, barefooted Adam standing before her. Shaking and spewing water like a wet dog, he slammed the door shut and dropped a long plank across it. Then he turned to her and smiled.

As the wood bar had thumped into place, the word Adam murmured in Henry Stanford's grape arbor flitted through Jonquil's mind as surely as if he'd uttered it aloud. *Gotcha!* The same word he'd spoken when he'd pulled her to him in the bubbly spring on their way north.

And indeed he did have her. Exactly where, in spite of a sudden case of shyness, she wanted to be. Here with this man, locked away from the world, with only the sound of raindrops on the tin roof.

"Get out of those clothes."

Taken aback by his order, Jonquil stared at him, stunned, as if she wasn't quite sure he was speaking to her. He stalked toward her, his own clothes clinging like an outer skin.

As his fingers worked to free the buttons of his shirt, he seemed not to notice that every bump and crevice of his beautifully proportioned body was visible for her perusal. Jonquil stood riveted to the floor, her eyes never leaving his hands.

He tugged impatiently at the shirttail buried deep in his clinging trousers. When his trousers refused to relinquish their hold, he began to unfasten his fly.

Unable to tear her gaze from his trousers, Jonquil gasped. At the sound Adam's fingers stilled, his dark eyes meeting hers across the small distance. In defense of her own clothes, Jonquil crossed her arms over her chest, and hot blood rushed to her face.

"It's time to get out of those," Adam repeated. Then, moving closer, he placed his hands lightly on her wet shoulders. "Now." Several wet curls fell forward over his forehead as he smiled down on her.

On their wild ride to the cabin, Jonquil's thoughts had been filled with only one thing—what would happen when they finally arrived? But now that the moment was upon her, her courage wavered. Her knowledge of what transpired between a man and a woman was nil. "You want me naked?" she whispered. "Right now?"

Most of what she knew she'd learned from her roommate during her brief stay in Hot Springs. Although Flo had made it clear that a man and a woman were supposed to put their private parts together, the way farm animals did, Jonquil in all her wildest imaginings never dreamed that she would perform this act without any clothes at all.

Adam turned and headed toward the wardrobe, calling behind him, "Unless you want to catch your death."

The intent of his words finally sank into Jonquil's brain. She couldn't stop a nervous titter. "Oh, yes, of course. I need to get out of these wet things."

Relieved, she worked the tiny buttons of her blouse, then froze. *Out of these . . . into what?* She sought out Adam again.

He'd opened one of the doors on the wardrobe and had disappeared behind it. From where Jonquil stood, she could see only his two bare feet, highlighted by the fire's glow in the dark shadows of the room.

"Here," he offered. "Put this on."

One bare, muscular arm snaked out from behind his makeshift screen and tossed a red flannel robe in her direction. Jonquil scurried to catch it, then buried her face in the dry, fleecy material. "Tell me when you're decent," he called, "and I'll come out." His wet trousers dropped to the floor.

Jonquil turned her back to the wardrobe. *Decent.* After tonight, she would never be decent again. A decent woman wouldn't scorn the rules of society to have a secret liaison with a man who was not her husband.

At the same time she knew deep in her heart, without completely understanding why, that this was the only man with whom she would ever do such a thing. Without knowing it, Adam had already stolen her heart. This time he had asked for her, and she would willing give herself to him. Her earlier resolve had become nothing more than a memory.

Jonquil discarded her clothing and draped it over the chair. Adam's flannel robe finally flowing around her, his musky smell enveloping her, she knew she'd made the right decision. She pulled the footstool closer to the fire, sat, and began to comb her fingers through her wet hair.

"Were you going to keep me behind that door all night?"

Adam's voice broke through her reverie. From behind her she could feel the heat from his legs warming her shoulders. Tilting her head back to look up at him, she rested it upon his thighs. "I'm sorry," she apologized. "I forgot."

His rich monotone caressed her. "Likely story."

His fingers moved to her shoulders and began to knead her tight muscles. Jonquil sighed, bending her head forward so he could work his magic on the nape of her neck. After a while she stopped his hand and drew him around to stand beside her.

Her heart thudded in her chest as she allowed her gaze to travel the length of him. Tiny russet hairs, hardly visible in the soft light, were sprinkled over his toes. Her own naked foot seemed so small in comparison to his—the two planted a few inches apart.

He'd exchanged his wet pants for a denim pair. The material, soft and worn from much wear, molded to his contoured calves and thighs. He was still shirtless, his chest bronzed by the firelight. Jonquil's gaze skimmed his muscles, lingering briefly on the dark areolas and the sparse hair around their wine-colored tips. Heat from the blaze warmed the laundered fabric of his jeans and a hint of fresh soap filled her nostrils.

"It feels so good to be warm again," she said, trying

not to stare at his naked chest when he squatted down beside her. Her breath caught in her throat at his perfection, and she fought the desire to reach out and touch his smooth flesh.

"Aren't you cold?" she asked, hoping he didn't notice the quiver in her words.

"Not really," he replied. In the dancing flames his dark eyes resembled fresh brewed tea.

Lifting her hand to his lips, Adam stared into the fire. "What now?" he asked, kissing each fingertip as though it were a candy stick to be savored.

Jonquil gave him a teasing smile. "Aren't you supposed to be the expert in situations like this?" She'd never felt so jittery.

He chuckled—low and huskily—then shyly looked away. "Would you believe me if I told you I haven't made love to a woman in well over a year?"

Sensing his unease, Jonquil sought to lighten his mood. "And would you believe me if I told you I haven't made love to a man in twenty-two years?"

In spite of where he'd found her, in the midst of rough-and-tumble carnival workers, he'd somehow known from the start that she was a virgin. And in Adam's other life, the one before the accident, he would have thought nothing of deflowering her. But this life was different. Jonquil was different. For the first time in his sorry existence he would not take. He would give.

How foolish he'd been to think he could seduce this woman for information. His brilliant idea had faltered long ago, along with his false denials that he cared nothing for her.

In truth, he ached for Jonquil in a way he'd never ached for a woman. She was like a beacon amid black doubts, when guilt had him on the verge of despair. He wanted her innocence to cleanse a corner of his soul, if only for tonight. But he would not force her. She had to want this act between them to happen as much as he did.

"Are you sure, Rose?" he asked hesitantly.

Jonquil stared boldly back into the face marred by doubt. "I'm sure," she confirmed.

On hearing her answer, a glorious smile spread across his features, gladdening Jonquil's heart.

"Well, then, my dear lady, it's time we rectified your lengthy problem."

Adam stood and scooped Jonquil into his arms. Walking to the narrow bed, he held her above its center and dropped her. The softness of thousands of feathers cradled her when she landed. A moment later Adam joined her on the downy cloud, hugging her close.

"Tonight, my love," he said, "you are the ruler. Do with me what you will." With those words he took her hand, licked her forefinger, and drew it in circles over his nipple. Tucked practically beneath him on the narrow bed, Jonquil felt her own nerve endings come alive at the tactile sensation.

"But it's too small," she complained, referring to the size of the bed, their bodies molded together.

Adam guided her hand to his buttoned fly. "It's anything but that." His voice was ragged.

Jerking her hand away as though she'd been burned, Jonquil hid her face against Adam's chest. With her hair for a cover, she peeked at the stretched denim over his swollen groin.

Adam lifted her face with his finger and looked into her eyes. "There's nothing to be ashamed of, Rose. This is all part of making love."

But from the way her heart pounded against her breastbone, Jonquil couldn't be sure she would survive what it took to make love. As she tried to still her own rapid breathing, Adam soothed her jitters with soft whispers of encouragement until she dared again to feel that part of him. Slowly she dragged her fingers down the center of his chest until they again rested upon the bulging protrusion.

With labored breath Adam whispered, "See what you do to me?"

He kissed her forehead, the tip of her nose, then touched his lips to hers. With his tongue thrust deep into her mouth, he covered her hand with his own and showed her how to pleasure him.

An astute learner, Jonquil followed his lead. Soon desire, raw and hot, steamed through her veins, evaporating all her inhibitions. This time she needed no champagne.

Her heart beat in cadence to the steady pulse of the rain overhead. No longer shy, and intrigued by her own curiosity, Jonquil explored with her fingers the rigid bulge of Adam's passion.

Through the softened denim she stroked him, wielding her power with a gentle caress. Back and forth, up and down, along his manhood. His trousers felt damp against her palm.

A soft groan escaped Adam's lips. "I can't take much more of that," he whispered, rolling her onto her back and pinning her down with his weight.

"But I thought you liked it," she teased, her woman's intuition telling her he'd loved every moment of her exploration.

"Oh, but I did," he agreed. "And I'd like it even more if we disposed of your clothes."

"And yours," she added, popping the top button of his denims. Fine, dark hair trailed down his abdomen and continued past the opened waist. He wore nothing beneath the trousers.

Adam sat up, straddling her knees, then pulled her to a sitting position. With one flick of his wrist the robe sash fell away, revealing Jonquil's secrets for his inspection.

A strip of porcelain flesh caught the firelight, then grew to a deep triangle when he peeled the robe down over her shoulders. At the sight of Jonquil's full, rounded breasts, their strawberry nipples budding with desire, Adam's breath rushed from his lungs.

Sitting erect and proud in the folds of his red flannel robe, Jonquil looked like a fairy princess emerging from the petals of a rose, her golden hair a gossamer veil around her shoulders.

"You're too beautiful," he whispered. He leaned forward, his hands curled around the sides of her legs.

All vestiges of modesty flew out the window with the disrobing of Jonquil. Adam's reverent inspection of her body made any doubts about her behavior evaporate in the warm, charged air of the cabin.

"Your turn," she announced, savoring the beauty of his naked torso. She trailed a finger playfully down his chest, hitched it around his opened waistband, and pulled him closer.

At her insistence Adam inched forward, his legs straddling her hips. He stopped, his smooth, hard torso a hair's breadth from her face. Like a dimple, his flat navel was partially hidden beneath a narrow strip of russet hair.

Overcome with a powerful need to kiss the crevice, Jonquil put her arms around his waist, then dipped her tongue into its depths.

A hungry growl escaped Adam's throat when her wet tongue made contact with the sensitive spot. Unable to control his response, he pulled her head closer, winding his hands through her hair, encouraging her to take more of him.

Slowly she feathered kisses down to the top of his waistband, her hot breath separating skin and cloth. As her lips trailed lower, boldly nuzzling his arousal through the constricting fabric of his trousers, Adam knew he had to slow down or he'd be embarrassing himself like some green-behind-the-ears schoolboy. With more purpose than he felt, Adam held Jonquil's face from his stomach and eased away.

Pressing a quick kiss on her lips, he said, "I'll be right back." He jostled from the bed and walked to the fireplace.

Exerting his will, he squatted before the hearth and busied himself tossing more wood on the low-burning fire. Funny, he thought, smiling at the irony, this fire he stoked, while the one raging inside him he had to quench. For the moment anyway, he reminded himself. Jonquil was not experienced in the ways of love.

With Adam's robe half-draped around her, Jonquil sat up in bed. She rested her head upon her drawn-up knees and studied the man squatting before the fire, his back to her. She found herself staring at his perfectly chiseled form. His dark curly hair, reddened by the firelight, was cut short, to the nape of his neck.

With each plunge of the stoker, his muscular shoulders moved with a grace of their own. Even the small, pink marks of healed tissue she'd noticed on his back the first time she'd seen him shirtless added to his look of rugged strength. She felt a staggering impulse to kiss each one.

Just watching him made her breasts tingle where they rubbed against the robe's fleecy material. The contact deepened her yearning for a touch of another kind. That of skin, Adam's skin, smooth and naked against her own.

Quietly, she stripped off the robe and tossed it to the floor. Her eyes never leaving Adam's back, she rolled down the coverlet and lay again upon the crisp linens . . . waiting. At last he turned from the fire and started toward her.

When he looked over at her, Adam's heart caught in his throat at the sight that awaited him. Jonquil lay uncovered, her body golden in the soft, flickering light. Her modesty as absent as her clothes, she could have been a model, posed for a barroom painting.

His eyes perused what he was eager to touch. Full, shapely breasts. Hardened, pouty nipples. Lush, rounded hips. And lastly, the triangle of shadowed curls at the apex of her thighs.

Her eyes, like magnets, pulled his attention to her face. An unwavering sensual smile seemed to give him her final consent. In response his body tightened, on the threshold of bursting with raw, undeniable need. He could no more stop its grip on him than he could stop the racing of his heart. What powers did this woman wield over him that no other had? In that instant Adam understood.

There wasn't a pretentious bone in her beautiful, desirable body. How many women, not having been trained in the art of love, could nonchalantly pose like a seductress while waiting to be deflowered? Her innocent curiosity, her willingness to experience, was as natural as breathing.

Eager and nervous, Adam dropped his jeans to stand naked before her. Jonquil's gaze slowly raked his exposed flesh, confirming his silent question as to who was seducing whom. More vixen than virgin, she seemed to have the upper hand on control while she tentatively explored, first with her eyes, then with her fingers, the dark hairy path that ran from his midriff to his engorged shaft. At her touch heat rushed from within Adam to burn his skin.

Whatever skills he'd learned in lovemaking had left him totally unprepared for what lay before him. For the first time in his life, the promise of fulfillment. Knowing this, he felt suddenly chaste and inexperienced.

"Bless it all, woman, must you stare?"

Jonquil's eyes met his, in them a sparkle of humor, before she fell back, laughing, against the feather mattress. From another woman the response would have been degrading, the idea that she'd laughed at what she'd seen. But then this was not just any woman. Her laughter was the seductive sound of a temptress—deep, rich, and enticing. Shaking his head at the wonder of it all, Adam crawled onto the bed beside her.

Their lengths bonded—her breasts to his chest, her womanhood to his maleness—and soon their merriment ebbed to intimate giggles. Both were consumed with feeling, touching and exploring each other.

Adam's hand slid to the nest of curls at Jonquil's thighs. Winding his fingers in the softness, he slipped them lower to caress the button that would unleash her pleasure. His own driving need continued to mount in exquisite anticipation.

Wrapping her arms around his back, she grasped him to her, impulsively opening her legs to allow him complete access.

"You're so wet . . . so hot." His words came through a haze of ecstasy, ragged and disjointed.

The heavens swirled behind her closed eyelids as Jonquil squirmed in mounting arousal. Her body begged for more of his delicious massage—faster, deeper—and the aching, blissful throbbing wrought by his magical fingers. Heat shot up from the depths of her being, tightening her nipples into hard buds. Adam tasted each tip before sucking on one and then nibbling it with his teeth.

His fingers played at the soft core of her body, plunging and receding, until Jonquil felt like a spring about to snap. She arched against his hand, trying to ease the alien longing that coiled inside her.

Finally he slipped between her open thighs, supporting his weight with one arm while guiding the head of his sex into her dewy softness.

"That feels soooo . . . good," Jonquil purred, pressing more firmly against him.

"Guide me, Rose," he whispered, his rasping words warm against her lips.

Adam repressed the urge to plunge into her molten depths, determined not to rush the inevitable. It was too important to pleasure her, to carry them together to heights accessible only to lovers.

Following Adam's instructions, Jonquil slid her hands between their moist bellies then lower, until they reached the downy curls surrounding his hard shaft. When her fingers touched the tip of his maleness, she heard Adam suck in his breath.

Hot, damp heat steamed their lower bodies. Moving her fingers farther, Jonquil settled the tip of his sex within the folds of her own. Slowly she guided him, up and down, until the tickling sensation turned to a gloriously wet, silken feeling. With each stroke, Adam's body settled deeper into the blossom of her core. With each slipping movement he forged deeper, his kisses becoming more intense.

Jonquil moaned in ecstasy, intense heat ripping through her body. Each liquid caress brought her nearer to uncontrollable surrender.

"It'll hurt, my precious," he whispered, pulling back slightly. "But only for a moment."

"Hurt?" She opened her eyes and looked deep into his own. "How could anything that feels so wonderful hurt?"

He laughed softly, then probed farther inward.

Jonquil's legs tightened around him, then relaxed and opened wider. Adam penetrated her slowly, easing himself into her tight canal. Then, as though she sensed a barrier that needed to be hurdled, she dug her fingers into his backside and thrust her hips against him, accepting his full length inside her.

His face buried against her neck, he slid fully into the wet, silken sheath of her womanhood. For Jonquil, a light, burning sensation accompanied his full entrance, but soon all pain receded.

"I'm sorry," he apologized.

"For what?" she returned, forgiving him with a

lover's smile. She lay motionless beneath him, savoring the fullness within her and the closeness of him.

Slowly, Adam trailed kisses along her breasts, her chin, and her lips. In the shadowed light of the burning fire, his eyes looked like whiskey. Jonquil ran a finger over his lips, then down through the deep cleft of his chin.

He'd been tender, gentle, and she'd been grateful for the moment. But a part of her remained strangely dissatisfied, wishing there'd been something more. What, she couldn't name.

As though he again read her thoughts, he tipped his forehead to hers. "We're not finished yet," he teased, planting a wet kiss on her lips.

She raised her brows in question, wondering how there could be more than this completeness, this linking of their bodies in such a glorious way.

Then Adam began again to move his hips. Bracing his elbows on either side of her, he cupped his hands beneath her shoulders and plowed deeper inside her with each thrust. Soon that same tickling sensation flared to life again and Jonquil's eyelids fluttered closed, relishing the heady invasion. She joined his rhythm, groping to fill the sweet, aching void inside her.

Adam knew his climax was upon him, but with Jonquil so close to her own peak, he fought for the stamina to pleasure her before seeking his own release.

Even as Jonquil's hands dug into the base of his spine, drawing him deeper into her fiery warmth, he tried to constrain himself—to endure—but his body surrendered to its own demand and he filled her womb with liquid fire.

Still he moved with her, taking her over the edge. Soon after, Jonquil's muscles contracted around Adam's spent body. Behind her closed lids, passion hurled her into a whirl of golden stars that resembled champagne bubbles.

Fulfilled, they both lay in exhausted languor. Rain no longer pounded on the roof. Only an occasional drop from the overhanging trees hit the tin. The only other sounds in the quiet room were the shifting of a log on the grate and the soft, calm breathing of sated lovers.

Adam eased himself from Jonquil and reached for the coverlet at the foot of the bed. Covering them, he lay back down and pulled her gently into his embrace. She said nothing, only smiled like a contented cat as his legs entwined with hers.

Snuggling closer to Adam, she drifted on the edge of wakefulness and sleep, savoring his warmth and the musky sweet smell of sex. Wafting in a cloud of serenity, her mind darted in and out of thoughts.

Gotcha, gotcha, gotcha. . . . The word resounded from the dark corners of Jonquil's mind. Her eyes flew open and she searched Adam's face, only to find him relaxed in slumber. Reminder or warning? Jonquil worried about the words. But only for a moment.

Adam shifted, settling her closer beside him. Soon her strange musings were crystal clear. He did indeed have her. Adam possessed not only her body, but also her heart.

Wrapped in that awareness, Jonquil sighed and drifted into a contented sleep.

Adam awakened slowly, his eyes on the smoldering remains of a fire that blanched the cabin's velvet darkness. Sometime during the night the kerosene lamp had gone out, its fuel exhausted, leaving only a halo of light reflecting from the coals in the fireplace.

Branches scratched against the roof like some giant claw. The eaves of the little house creaked and groaned with the wind's invasion, breathing cold air into the once warm cabin.

Fully awake now, Adam became aware of the room's chill against his face. In contrast, beneath the wool coverlet where Jonquil lay pressed against him, he felt hot as a warming brick. In the amber light, Jonquil's golden hair resembled spun brass. As breathtaking as she'd been in the throes of passion, she was even more beautiful in sleep. With the memory of their lovemaking still fresh in his mind, Adam felt a soft stirring of desire where Jonquil's silken thigh rested against his groin.

He knew he should tend the low-burning coals but he hesitated. He didn't wish to disturb Jonquil, to awaken her from sleep, and he wanted to savor her nearness, undisturbed, for a few more moments.

A million confusing thoughts spun through Adam's head. Never could he recall a time when he'd wanted to share the aftermath of passion with a woman. In the past, if he'd paid for female company, he'd leave money and quietly excuse himself. The woman who'd obliged him—and the act itself—would be forgotten with the closing of her door. It had been the same with the few other women that he'd known. He just hadn't left gold. But with Jonquil, his aloofness had disappeared.

And what of Katherine, his betrothed? His mind dredged up painful memories. Their discreet couplings had satisfied his physical needs but had left him feeling empty, alone, and guilty.

Poor, lost, misguided Katherine. She'd loved him and accepted him in spite of his faults. But Adam had felt certain she knew his true reasons for wanting to marry her.

Katherine Ahearn had possessed everything money could buy, and that same money had bought her a fiancé, the stepson of a prominent Chicago lawyer. Looking back on the bargain he'd struck with the

273

heiress those many years ago, Adam knew if she'd lived her purchase would have bought her nothing but heartache and loneliness.

She'd wanted love, but money couldn't buy Adam Coulter's heart. He'd wanted satisfaction, security, and revenge on a stepfather who'd tried to show him the error of his ways.

He'd resented the man for pointing out what he himself refused to see—that a man reaped only what he sowed, whether that be blessings or curses. And he'd resented Katherine for making it so easy for him to walk on her. The memories stabbed at his gut, and he wished again that he'd had a chance to put things right between them.

Now, as he basked in warmth beside Jonquil, he knew he'd been granted a second chance. What had drawn him to her, he still couldn't explain. From their first meeting, she'd made rubble out of the wall of aloofness he'd built around himself. Even now his body burned to connect with hers again.

Adam tried to curb his rising desire by not thinking about her soft, satiny breasts pressed against his chest, or the steady beat of her heart against his ribs. As her warm breath rippled the hair in the hollow of his arm, ripe sensations flowed through him. Releasing an erratic sigh, he tried to ignore her lushness—to think of something else—but found his efforts futile. He wanted her.

She stirred beside him, her eyes seeking his in the soft darkness. When she smiled shyly at him and snuggled closer, it was nearly his undoing.

"Sleep well?" he asked, brushing back a lock of her hair.

Slowly, she stretched full-length, then answered, "Loved better."

"That response can only get you into trouble." He pulled her tighter against his chest, enjoying the feel of her.

"How?" she asked with wide-eyed innocence, resting her chin against the top of his ribs. She traced his nipple with her finger and watched it peak. "You mean like this?" She followed her finger with her tongue.

A hot current raced through Adam's blood. "Siren," he teased approvingly.

When Jonquil moved lower to lick a trail of moist fire down his stomach, Adam had to restrain himself to keep from whistling with pleasure.

Slipping down over his extended staff, carefully enough to bait him, she settled her bottom on Adam's thighs, and sat upright. With her hands planted on her hips, she let her gaze travel up his length before focusing on his very obvious erection.

"This little fellow doesn't appear too sleepy," she replied.

"You mean big fellow," Adam answered, feigning indignation.

Even in the dark Jonquil found herself flushing profusely at her newfound boldness, though she felt giddy with power.

Rising to meet her, Adam silenced any snappy retort by placing his hungry mouth on hers. Jonquil eagerly responded, tasting and probing, teasing his own tongue with hers. A low, deep growl confirmed his hedonistic pleasure.

He moved to nibble her throat, her ear, and then grazed a path to each breast. His voice, husky with desire, breathed a lover's whispers as he went.

His hand dipped to her silken sheath, teasing and moistening, until her body once again ached to feel his length buried deep inside her quaking flesh. Finally he lifted her hips and settled her over his hard length. Jonquil's heart beat with such an erratic tattoo she was certain it could summon a small army were one within hearing distance.

"Mmmm . . . he's exquisite," she mumbled when

he slid fully into her wet, tight space. Scalding heat saturated the expanse between their bodies.

Jonquil clasped herself to him and rode him with reckless abandon. Her head thrown back, her breasts jutting proudly forward, her movements matched each upward thrust of Adam's hips. Taking him deeper into her woman's core, her muscles tightened around him, caressing him from within.

"Oh, Rose, I love . . ." he moaned, filling her with the boiling juices of his passion.

Feeling his body tense, Jonquil moved against him until she, too, spun into the turbulence of fulfillment.

Winded, she cradled Adam's head against her breasts, his exhaled breath hot against her already heated skin, and for the first time she felt the prickles of a beginning beard. Savoring the feel of him against her, Jonquil opened her eyes and peered through the dancing shadows of the room.

And then she saw it—reflected from the wardrobe's mirror, the image of two lovers in the throes of sated passion. A feeling of intense happiness settled in her.

Mirrored in the glass, their bodies glistened with the dampness of their mating, as close as man and woman could be. Evidence of this miracle shimmered before her. The image of Adam's bronzed body entwined with her paler one would be engraved in her memory forever.

She lifted his head from her breasts and urged his gaze toward the looking glass. Upon seeing their image he smiled, his eyes meeting hers in the mirror. They clung to each other, no words necessary.

Jonquil's tangled, golden hair fell over her arm, encasing them both, and Adam thought that in all the world no work of art could compare with the perfection in his arms.

"You're so beautiful," he whispered to her reflection.

"No," she responded, hugging him to her bosom. "We're beautiful."

Adam's face blossomed into a broad smile. How complete she made him feel by such a simple observation. "Oh, my sweet, sweet Rose," he whispered and, pulling her with him, fell back against his pillow.

Together they lay wrapped in each other's warmth, exchanging playful kisses and teasing explorations. Sometime later, Adam reluctantly tiptoed to the fireplace to stoke the dying coals. Then, returning to Jonquil, he climbed back in beside her and the two lovers drifted into a satisfied and exhausted sleep.

Hours later they both came awake at the same time. The alarming sound of a bell tolled through the windy darkness. Jumping up from the bed, they raced toward the window. In the distance, above the surrounding trees, the sky glowed with an aurora of red light. Urgently, the bell continued to peal across the hills. Up the mountain, away from the safety of Adam's cabin, fire raged in Eureka Springs.

Chapter Sixteen

Adam jerked the carriage to a stop at the foot of Mountain Street. Fleeing wagons, frightened horses, and terror-stricken pedestrians rushed toward them, the fiery sky illuminating the race to escape.

Jonquil sat beside Adam, watching clouds of black smoke surge upward into a sky that looked like a blazing ocean. For the first time since she had heard the alarm, fear gripped her. Somewhere in that maze were the people she cared about. What if something had happened to Gabriel? Or the Stanfords? Frightful thoughts flashed through her mind as she stared at the fleeing mob.

"Please," she yelled to a woman who ran by the buggy, her small toddler locked in her arms. "Do you know if the fire is near the Stanfords' boarding house?"

The hysterical woman didn't respond, but kept running, crying as she went, "I've got to save my baby, I've got to save my baby!" Jonquil watched her until she disappeared into the midst of the noisy crowd.

Above the din of braying horses, shrieking adults, and crying children, Jonquil gave Adam a pleading glance. "We must go to the boarding house."

Her uppermost thought was to find Gabriel.

Jonquil knew it would be the first place he'd check when the fire alarm sounded. When he didn't find her, he'd be sick with worry. She grasped Adam's arm and began shaking it in desperation. "Please," she begged, "go to Liz's."

"All right," he said, "we'll try to get through. But I think we would make better progress on foot."

Urging the horse forward and swinging onto Center Street, they headed north, away from the fire. People still ran in every direction, but the traffic had thinned enough to allow them to pass. "We'll have to find a place to leave the buggy. The horse is upset enough as it is."

"There!" Jonquil pointed to a vacant lot.

Leaving the road, Adam guided the animal to a stop on the blind side of a two-story building. Leaping from the carriage, with Jonquil close on his heels, he tied the horse to a nearby tree.

"My guess is we will fare better staying off the main thoroughfares." He patted the skittish beast and pointed up the hill. "We'll cut through alleys and vacant lots. Hopefully we'll be able to approach Owen Street from the rear."

"What will we find . . . ?" Jonquil's voice trailed off, her worst fears ready to surface.

"From where we were on Mountain Street, it looked as though the fire burned south of the Stanfords' home."

"But with the wind, all it takes are a few cinders."

Adam grabbed Jonquil and pulled her to him, silencing her with a finger pressed against her lips. "I know," he said. "But the wind is blowing south, away from Owen Street."

He hugged her close. "Are you warm enough?" he asked, pulling the collar of his sheepskin jacket up around her neck.

Jonquil nodded. With nothing but the light-weight clothes she'd worn on the picnic, Jonquil had acceded to Adam's insistence that she don his heavy coat. So large it swallowed her, it at least offered her protection from the frigid air that had come in on the tail of the rain.

"I want you to promise me something." Adam steadied her chin with his fingers, his eyes drilling into hers. "If we should get separated and they evacuate the area, you must go, whether I'm with you or not."

"But—"

"Your word, Jonquil." His voice brooked no further argument. "With all the wooden buildings, this town could become an inferno in a matter of minutes. I saw it happen in Chicago."

The air was charged between them as Adam waited for Jonquil's answer.

"I promise."

"That's my girl." He pulled her into his arms and sealed their bargain with a kiss.

Together they walked back toward the street while Adam issued further instructions. "We'll meet back here when everything is under control."

"Only if we get separated," she reminded him.

Linking fingers, he pulled her along beside him, and they headed in the direction of the blaze. Walking between the houses turned out to be easier than Adam had anticipated. But the closer they got to the fire, the brighter the sky became, and the smell of burning wood clogged their throats.

At last they reached the boarding house to find the fire was a good distance below them. From the houses that lined the street, old men and women and young children watched from porches and upstairs windows. Everyone else, it seemed—including the Stanfords—was down at Mountain and Eureka streets, helping the fire warden and joining the bucket brigade to fight the flames.

Adam kissed the top of Jonquil's head and turned

280

to leave. "Stay here where you'll be safe."

Tugging at the tail of his jacket, Jonquil stopped him. "You won't get rid of me that easily, Adam Coulter. I'm as able as the next person to help, and I won't remain here."

"It's too dangerous."

"Is Liz cowering here because it's dangerous?"

"Jonquil, you don't understand. A fire like this is so unpredictable, anything can happen."

The memory of the Chicago fire blazed again in Adam's mind. The destruction, the panic, the loss of life. Katherine's life. If anything happened to Jonquil, he didn't know if he could handle it.

"I'm going," she added, "with or without you." She crossed her arms against her chest and set her chin at a determined angle.

Adam breathed a sigh of resignation. "You are the most stubborn of females," he insisted. Grabbing her arm, he nearly dragged her down the street, issuing warnings as they went.

Having never witnessed anything more than a brush fire, Jonquil couldn't believe the holocaust that she faced when they finally reached the scene.

Licking at and then devouring whatever they touched, flames leaped from one wooden structure to the next, the fire's spark-filled breath carried on the prevailing wind. A snapping, crackling sound, much like that of an enormous bundle of twigs burning, filled the air, along with the screaming of the horses that hadn't been lucky enough to escape the burning livery. Holding tight to Adam's hand, Jonquil entered the maelstrom of people, many yelling from fear and excitement as they tried to help wailing children locate their parents.

Cinders fell thick and fast, like a firestorm. Feeling the intense heat, Jonquil shrugged off the heavy jacket Adam had insisted she wear. Several people she recognized from the boarding house hallooed to

281

them as they passed, but Jonquil and Adam kept walking, searching for any sight of Liz or Gabriel.

"Rosie! Rosie!"

Jonquil heard the calls above the amorphous cacophony. She halted and turned toward the familiar sound.

"Thank God, Gabriel, we've found you."

It took all of Jonquil's willpower not to throw herself into her friend's arms. But even in a crisis such as this, she couldn't risk shaming Gabriel. A white woman simply could not openly show her affection for a man of color. Instead, she smiled into her dearest friend's face.

"I went to the boardin' house. Miz Stanford, she said she ain't seen you since early afternoon."

"A storm came up," Jonquil replied, trying to explain her absence.

"Said you were a-picnickin'." Gabriel noted for the first time Adam's presence beside Jonquil and shot him a disapproving look.

"She was with me . . . and she's fine."

"I can see she survived the fire," Gabriel harrumphed, "but I don' know how fine she is." His gaze never left Adam's.

Sensing an animosity brewing between the two men, Jonquil tried to ease the air between them. "Oh, Gabriel, I'm so glad you're all right. But tell me, have you seen Liz?"

"She's over there."

He pointed to a chain of women and young girls passing buckets of water to the men who formed a ring around the entrance of a large three-story structure. These men threw the water against the porch, but rivulets of flames already gobbled at its floor boards.

Gabriel turned back to Adam. "We could use your help movin' furniture from the street." He motioned toward a large stack of goods piled high in the middle

282

of the road, a short distance from where they stood. Then he turned his eyes back to Jonquil.

"You'll be all right, missy?" he asked.

"She's fine." Adam curled his fingers possessively around Jonquil's arm, answering for her himself.

"I'm fine," she affirmed.

Gabriel noted Adam's hand on Jonquil's arm, then excused himself before heading down the street.

"Take care," she called to Gabriel's retreating back. Then to Adam she said, "You didn't have to be rude."

"He wasn't exactly delighted to see me, either."

"But you don't understand."

"I understand plenty." Adam pulled her closer and steered her in the direction of Liz. "More than you know," he mumbled beneath his breath.

About to question what he meant, Jonquil forgot to do so when Liz called to her from the chain of women.

"When the alarm sounded, Mr. Stanford and I rushed over here immediately. Didn't have time to rouse you, but figured you'd be down shortly."

She beamed a smile toward Jonquil and Adam, but never stopped passing buckets down the line. "Come join me. We need all the help we can get."

"That's a good place for you," Adam agreed, guiding Jonquil toward Liz's side. The older woman made a space for her.

"Take care of her, Liz," Adam charged. He gave Jonquil's shoulders an affectionate squeeze and gently shoved her in Liz's direction.

Jonquil looked back at Adam for reassurance. She couldn't bear his being out of her sight. What if he were hurt?

"But—"

"No buts. Remember?"

At Jonquil's reluctant nod Adam excused himself and strode off in the direction Gabriel had taken.

283

Soon Jonquil was caught up in the backbreaking task of passing buckets of water to the front of the line. It seemed like hours later, though less than one, when dawn lightened the sky over the eastern mountains.

The fire warden announced the fire on the porch had been extinguished because of the volunteers' efforts. Again he enlisted their help, directing them to another area farther down the street. Jonquil and Liz marched with the others, cheered on by their success, their spirits lifted.

The burning area extended to both sides of Mountain and Eureka streets. People who'd fled when the fire first broke out began to dwindle back to help. Under the leadership of the fire warden, stalwart citizens of all ages worked side by side with the volunteer bucket brigade to put out the conflagration that threatened to level the whole town.

After several exhausting hours of labor, with only short breaks to rest their aching muscles, Jonquil and Liz stepped from the line. Together they walked toward a table on which someone had set up refreshments for the volunteer fire fighters.

Never had coffee tasted so good, Jonquil thought when she had swallowed the last dregs from her cup. The small crowd that gathered around for a quick snack were a weary, ragtag lot. With soot-blackened faces and clothing dotted with burn holes from flying sparks, they looked as though they were penniless. Sadly, Jonquil realized that many of them likely were. Some had probably lost everything they owned to the fire.

She ran her fingers through her mussed hair. It felt wet from her own perspiration. Her shirtwaist was no longer white but pocked with tiny holes and dusted with light gray ash. She looked no different from the others gathered around her, and the realization suddenly gladdened her heart. For the first time in Jonquil's life she felt as though she belonged.

She turned to thank a woman who was pouring from a large canteen and accepted a tall drink of cold water. Then her eyes searched the street for some sign of Adam. She hadn't seen him since he'd left her with Liz earlier.

"Saints preserve us," Liz declared beside her.

Farther up the street they watched a whole side of a building collapse, like a fiery shield, to the street. Men scampered to escape the falling debris and shooting sparks thrust heavenward when the wall hit the ground.

Through the monstrous noise, Jonquil imagined she heard a scream of agony near the downed partition. Exchanging anxious looks, both she and Liz thought of their loved ones working in the vicinity where the fire was at its worst.

Mouthing a silent prayer, she bargained, God, please don't let it be Adam or Gabriel.

No matter how hard she tried, Jonquil couldn't shake the uneasy feeling that settled in her stomach at the haunting sound. Though she couldn't possibly have distinguished a scream in the midst of the roaring blaze, some unknown force nevertheless propelled her into action. She started running. If Adam and Gabriel were hurt, she had to get to them.

"Jonquil, no!" Liz shouted, trying to stop her.

But Jonquil ran as though the hounds of hell were nipping at her heels.

The closer she got to the downed building, the more intense the heat became. It sucked the moisture from her face, parching her skin as surely as a desert sandstorm. But nothing could deter her. She had to make sure Adam and Gabriel were safe.

A downpour of ashes rained upon her through the clouds of smoke. Fire still licked away at the skeletal remains of partially standing structures, but Jonquil kept moving toward a large crowd gathered before a building that looked beyond saving.

A man tried to grab her. "Lady," he shouted, "you can't go over there!" But Jonquil jerked free of his hold.

When she reached the edge of the group, she saw these people were pointing at the blazing structure that loomed up from the street's edge like a wounded monster. Flames ingested the monster's insides as it belched its last smoke-filled breath through hollow windows.

Again the hair-raising scream cut through the bedlam of noise. She had heard it after all. It sounded like a wild animal trapped in the throes of a painful death.

Jonquil searched about her for the victim, but saw only the crowd whose gazes were concentrated on the burning structure. Then, in a third-story window, the room behind her lit with flames, she saw a woman draped over the sill, reaching with her arms toward the crowd below.

Panic rumbled through the spectators. "God help her, no one can get to her. If she jumps, the fall will kill her."

Jonquil's heart went out to the trapped woman. She herself could see a rescue attempt was impossible. Anyone who entered the blazing inferno would certainly meet with his own death.

Some folks held onto outstretched blankets, urging the woman to jump. It was the only chance she had, but the woman didn't seem to understand.

"Save me. Oh, please, someone help me," she begged, her hysterical sobbing silencing the onlookers. Then she slumped against the window sill, her arms dangling on the outside of the smoke-filled building. Now she had no chance at all.

A painful wail escaped a man who stood nearby in the crowd of spectators. "Oh, my God. Katherine."

Dear Lord, Jonquil thought, he must be her husband.

The man rushed toward the front entrance of the house, shoving aside several people as they tried to stop him. "I'm coming, Katherine. Hang on." As though in a stupor, and with no regard to the danger to himself, he yelled assurances to the woman as he went. "Hang on, I'll save you."

Jonquil turned as the man pushed past her, and she gasped. A shiver of panic rushed up her spine. Adam Coulter streaked toward the burning building.

"Adam!" she screamed, but the word barely carried past her lips. He never turned around.

Shoving would-be obstructors aside, he continued to shriek out words of reassurance. "I'm coming! Hang on!"

"Man, you can't go in there," someone in the crowd yelled, trying to halt Adam's advance. "It'd be suicide."

Adam punched him hard in the face and kept running.

"Oh, God, no!" Jonquil cried, bolting after him.

Strong arms grabbed her from behind. "Woman, are you as crazy as he is?" With every ounce of strength she fought to tear herself away from her captor, but to no avail.

"Please, Adam, oh please," she wailed, collapsing against the man who held her fast. But Jonquil's plea fell on deaf ears.

Adam bounded up the outside stairs of the building and, as if it were a battering ram, slammed his shoulder against the burning door frame. Jonquil watched in despair as he disappeared within, then she slumped into unconsciousness.

"Rosie—gal, wake up."

Inhaling the startlingly pungent solution passed

beneath her nose, Jonquil fought her way back to wakefulness. Her head was cradled in Liz Stanford's lap, and Gabriel peered down at her from worried eyes.

"Gal, you gave us a scare."

Hardly focusing on his words, she wanted only to join Adam in the inevitable death she knew he'd met. Tears rolled freely down her face. She could feel Liz wiping them away as quickly as they came. "Adam?" she asked, barely able to say his name.

"He's going to be fine, child." Liz gave her a bright smile. "He saved that poor woman."

Jonquil shot upright, trying to absorb the blessed news. "Where is he?" She held her head to slow the spinning of her surroundings. "I must see him. Please."

"All right, missy, come on. I'll take you." The resentment Jonquil had read in Gabriel's eyes was gone, replaced by a gentle expression of respect for the man who had defied death to save a stranger.

Gabriel helped her to stand, and together they made their way to a cordoned-off area. There Adam lay stretched out upon a blanket. One man wiped his brow with a wet rag while around him others milled about, describing the marvel they had just witnessed.

His eyes were closed, his skin looked chalky gray. Jonquil crumpled to her knees beside him, her tears flowing freely as she stroked his hair back from his face.

"Doc says he's gonna be fine," the man attending to him said, "just suffering from breathin' in too much smoke."

"He acted with valor," Liz added, admiration in her voice.

"'Twas that old rug that saved them both."

Jonquil looked toward a discarded rug Gabriel pointed out. Once beautiful, it now lay in a wet and charred heap beside the road, several holes burned

288

into its patterned surface.

"Yessir," another man offered, "he come flyin' through that door like some avenging angel. He had that little lady draped over his shoulder. That rug, pulled over their backs and heads, was flappin' like some giant wings."

Jonquil reached down and curled her fingers through Adam's.

"Yessiree," Gabriel added, "that rug shore saved 'em, that and Mr. Coulter's quick thinkin'."

Jonquil felt Adam's fingers tighten around her own. She looked down to see him watching her, a weak smile on his face.

Her heart gave a lurch. She now saw for herself that he would be all right, but his rapid, shallow breathing worried her. "Hello," she whispered. "Welcome back."

"Doc says he needs to rest."

"We can take him back up to our house," Liz offered.

"No," Jonquil replied witout hesitation. "You're needed here. I'll take him back to his cabin. It's quiet there and he'll be fine."

At her words she saw Gabriel's eyes light up, but Liz acted as though she had heard nothing. Adam tried to sit up and began coughing.

"Gabriel," Jonquil instructed, "go to the vacant lot on Center Street. Adam left the carriage there. Bring it back here, or as close as you can get."

"I can walk," Adam argued.

"You can do no such thing, not yet anyway. We'll wait for the carriage."

Ten minutes later Gabriel returned. "I've got the buggy parked in the next block. Couldn't get any closer."

Jonquil gave her friend a smile of gratitude. "That's fine. We'll get him there from here." Hoisting Adam to his feet, she took one side while

Gabriel took the other. Liz took the lead, ordering everyone out of their path.

When they reached the buggy, Adam insisted on climbing in by himself, but faltered halfway up. Gabriel lifted him the rest of the way and threw a blanket around his shoulders to ward off a chill.

"You go on with Liz," he said, "and I'll see him back to his place." He paused in front of the two women, his eyes holding Jonquil's.

"No," Jonquil stated, her stance firm. "I'm going with him."

"Gal, you can't be in no cabin alone with a man, sick or not."

"Gabriel, I'm going."

"Rosie, gal, it ain't proper fer you to attend to him."

Jonquil placed a hand on Gabriel's chest and looked up into his eyes. "I love him, Gabriel, and I'm going with him."

Shocked into silence by this admission, Gabriel stood rooted to the ground.

"Let her go, Mr. Sims. She'll be fine." Liz took Gabriel's arm, patting it as if he were a child and steering him away from the carriage.

Jonquil climbed onto the seat beside Adam. Looking down on Gabriel and Liz, she whispered, "Please understand."

"Get on with you, child," Liz intervened. "See that our hero there gets the sleep he needs to recover."

Jonquil smiled at her dear friends and, with a flick of the reins, started the buggy into motion.

As it moved away, Liz Stanford turned to Gabriel. "Mr. Sims," she said, "it's never easy to let go of our children." She spoke in a consoling tone. "Believe me, I know. I lost one to death, and the other is married and now living in New York."

Gabriel stood in silence, listening to the woman who had befriended him, a man of color, just as she

290

had befriended Jonquil.

"Yes'm, but I can't bear to see that gal get hurt."

"I understand your concern. But believe me when I say Adam Coulter is a fine man. Although he may not know it yet, he's in love with Jonquil. When he discovers this, there will be no keeping those two apart."

"And in the meantime?" Gabriel asked, his spirits somewhat lifted by her wisdom.

"In the meantime, Mr. Sims, we'd better get back to that fire and see if we can be of any further help."

Adam's breath, still raspy from the punishment his lungs had endured, resonated from the bed clear across the small cabin. Jonquil watched the rhythmic rise and fall of his chest, amazed that he breathed at all.

He'd tried to help when she'd stripped him of his grimy clothes, but his arms had hung heavy, deprived of all energy. Having washed away much of the dirt from his face and hands, Jonquil had urged him into a clean nightshirt and into his bed.

The little bit of broth and warm tea she'd attempted to feed him, however, had seemed to burn paths down his gullet, and Adam had finally given up trying to swallow. He'd been so weak and depleted Jonquil had been glad when he'd finally closed his eyes. She'd hoped he would drift off, for from the painful squinting of his eyes she could see that every shallow breath he drew brought on new, suffocating pressure.

Now satisfied that her patient slept soundly, Jonquil took care of her own toilet. She stripped away her soiled garments and, without benefit of a real bath, wiped away as much of the dust and soot as she could. She donned Adam's red robe before collapsing into the big chair in front of the fire.

Mercy, I'm tired, she thought, massaging her upper arms. Her joints ached. Her muscles felt as stiff as an old woman's. During the night she'd passed along so many filled buckets, at times she thought her bones might break. She was certain that, undisturbed, she could sleep for a week.

But now that Adam was settled, she found the most she could allow herself was a light nap, curled up in the comfort of the old chair. In the night, Adam might need her. Closing her eyes, she drifted on the edge of slumber.

"Jonquil."

Hearing her name, she lifted her head from the chair arm and looked to the bed. Had Adam called her or had she dreamed it?

"Come here," the voice called again. It sounded as dry and brittle as dead leaves looked.

This time there was no doubt in her mind, Adam had summoned her. She jumped up from the chair and ran toward him.

"Sleep with me," he whispered, patting the sheet.

"You'd rest better alone."

"I'd rest better with you here."

Jonquil needed no further prodding. With the robe still wrapped around her, she lay down beside him and curled up against him. Soon she drifted into a restless slumber.

Her dreams were filled with sporadic scenes from the fire—people running and screaming; a woman crying, her baby clutched in her arms; then Adam dashing into the burning building. She relived those awful last moments when she'd thought she'd never see him again. . . .

Hours later, Jonquil's mind snatched at wakefulness. Disoriented, her thoughts tumbling in and out of darkness, she finally realized she was awake and that night had settled around the little cabin. Soon alert to her surroundings, Jonquil realized she lay beside Adam's sleeping form. The nightmares of the previous day drifted from her mind.

Embers glowed red on the grate and the air that circulated around her face felt chilly. Easing herself from under the covers, Jonquil tiptoed to the window and looked toward town. Nothing but darkness shrouded the nighttime sky, and Jonquil sighed with relief, knowing the fire had been extinguished.

Pattering across the floor, she poked at the dying coals and threw more wood upon the fire. Soon, bright blue and yellow flames restored warmth to the room.

The words *Katherine, Katherine* echoed through Jonquil's consciousness while she stared, mesmerized, at the flames. Adam had repeatedly called out that name before he'd plunged into the burning building. Who could this Katherine be?

"Did you mean what you said?"

Jonquil nearly jumped out of her skin. Turning around, she found Adam standing behind her, his dark eyes caressing her own, his curly hair tousled from sleep.

"What I said?" she questioned, uncertain as to what he meant. "You shouldn't be up," she scolded.

"That you love me." Adam answered, dropping into the chair and pulling her onto his lap.

Suddenly recalling the words she'd uttered to Gabriel, Jonquil felt shy and unprepared to answer his question. That had been the first time she'd acknowledged her love, even to herself. But she hadn't realized Adam had heard.

"The doctor said you needed your rest."

Trying to skirt the issue, Jonquil moved to escape from Adam's lap, but he held her fast.

"Don't avoid my question, Rose." His finger

293

tipped her chin so he could read her eyes. "Do you love me?"

Unable to deny her feelings a moment longer, she replied, "Yes, with all my heart."

Adam pulled her closer, his lips seeking hers as a small sound of wonder escaped from deep in his throat. "Oh, my sweet, sweet Rose . . . my heart."

He held her so tight that Jonquil could feel the thumping of his heart against her own. Parting her lips with his tongue, he took possession of her mouth. Seeming satisfied at last, he broke off the kiss and leaned his head against the chair's back. Gently he cradled her, his hand caressing her arm and shoulder as though he were soothing a small child.

Jonquil relaxed against him, happy that she'd admitted her love for him. But, considering all the problems loving him would cause, her happiness was mingled with worry. There were so many things she needed to tell him, but she was frightened. Afraid he'd turn away from her when he learned the truth about her past. If it were just her problem and she didn't have Gabriel to protect, she'd tell him everything. But she couldn't risk Gabriel's safety.

. His eyes closed, Adam held Jonquil fast in his arms. God, how he loved her. And love was a strange companion for a man who'd thought himself incapable of such an emotion.

How simple it would be if this were any other woman in his arms. But she was his quarry, a suspect in a brutal murder. His brother's murder. And, ironic as it was, this woman was also his love.

In spite of the evidence thus far, Adam knew in his heart that his Rose was neither crook nor killer. Hell, she couldn't harm a fly, much less murder a man in cold blood.

"Who is Katherine?" Jonquil's eyes grew big and liquid.

"Katherine?" He looked at her vaguely, trying to

remember when he had mentioned the name.

"You ran into that house calling out her name. Whoever she is, you must love her a lot."

He nodded wearily. It was time, he decided, to reveal something of his past. Perhaps after Jonquil heard his depraved tale, she would no longer love him. But he had to take the risk. She might not know he was a detective, but she deserved to know who he really was deep inside. Or rather, the sorry fellow he had been in his other life. If she turned her back on him, he wouldn't blame her.

"Katherine was my fiancée," he started to explain. "But love? No, I never loved Katherine. I needed her fortune so I could continue to live the wild life I'd chosen for myself." Adam's voice held a trace of bitterness.

"You see, my esteemed stepfather had decided it was time for his wayward son to settle down and become responsible. With my law studies completed, I was expected to join his law firm. When I wouldn't, he stopped my allowance. Katherine's money was my way out, and she died because of it."

Adam expected Jonquil to pull away, to be repulsed by his confession. But she didn't move or speak.

She felt his body tense. But rather than experiencing disgust, she ached at seeing the raw pain in the depths of his eyes.

"Please, go on." Jonquil's gaze never wavered from his.

"It was during the great Chicago fire that she died. That evening—I remember it well—we had a party to attend, a big social affair in her honor. Not only was Katherine an heiress with a sizable fortune, she was a philanthropist as well."

He paused, searching Jonquil's face as though waiting for her rejection. When none was forthcoming, he continued.

"When I didn't show up at her home to escort her, she went to my apartment on the Southside to find me. Not the best address," he digressed, "but when one doesn't have a lot of money, one makes do."

Jonquil caressed his arm, hoping to ease the pain reflected in his eyes.

"It was down in the Irish quarter, a section of rickety wooden structures, a tinder-dry fuse waiting to be ignited. Because of the very dry weather we'd had that summer, not to mention a four-block alarm the day before, the exhausted fire department was slow in responding. Within minutes the blaze had raged out of control. As if that wasn't enough, a dry prairie wind from the southwest drove the fire to the heart of the city." Adam hesitated. "I'm sure you know all this."

Jonquil vaguely remembered her mother and Gabriel discussing the disaster. "I'm sorry," she said, trying to show her sympathy. "I was much younger then."

He gave her a rueful smile and tweaked her nose. "Of course you were. Well, to make a long story short, Katherine escaped the roped-off area and rushed into my building, thinking I was trapped inside. You see, in those days I drank rather heavily, so she automatically expected the worst."

His fingers tightened on her arm, but she refused to flinch despite her discomfort. He looked down at her, a grim expression on his face. "Are you sure you want to hear this?"

"Please," she whispered. "Whatever you want to tell me."

Adam stared at the ceiling as though trying to recall every detail of that fateful night.

"I watched from the street, and when I caught sight of her I tried to follow. But several onlookers held me back. I yelled her name, trying to get her attention, but in the confusion she didn't hear me. Finally I was able to break away enough to run into the building. By then the first floor was as far as I got."

His jaw clenched, and his mouth thinned into a blanched line. "I remember holding my hand in front of my eyes, to shield my face while I tried to find the stairs. Flames had caught hold of my shirt. All I could see was the horror of hell. Then a fire fighter grabbed me from behind and pulled me out."

Jonquil remembered the mysterious scars on his back. So that was how he'd received them. She tried to absorb his painful memory as if it were her own. "I'm so sorry," she whispered.

"Jonquil, I tried to get to her." Adam's voice was filled with raw emotion. Tears welled in his eyes, and he fought to repress them. "As God is my witness I tried. If I hadn't stood there like some limp-assed coward until it was too late—" He choked on the word, then expelled a deep, mournful sigh. "The building collapsed, and suddenly there was nothing where it had stood but a pile of charred and burning rubble."

Adam's tears flowed freely now and Jonquil kissed them away as they slid down his cheeks. Pressed so close to him, she could feel his body tremble when he gulped back a sob.

"You know, the really sad thing was I never realized until years later that she loved me. Before that time, I was too damned selfish." Self-hatred replaced his sorrow.

"I didn't love her and because I didn't, I never considered that she might love me. Not until she ran into that inferno looking for me. I can't even remember mourning her passing, but by all that's holy, I've lived with her death on my conscience. And it will haunt me forever."

"But today you redeemed yourself," Jonquil answered, pushing the curls back from his forehead. "You risked your life to save that woman, just as you would have saved Katherine if you'd been given the chance."

"Maybe. God only knows I couldn't stand by and let her die. For a moment it was Chicago all over again. But now, after knowing you, I believe I understand the power of love. Katherine was willing to risk her life for me, and she lost it. Now, since I've loved you, I know why she was driven to save me."

"Oh, Adam. My dear, tortured Adam."

Jonquil sought his lips, hoping to draw out some of his pain, to shoulder some of his burden. His tongue moved into her mouth with such urgency that she was shaken. Desperation was in his kiss, then passion.

Adam took her there in the chair. In a raw act of possession, he lifted her naked bottom hidden beneath his robe and, without the luxury of foreplay, pulled her down upon him. Greedily Jonquil responded, ready for him, her urgency matching his own. Their tongues dueled with fevered hunger, while with his every thrust, she became one with him. When at last their frenzied release had come, they gravitated back to earth, breathless and satisfied. Their bodies had bonded in the physical sense, their hearts in the spiritual.

"What now, my Rose? Do you love me still?"

Ebbing spasms keeping their bodies joined, Jonquil held him tight within her woman's core. "I'm powerless to do anything else."

"Promise?" he asked as though he craved the security of the word.

"Promise," she confirmed. And she buried her face in the hollow of his neck until the last of the spasms had subsided.

Chapter Seventeen

Finally easing Jonquil from his lap, Adam stood and peeled the robe from her. Her body was still flushed and glowing from their lovemaking, her nipples erect, forming tight little buds.

Adam's eyes trailed the length of her. "You, my sweet, are so beautiful."

He scooped her into his arms and carried her back to the bed. Stripping off his nightshirt, he lay down beside her and pulled the coverlet up over them.

"Tell me, my pretty flower, how did you ever get such a name?"

Jonquil contemplated his question. If this relationship between her and Adam was to grow, she had to allow him access to some of her secrets. Her name, she decided, was a good place to start.

"My mother named me. You see, she loved flowers, especially roses. Some of her fondest memories were of the beautiful rose gardens she'd known as a young girl on her father's plantation in Mississippi. Yellow roses were her favorites."

For a moment, Jonquil fell silent, transported back to when she was a little girl, thrilling at the story of how she had nearly been named Yellow Rose. "When I showed up with a shock of golden hair, Mama started calling me her yellow rose. But Gabriel argued that Yellow was no fit name for a proper young lady. Since he'd delivered me, he figured he had as much say in my name as Mama did. So they settled on Jonquil Rose."

Jonquil ran a finger playfully along Adam's hard chest. "But Rose is my special name. Only special people call me that."

"Thank you."

She looked questioningly into his eyes. "For what?"

"For allowing me to call you Rose," he said. "For allowing me to feel special."

"You're welcome." Jonquil's hand stilled. "My mother's dead, you know."

"Yes, I heard you tell Liz. I'm sorry." Adam placed a light kiss on her forehead, then waited for her to continue.

"Me, too," she replied, trying not to recall the pain of losing her mother. Then, on a positive note, she added, "But God rest her soul, she's now at peace."

She trailed her finger along Adam's mouth, savoring the feel of him. "I can see now that I was the only good thing left in my mother's life—from the old days. She loved my singing, she loved yellow roses, and she loved my dead father. He died in the war."

Adam listened intently, his detective's mind intruding even now. It was as he suspected—Jonquil didn't know Innes Ball was her father.

"I didn't know," he fibbed.

As if he hadn't interrupted, Jonquil continued. "So when Gabriel and I went on the road, I made a vow to myself: out of respect for her memory, I would always wear black when I performed . . . and a yellow rose. A reminder to me of the roses my mama loved so much."

"So that's why you insisted your concert gowns be black. That's right admirable of you, Miss Trevain. And thank you for sharing your reasons with me."

Adam jumped up and went to the wardrobe. "As much as I hate to do this, I'm taking you back to the Stanfords." He took out a clean shirt and pants, and started to dress.

"I figure we have a few more hours before daybreak, and I want you back in Liz's boarding house before someone discovers you're missing."

"But—"

"No buts. Remember?" Adam reminded her. "I'll take you home and join you for breakfast later. And by the way, that broth you forced down me earlier was awful. I'm starving—for real food."

"Well, your food stock is sadly lacking," Jonquil quipped, reaching out to catch the pants and shirt Adam hurled her way.

"Put those on," he ordered. "It's cold outside."

Eyeing her filthy garments strung across the chair, Jonquil slipped obediently into the clean clothing.

Thirty minutes later, dressed again as a boy, Jonquil stole up the outside stairs of the Stanfords' boarding house. Once on the top landing, she paused to wave before disappearing through the back door.

From the street below, Adam watched her until she was out of sight. He turned back to the buggy, mounted it with one quick stride, then guided the horse down the street.

Moving past the silhouettes of darkened buildings, he was glad to see most of them had escaped the conflagration of the night before. The wind shifted and slapped against his face, bringing with it the acrid smell of scorched wood. The scent reminded him of old ashes in a cold fireplace, but on a much larger scale. Off in the distance a dog howled and a baby cried, then quieted, leaving only the steady clopping of the horse's hooves on the packed road.

Tomorrow all the people who'd lost their possessions would have to start rebuilding from scratch. Adam knew he, too, had some rebuilding to do.

He was anxious to put this Ball case behind him, to bring his brother's killer—whoever that was—to justice and to build a new life with Jonquil. But like the other victims of Eureka Springs, he knew the coming days would not be easy. He only hoped his and Jonquil's fragile foundation would be strong enough to withstand what was sure to come.

"The Lord has a day of vengeance!"

With bombastic eloquence, the preacher's voice rang out over the small crowd of onlookers.

"Streams will be turned into pitch, dust into burning sulfur. The whole land will blaze."

"Amen," the crowd replied in unison.

The remains of a scorched tree stump served as the dais for the traveling minister. He stood upon its charred surface, his arms outstretched in supplication, his words charged with emotion.

"The fire will not be quenched night or day; its smoke will rise forever."

Again his enraptured crowd responded.

"Sinners, the fire you witnessed last night"—grandiosely he waved his arms and cried out even louder—"*this* is smaller than a needle's eye in comparison to *His* fire. Repent, repent you sinners!"

"Someone should put a muzzle on that man," Adam complained to Jonquil as they worked side by side picking up rubbish. "It's not enough that some of these people have lost everything they own, they have to listen to him expound on the devastation of the world."

Ahead, in the distance, Jonquil could make out a black-suited man surrounded by listeners. "I'm sure he means well," she responded. Bending to pick up a piece of crockery that had survived the fire, she showed it to Adam. "We'll put this with the other things. Hopefully some of these possessions will be restored to their owners." She placed it in the wagon being steered down the street.

"Yeah, if the scavengers don't get to it first. Like those." He pointed to several seedy-looking characters plying through the rubble, burlap bags flung over their shoulders. "Looters," Adam mumbled in disgust before he turned away, "they should be run out of town."

Jonquil and Adam continued walking, following the wagon while they and others sifted through the debris. Though it was fatiguing work, Jonquil was gladdened to see that most of the townspeople had united to help clean up the ravished area, and to salvage what was possible from the remains. She felt a real part of the community.

Straightening, she scanned the horizon, recalling the *Morning Echo*'s reports on the fire. Five acres of the town had burned, with an estimated damage of around twenty-five thousand dollars. Thank the Lord there had been no fatalities. Stealing a look at Adam, she shivered to think what might have happened to that poor woman and to him as well.

"*Salvation* is the answer." The preacher's voice floated to Jonquil's ears. "Salvation is yours by casting out your wicked ways."

The voice carried a familiar ring, but Jonquil shoved it to the back of her mind, instead ruminating upon those who heeded his words. Walking slowly, eyes focused upon the ground, she saw the remains of a porcelain doll. Its golden hair had been singed to a sooty gray. Deciding it was unsalvageable, she ignored it and kept moving.

Soon the cart stopped several feet away from where the preacher stood. His fold had increased, making the street nearly impassable.

"Salvation indeed!" Adam grumbled. "The good reverend there should be using his energy to help clean up this town instead of worrying these poor homeless folks about the destiny of their souls. Let's get out of here." He took Jonquil's arm and tried to steer her away.

Nodding in agreement, Jonquil turned to take one last look in the direction of the assembled crowd. When she did, her knees threatened to buckle and she grabbed Adam's arm for support. Her pulse raced as she drew a calming breath.

"Rose, what is it?" Adam stepped closer, holding her elbow to steady her, concern written on his face.

Not wanting Adam to know what had upset her, Jonquil did the only thing she could. "I must be more tired than I realized," she fibbed. "I need a moment to rest."

"Come with me." Leading her to the edge of the road, Adam ordered her to sit upon a stone wall. "Wait here. I'll get you some water."

"No!" She started after him.

At seeing his puzzled expression, Jonquil tried to smooth over her response. "I'll be fine, honest. Too much excitement, I imagine. I'll go back to my room and rest awhile." She turned to leave.

"You'll do no such thing until I bring you some water. Now wait right here until I return." Allowing no further argument, he left her in search of refreshment.

I have to get away, Jonquil thought, burying her face in her hands. I have to find Gabriel and warn him that Cates is in town.

Then she remembered Gabriel had gone with others to nearby Berryville for a load of lumber. For now, anyway, he would not be recognized by the minister.

When Jonquil had run with Gabriel from Prater, she had never expected to see Reverend Cates again. This was the other end of the state, for heaven's sake. What if he recognized her and questioned her about her mother's death? Or the reason for her sudden disappearance from the farm?

Out in the open Jonquil felt exposed and vulnerable. A cold dread knotted her stomach. She simply couldn't take the chance of his recognizing her. It was too much of a risk. *I must get away now!*

Moving from the rocky ledge, Jonquil turned to flee. She'd taken only a couple of steps when she felt a restraining hand upon her shoulder.

Cold, bony fingers dug into her flesh, jerking her to a standstill. Whipped around, Jonquil looked into the colorless eyes of the minister.

"I thought I recognized you."

Cates released her shoulder and rocked back upon his heels. Determined not to cower in his presence, Jonquil met his stare defiantly.

"Still no respect for your elders, I see." The man lowered his hands over his midsection, holding a black Bible like a shield across his front.

"Elders like everyone else should earn respect," Jonquil answered, her chin held high.

In all these months the preacher hadn't changed a bit, she decided, taking in his pose. He was still the sanctimonious clergyman who'd frequented their farm in Prater. The man whose visits had left her mother withdrawn and depressed. The man who'd pestered her mother for the deed to their small farm.

And the man Jonquil had ordered, on his last visit, to leave and never to return.

"What do you want?" she asked, meeting his icy stare with her arctic blue one.

"Why, Miss Trevain, I believe you know what I seek." He leaned closer, not to be deterred. His stale breath wheezed into her face. "Honor thy father and thy mother." He smiled wickedly and hovered near her like a dark, evil shadow.

"I do honor my mother," she replied, drawing her shoulders back, ready to do battle against the sinister man. "It was you who dishonored her, and the faith. Posing as a man of God and badgering her in His Almighty name. You, sir, would do well to remember

305

the Commandments. 'Thou shall not covet thy neighbor's house.'"

Cates's eyes glistened wildly. "You, young woman, listen with deaf ears," he accused. Again he recited the Fourth Commandment, "Honor thy *father* and thy mother."

The emphasis on the word *father* did not go unnoticed. Jonquil retorted by staying, "I honor my father's memory. He died in the war. But this conversation has nothing to do with anything. Now if you'll excuse me . . ." She turned to leave.

Cates bounded in front of her, walking backward as she proceeded.

"Your earthly father, Miss Trevain, is not dead and never has been."

He paused to allow his words to sink in. Throwing his head back, he caused his long, stringy hair to flutter over the bald spots on his head. Then he stared down his beaky nose, adding, "He is alive and well and resides in New York City."

"I beg your pardon?"

Jonquil stopped dead in her tracks. Had she and her mother not endured enough pain at this man's hand? She wondered what new evil he had called upon to make her suffer more. Recalling how her heart would break for her mother after his visits to their farm, she said coldly, "Certainly you lie."

"Lie? Never," Cates rasped between yellowed teeth. He hulked over her, seething with restrained fury. "Your mother was a whore. She gave birth to you out of wedlock. You, my dear, are a misbegotten child."

"A bastard?" Jonquil choked out the word. Then her anger took over. "How dare you soil my mother's name with your blasphemous lies!"

"Nothing more than the devil's spawn," he continued as though she had not spoken, "Lucifer in the guise of Innes Ball." Seemingly pleased with his deduction, Cates crossed his arms over his chest and smiled at her.

Jonquil gave him an incredulous look. "Why would you say such a thing? Are these the same ugly lies you taunted my poor mother with?" If they were, Jonquil could at last understand her mother's depression.

"Your mother, she knew her transgressions were many and had accepted her fate. But I must admit, I admired the old woman's spirit. She never gave me the deed, no matter how much I badgered her for it."

"The deed?" *The same piece of paper the tres-passers were willing to kill for?* "Why on earth did you want the deed? It's only a title to a little farm that means nothing to anyone but us."

"Oh, I never wanted it."

The man was clearly enjoying his cruel mission. "Your father, Innes Ball, wants it. He's desperate to own that worthless piece of land. Why in the devil, I can't imagine. It's only trash." He added for empha-sis, "Like its occupants."

Jonquil did her best to hold her temper. "And what part do you play in this man's ruthless scheme?"

"Money. What else?" He let that piece of informa-tion seep into Jonquil's consciousness before con-tinuing. "And for a while the old man paid me well, knowing my position would allow me to speak of such things to your mother. But the bitch turned out to be more stubborn than your manipulative father had suspected she'd be. So he dumped me and employed other, more persuasive means to get what he wanted."

Other means! The realization hit Jonquil like a sledgehammer. Suddenly everything became clear. The men who had raided their farm and caused her mother's death had been paid to steal the deed to their home. What kind of evil, malicious man would treat his cast-off family that way?

As if a tightly wound spring uncoiled inside her

brain, releasing her from self-control, Jonquil hurled herself against the preacher and flailed him with her fists.

"Evil! Evil! Evil!" she wailed, punctuating each jab to his chest.

"Jonquil, what's the matter with you?"

Suddenly Adam's strong arms encircled her and drew her away from Cates. Collapsing against him, she succumbed to her anguish, her body wracked with great, jerking sobs.

Straightening his frock coat over his skinny shoulders, the preacher swiped at the places where Jonquil had delivered her blows. Intent on having the last word, he added, "If you don't believe me, ask your freedman. He knows the whole story."

"What's the meaning of this?" Adam charged the preacher.

He felt like grabbing the scrawny man and shaking the truth from him. Whatever this stranger had said to Jonquil, the pain of it had caused her terrible despair. Her narrow shoulders shuddered as she let out heart-wrenching moans, and he feared if he released her she'd drop into the street.

"'Tis nothing, brother," Cates explained, then turned toward the curious who'd gathered around them.

"Just another sister," his voice boomed out, "repenting of her sinful ways."

With his hands uplifted, his face turned toward the heavens, Cates led his small flock down the street and away from the couple. His words resounded like a prophet's through the narrow street. "Seek and ye shall find; knock and the door will be opened."

Seek. You can bet your sweet ass I'll seek out your righteous hide before this night is over, Adam silently vowed. Repulsed, he turned his head from the retreating preacher.

First things first, he decided. Looking around, he realized they were only a block away from the

Stanfords'. "It's all right, Rose, I'm here. That son of a bitch won't hurt you again." Without trying to make her stand, Adam scooped her into his arms and carried her to the boarding house. At the door they were met by a concerned Liz.

"Child, what happened?"

But Jonquil kept her face buried in Adam's jacket, sobbing quietly as if her heart would break. "Hurry," Liz instructed, "bring her upstairs."

When they reached the third floor, Liz pushed opened the door to Jonquil's room and allowed Adam to precede her inside. When he had settled Jonquil on the bed, he sat beside her, refusing to budge. Liz stooped to wipe Jonquil's brow with her hand. "Now, dear"—she spoke soothingly—"you're home. Everything will be all right."

Hurrying to the washstand, she poured a bowl of water from the pitcher and brought it back to the bed. Like a mother hen worrying over her young chick, she unfastened the top buttons of Jonquil's shirt-waist, then began sponging her face and neck with the cool, water-soaked rag.

Exchanging worried glances with Adam, she asked, "Whatever happened?"

"I'm not certain," he answered, explaining what he'd seen of the encounter between Jonquil and the preacher, "but I sure as hell plan to find out."

Jonquil's sobs had quieted now, and she had turned her head away, continuing to whimper like a wounded animal. Adam sat beside her, holding her cold hand in his as Liz administered to her. He felt so useless. What could the man possibly have said to cause his beloved such overwhelming grief?

"Should I get Gabriel?" he asked.

"Mr. Sims is in Berryville. He stopped by here this morning and told Jonquil he wouldn't be back until tomorrow. Something about lumber."

Adam leaned over Jonquil and whispered into her ear. "Rose," he pleaded, "can you tell me what's wrong?"

For a response Jonquil only rolled farther away from him and buried her face in the pillow. Her shoulders shook convulsively.

Liz moved away from the bed and placed the rag on the washstand. "You stay with her a few moments," she said. "I have some laudanum downstairs. It should help her sleep."

Adam paced the room, stealing glances at Jonquil who seemed in torment. No manner of coaxing from him could rouse her from her suffering, and relief came over him when Liz finally returned.

The older woman placed a hand upon Adam's shoulder. "Leave us now. I'll help her to change for bed. I'm sure it's more exhaustion than anything else." She flattered him with a reassuring smile. "You can check on her later this evening."

Adam looked over at the landlady. "Before I went for the water, she did say she felt tired. Maybe she is just exhausted." He scratched his head in contemplation before turning to leave.

From the doorway he looked back at the desolate woman on the bed. "Take care of her," he whispered. "I'll see you both later."

Adam exited through the back door of the house and loped down the long back stairs to the street, all the while considering Jonquil's actions. Her problem involved more than fatigue. Now all he had to do was find the mealy-mouthed reverend and get his answers.

With a lighted match Adam checked his timepiece. Midnight. He dropped the watch back inside his pocket. His legs were stiff from having waited in the alley for so long. After what seemed half the night, the lights in the Stanfords' boarding house were finally extinguished, save the one that shone from Jonquil's room. Still he waited, to be certain everyone inside was fast asleep.

The minutes passed slowly. Adam snuggled deeper into his jacket, scanning the town wrapped in a blanket of cold air. A thousand stars twinkled in the clear sky. A half-moon reflected silvery light on the tin rooftops that dotted the hillsides.

Adam's breath rushed out in steamy, white clouds while the events of the day crawled in and out of his thoughts. His search for the minister had been easily accomplished. However, pulling information from the man had been another story. It was as though the preacher suspected he was more than a concerned friend.

Spouting Biblical lore instead of answering questions outright, the high-handed preacher had irked Adam. In the end, all he had learned was that Cates had visited Jonquil's farm in Prater. The man had suggested that his reference to her parents had probably upset the girl and went so far as to offer his condolences.

That the preacher had mentioned both her parents had seemed strange, for Jonquil never referred to her father. Whatever it was, this man seemed to have some link to Jonquil's past. Maybe even to Innes Ball. And Adam had no intention of quitting until he knew the whole story.

The light still burned in Jonquil's window, and Adam wondered if she was still asleep. When he'd dropped in to check on her before dinner, she had slept through his entire visit, never waking, never giving him an opportunity to ask her any questions about what had distressed her so. He'd not had the chance to hold and comfort her.

But now it was time. Jonquil knew well enough how Adam felt about her. If they were to have a future as a couple, she had to confront her past and share her plight with him. If she knew anything at all about Innes Ball, it was time to say so. Adam loved Jonquil, and he was certain any problems they had could be worked out together.

Deciding he'd waited long enough, he stepped out from the black shadows and headed for the light at the top of the stairs.

Jonquil lay awake, staring at the ceiling. At the round pattern of light given off by the small lantern on her bedside table. Unsolicited tears slipped from her eyes, trailing hot paths down the sides of her face before disappearing into her hairline.

Cates's cruel words resounded over and over in her brain—*Whore . . . bastard . . . Innes Ball.* Jonquil knew in her heart that her sweet and gentle mother could never be a whore. But what of the man named Innes Ball? Was he truly her father?

She had so many unanswered questions about her past. Living in the security of her mother's and Gabriel's love, she'd never thought to look beyond their explanations of her situation. Now, since coming to Eureka Springs, Jonquil knew there were pieces of her mother's past she should have insisted be revealed.

Another sob choked her, and she bit the back of her hand to control it. Recalling that horrible day, she was again uneasy. Had this Innes Ball sent those ruffians to the farm to murder them?

And was she really his bastard child? If so, how could Adam love her when her own father had tossed her aside as though she were nothing? Her stomach churned with shame.

"Oh Adam. My sweet, sweet Adam."

Feeling that her heart might break, she whispered to the silent room. How could she ever face him again, having learned these horrible truths about herself? "I'm so unworthy," she groaned.

When Adam had visited her before dinner, she'd wanted to run to him and have him chase all the ugliness away. Instead, like a coward, she'd feigned sleep so she wouldn't have to talk with him.

But he deserved better than that. Although it would be easier to escape inside herself to keep from facing him, Jonquil knew she couldn't. If she did, then her worst fears would be realized. She would be like her mother. No, she raged. She would confront him soon, regardless of the outcome.

Her thoughts now spun off in another direction. Gabriel. She had to talk with him. Poor, sweet man. All these years he'd done what he could to protect her. Now the time had come for truth. She had to know.

"Rose, it's me."

Adam whispered to her from across the room, but she was certain she dreamed it, that it was nothing more than her heart's longing surfacing in her mind.

"Rose, it's Adam. Are you awake?" Again his voice possessed her.

The translucent waves on the ceiling shattered into a million pieces. The shadow of a man darkened the lighted space.

"Rose."

Jonquil directed her eyes toward the voice, suddenly aware of puffed and swollen lids. Adam materialized. Her heart's deepest yearning had summoned her love.

"Adam?"

In an instant he was beside her, and she was in his arms, sobbing against the solid warmth of his chest.

"Rose, oh, Rose. I was so worried."

He kissed her lips, then his mouth stopped the fresh tears as they slid from her eyes. "You mustn't cry anymore."

"Oh, Adam," she responded in a low, suffering voice. "I've missed you so."

"I'm here now. Won't you please tell me what that man said to upset you?"

Jonquil felt so vulnerable, so fragile, like a feather in the wind. Adam held her now, cradling her, inviting her to share her heartache. But would he still

313

want her when he learned that she might be a bastard child?

"Tell me, please," he whispered. His expression mirrored her own sorrow and gave her the support she needed to tell him.

"The man we saw is named Reverend Cates. He used to come to the farm."

Jonquil told Adam about the preacher's upsetting visits to her mother. "But today he said my real father lived. That he did not die in the war as I'd been led to believe."

Adam settled Jonquil in the crook of his arm, his head propped against the pillow. She lay sideways against him, her face turned upward toward his. Beneath her palm, which lay on his chest, she could feel the muffled beating of his heart. He said nothing, but waited for her to continue.

"He said my mother was a whore. That I was born out of wedlock." Voicing Cates's insinuations only renewed her pain, but Jonquil forced herself to continue.

"He said my father's name is Innes Ball, that he lives in New York." In her grief she collapsed against Adam.

So Cates had said more to Jonquil than he'd indicated. Adam told himself he should have known. He had never trusted roadside preachers, self-ordained, or whatever else they elected to call themselves. Most had never set foot inside a church, but they preached to and preyed upon the less fortunate. They traveled from one backwater to another, promising people salvation for a return on their contributions.

Preaching fire and brimstone, these men convinced the poor souls they attracted that the more they gave, the better their chances of not burning in hell. Adam should have realized Cates was no different from the countless others he'd come across. The preacher's heartlessness proved he lacked the grace of God.

314

"Why would my mother and Gabriel have lied to me all these years?" Jonquil asked.

"I'm sure they were trying to protect you, to keep you from being hurt," Adam offered, stroking her back.

"But even so," she insisted, "I had a right to know."

"Yes, you did. Nonetheless, whatever Cates said about the circumstances of your birth doesn't affect the kind of person you are."

He lifted her chin and looked deep into her eyes. "You're a beautiful and caring woman, just as I'm sure your mother was before you."

"Do you really think so?"

"I know so. Why else would I love you and want to spend the rest of my life with you?"

Jonquil took in his words, hearing for the first time that Adam wanted a future with her. Any woman would have given all her tomorrows to hear this admission. But his words, reassuring though they were, also troubled her.

She wanted to tell him everything . . . about that fatal day on the farm, what had happened when the strangers had come, and about the deaths of those three men. She wanted to tell him about the U.S. marshal who had intervened to save her life, and about why she and Gabriel had chosen to run.

He had to hear it all. If they were meant to be together, there could be no more secrets between them. Tomorrow, after Gabriel returned from Berryville and she'd had a chance to speak with him, she would make a clean breast of it, she decided.

"There's more," she continued, "and you need to hear it. I've told both you and Liz about my mother's depression, but never how her condition deteriorated toward the end of her life."

While Jonquil talked, Adam listened, his fingers comforting her as they stroked her back.

"She'd go for weeks as lucid as you and I are right

315

now, and then she'd have one of her spells." Jonquil smoothed a strand of hair from her face before continuing.

"Then she'd take to her bed and wouldn't speak for days. When she finally got up, she'd be withdrawn and distant, almost as though she were frightened of something or someone. Now, when I think back, I realize she usually had a spell after one of Reverend Cates's visits."

Adam nodded, encouraging her to continue. Interesting, he thought, maybe Jonquil's mother had good reason to be frightened after Cates's calls. Maybe he'd threatened her in some way. The more he thought about it, the more convinced Adam became that Cates and Ball were connected.

The possibility that Cates had killed his brother jelled in his mind. At last everything seemed to be falling into place. Soon he'd be able to wrap up this case and he and Jonquil could get on with their lives.

"So you see"—Jonquil's voice pulled him back from his preoccupation—"if her illness is hereditary, then it's possible I might pass the same disorder on to my children."

"Don't believe it," Adam assured her. "I'm certain your mother's condition was brought on by the terrible things that happened to her."

"That's exactly what one of the doctors at the Invalid's Association told me. He said distress caused all kinds of problems, both physical and mental."

Adam smiled. It was the kind of smile that said, "I believe in you," and it reached clear to the bottom of Jonquil's heart.

"I'm not saying what Cates told you is true, but say it was," Adam went on, "your mother had a big burden to shoulder alone. I think that responsibility would be enough to depress anyone at one time or another."

"Then if we had children . . . " Jonquil blushed at her own impulsiveness.

Laying his finger upon her lips, Adam pulled her to him. Picking up where she had left off, he said, "Not a chance." He sealed this opinion with a heart-stopping kiss.

In very few words, Adam Coulter had made Jonquil feel reborn. She marveled at his ability to lessen her pain, to make her focus on their tomorrows. She supposed that was part of the power of love.

Her mood lightened once again, Jonquil teased, "Not a chance that they would inherit my family curse, or that we would have children?"

"Definitely the first. I intend to work very hard upon the latter." And Adam proceeded to show her where to begin.

Soon all their garments lay upon various furnishings around the room. Jonquil's lawn nightrail swagged over a curtain rod, a cast-off valance above the lace panel. Adam's ruffled shirt puddled atop a pie table, mimicking the finest of table linens in the soft glow of the lantern light. His black wool trousers made it only as far as the bedpost, where they hung like a drooping flag. His socks remained upon his feet.

Together the two rocked in the throes of passion, their moans and sighs music to the once-quiet little room. At the very culmination of their act of love, the lamp sputtered into darkness. And the lovers floated back down to earth embraced by velvety blackness.

Chapter Eighteen

Adam rolled over onto his side and stretched out his arm to feel Jonquil's warmth. Instead, it met a cool void where she had lain only a short time before. Ascending through a sleepy haze, he came fully awake.

It was early yet, the room still cloaked in the subtle light of a late autumn dawn. Nevertheless, morning had arrived and with it Jonquil's responsibilities downstairs. She'd dressed so quietly, he'd never heard her, although he thought he remembered a feather-light touch to his forehead, nothing more than an angel's kiss.

Already he missed the sweet feel of her nestled against him in sleep. On impulse he leaned over and buried his face in her pillow, savoring the lingering fragrance that was uniquely hers.

Rolling over onto his back, his hands beneath his head, Adam stared at the ceiling. He couldn't remember when he'd felt so rested. Ever since Jonquil had first lain with him, he'd begun to know an inner peace he hadn't believed existed.

Memories of the past night flitted through his mind—the trust she'd shown in disclosing her innermost fears, her gentle loving, and lastly her full acceptance of him, flaws and all. There remained only one cloud between them.

She didn't know he was a detective.

This weighed upon him like an anvil. But having heard Jonquil's admissions, having watched her sob against his chest, he found that the puzzle's pieces were finally slipping into place. Before long, he would be able to tell her everything.

It had taken quite a while to calm her. At learning she was illegitimate, she'd assumed a shame that until now had been foreign to her. The fact that her old friend, Gabriel, had known all along had shaken the world off its axis.

During the night Adam had held her close, reminding her that any facts kept from her had been held back out of love. Finally her tears had subsided, and he had turned her thoughts to their future.

As far as he was concerned, nothing in her past mattered other than that she was a survivor, that she was strong and good. He was glad he'd sneaked up to her room. The townspeople, had they known, might have been prepared to throttle him for ruining their new singer's virtue, but he knew he'd made a wise move.

Adam swung his bare legs out of bed and picked up his pocket watch from the nightstand. Seeing the time, his brows shot up in astonishment. Jumping jackrabbits, he'd slept till eight o'clock.

Looking at the half-opened curtains, Adam saw the drab light beyond. Must be fog on the mountain, he thought. It wouldn't burn off until the sun hit it. Hopefully the other boarders on this floor would still be at breakfast or would be gone for the morning. Otherwise, how he'd manage to escape being seen he had no idea.

Hastily he took a sponge bath, grateful for the water bowl left on the dry sink. Checking his face in the overhead mirror, he ran a hand over his stubbled chin. There'd be no calling on Jonquil today, or

319

anyone else for that matter, until he'd cleaned himself up properly at home. Besides, with the information his beloved had furnished, he had a lot of thinking to do before passing it on to Clayton.

As he put on pants and boots Adam decided this case was nearly solved. After last night, he could turn his thoughts to more likely suspects in his brother's murder than the fragile flower who had lain sobbing in his arms.

In revealing to Adam that he had asked about Jonquil's parents, the bombastic Reverend Cates had unwittingly dropped one hint too many. Adam was certain the man knew much more than he had intimated.

Jonquil was no more a murderer than Adam himself. But Cates or Ball might be. Deciding this, Adam let his heart open to the rays of sunlight that had been denied him for so long. Soon he would have nothing to concern himself with but planning for his future with Jonquil. He felt so good he wanted to shout out the happy news.

Slipping into his shirt, he found himself humming—something he couldn't remember doing in years. She did this to me, he thought. My beautiful yellow Rose. She'd made him happy, made him want to hug the world. By God, he was reincarnated.

He remade the bed, smiling at the rumpled sheets. Then, taking his Stetson and jacket from the trunk at the foot of the bed, he started for the door.

A thought suddenly struck him. He had to make himself scarce so no one saw him leave, but he hated to go without one last kiss. If he couldn't deliver it in person, he most certainly could set it down in prose. Flinging his hat back down on the trunk, he walked over to the writing desk and pulled out the chair.

A blank notepad lay before him. Still humming, he picked up the black pen beside it, mulling over the words he would write. Because they'd both be busy this morning, helping out where they could, Adam's invitation for a one o'clock rendezvous had been enthusiastically received.

Perhaps they would shop for some necessities for a few of the homeless. At any rate, it would be an excuse to be together. Jonquil had said she'd be busy until then, working with some of the women and serving the noon meal, but by one o'clock she'd be ready for a break and a good meal herself.

Prepared to confirm their date, Adam started to plunge the pen's tip into the inkwell. Then his arm stilled in midair.

On the desk, amid stacked books, stood Jonquil's inkwell. Not just any inkwell, not like the one he'd offered to buy her in the dressmaker's salon. This one was unique. Faceted like a crystal bowl, it was topped by a filigreed silver lid. It was beautiful.

It was his brother's.

Adam heard, rather than felt, the pen drop to the desk. With a shaking hand he reached for the inkwell that Simon had brought back from Mexico. Embellished in curlicue script were the initials *SHT*, like those on his belt buckle engraved to hint at Simon's favorite expression.

Oh, Lord, I'd know it anywhere.

He placed it upon the desk for fear his trembling would cause it to fall and shatter, as he felt himself about to do. No, he told himself, this can't be happening. How in God's name did Jonquil come to have this in her room? Where did . . . ?

And all at once he knew. All the explanations she'd given him—all the excuses he'd given himself—simply didn't add up. Not anymore.

Not with Simon's inkwell on her desk.

For a moment longer he stared at the incriminating evidence before his mind hurtled into action. Searching the desktop, he fumbled among the books, looking for something—anything—that might refute the proof he'd just seen with his own eyes.

He ran his hands along the front of the desk, finding a wide, shallow drawer. His mind screamed, Open it, open it! His heart threatened to break if he did.

Slowly he pulled the drawer forward against his waist, then rummaged through the contents. Inside he found more paper, envelopes, and a Bible. Pulling out the Testament, he ruffled through the pages, finding no further evidence of Jonquil's implication in Simon's death. Interesting, he thought, laying the holy book atop the notepad, people usually kept important papers within its pages. All that had drawn Adam's attention was the inscription inside the front cover: To my beautiful daughter. Mama.

Still his fingers roamed, lifting and shuffling sheet music, until he touched a flat suede pouch about the size of a woman's reticule. He hated himself for digging into Jonquil's private belongings, but more for the fact that, in so doing, he was destroying any future they might have had. But whatever secrets she had left, Adam had to know, regardless of the damage done to his heart.

He was, first and foremost, a lawman.

Opening the pouch, he dumped its contents onto the desk. Out fell a folded document and a hard, linen-wrapped object. Even as he reached for the first item, Adam had a premonition. After reading only the first two lines he knew he'd found the missing deed to Margaret Mary Trevain's property—the missing paper that Innes Ball so badly wanted.

Almost as an afterthought, he laid down the paper and picked up the flat, rounded object wrapped in a handkerchief. Curious, he unfolded the edges of the cloth and heard a pained whimper escape his lips.

There, cupped in the linen like a Communion wafer lay the silver badge of a federal lawman. Simon's badge. Not the six-pointed star of a deputy

322

United States marshal, but a five-pointed star surrounded by a circle and marked U.S. Special Deputy. Simon had been proud of the distinction.

Cold certainty shot through his veins. Jonquil Rose Trevain had, after all, killed his brother.

Still holding the badge, Adam laid his elbows on the desk and buried his head in his hands. Not in all his life, not even when his father had left home when Adam was but a child, or when his fiancée had perished, had he felt such total despair.

So this was what his stepfather had meant when he'd said Adam would one day earn his due for all the misery he'd caused those who loved him. So this was how it felt to love.

But despite his pain, Adam knew he'd never hurt anyone as badly as he had just been wounded. It felt like being buried alive.

He retrieved the inkwell, the document, and the badge, and placed all three in the pouch. Rising from the desk, he slipped the small bag into his coat pocket, then picked up his hat. While it had, indeed, been a wise move he'd made in coming here last night, he knew it had also been the worst one he'd ever made.

Powell Clayton stared at him across the threshold. "What the devil happened to you?"

"Nothing." Adam stormed past the general into the foyer, his shaky voice barely audible. "Hell, everything."

He looked around, half-expecting Addie to come pouring into the hallway, greeting him with her usual, bubbly smile. He didn't think he could stand it.

The lilt of feminine voices trailed through the closed double doors leading into the massive parlor. Adam started to back off toward the front door. "I'm sorry," he apologized. "This may be a bad time."

Clayton shook his head. "Addie's having a meeting with some women. The fire may be out, but there's still a lot to be done." He added, "The children are next door."

Clayton looked tired, as though he had aged overnight. The fire had been devastating. So many people had been displaced. But the expression on his face held more than fatigue, it was fraught with grim expectation, as if he were braced for a powerful kick to the stomach. God, if only I had been so prepared, Adam silently protested.

"It's all right," the older man said. "We can talk. Let's go into my study."

Adam followed Clayton into the small paneled library on the opposite side of the hall, then waited for him to close its double doors behind him.

He held his Stetson in his hand, hardly able to keep his trembling under control—fury mixed with anguish. At any moment he was certain his heart would rip into a thousand jagged pieces.

"I've got our killer."

He slammed his hat against his knee and began to pace.

"Sit."

Clayton gestured to the two chairs on which only weeks ago they had sat discussing their suspicions of Jonquil's guilt and the possibility of her innocence. That possibility had now dried up, vanished. And along with it, Adam discovered, so had his soul. He had believed in this woman—his woman, he'd come to think—only to learn she was nothing more than a clever, cold-blooded killer.

And all this time he'd blamed himself for his masquerade. Compared to her he was a babe in the woods.

So intent was his focus on his pain, he didn't see that Clayton had poured him a whiskey until the man shoved it into his hand. He also didn't realize he'd nearly recreased his Stetson until Clayton gently tugged it from his grasp and laid it on his desk.

The general seated himself. "All right, son, drink that down, then tell me what's happened."

At his behest Adam took a throat-scorching gulp and let the whiskey slide down his gullet. Clayton sat quietly waiting, as though he had all the time in the world for his guest.

After Adam had drained the small glass, he felt slightly less trembly though far from calm. But he needed to talk, to come to grips with this damned, sordid case. From his coat pocket he pulled out the leather pouch and thrust it at Clayton.

He'd wished a thousand times over in the last hour that he'd never heard the black-gowned, black-hearted temptress sing. That he'd never seen in her lying eyes a look of innocence. That he'd never fallen in love with her.

He, the young renegade who had used women for his own means, now had been exploited. In the name of duty he had planned to seduce a suspect only to be violated himself. Adam could have withstood being professionally thwarted, but such a personal betrayal sapped the life blood out of him more effectively than a Bowie knife in the back.

I swear to you, Simon, I'll bring her in. It's as good as done.

"Son," the general was saying, "I think you'd better begin at the beginning."

Pulled from his thoughts, Adam looked over to see that the man had emptied the pouch. In his hand he held the incriminating deed and Simon's belongings. Oh, God, Adam muttered, running his hand down over his chin, he'd never dreamed the truth could hurt so badly.

*   *   *

325

The Stanfords' buggy headed toward the Clayton House. Inside, Jonquil fairly bubbled with anticipation. The breakfast dishes finally put away, she had hopped into her landlord's equipage as Henry Stanford headed out to do some errands.

Her hands still carried the wrinkles resulting from soapy dishwater, temporarily. They looked to her much as her soul had felt all these months while carrying her menacing secret. At times her heart had been so heavy, she was sure it affected her breathing.

Not anymore.

This afternoon her burden would be lifted. She was so eager for one o'clock to come, she had Henry pull out his pocket watch for a second glance, just to make sure time hadn't stood still.

"You probably haven't missed much," Henry was saying, referring to the meeting going on at Addie Clayton's. "It's barely after nine."

Jonquil knew a tinge of guilt at her own preoccupation while at this very moment every respectable citizen in town was trying to help in the aftermath of the fire. She gave him a fervent tilt of her head, "But there's so much to be done. I just want to do my part."

This was not a day for daydreaming. There were people to be helped, homes to be reconstructed, lives to be rebuilt.

Jonquil looked around the street teeming with wagons and pedestrians. Along the boardwalks women carried baskets, presumably filled with much-needed clothing and foodstuffs. Men ambled out of stores with burlap sacks slung over their shoulders, calling to one another to load up lumber and supplies for another trip to the devastated area.

After today, when she finally would open her heart and guard no more secrets, nothing would stand in Jonquil's way to becoming a respectable citizen. When she confided in Adam, he would know what to do to turn everything right.

For so long she had wondered if she ever could share her past with someone she could totally trust. Finally, she had found that someone. With Adam at her side, she would be able to face any demon who threatened her . . . including the man who had abandoned her mother.

The buggy pulled to a stop in front of the ex-governor's home. Jonquil gathered her skirts around her and alighted. On the driver's seat Henry Stanford checked his watch one more time, supposedly for his own sake. Jonquil knew that instead it was for her.

"Nine twenty-two," he said. "Not so bad considering all this traffic." He gave her a satisfied nod. "Shall I return for you later?"

"Thank you, no," Jonquil called, pulling her cape around her shoulders. "I can walk back after we're finished." With that she waved him off and started up the walkway. For the number of women expected this morning, she noticed a marked absence of conveyances out front. Obviously, other drivers had deposited their passengers and had gone on their way.

At the hitching post beside the fence stood one lone horse, a handsome mahogany stallion with a white blaze on his face. She immediately recognized Adam's Ranger. Her heart gave a sudden lurch at the thought that her beloved might also be inside.

From the time he had met the Claytons, Adam had seemed fond of the likable couple and their children. Perhaps even now he was, at Addie's request, offering suggestions to the assembled ladies.

Come right in, read the note on the front door. Jonquil turned the knob, understanding the greeting to be addressed to the women who would be arriving. Once inside, she quietly closed the door and headed for the massive hall tree just outside the closed doors to the study. Coats and hats adorned its hooks, and more were stacked in a mountainous pile on the bench beneath, half-covering the tree's oversized mirror.

Jonquil fumbled with the buttons of her cape, checking her appearance in the mirror's reflection. From the parlor drifted the enthusiastic voices of the assembled ladies, and she strained to hear Adam's. What a sight for sore eyes he would be. Her hands shook while she unfastened the last button on her cloak, then stilled. Adam's voice filtered into the hall, but not from the parlor. It came from the study instead.

Jonquil inched toward the closed entrance to the study, waiting for his next words. He must be here not for the women but for business with Addie's husband. Without thought of eavesdropping, she quietly held her ear to the juncture of the double doors.

From within she could hear the low, quiet voice of the general. She could also hear Adam's—loud, distinct, and angry.

". . . damned woman didn't have the sense . . . " he roared, startling Jonquil with his intensity.

Dear Lord, she thought, her fingers going to her mouth. Truly someone had upset him. What woman had insulted him to the point that he had to take his complaint to Governor Clayton?

Jonquil eased away from the door, wondering if she should intervene. The general didn't seem able to calm him down. Perhaps she could. She'd wait just a moment more.

"Simon never deliberately hurt anyone in his life." The fiery words were Adam's.

Simon? Who in the world was Simon? she wondered. Obviously someone close to him. Adam sounded anguished. He must have received bad news. This Simon—possibly he was a good friend, a relative—and the woman were having marital prob-

328

lems . . . or some ill had come to them.

Jonquil could understand Adam's seeking advice from a wise, older friend. But now that they were so close, she wanted to be the one to comfort him. If he hurt, then so did she. Raising her hand to knock, she debated whether or not to do so.

Perhaps she shouldn't interfere, after all. The last thing she wished was to embarrass him. Besides, unless he asked for sympathy from her, it really wasn't any of her business.

She started to move away.

". . . and I, a self-respecting detective, believed a cock-and-bull story like that? When all the time she had the evidence in her possession?"

Jonquil froze. Still, she tried to think of other explanations for his statements.

". . . My brother went to his Maker for this?" By now Adam was practically yelling. ". . . his inkwell, his badge, and a damned, sorry title to a worthless piece of land."

At his last words Jonquil's knees turned to water. Adam's tormented remarks struck her like lightning, and she reached out to steady herself against the adjacent wall.

Oh, my God! He knew. Before she'd had a chance to explain.

Jonquil's hopes for the future crumbled into nothingness. He'd found everything in her room. His words ricocheted around in her head, colliding with one another in complete pandemonium.

She had to make some sense of this. She gathered her cape around her, numbly stumbled to the front entry, and opened the door.

Adam. Simon. Brothers.

She spoke their names, attempting to form a new sense of reality. Adam was a detective. Simon had been a marshal. The man who had died trying to save her finally had a name. And now his brother had come after her, thinking she had killed him.

This man she'd allowed into her life, into her heart, had tricked her. Tricked her into loving him. In a daze, she started walking, down the steps and to the street.

Detective . . . detective . . . detective . . . The word thundered through her brain with every step she took.

At the end of the street she turned the corner and headed up the hill. The farther she walked, the faster she climbed, heedless of the wind that rippled through her cape and flitted through her upswept hair, of the crowds who passed her on the street. Heedless, even of the icy numbness spreading through her stomach. Later she would cry, when she had the time. For now, time was running out.

Lest she encounter Liz or one of the roomers, she chose to enter the boarding house by the back steps which started at street level. Purposefully she took them two by two until, nearly oxygen-starved, she reached her landing.

Once in her room she packed, methodically opening drawers and shoving their contents into two large carpetbags. Her fancy gowns she left in the large pine wardrobe. That part of her life was now over. She took one last look at them before closing the wardrobe doors.

From the secret compartment in her trunk she retrieved half of her saved money. She hastily scribbled a note to Liz, asking her to have the trunk delivered to Gabriel. Their trunk, it was filled with memories and meager possessions.

She thought of her beloved friend, her protector. He couldn't save her now. But she could try to protect him.

Jonquil wilted onto the bed's counterpane beside the open luggage. In the confusion she had not once thought of her defender.

She steadied herself by grasping the bedpost and devised a hasty plan. Adam might have questions for Gabriel, but he would come looking for her. To him, Gabriel was her servant, loyal to his mistress. And if Gabriel didn't know where she had gone, he wouldn't have to lie about her whereabouts.

Now she was on her own. No more would her guardian be forced to run from something he had never been able to prevent or disprove. If she was caught, Jonquil would plead her case and seek the court's mercy. She might serve years in prison, but she would not be hung. Of that she felt sure. She was a young woman, and white.

Not so with Gabriel. He was a man, and black.

And he deserved this new beginning. A talented musician, he had made friends here. Jonquil's only regret was that he still longed for his Keely, back home in Prater.

She rose from the bed and walked over to the corner where her banjo stood in its black leather case. Like a mother bidding goodbye to her dead child, she reverently laid it into the trunk and closed the lid, setting the lock in place.

At precisely eleven o'clock, in front of the Basin Hotel on Spring Street, Jonquil climbed aboard the stage headed south. The driver tossed the last mailbag atop the coach and saw that her luggage was secured. It seemed forever before he finally mounted to his own seat.

Within seconds the coach jolted forward along the dusty street, marking the start of Jonquil's long journey. Alone inside, she watched the hotel fade into the distance, saw that the town and its people were carrying on business as usual. For them nothing had changed.

For her everything had.

No longer was she whole, with hope for a future. No longer did she have the security of being loved, of trusting Adam, a man who had lied to her from the moment they had met.

Only two hours remained until one o'clock, the magic moment she had naively thought would change her life. By then the miles she'd covered would prove a slight advantage over Adam Coulter, the hunter, when he finally began looking for her.

She hoped it would be enough.

Within the same hour Adam took the back stairs to the third landing of the Stanfords' boarding house, reliving with every step his earlier ascension to Jonquil. At that time he had known such fulfillment he'd thought it too good to be true. Obviously, it had been.

This time he lunged up the stairs, determined to catch his quarry before she suspected his discovery.

Moments later, he stood stupefied in Jonquil's old room, now bare except for the finery in the wardrobe and the large, wooden trunk. So his angel in black had disappeared. And she had taken his soul with her.

He moved to the desk where he had discovered Jonquil's treachery and read her note to Liz. According to this, Gabriel would still be around. Why the hell Jonquil had left in such a rush he couldn't guess, but for the moment he would head for the nearest source of information.

He knew better than to go himself. If he frightened the man, he would never extract any details from him. And the way Adam felt at the moment, he simply could not risk losing control and taking out his anger on Gabriel.

Downstairs he found Henry Stanford, who had just pulled up in his buggy. "I need a favor, sir, if you have the time," he requested, trying to keep his voice under control. "Would you mind riding over to the bath house? Jonquil has a trunk in her room that Gabriel Sims must pick up this morning." He looked nonchalantly at his watch. "He should be back from Berryville by now." No need in upsetting Stanford who seemed unaware that a problem existed. "I'd go myself, but I'm to meet someone here."

"No trouble, son. Be happy to. I'll even help him load the trunk and take it where it's to go, since Miss Jonquil doesn't require me to pick her up."

Adam stared at the man. In a forced, even voice he asked, "Oh, and where might she be today?"

"Over at the Claytons'. Some of the ladies are meeting there this morning to try to help with relief. Took her there myself." With that, Henry Stanford stepped back into his buggy. "We'll be back soon."

"Thanks," Adam answered. "Just send Gabriel up to Jonquil's room. Liz showed me where it is. I'll wait for him there."

Adam's insides turned to stone. Jonquil had been at the Claytons'. She must have overheard him. It was the only explanation he could think of. And now she was gone.

This time he took the inner stairs up to Jonquil's third-floor room and closed the door to wait. Pulling the ladderback chair from the desk, he sat and propped his feet on the trunk at the end of the bed. The empty room held echoes of his night with Jonquil and whispers of what a fool he'd been to open his heart. His chest tightened with acute and primitive grief.

He closed his eyes, reliving the hours when they had shared this bed. How desperately he'd needed her, and today she'd thrown that need in his face. Jonquil Rose Trevain would pay for this betrayal, by God. He'd see to it.

Before long he heard Gabriel on the stairs,

humming lightheartedly. Pushing his Stetson back on his head, Adam laid his gun across his lap, then waited for the light rap.

"Come in," he announced, keeping a tight rein on his temper.

The door opened and Gabriel stepped inside, holding his black felt hat in his hand. Taking in the deserted room, his face froze. He looked over at Adam, his visage becoming stony. His breathing quickened in fear at the sight of the drawn gun.

Deliberately, Adam removed his boots—one at a time—from the top of the trunk, as if he'd just awakened from a catnap and was about to resume his daily routine. When he stood, the two front legs of his chair hit the floor with a dull, scraping thud.

He nodded toward the locked trunk, gazing with an air of empty conquest at the dark, rugged face before him.

"You got a key to this thing? Or do I have to shoot off the damned lock?"

Chapter Nineteen

Gabriel stood before him, looking lost and bewildered. His quick eyes scanned the room. "Where is she?" he demanded. It was a simple question, delivered with the anxiety of a parent looking for his child.

"Ha!" Adam roared. "That's a good one." He took a threatening step forward. "I'm asking you the same question."

His pistol drawn and within Gabriel's sight, he stood no more than a whisper away from the man who until recently had been Jonquil's shadow. Though Adam delivered no blow, the man he confronted looked as though he'd been struck in the face.

To Adam, Gabriel Sims had always seemed tall, lean, and strong as an oak. But now, as he looked into those coal black eyes, the man visibly shrank before him.

Unable to retreat any farther, Gabriel made no move to fight Adam off. He choked out a throaty answer. "I-I don' know what you mean."

"Like hell you don't," Adam accused, his voice icy. He stepped back. Reaching for the paper on the desk, he thrust it into the man's hands. "Read that," he growled, "then tell me you still don't know anything."

Gabriel scanned the paper, then looked back at his accuser. "Please, Mr. Coulter," he begged, "I still don' know what's happened here. I ain't seen Rosie since yesterday." He shook his head, his hands trembling. "Everything seemed fine then."

He suddenly looked Adam square in the eye with an accusing stare. "As I remember, she was with you . . . and happy enough. So what'd you do to run her off?" He started forward. "Did you hurt that gal?" His eyes took on a fiery expression.

Hurt her? Adam thought. The first woman to bring life back to his soul had yanked it right out from under him with her lies. "I'd say not," he returned, the gun still braced in his fingers. "I wish I'd never laid eyes on her."

"You're not makin' any sense."

"Then let me see if I can clear this up for you." Adam pasted a callous smile across his face. "Allow me to introduce myself. Adam Coulter of the Pinkerton Detective Agency, brother of one Simon Hector Thompson of the United States Marshal's Service." His gaze burned into the black man's face. "Ever seen anybody else with these eyes?"

At his revelation, Gabriel stared back, first at Adam's face, then at the fancy ruffled shirt that had become his trademark over the last weeks. "You ain't . . . ?" He ran his fingers through wiry, graying hair. "You told us you was a manager. You made us believe in you. And all this time . . ."

Gabriel's voice trailed off, his shoulders visibly slumping under the barrage of facts Adam had just slung at him. Then he straightened. "You lied to us."

If Adam had thought the black man would cower when confronted, he had been wrong. Now, as he watched Jonquil's guardian regain his dignity, he grudgingly admired the man. If nothing else, Gabriel was loyal to his charge.

"I don' know no Simon Hector Thompson." Gabe cocked his head as if trying to remember some vague detail. "And I don' understand your riddles, either. What do you mean about your eyes?"

Gabriel put up a brave enough front, all right, acting the innocent. Adam had to give him credit for that. But he was convinced that with his memory triggered, the man would remember every detail Adam wanted to hear.

Quietly, he moved over to the window, pulled back the curtain, and looked out. "Simon and I were half brothers," he explained, scanning the street below. "But our mother always said she could tell her two sons were related because of our eyes. They were so dark, she always said they looked like two burnt holes in a blanket."

He turned back to the other man in the room. "But maybe you didn't have time to study his eyes before you and your female companion killed him."

Recognition dawned on Gabriel's face. His shoulders heaved. The gasp that escaped him was strangled, like the final breath of a dying man. "No," he muttered, crushing his hat to his stomach, "it didn't happen that way."

"No?" Adam's taunt was as light as an invitation to a Sunday School picnic. "You're telling me you didn't deliberately shoot down a United States special deputy marshal?"

For the second time that day, Governor Clayton ushered Adam into his house, this time in silence when he saw Gabriel at Adam's side. When the door was closed behind them, he showed the two men into his study. The house was quiet now, Addie's meeting having ended.

"Sims." The general acknowledged the black man.

"Sir," Gabriel replied, his face wan. He stood as though defeated, his eyes downcast, his hat hanging from a lifeless hand.

"She's gone," Adam stated. "We've just come from

the hotel. The clerk said she boarded the morning mailcoach." Adam felt defeated himself, knowing that while he'd been revealing his discovery to the governor, his quarry had been within easy reach.

"Stanford said he dropped her off here earlier for the meeting. She must have overheard our conversation, then taken off as though the devil were on her heels." Adam looked over at Gabriel. "Lord only knows where she's headed."

The general leaned against his desk and looked at Gabriel. "Do you know where?"

"Not for certain," Gabriel answered, shaking his head. "I had no idea she'd run off and do somethin' like this. Not without me, anyway." His words a mere whisper, the man muttered, "Not 'n' leave me here."

He sounded desolate, the pain of abandonment emphasizing the tight, thin line of his mouth. He looked like a man about to cry.

"She left her trunk," Adam said, directing his words to Clayton. "It was locked. She also left a note saying it was to be delivered to Sims." He jerked his head in Gabriel's direction. "I took a chance that he might have a key."

Back in Jonquil's room Adam had waited with malice for her trusted friend to appear, to revel in Gabriel's anguish when he was forced to open the trunk. The lawman in him wanted the black man to come clean about what he knew. The betrayed lover in him wanted him to share in his gut-wrenching pain.

But when Gabriel had lifted the lid and found Jonquil's banjo, his hurt had been deeper than Adam had envisioned. In his eyes had been profound despair, as though he'd found on some shore the discarded clothing of a beloved friend who had walked into the sea. "We gotta find her," was all he'd said.

Clayton showed Gabriel to a chair. "We might as

338

well sit. I think we'll be here for a while." Rising from his desk, he reached behind him for the leather pouch and handed it to Jonquil's companion. "I think you'd better start by explaining what you know about what's in here."

Gabriel stared at the pouch as though facing Armageddon. Without touching the contents, he began describing them in pathetic detail. His words suddenly gushed forth as readily as the springs that flowed from the rocks around the town. "I'll tell you whatever you want to know," he pleaded, "but please help me find her."

"Oh, we'll find her, all right," Adam retorted, "if I have to hunt her to the ends of this earth." But the more he studied Jonquil's faithful companion, the more he questioned his own accusations. Could this woman he'd come to love be an innocent victim, after all?

As succinctly as he could, Gabriel revealed the events leading up to the tragedy on the farm. He recounted the unbidden appearance of surveyors on their land, the subsequent visits of the persistent minister, all the while declaring his bewilderment at these situations. He described the somewhat unstable condition of Jonquil's mother, and said he had feared for her mental state whenever the preacher would come.

"I tried to stay out of it," he told them, "but I couldn't stand hearin' that preacher badger her for the deed. All he did was make her cry." He shrugged his shoulders. "Why was he so all-fired interested in stealin' our place? 'Twasn't no good to anybody but us poor folks. All we wanted was to be left alone."

But the tale he wove about the fateful day the three strangers arrived and the gunfight occurred left both Adam and Clayton staring at him in awed silence.

So, Adam concluded, Simon had walked onto that property while working under cover for Judge Parker. And when all the chips were down, he'd gone and made himself a hero. His little brother had tried to save a family and had gotten himself killed in the process. Simon, who always saw the bright side of life, who found good in the worst of men, even his own older brother. How Adam had loved that rascal.

If only he had told him so . . .

One gaping hole remained in this sordid case, one that had to be closed before Adam could begin to heal. He had to know that Jonquil's reaction to learning she had a father had not been false.

While she might not be a murderer, she could still be a conspirator. Otherwise, his brother might not have found himself in the wrong place at the wrong time. Did she truly know nothing about the man being investigated by the government?

Adam posed one last question. "What can you tell me about a man called Innes Ball?"

At the name Gabriel's head snapped up. "Ball, did you say?" His brows lifted in surprise. "Innes Ball?"

"Innes Ball."

For a moment the air tensed as the three men looked from one to the other.

"Man," Gabriel finally said, "I ain't heard that bastard's name in a lifetime. Sorry, General," he amended. "What you want with him?"

"Then you have heard of him," Adam prodded.

"Heard of him? I've spent every day of my life tryin' to forget he ever lived. He was the meanest creature ever to walk this earth. He only did one good deed in his miserable life." Gabriel uttered a sharp, cynical laugh. "And he didn't even realize he'd done that."

Adam held his breath. "What do you mean?"

Suddenly Gabriel became quiet, as if weighing his words.

"Come on, Sims," Adam said. "You want to help Jonquil? We need to know."

"I promised Miz Margaret I'd take this to my grave." Again Gabriel looked from Adam to Clayton.

"But it's Rosie I gotta worry about now. That bastard—Ball—is Rosie's father."

Adam jumped from his chair. "That's all I needed to hear."

"Wait," Gabriel pleaded, holding his arm out. "There's one more thing you need to know."

"What is that?"

"Rosie doesn't know. She's never heard of him."

Adam gave him a grim look. "She has now."

Gabriel exhaled in a loud gasp. "How?"

"Your preacher, the Reverend Cates, is in town." Adam's voice was filled with contempt. "He made sure Jonquil learned the ugly truth."

Gabriel vaulted from his chair. "I'll kill him," he seethed. "He had no right."

When he stood, the pouch fell from his lap to the floor, some of the items it contained escaping it.

Distressed, Gabriel looked up at the general. "Sorry, sir." He dropped to his knees. "I hope I didn't spill any ink on your rug."

As he lifted the inkwell, the ink bottle fell out, along with several small, translucent pieces of river rock that had been beneath it.

"What's this?" Adam stooped to pick up the smooth, clear stones.

Clayton gathered up one and held it out to the light. "Good heavens, Coulter. Do you know what these look like?"

"Diamonds!" they exclaimed in the same breath.

Adam couldn't believe his eyes. "Where on earth did these come from?"

Gabriel studied the stones, his eyes wide. "Probably at our place," he said. "Man, I got a whole cigar box full of them things."

Both men turned to him. "What!"

"That's right." He laughed at the twosome as if they were foolish children. "But I don' know about these bein' diamonds." He took one stone from Adam's palm and held it to the window. "See here," he said, "these are real cloudy. Diamonds are bright and so sparkly you can see right through 'em."

Clayton could hardly repress a laugh. "That's exactly right, Mr. Sims," he said. "But that would be after they've been cut. I feel certain we're holding a small fortune."

Adam's thoughts reeled. "Wait a minute!" he exclaimed. He suddenly remembered the letter Parker had given him, written shortly before Simon's death.

"I used to tease my brother about being a marshal. It was dangerous work and didn't pay a lot. I'd remind him if he didn't settle down, he'd answer the last roll call alone and broke."

Adam shook his head sadly, remembering his brother's excitement when he'd receive special assignments. "In that last letter he said he might die alone, but he had no intention of dying broke." He looked at the stones in his hand. "Could this be what he meant?"

"It would certainly explain a lot," Clayton offered, "to start with, why the preacher kept insisting on getting the title to the property. Did Miss Trevain say any more? Obviously Cates has more than one master."

The three men stared at one another, the name Innes Ball on the tips of their tongues.

"But we must go slowly here," Clayton pointed out. "We don't know with absolute certainty that these are valuable. Just as Sims here says, they could be fancy river rock. Besides, who ever heard of diamonds in this country?"

While the general discussed a plan of action, Adam could think only of Jonquil. Right now, she might be miles away, alone and sick with fear. He only hoped she was headed home. It would be the one place that held any security for her.

He pulled out his watch. "Look. I don't mean to be rude, but I don't give a tinker's damn about these rocks. My woman is out there somewhere, innocent and frightened. Heaven help me, I only hope she's safe."

Gabriel and Clayton exchanged glances before turning their attention back to Adam.

"I understand, son," Clayton sympathized, "and we'll find her. Remember, she's a hill girl, a survivor. She's nobody's fool. We've come this far, and if my guess is correct, these stones are not only going to prove her innocence, they're going to make her a very wealthy woman."

But all Adam feared for was Jonquil's safety and her mental state. What good would wealth be to a woman who thought she'd lost everything that mattered in life? It would be poor compensation at best.

She'd been so fearful that her mother's depression could affect her. Well, if it did, he had only himself to thank. By heavens, he'd all but shouted to the world that Jonquil was a murderess.

"Look," he said, "you two stay here and jaw all you want. I've got to find Jonquil." He turned to leave.

The general gave Adam a sympathetic look. "And what will you do after you've found her?"

"Keep her out of Ball's clutches—and try my damnedest to make things right between us."

"Then we need a solid, logical plan." Clayton draped an arm over Adam's shoulder, friend to friend. He looked at the clock on the wall. "We've already spent a good part of the afternoon unraveling this mess, and if these rocks turn out to be what I think they are, we'll have Cates rounded up before he has a chance to leave town."

Adam gave the older man a grateful but determined look. "Fine. You take care of that end. I'm riding out as soon as I can get my gear together."

"Not without me you ain't."

Adam caught the equally determined expression

343

on Gabriel's face.

"I been responsible for that girl since before she was born, and I ain't lettin' her down now." He moved, tightlipped, toward the door. "Anybody goin' anywhere, I'm goin' with 'em."

"I agree," Clayton suggested. "Adam, Judge Parker expected you to bring these two in to Fort Smith when the time was right. We just didn't know they'd be going under protective custody. But since they are, it's your responsibility to keep them both safe until Ball can be charged."

He turned to Gabriel. "I don't mean to frighten you, Mr. Sims, but from everything you've told me, you and Miss Trevain are the only witnesses to a heinous crime. I think we'd all rest better knowing you were together."

"Yes, sir," Gabriel agreed. "But I think there was another witness, too. And I gotta make sure nothin' happens to her."

Adam stepped forward. "Another witness?"

Gabriel nodded. "Her name is Keely Watts. She was out visiting me the day . . ." His voice trailed off. "And it's possible she saw what happened. She was gone when it was all over." He gave Adam a pleading look. "Mr. Coulter, I gotta see to it nothin' happens to her either."

"Mr. Sims," Clayton interrupted, "if you've had your own witness all these many months, then why in heaven's name have you been running?"

The look Gabriel gave the older man showed disbelief of his ignorance. "General," he said, "Keely's skin is the same color as mine. This may be eighteen eighty-two, and we may be free. But as far as pointin' a finger at a white suspect, we're never gonna be believed."

Adam smiled at the brave but foolish Gabriel, who had forfeited his own freedom and happiness to see that Jonquil had a chance to start over in a cruel and unfair world.

"I think you're going to be pleasantly surprised," he declared with a warm smile. "We're going down to Prater, you and I, and when we bring Jonquil back to Fort Smith, we're bringing Keely with her. Parker has a healthy respect for honest folks, and he doesn't care one whit what color their skin is."

When the three o'clock stage pulled out of Eureka Springs, Adam and Gabriel were still out of breath from running it down.

Much as Adam would have preferred riding his horse, he knew he couldn't force another man to keep up with him. And the stage, trading for fresh horses along the way, would travel through the night, whereas Adam knew Ranger could not.

Along with the possible discovery of diamonds on Jonquil's property came suspicion of treachery from another source. Her father, the flamboyant railroad magnate from New York.

The probability of charges being made against Ball loomed larger and larger, and for the first time Adam realized just how dangerous this man could be. When instant wealth was within Ball's reach, he would stop at nothing until he grasped it—even pointing a finger at a woman he'd never seen. Or harming his own daughter.

So Adam sat, marking each mile with his watch, praying that his woman would be safe until he found her. If he found her . . .

For Jonquil's sake and his own, he prayed that the rocks Simon had found were indeed diamonds.

Chapter Twenty

Jonquil, squeezed into her space in the Concord coach, forced herself to return Keely's smile. Though the two women had left Prater in the company of Adam and Gabriel only yesterday, it now seemed like a lifetime ago. Hopefully, within the next hour, before the sun set, they would arrive at Fort Smith.

It would be a relief, she thought, to leave the confinement of the jouncing coach. The stage had been packed to capacity, each of its nine passengers vying for the allotted space of fifteen inches across.

After their last stop, Jonquil had taken her rotation at the window. She now had her head propped against the back of the upholstered seat, the leather curtain rolled up to allow air to circulate through the coach.

Judge Isaac Parker, the hanging judge. So she would finally come face to face with the man she'd feared for the last eight months. And though she'd not be spending her life behind bars, her punishment was to be just as enduring. She was a lover betrayed.

From her seat Jonquil heard the *jehu* urging the horses to keep up their pace as they approached a hill. With the whip cracking just above their heads, the six-horse team raced across the countryside at breakneck speed.

Her vision blurred with tears when she thought of

the man riding shotgun. Who better, she thought bitterly, than a Pinkerton Detective on special assignment for Judge Isaac Parker? At least this way she didn't have to endure looking at him. Gabriel, on the other hand, hadn't seemed to mind Adam's presence. The easy manner between them since they'd found her at the farm only confused Jonquil more. Fact was, the lawman had betrayed both of them with his deceptive lies.

Keely leaned across the narrow distance and patted Jonquil's knee. "Miss Rose, you don' look so good." Her coal black eyes delved into Jonquil's teary ones.

"It's the alkali dust," Jonquil replied, not wanting to admit she mourned her lost love.

Keely unscrewed the lid of her canteen and doused a hanky with water. "Here. This might help." The black woman pressed the wet cloth into Jonquil's hand.

"It might, thank you," Jonquil replied. But she knew there weren't enough hankies in the world to absorb the amount of tears she'd shed since leaving Eureka Springs. Holding the cool cloth over her eyes, she leaned her head against the basswood side panel and tried to relax.

Events of the last few days flipped through her mind like shuffled cards—the desolation she'd experienced on returning to the little farm after having been gone for so many months, the pain at visiting her mother's grave again, and the torture of waiting for Adam.

She'd known he'd come looking for her. Gabriel would have been forced to tell him where he'd thought she'd run. Adam's heated words in Clayton's study had said it all. He'd used her to solve his case, manipulating both her and Gabriel. But what had hurt more than anything was that Adam had believed she'd murdered his brother.

The coach's wheels dipped into a deep gully, launching the passengers toward the ceiling. Shrieks and groans assaulted Jonquil's ears, averting her thoughts. When everyone had settled back into his or her allotted space, Jonquil's mind spun off in another direction.

Had the shack and barn always been in such disrepair, or had they worsened with time? Strange, she'd lived most of her life on that little farm, wrapped in a protective cocoon of Gabriel's and her mother's making, never once questioning their meager existence. Now, having lived in a real town like Eureka Springs and been part of a community, Jonquil knew she could never go back to her former life.

But what did the future hold? At the moment it stretched before her like the barren fields that surrounded her small home. Fallow was how she felt—plowed, tilled, but left unseeded during a growing season.

To Jonquil, Adam's love had been the promise of growth, of caring and sharing. His duplicity had been the rain that washed away any chances they had to garner that happiness. Now, all that remained to her of that brief union were painful memories and the realization that it was over.

She had laughed in Adam's face when he'd arrived and asked her forgiveness. With what little dignity she had left, she'd refused him a second chance to prove his love. What did he know about real love, anyway? And the pain it could cause. Hadn't he already confessed his failure in another time with another woman? She'd even refused to listen when Gabriel pleaded his case.

She would not end up like her mother who, over love, had become a prisoner of her own making. At one minute Adam had sworn his love; he'd believed the worst of her the next. Jonquil could never forgive him for that betrayal or for breaking her heart.

"Fort Smith."

The driver's voice carried to them as he pulled the

stage to a rocking halt at the depot across from the high-walled Army fort. Sighs of relief echoed throughout the dusty interior. When the door opened, the station keeper lowered the step, then stood by to help the passengers to alight.

Jonquil took his hand and stepped down. Five hours since the last coach stop. Her legs threatened to buckle, but sheer willpower kept her upright.

Gabriel took Keely's arm until she was able to move under her own power. But when Jonquil saw Adam start her way, she quickly turned and began talking with a fellow passenger.

"Mr. Coulter?" a young man in military dress called.

Adam acknowledged the summons. "Here I am."

"You and your party are to come with me, sir. I'll have your bags brought later."

Following Adam and the soldier, Jonquil fell into step between Keely and Gabriel. As they crossed the road toward the fortress, a damp gust off the Arkansas River snapped the guardhouse flag like a ship's sail. Jonquil's cloak whipped around her legs as wind propelled her forward.

At the sentry post, a knot of dread settled in her stomach. Even under protective custody she couldn't help feeling like a prisoner about to meet her doom.

Where, she wondered, would they be boarded? At this point she'd gladly accept any quarters—a cell if necessary—as long as she didn't have to be near Adam Coulter. The less contact she had with him now, the easier it would be for her to sever the fragile ties that linked them.

"We've been expecting you, sir," the sentry confirmed. "The women"—he looked at Jonquil and Keely—"will be quartered over the courtroom. Your man, he's to stay in the enlisted men's quarters, and you, sir, are to report to the judge's chambers. He's been waiting for your arrival."

When the group entered the compound, the gate

clanked shut, its metallic sound jarring Jonquil's teeth. She glanced around the dusk-blanketed grounds, but saw only the shadowy silhouettes of rectangular buildings, their windows aglow with buff light. The smell of cooked cabbage, potatoes, and ham hung in the air and made her stomach rumble with hunger.

"Follow me," the guard instructed.

The foursome dogged his footsteps to a large brick structure with a wide porch flanking its front. Bounding up the stairs, he opened the door.

"Miss Trevain, you and your maid will be staying here."

"She's not my maid, but thank you anyway."

Jonquil stood on the steps, waiting for Keely to say good night to Gabriel. Irritated by the young man's presumption, Jonquil questioned why most whites assumed coloreds could be nothing more than servants. Glancing over at Gabriel and Keely, who were having a quiet conversation, she regarded her guardian with respect. She'd never thought of him as a servant.

For as long as she could remember Jonquil had looked upon him as a child looks upon a father. But now, seeing him reunited with Keely after she'd shared her own heart with Adam, Jonquil suddenly realized that perhaps she and her mother had been selfish in their demands on their faithful friend.

Both had always expected Gabriel to be there for them, never considering that he might have wished to marry and have a family of his own. Had they really been no different in their thinking than the rest of society? Had they, too, considered the black man as nothing more than a servant?

Now that she knew the complete story of her past, she realized that Gabriel had never truly been set free. While he had long ago been returned his dignity and granted a release from slavery, he had never freed himself from his emotional bondage to an unwed mother and her little girl.

Jonquil's heart ached at the thought that her love for him had deprived Gabriel of a life of his own. When this business in Fort Smith was concluded, she would set him free at last.

Although she could not see Adam's eyes through the darkness, Jonquil felt his gaze upon her as distinctly as though he'd caressed her.

"Jonquil, may I speak with you?" he asked.

She shifted her feet nervously, not certain how to respond and not trusting herself to be left alone with him. In this strange and alien place she felt quite vulnerable, but she wouldn't allow herself to give in and take refuge in Adam's arms.

She'd trusted him once and he'd betrayed her. Never again would she be weakened by romantic notions. She wouldn't fall into the same trap twice.

Her voice stiff and final, Jonquil replied, "I'm sorry, Mr. Coulter, it's been a long two days and I'm very tired. If you'll excuse me . . ." She turned her back on him and walked to the door.

With her hand on the knob, she paused and called to Keely. "I'll wait for you inside."

Then, without glancing in Adam's direction, Jonquil entered the wide, empty hall.

From the bottom of the steps, Adam watched Jonquil disappear into the dim corridor, his heart nearly breaking at her cold dismissal. But what had he expected her to do? In Jonquil's shoes wouldn't he have acted the same way?

He'd been furious at Clayton's house, where she'd overheard his bitter words. He'd accused her of being a thief, of murdering his brother. If that had not been bad enough, she'd then learned his identity and his mission. What person wouldn't feel betrayed at such discoveries, especially the woman he'd held only hours earlier, declaring his undying love and encouraging her to trust him?

Damnation, he hoped the judge had a good stiff drink. He needed one right about now.

"Boss."

Adam smiled at Gabriel's form of address. Over the last few days the two of them had made their peace, had become friends. Now Gabriel was taking particular pride in the fact that he was working for Adam, helping to bring Innes Ball to his knees.

"Rosie, she'll come around. Give 'er time."

The words penetrated Adam's thoughts. "I hope so." He shook his head in remorse. "The things she must have heard me say in Clayton's study . . ." He paused, groping for words. "I deserve her hate."

"No, sir, you was upset, didn' know what to believe." Gabriel held his felt hat in his hands, Keely's fingers resting on his arm. "I raised that gal, and I know my Rosie. Once she sets things straight in her mind, she'll come around. Rosie ain't one for holdin' grudges."

"I hope you're right," Adam replied. "I love her. I've tried to convince her, but she won't listen. Now she won't even speak to me alone."

"Tomorrow's another day. We's all tired after our journey. You'll see, boss, she'll come around."

Not quite so confident, Adam had no choice but to hope Gabriel knew his charge as well as he claimed. Tonight he didn't wish to dwell on the possibility that Jonquil might not have a change of heart.

"If you two will excuse me, I'll see you both in the morning," he said. Then he walked toward Parker's chambers. Soon, he thought, this mess would be behind him. He'd had enough of intrigue and collusion to last a lifetime.

"Sympathy should not be reserved wholly for the criminal."

Judge Parker paused, pinched the bridge of his

nose, and continued to address his audience. "I believe in standing on the right side of the innocent —the quiet, peaceful, law-abiding citizens such as yourselves."

Parker's deep, articulate voice complemented his imposing size, Jonquil decided from her chair in front of the judge's desk. She'd deliberately refused Adam's offer of a seat beside his own, and instead had positioned herself between Gabriel and Keely. With them flanking her, she felt safe from Adam's scowling presence.

Even now, when she peeked at him from beneath lowered lashes, she felt as though her heart might burst with love. Jonquil had lain awake most of the night, willing herself to think of what she'd do when this ordeal was behind her. But her thoughts always returned to what might have been. Even in her fitful sleep, Adam surfaced in her dreams.

"You, young woman, and you, sir"—Jonquil snapped out of her reverie when she realized the judge was speaking to her, his eyes connected first with her and then with Gabriel—"deserve both sympathy and prudence."

The way he demanded their attention, she thought, he might be a father lecturing recalcitrant children.

"Sometimes you will find good men involved in things they normally wouldn't participate in. It's because they have lost confidence in the courts and juries."

Jonquil and Gabriel exchanged conspiratorial glances, each silently identifying with the judge's opinions.

Parker's regard focused upon Jonquil. "You, Miss Trevain, what do you have to say for yourself?"

Temporarily at a loss for words, she mumbled through frozen lips, "Me, sir?"

"Adam here tells me you're a very talented young woman." The judge studied her before continuing. "I believe his exact words were 'she sings like a

353

canary.' Should I have someone bring you a banjo?''

Underneath the booming voice Jonquil recognized a calming wit, and she smiled. Her fear of the revered man had vanished.

"I know we were wrong in running," she returned, "but at the time, we felt we had no choice. Our small family was estranged from the town. The people there thought my mother was crazy, possibly dangerous. I felt no one would believe our story, or that Gabriel, a man of color, had shot a white man in my defense. Especially if that man rode with a special deputy United States marshal." Her eyes met Adam's before she looked back to Parker.

"Miss Trevain, I understand your situation, but that doesn't excuse your actions or allow you to run from your obligations.''

"Under the circumstances, sir"—Adam stood up, hat in hand, and faced the judge—"I believe they had no other choice.''

Parker leaned back in his chair, crossed his fingers over his stomach, and listened to Adam's opinion.

"From the eyewitness accounts, it would seem Miss Trevain and Mr. Sims were victims of a heinous crime. Not only were the men who rode with my brother intent on murder and rape to secure the deed to their meager farm. But the townspeople mistreated a frail woman whose nervous condition they believed posed a threat to them.''

"Son," the judge intervened, "no one is on trial here." His gaze locked on Adam in understanding. "I merely wish to make it clear to these good people that laws are made to protect them. Our system will only work if we, as citizens, exercise the rights spelled out to us in the Constitution. You above all others should know we can't turn our backs on justice.''

"Sorry, sir, I didn't mean to imply—''

Parker silenced Adam with his hand. "Maybe, son, you should put your legal training to work. The courts need all the good attorneys they can get.''

"I've been thinking about it, sir." Adam sat and rested a booted foot upon his knee. He balanced his brown Stetson on the raised boot.

Attorney. So Adam had decided to practice law. Jonquil recalled the night in the cabin when he'd mentioned studying law. He'd make a good lawyer, she thought, then questioned her own sanity. Lawyers shouldn't lie!

Again her thoughts were interrupted by Parker's words.

"Our witnesses are sound. Miss Watts here saw the whole scene from behind a thick bramble bush. Is that not so, ma'am?"

"Yessir, that's so. I was so scairt I was sick. After it were over, all I wanted to do was skedaddle. And after my man left town without no words, I jes' nearly died." Keely's black eyes locked on Gabriel. "I coulda kicked myself to Little Rock and back fer not comin' forward."

"Your plight is understandable, Miss Watts, but again I must remind you of the seriousness of not reporting a crime."

"Yessir, I know, sir."

"Our other witness, the so-called Reverend Cates, whom I chose not to invite to this session, has also agreed to cooperate. Of course Mr. Cates is more interested in saving his own neck than in seeing justice done. Our fine jail will accommodate him until you return, Adam. I've been told he's busy converting the souls of our inmates."

Return? The judge's words finally sank into Jonquil's brain. Adam was leaving. But then, wasn't that what she'd wanted all along? The sooner, the better.

"When you reach New York," the judge continued, "be sure Mr. Ball understands it's essential that he return to Arkansas. Tell him that without his testimony and his identification of the woman who stole the deed, we'll have no case. It's his word against hers. If he knows the value of the property, which I suspect he does, I'm sure greed will bring him back."

"I'm certain of that, too," Adam replied. "It will be my pleasure to outwit the old fox."

"Well, then, I'll see you when you return. After the hearing I'll only need your deposition for the trial." Parker nodded understandingly, "In case you have to leave."

The judge walked around his desk and shook Adam's hand before turning to the others.

"I hope your stay here will be comfortable, but you will be asked to remain inside the garrison. Innes Ball is a very powerful man with connections, good and bad. Your safety is very important to us, and we don't want Ball to get wind of what we have planned for him. We need him here in order to charge him."

A knock sounded on the chamber door. A young clerk pushed it open and stuck his head in. "They're waiting for you in the courtroom, sir."

"Thank you, Bill. I'll be right along."

Turning back to Jonquil and Gabriel, Judge Parker made a request, "I hope you'll both be kind enough to offer us an evening's entertainment before you leave us." Bidding them both good day, he paused before Adam. "Good luck in New York," he said, and then he turned and exited his chambers.

New York. Adam was going away, he was going to leave her. Jonquil walked outside the commissary with the others and stood for a moment in front of the stone building, trying not to listen to the conversation between Adam and Gabriel.

"How long you be gone, boss?" Gabriel asked.

"No more than two or three weeks, I hope." Adam looked toward Jonquil, then pulled his watch from his vest pocket. "I leave on the one o'clock stage."

"One o'clock? That don' give you much time then."

"Not nearly as much as I need."

Jonquil knew Adam's reply had been intended for her. She felt the heat of his gaze through the many layers of clothing she'd put on that morning. During the night the weather had become damp and penetratingly cold, and she'd been chilled—until now.

The foursome stepped down from the grassy rock terrace and walked toward the courthouse building where Jonquil and Keely were quartered. Purposefully, Gabriel and Keely slowed their pace, leaving Adam and Jonquil alone.

When they reached the porch, Adam grabbed Jonquil's hand and dragged her toward the end railing, away from the wind and curious passersby.

With one hand on either side of her head, he pinned her against the wall. "I know you don't care to listen," he said, "but I'm going to say my piece one more time before I leave here."

He sighed and shook his head. "You have every right to be angry with me, but I also have a right to plead my case. I love you, Rose, it's that simple. I'll always love you."

It's not simple at all, Jonquil thought. She would never be able to believe this man who'd lied about his identity, who had condemned her as guilty without a backward glance. Guarding her heart against another emotional assault, she snapped on a mask of aloofness, unwilling to meet his eyes.

Not to be deterred, Adam continued. "If I could take back those words you heard in Clayton's house, I would. They were cruel and selfish, and I'll never forgive myself for condemning you before I heard the truth from your own lips."

Jonquil tried to pull away from Adam's hold. "Please," she begged, unbidden tears threatening to fall.

"Not until I'm finished," Adam replied. "I can't explain what happened to me that day when I saw Simon's personal things in your possession. I just went crazy. Maybe it was my own guilt over never patching things up with my brother when I had the opportunity. The knowledge of his death made me realize that chance was gone forever."

"Please, I don't want to hear this."

But Adam ignored her plea. "Look, my mistakes are many. I've tried to tell you most of them. Simon always loved me, idolized me." He laughed thinly. "Can you believe that? I was too pigheaded to accept him. Why is it I always hurt the ones who love me the most? Simon, my stepfather, my mother, and now you."

The pain in Adam's face chipped away at the ice in Jonquil's heart. Even though she realized the gulf between them was too wide to be breached, she couldn't bear to see his hurt.

"Don't," she whispered, trying to silence him with her fingers. But he brushed them away.

"No. I want you to hear me, dammit! I can't explain why I carried so much hate inside me all those years. I'd always felt like the outsider in my family, like the fifth wheel. And no matter how hard the others tried to make me feel I belonged, I still resented them."

"Adam, please don't torture yourself with such memories. I'm truly sorry I can't be more forgiving." She simply could not chance having her heart broken again.

Adam's hand caressed her face, his thumb catching the tear that trailed down her cheek. "I love you, Rose. Please don't make any decisions about us until I return. Maybe after you've had time to think we can start afresh."

Jonquil clasped his hands between her own, holding them against her chest. "But I'm so confused."

"Shhhh." He pulled her into his arms wanting to comfort her. "Without you I'm nothing, with no reason to live."

Jonquil looked up into his dark eyes. She wanted to believe him, wanted to trust this man who held her prisoner—body and soul. Maybe, as he said, after she'd had more time to think . . . Maybe . . .

Adam's head bent lower, his mouth mere inches from her own. They were so close, Jonquil's insides turned to water. She wanted to melt into his arms and forget the pain of the last week. Would he always make her feel this way?

"Boss, you tell her yet?"

Gabriel stood on the ground below, his lips turned up in a wide grin beneath the old felt hat. From where he stood, it looked as though Jonquil and Adam had patched up their differences. Excited by the prospect, he continued, "You tell her she's as rich as Queen Victoria?"

Jonquil stiffened; her expression clouded. She looked from Gabriel's gladdened face to Adam's troubled one. "What is he talking about?"

Adam's palm made contact with his forehead. "I almost forgot. We only found out this morning. I planned to tell you, but this needed to be said first. I wanted you to know how I felt before I left."

"Tell me what?" she demanded, pulling back until he was forced to release her.

Gabriel, below, looked as though he'd just swallowed rotten food.

"Diamonds, my love. Your farm sits in the middle of a diamond field. You're rich. Very, very rich. That's why Innes Ball wants your land."

"My land . . . diamonds?" Impossible. She and Gabriel both knew their farm was worthless, barren.

"It's true."

Adam raised his arms in excitement. He'd finally given her the news. "After you fled town, we found a secret compartment in the bottom of Simon's inkwell."

Jonquil looked at him as though he'd lost his mind.

"I know this sounds absurd, but Simon must have found the rocks when he was surveying for Ball. The old man must have known. His story about the railroad was merely a hoax. Simon probably planned to disclose his find to Parker, but he got caught in the crossfire of the no-goods he traveled with. He went to his grave with the secret."

Jonquil watched Adam's lips move, but surely she hadn't heard him right. *Rich . . . impossible!* And to think her mother had lived the life of a pauper, not knowing she owned a diamond field.

"Before I left Eureka Springs, I sent those rocks to an assayer. We couldn't make any statements until we knew for sure. Just this morning I received word they were genuine."

Instead of an expression of happy surprise, Jonquil had turned ashen, as though she might be sick.

"You're rich," Adam whispered, trying to get through the significance of his news. "I just wish I could have told you sooner."

"Stage is coming," the sentry yelled from the guardhouse.

Jonquil gave Adam a wounded look. "Gabriel had to remind you of something as important as this? When would you have told me?" she accused. "When, Adam? After you had married me? When you, too, were as rich as the Queen?" Her words were raw and angry. "You never wanted me. You want only the diamonds, the wealth." Her voice was sharp as a stiletto.

"What are you talking about? Of course I love you."

"You wanted me to accept your declaration of undying love before you left—before you told me about the jewels." She turned from him. "Well, you nearly had me convinced."

"Wait a minute—"

"It wasn't me at all, was it, Adam? And to think, I almost believed you did care."

"Damn it, Jonquil, I do." He grabbed her shoulders.

"Why, I'm no different than Katherine."

Jonquil choked out the words. "You planned to use me—my wealth—just as you would have used hers if she'd lived." Prying his fingers from her shoulders, she glared at him, disbelief stamped upon her face. "Well, I'm not like my mother."

"Boss, the coach is waitin'."

Adam felt as if he'd been slugged in the groin. Did she loathe him so much that she'd believe him capable of such an act?

"Rose, please, don't say these things. It's not like that at all." But Jonquil was beyond reason.

Her voice filled with uncontrolled emotion, she flung the hurtful words at him. "Don't ever call me that again. My name is Miss Trevain to you. I want you out of my life. I never want to see you again."

Rebuffed, Adam backed away. Further words would be useless. He'd opened his heart, told her about Katherine, his guilt—things he'd never spoken of to another living person. And Jonquil had defended his actions, making him feel worthy at last. But now she'd turned his revelations against him, choosing only to believe he'd used her the same way.

"As far as I'm concerned you're dead, Adam Coulter. As dead to me as your precious Katherine is to you."

Jonquil's words sliced his soul. Turning away, he headed blindly for the stairs. He sailed down into the yard, feeling like a man attending his own funeral.

"You'll never touch my diamonds, Adam Coulter!" Jonquil yelled. Following as he cut across the yard, she ran the length of the porch. "I'll see you in hell first."

Adam strode across the field, never once looking

back. When he passed the guardhouse, the metal gate banged shut behind him with a finality that echoed across the compound.

Jonquil collapsed onto the porch floor, clinging to the railing. "Never . . . never . . . never . . ."

Keely ran up the porch stairs and knelt beside her. Holding Jonquil, she helped her to rise.

"Come now, child," she crooned, "you musn' upset yourself this way."

Numb, Jonquil allowed Keely to escort her inside the building and into the privacy of their small room. Once inside, she fell upon the bed, certain her heart would break.

The Butterfield stage left Fort Smith at precisely one-ten, heading north over the Butterfield Road. Inside the crowded coach the one male passenger sat looking out the window, without seeing. To those around him he appeared calm and composed, but within him a battle raged.

Adam Coulter had lived with pain and rejection most of his life, enough to know this, too, would eventually dull to a mild ache. And though it would be the hardest thing he'd ever do, this man would never again allow Jonquil Rose Trevain to stomp upon his empty heart.

Chapter Twenty-one

Nearly two weeks had passed since Adam's departure from Fort Smith. Weeks of agonizing regret over the cruel barbs Jonquil had flung at him before he left.

She stood now in her small room, alone, looking through the one square window. A bright patch of sunshine beamed through the pane, reflecting light on the crystal stones she held.

Rotating her palm, she studied the almond- and triangular-shaped stones; yellow, pale green, and brown. To Jonquil they looked like nothing more than colored pieces of gravel. But a copy of the assayer's report accompanying them from Eureka Springs convinced her they were much more than just pretty baubles.

In her hand she held considerable wealth. In addition there were the stones Gabriel had found on the property and stored in a cigar box . . . and the ones that still lay buried in the deep wrinkles of the earth on her little farm.

Jonquil glanced out the window toward the fort's gallows at the far end of the compound. Only the very top of it was visible from her room. For that she was thankful.

Executions of condemned prisoners were carried out with regularity. There had been two since she'd arrived. For as long as she lived, she'd never forget the sound of the trap door in the platform slamming open and banging against the supporting wood. She only had to hear that sound to imagine the macabre scene taking place less than two hundred yards away.

It was rumored that six men could be hung at once, six lives snuffed out as quickly as a candle's flame by the executioner, George Maledon.

His dry remark to her the day she met him, "I never hanged a man who came back to have the job done over," had sent prickles up her spine, for only months earlier she'd envisioned her dear friend Gabriel being hanged.

Turning away from the window, Jonquil dropped into a straight-backed chair. The gems nestled in her palm again caught the rays of the sun. Diamonds.

She now had enough wealth to go anywhere and do whatever she pleased. She could even build a beautiful home near the Claytons in Eureka Springs. She should be ecstatic over the wondrous turn of events.

Why, then, did this knowledge leave her feeling as lifeless as the men who swung from the nearby gallows?

Unable to deny the truth a moment longer, Jonquil recognized that her pensiveness stemmed from her need of Adam. The first few days after his departure she'd been too numb to think. She'd stayed abed, pleading illness, until Gabriel had reminded her that her actions mirrored her mother's. His words had kindled the spark that had gotten her up and about, but even they had not expelled the depression that threatened to consume her.

Every day she lived with the memory of her accusations. If today she and Adam were both tried for crimes of love, his guilt would be decreed the lesser. Like a knife striking a vital organ, her words had pierced and ripped. Had broken his pride.

Many thoughts had come flooding back in the last

few days, one always remaining at the surface. She was as guilty of telling untruths as she'd found Adam. Her excuse, to protect Gabriel. His excuse, allegiance to his job.

Throughout their relationship Adam had been the giver and she the taker. More times than she could count he'd saved her from the clutches of men who'd meant her harm.

He'd taken her to a life that she and Gabriel never knew existed, introducing her to honest, accepting folks. And now, because of him, she and Gabriel could live out their lives with no more fear of the law—and no more poverty.

Jonquil straightened on the stiff chair, rested her head against its high back, and closed her eyes.

They had both failed miserably when it came to trust. After all they'd shared together, each had believed only the worst about the other before all the evidence was in.

Jonquil would go to her grave regretting the charges she'd thrown in Adam's face. She'd used his heart-rending revelations about his past to incriminate him. She was ashamed.

The door opened and Keely slipped in quietly. "You feelin' better, Miss Rose?"

"I want to, Keely, but I feel so guilty."

Jonquil stood and walked to the window. Tufted clouds skidded across the sun's surface, temporarily enveloping the room in gray shadow.

Keely came to stand beside her. "You need to talk?"

"I've so many regrets. I wouldn't know where to begin."

"My ol' mammy always say, 'start at the beginnin'.'"

"Your mother, Keely?" Jonquil asked, looking into the shorter woman's eyes. "You know, until this moment I never thought about either you or Gabriel having family—or any—ties for that matter. He was just always there for me." She shook her head. "How

365

selfish I've been."

Keely ignored Jonquil's self-recrimination. "She weren't my real mama. I was sold downriver before the war and never saw my family again. The mammy I refer to was everybody's mammy on the plantation. She was the wisest ol' woman I ever did know." She smiled then and her teeth sparkled like pearls in her ebony face.

A rush of regrets swirled through Jonquil's brain. "I've made so many mistakes. With Gabriel, with Adam, even with my poor mother. Maybe things would have been different for all of us if I'd insisted—"

"Ain't too late unless you let it be. Child, I'm near fifty year of age, and now my future's just so bright and full of hope."

"I'm so happy for you both." She hugged the older woman. "I can't help but believe, though, if it hadn't been for me and my mother, you two could have been together years ago."

"Weren't no decision to make. We both did as we saw fit. Gabriel had a responsibility, and I had my job and place in the community. We was happy living the way we did."

"And then I took him away from you."

"Not your doin', girl. You was a victim of circumstance beyond your control. You did what you thought was right. If you hadn't left, my Gabe might be swingin' from some tree. Whadda we country folk know anyway?"

"But if we'd had more confidence in the system, as Judge Parker pointed out—"

"No insult intended to the good judge, but he ain't livin' in this here black skin, and he don' know the power of the white hatemonger in the South."

"I know, Keely. But from now on I believe I'll think twice before I run from the law."

"Maybe me too, child, I jest ain't decided yet. But I do know when I thought I'd lost my Gabe forever, it weren't no life without him. So I planned, if the good Lord saw fit to give me another chance to be with my man, there'd be no way he gonna git free of me again."

Jonquil couldn't help but smile at her friend's exuberance. "Is there a message here, Keely?"

"Plain as that nose on your face. Adam Coulter's a good man and he loves you. But you dealt him a powerful blow the way you went on at him. A man has pride, and once that's broken it's hard to repair. But if I was you, I'd die tryin' to mend it."

The cloud that covered the sun earlier drifted away and spilled bright sunshine through the window. "Keely, I believe you're as wise as your old mammy."

"I've also come with news—good and bad." Keely hesitated, allowing Jonquil to brace herself for both. "Gabriel sent me to tell you. The judge stopped him earlier and said he'd had a wire. Mr. Coulter and Mr. Ball will be here in the mornin'."

"Tomorrow?" The word escaped from Jonquil's clenched teeth.

Keely nodded. She opened the small wardrobe they shared and pulled out one of Jonquil's gowns. Of deep indigo blue, it had been made in Eureka Springs for cooler weather. Jonquil had never worn it.

"I'll take this down to the laundry and press it. You gonna look your best in that courtroom." Keely draped the dress across her arm. "By the way," she added, "Gabe said the judge cleared his calendar for tomorrow afternoon. He's as ready as the rest of us to get this Ball business over with. We all needs to get on with our lives."

Jonquil trembled at her words. Ball. The father she thought had died long ago. "Wait," she called.

"Cain't wait. They'll be locking me outa the laundry if I don' go now." She patted Jonquil's outstretched hand. "We'll talk about this later." Keely hurried from the room.

Tomorrow, Jonquil thought. She'd meet the man

who had fathered her, then run away. The man who'd cared nothing about her, and who even now sought only to regain the property he'd signed over to her mother—property he'd believed to be worthless.

From what she'd so recently learned from Gabriel, the man who was her father had never possessed a heart. Her gentle mother had loved him until she'd seen his cruel and vindictive side. Jonquil expected nothing from their meeting but the satisfaction of knowing that at last he'd pay for his crimes.

Her larger concern was for the other man who would arrive on tomorrow's stage. She loved Adam Coulter with all her heart. And if she had to move the Ozarks to do it, Jonquil would do all in her power to mend the hurt she'd inflicted on him.

The stage was set. The preliminary hearing would begin in ten minutes. Adam sat beside Innes Ball inside the courtroom, waiting for the judge to take his place at the bench.

When they'd arrived that morning in Fort Smith, Adam had escorted Ball to one of the better hotels on the presumption that he would wish to freshen up after his tedious journey south.

After Adam had taken his leave of him, Ball had been under constant surveillance. Parker's deputies, in the guise of travelers and hotel employees, had kept their eyes on the man they knew to be responsible for the death of a respected colleague, Special Deputy United States Marshal Simon Hector Thompson.

Adam didn't wish to think about the woman he'd soon meet again face to face. Deliberately avoiding any chance encounter with her, he'd sought out the judge immediately upon his return, then had come and gone as prudently as possible.

In the past two weeks he'd worked overtime to condition himself for this meeting. Beneath his rib cage, in the place where his heart once beat, now dwelt an empty shell, as hard and cold as petrified wood.

Never again would he fall victim to her pretty face and winning smile, nor would he trust any other women for that matter. After today Adam would head West. Another chapter closed and forgotten, like the pages of a bad book.

The room was beginning to fill up with people. Adam recognized some of the deputies he'd met on his earlier visit. Because Parker wanted this hearing to appear as natural as any held in his courtroom, the men dressed as civilians.

Jonquil and Gabriel would sit at the front table, situated across from him and Ball, supposedly to be charged with the stealing of the railroader's deed. Under the assumption that he was needed to identify the thieves, Ball had eagerly come to court.

Adam looked forward to seeing him point at the accused. If it would allow Ball's greedy fingers access to the diamond field, the man would probably swear that God Himself was the culprit.

Cates's and Keely's appearance would be saved until the end. Their corroborating testimony would slip the noose around Ball's scrawny neck, and he'd be charged with federal racketeering. The state would bring another charge, conspiracy to commit murder.

Adam stole a look at the man who sat beside him. His sandy hair was streaked with gray, as were his muttonchops and mustache, and regardless of what Ball might deny, his eyes were a giveaway that he had fathered Jonquil Rose. Every time Adam looked into those blue jay–colored eyes, he was reminded again of his lost angel.

The entrance door opened, and all eyes turned to the last people to enter the courtroom. Their footsteps echoing on the hard pine floor, the young woman and her two black companions walked to the front to take their appointed seats.

Out of the corner of his eye Adam saw Innes Ball shift restlessly and absently grope for his stiff collar. All the while Adam remained conscious of the woman across from him.

"Please rise for the Honorable Judge Isaac Parker." The proceedings were about to begin.

All stood, waiting until the judge had taken his seat before returning to their own. Parker's gavel signaled for quiet to settle again in the small room.

Without turning his head, Adam sought Jonquil out. She was more beautiful than he remembered— thinner perhaps, but soft curves were still evident beneath the indigo dress. The color complemented her porcelain paleness, and the mull lace trim at her neck reminded him of a ruffled blouse she'd once worn in his presence.

Her golden hair, all but hidden beneath an indigo felt hat, was adorned with her trademark, a velvet cluster of yellow roses. Although Jonquil's eyes were nearly concealed by her hat brim, he had sensed her look his way when she'd taken her seat.

Adam's heart thumped so loudly in his chest he felt certain it could be heard across the quiet room. Willing his gaze forward and resuming his frosty mask, he concentrated on the judge's words.

He hates me so much he can't bear to look at me.
From beneath the rim of her hat, Jonquil studied the man who sat in stilted indifference across the aisle. Since yesterday, when Keely had informed her of Adam's return, she'd both dreaded and anticipated this moment. But never had she dreamed his appearance would cause her such pain.

She'd glimpsed him earlier in the morning when she'd stood by her window. He'd walked across the yard to Parker's chambers, never once glancing in her direction.

Her heart now willed Adam to look at her, and when he didn't, Jonquil bypassed him to study the man who sat with him, leaning forward in his own chair.

So, Father, at last we meet.

Her gaze traveled from the top of Ball's head down, over his tailor-made suit and to the tips of his patent leather shoes. If his clothes were any indication of his finances, it appeared her father had not lived for the last twenty-two years in the dire need she and her mother had known.

"This court is but the instrument of the law," Parker stated, "executing its mandates." The judge's voice droned on, pulling Jonquil's attention back to the proceedings. He turned to the clerk. "Could we see the evidence?"

Innes Ball straightened in his seat when the clerk walked to the front of the courtroom and presented the judge with a faded piece of paper. After the judge had studied it, he turned toward Jonquil's father and issued his request.

"Mr. Ball," he asked in a friendly voice, "will you please approach the bench?"

Jonquil's gaze followed Ball as he swaggered forward. He was a runty little man, not at all the father she'd envisioned. In her descriptions Margaret Trevain had created a tall, handsome hero not unlike the male who now possessed Jonquil's heart. Again she glanced over at Adam, but he continued to stare straight ahead.

"Is this the deed?" the judge asked, leaning over the bench.

Ball examined the paper with a triumphant gleam in his eyes before the judge snatched it from his grasp. Then Parker bent closer and whispered something into his ear. Jonquil held her breath when Ball turned to face her.

"The woman you claim stole this deed from you, is she in this courtroom today?" Judge Parker's booming voice echoed throughout the large room.

Seeming to enjoy the attention bestowed upon him, the invincible Innes Ball approached Jonquil's chair. Gabriel stiffened beside her, his fingers balled into tight fists.

"We're waiting for your answer, Mr. Ball."

Jonquil's eyes were riveted upon her father's face. For a moment the man seemed to waver, as though he recognized a part of himself in her gaze. But his greed outweighed his trepidation.

He pointed in her direction. The large ruby ring on his finger sparkled when it caught the light. "That's the one, your honor. I'd recognize that woman anywhere."

As though the audience had been prompted, noise erupted among the spectators. Jonquil's hand automatically went to her chest in response to Ball's vehement look.

Then the outer doors of the courtroom swung open, and all eyes turned to the bailiff ushering in another party.

Reverend Cates, looking every bit the minister in a black suit and high, white collar, his Bible in hand, walked pretentiously into the courtroom as though he were about to conduct a ceremony.

Innes Ball faltered. Irresolution flickered across his face. "What's the meaning of this?" he roared.

"The meaning, sir, I believe is clear. You, Mr. Ball, are to be arraigned for fraudulent use of government funds, conspiracy to murder one Margaret Mary Trevain and her daughter, Jonquil Rose Trevain, and as an accessory to murder."

"Surely you jest," Ball countered, his cheeks puffing with rage. "I'm a very influential man."

Judge Parker glared down from the bench. "Need I remind you, Mr. Ball, I, too, am influential."

"Who instigated this lunacy?" Ball demanded, searching out the faces of the crowd.

Reverend Cates jumped to his feet. Pointing a

bony finger toward Ball, he let loose with some inspired advice. "Ye cannot serve God and mammon."

"You old coot, you can't serve anything."

Ball lunged toward the preacher and nearly had Cates by the collar before several deputies restrained him.

"Order! Order in this court!" Parker banged the gavel on his desk. "I'll hold you in contempt, Mr. Ball, if we have another outbreak such as this."

"My New York lawyers will rake you crackers over the coals," Ball threatened. "You can't charge me with anything."

"Oh, I believe, sir, we can charge you with quite a few things. The United States Government has been investigating your business practices for well over a year now. Reverend Cates is willing to testify as to how you tried to swindle Miss Trevain and her daughter out of their property, even ordering their deaths if necessary."

"Lies, lies!" Ball shouted. "Everything he says is a lie."

"Do you, sir," Parker interrupted, his fingers laced across his chest, "recall a surveyor you hired? One Simon Thompson?"

The judge's eyes narrowed, his gaze locked on the fuming man. "Mr. Thompson worked for me, undercover. He was a special deputy marshal. One of your cutthroats murdered him when he accompanied them to the Trevain farm."

The judge nodded toward the minister. "Cates, here, witnessed the whole ugly incident."

Ball stilled at the words, red splotches creeping up to his hairline. He looked like a volcano about to erupt. A vicious laugh escaped his lips. "Ha!" he snorted. "Who's going to believe a fanatic, a man who considers himself a divine prophet?"

Judge Parker seemed unperturbed. "We have another witness," he said, "who witnessed Cates witnessing the deed. I believe, Mr. Ball, you're going to need a very good New York lawyer to protect yourself against us *crackers*."

With that, Parker slammed his gavel upon the desk to quiet the outburst in the courtroom. "Trial is set for one week from today. In the meantime, Mr. Ball, I trust you'll enjoy our jail."

The bailiff, surrounded by deputies, moved to escort the shaken Innes Ball from the room. When they reached Jonquil, she stood before Ball to block his way. "May I have a word with him?" she asked.

Gabriel rose to stand beside her, an unspoken warning on his face.

Adam, following close in Ball's footsteps, motioned for the guard to stop.

The railroader drew himself to his full five-foot, six-inch height. "Who are you anyway, young woman?" he accused. "Someone paid to lie for this court?"

"I'm Margaret Trevain's daughter." Jonquil paused to allow her words to penetrate.

"I should have guessed," Ball answered with a pugnacious snort. "Are you cut from the same cloth as your she-bitch mother?"

Gabriel lunged forward, but a deputy restrained him.

Ball laughed—the sound was shrill, ugly—as he looked the black man up and down. "And I suppose you're that young buck Margaret's mother insisted she bring with her when we left that fine plantation behind. Always wondered about such devotion from a young stud." He looked closer at Jonquil. "Are you sure I'm your daddy, gal?"

Jonquil gasped at the insult and fought back the tears that threatened to steal from her eyes.

Adam stuck his face into Ball's, daring the man to utter another lewd word. "We'll have none of that talk." He turned to the bailiff. "Get him out of here."

"Please . . ." Jonquil stopped their retreat by

placing her hand on Ball's arm. "Have you never felt regret for leaving my mother, or wondered how she fared?"

"Regret?" He snickered. "My only regret is that I signed that damned piece of property over to her. As for your other question, one whore is as good as the next."

Again Gabriel had to be restrained. Keely wrapped a protective arm around Jonquil. "Let 'im go, girl. He ain't fit to set eyes on you."

Jonquil turned into Keely's arms, feeling as though she'd been slapped in the face.

Adam motioned for the deputies to escort the prisoner from the room. He looked over at Jonquil, wrapped in Keely's embrace, and fought the urge to hug her to himself. But he realized his time for comforting had ended. Right now, he'd just as soon use her father's head for a punching bag.

When the men had nearly reached the door, Ball skidded to a stop. He swung around, his hate evident. "When I get out of here," he yelled, "I'll come for my land. It belongs to me. No split-tail bitch is going to have what's rightfully mine."

Adam lunged for him then. Grabbing him by the collar, he yanked Ball up like a ragdoll, leaving the man's toes barely touching the floor.

"If you so much as attempt to lay a finger upon this lady, or her land, I'll come after you. I swear it. If you haven't already swung from a rope, I'll hang you from one myself." He lowered the now-cowering man and shoved him across the floor.

Brushing his hands off and bending to pick up the hat he'd dropped, Adam stood erect again. With eyes as cold as the Arkansas River outside, he looked at Jonquil.

"Miss Trevain," he said, "I wish you the best in your future." Then he turned and walked away.

*   *   *

Jonquil cried herself to sleep that night. The next morning she awoke with bloodshot eyes; her face puffed and swollen. Though she moved with the living, she felt dead inside. Her life had ended the second Adam had walked out of the courtroom without a backward glance. And she had no one to blame but herself.

Her actions had been deplorable, unforgivable. But she had seen the look in Adam's eyes when he'd grabbed the man who had taunted her. It revealed that he had taken her own pain to himself. Without a doubt, he had needed great control to prevent his killing Innes Ball on the spot.

Adam loved her, of this Jonquil was certain, just as she loved him. But she was not so certain of how to convince him she was worthy of his love.

Judge Parker had told them that for the trial Adam's deposition alone was required. This meant he could leave at any time.

Jonquil had to think fast.

"Are you sure?" Jonquil whispered, not yet fully awake.

"That's what he told Gabe last night. He bought a new horse in town and plans to set out at first light. Said he was headin' west, by the Texas Road."

"Bring me my clothes," Jonquil ordered, rolling from beneath the covers.

Keely lit a lamp and hurried to the trunk in which yesterday she'd stored certain items as Jonquil had requested.

Dusk was nearly upon her when Jonquil realized that Adam had outdistanced her. Tonight she wouldn't overtake him after all. Maybe he knew a shortcut to Dallas.

Now she had more immediate things to consider,

376

such as where to camp, and the awful comprehension that she'd be camping alone.

Water gurgled nearby. Seeking its source, she guided her horse off the road. Some thirty minutes later she sat before a small fire while darkness settled around her.

Strange, Jonquil thought as she nibbled on a piece of hardtack, she'd camped for months in woods no different than these. But never before had she been alone. If only she'd caught up with Adam earlier.

In the shadows beyond the campfire, low-slung tree branches swayed like menacing arms in the cool night wind. The high-pitched trilling of crickets and the hoot of an owl heightened her senses, sending shivers up her spine. In the deepening darkness she imagined all sorts of predators stalking nearby.

Finally exhausted from having battled to keep her eyes open, Jonquil threw a new log on the fire, determined not to sleep long enough to let it burn out completely. She then settled into her blankets, hugging a large piece of wood to her chest. Not much in the way of a weapon, it would nonetheless serve as a club if needed.

Pulling her hat over her face, she willed the frightful world away and drifted into a fitful sleep.

Adam sat against a tree, listening to the night sounds, waiting for the stranger to fall asleep.

For all the changes brought about, this was still rugged country, hardly safe for a lone traveler during the day. At night it could be described as perilous at best. But if he had any say about it, no man was going to sneak up on him and send him to a premature grave.

Shortly after noon he'd discovered he was being followed. Keeping his distance, he'd circled behind the lone horse and rider, careful not to give away his position. Experience had taught him never to give up the advantage.

Tonight was no different. He'd wait until the man had fallen asleep before he paid him a surprise visit.

Long after the noises of activity around the campfire had ceased, Adam made his way through the brush toward the stranger who had dogged his trail. Creeping forward across the forest floor, he came within sight of a dying fire and the bulky backside of the man lying next to it. The man's hat shielded his face.

A twig cracked beneath Adam's boot and he stopped, holding his breath. The man never moved. Good, he thought, he must be fast asleep. Slowly, Adam inched forward on silent footsteps until he stood looking down at the burly form.

His booted toe dipped into the man's cushiony backside. No response. Again he urged his boot against the unmoving body.

Damnation, was the man dead?

Stooping low over the reclining form, Adam's fingers curled around a shoulder. At that precise moment the stranger rolled over, swinging a club at his head.

But Adam was too fast.

His fingers locked around the attacker's wrist, hurling the wood from his grasp. Without waiting for a response, Adam fell on top of him.

Trying to pin the stranger to the ground, he thought he'd landed on a downy cloud. Had he gotten hold of some kid still in knee pants and baby fat?

Arms and legs flailed helplessly beneath him.

"Get off me, you cussed, rotten lout!"

From underneath the scrapper's overalls, goose feathers fluttered upward into Adam's face.

"What the—?"

Straddled across the puffy torso, Adam sat up, stunned, and attempted to extricate a mouthful of feathers. Beneath him, amidst layers of fluff, her wrists captured in his hands, lay his Jonquil Rose.

"Jonquil?" He dropped her arms and stared, stupefied. "Good heavens, woman, what are you doing out here?"

"Adam? Is it really you?" The words came in a rush.

Sitting up, Jonquil flung her arms around the welcome intruder astride her lap. "Oh, thank God it's you. I've been so scared."

"Well, you should be," he bellowed, pushing her away to make his point. "Don't you have any more sense than to be out here alone at night—with no protection but a pathetic piece of wood? For heaven's sake, woman, you could have been eaten alive. Or worse."

"Worse?"

"You addleplated numbskull. Trouble rides up and down these roads day and night." He held her at arm's length, his hands digging into her shoulders. "Woman, you could have died."

Jonquil gave Adam a bittersweet smile. "I already did. The minute you walked out of that courtroom."

Biting her lip, she swallowed hard. "I had to come after you. I've come to tell you I'm so sorry for those cruel things I said. I've wanted to take them back, to apologize, to tell you that without you I'm nothing, that I don't want a fortune—or anything. Just you."

She paused to catch her breath. "I've wanted to talk to you, but you completely ignored me, which, of course, you had a right to do." Her words tumbled out like a child's scattered blocks. "But if you had talked with me, I wouldn't be out here in these ridiculous clothes, thinking some unknown creature was about to kill—"

Adam put his fingers to her lips. "Jonquil," he whispered, "hush up. It's all right."

"No!" she retorted, swiping at his fingers.

"No?"

"No. You can't call me Jonquil."

At her words Adam stiffened, his expression turning stony.

"Please," she amended, "to you my name is Rose."

In the light of the dying campfire the beginnings of a smile touched Adam's mouth.

"Rose."

At the sound of her special name on his lips, Jonquil flew into Adam's arms.

Claiming her mouth, Adam crushed her to him. His tongue dipped into her warmth, possessing her, and its sweetness sent Jonquil's senses reeling.

Cradled at last in his arms, she breathed in his special essence and felt his heart race against her cheek. "I love you, Adam Coulter," she confessed. "Can you ever forgive me?"

In response, he wrapped her more securely in his arms, burying his face in the hollow of her neck. "If you promise not to send me away again."

Jonquil pulled back to bask in the warmth of his dark, compassionate eyes—so like another's she remembered. "Never," she whispered.

And never, she vowed, would she fear the night again.

Epilogue

Eureka Springs, five years later

"My gracious," Flo commented, rising from her knees beside the baby blanket. "I just can't believe how much little Simon has grown. Why just yesterday, I swear, he was only a little chickabiddy."

Flo removed her white apron and poured herself a cup of coffee from the sideboard. Placing the cup on the round oak table, she settled herself in a chair and rested her feet on an empty one nearby.

Jonquil and Liz chuckled at the woman's choice of words.

"Honestly, Flo," Jonquil said, "you never cease to amaze me with your language."

"Keeps the boarders on their toes, I'll tell you," Liz added. "Seems every morning they take longer and longer to eat, just listening to her pearls of wisdom."

She gave Flo a genuine smile. "And I wouldn't have it any other way. I do hope you're happy working here, my dear."

"Happy as a cow in a cornfield," came Flo's reply. She tugged at her shirtwaist. "I'll be as big as one, too, if I don't stop eating my own cooking. These clothes already fit like sausage skin."

The other two women nodded with understanding. The front door slammed and childish laughter filtered toward the back of the house. "Mama, Mama." The calls resounded as a little girl entered the dining room, tugging her father by the hand. Blond and blue-eyed, she resembled her mother in miniature.

"Morning, ladies."

"Mama," the child squealed delightedly and ran to Jonquil. "Daddy says we're going to see Uncle Gabe tomorrow. He said Uncle Gabe's gonna take me diamond huntin'. Can Simon go, too? Can he?"

"Not so loud, Gabrielle," Jonquil cautioned. "You'll startle your brother." She took her daughter's hand. "Of course we'll take Simon. Gabriel and Keely want to see both of you. And we all want to see their big, new house."

Jonquil smiled up at her husband. "So you can close your office tomorrow, after all?"

"Sure can," Adam said with a broad smile. "The circuit judge delayed his trip, so we leave in the morning. I picked up the train tickets a little while ago."

While Jonquil gathered her belongings, Adam walked over and picked up his son to leave, handing Gabrielle the baby blanket.

"Well, you two," Jonquil said, addressing Liz and Flo, "I have packing to finish. We'll see you in a couple of weeks."

"Give our best to Gabriel and his wife," Liz said.

Flo stood and chucked the infant under his chin. "And tell Gabriel to tune up that banjo of his," she teased. "I might just have to start dancing again if I want to shuck a few pounds."

"We'll see about that," Adam announced. "I recall a performance that nearly set this town on its ear. I'm not at all sure we're ready for another one."

He stole a glance at his wife, his eyes betraying his ardor. "You naughty, naughty girl."

At Jonquil's demure blush and the other women's laughter, a devious smile crossed his face. "But I wouldn't have missed it for the world."

Author's Note

Research for this book led to the only place in the United States where diamonds have been found in their natural matrix, Crater of Diamonds State Park near Murfreesboro, Arkansas.

In the late 1800's, geologist Dr. John C. Banner recognized the soil as similar to the diamond-bearing kimberlite clay found in Africa. Not until 1906 were diamonds actually discovered in this area by a farmer named John Huddleston.

Research also led to the authentic Victorian town of Eureka Springs, located in the northwest corner of the state. During the period covered in this book, the town, high in the Ozark Mountains, was a fast-growing city of culture and refinement, as fashionable as any health spa in the country.

Those who had come as invalids and found the healing they sought in the water stayed to build a unique community. General Powell Clayton, first Republican governor of Arkansas, played a vital role in the growth of Eureka Springs.

A destructive fire actually did occur in the early morning hours of November 3, but sources differed as to the year of the catastrophe. One claimed the fire happened in 1882; the other, 1883. The 1882 date fits this story better.

During this period Fort Smith was an important

place. The site of the Federal Court for the Western District of Arkansas, it also served to protect the inhabitants of the Indian Territory to the west. From 1875 to 1896, the court was presided over by Judge Isaac C. Parker, also labeled the hanging judge.

As with many legendary figures, the image does not always fit the man. He was described by a reporter for the *St. Louis Republic* as being ". . . the gentlest of men, this alleged sternest of judges. He is courtly of manner and kind of voice and face, the man who has passed the death sentence upon more criminals than has any other judge in the land. The features that have in them the horror of the Medusa to desperados are benevolent to all other humankind."

After careful research of the lives of both General Powell Clayton and Judge Isaac Parker, we determined this is how they might have acted in the given situation.

We hope that our characters' story pleased you as much as it did us. They directed it, and we recorded it.